OTHERWORLDER SURVIVAL GUIDE

SAL MONROE

Otherworlder Survival Guide

ISBN (paperback): 979-8-88993-111-9
ISBN (e-book): 979-8-88993-112-6

Edited by Jimi Iyiola
Interior Design by Tangcu LLC

Published 2026 by MoonQuill®
Arlington, VA

www.moonquill.com

Table of Contents

Table of Contents Continued

Dedicated to my lovely wife.
There isn't much I do that isn't.

Chapter 1

Remember to Have Fun

The teenager fell from the sky, as teenagers occasionally did in this world. It was common knowledge for citizens of Astranta that if they spotted any human spontaneously appearing from the sky, they should take extreme caution not to approach the situation and simply report the incident to the nearest government official.

I didn't consider myself a stupid girl, nor did I think that I lacked any sort of common sense, but unfortunately, I hadn't actually managed to see the young teenager falling.

When I heard the boy screaming, it just sounded like someone was injured and needed my help. I moved without thinking, not wanting to ignore the sound and have my conscience plagued forever for abandoning someone in their time of need.

Consciences are stupid. I should've plagued mine away.

By the time I noticed the quickly closing magical rift in the sky, I had already locked eyes with the boy, sealing my fate. My first instinct was to sprint away as fast as I could. He was sprawled out on the floor, and judging from the number of branches stuck in his clothes and hair, he'd fallen from quite high up. For a normal human, it would've likely broken their bones or given them a concussion—something that would stop him from getting up and chasing after me if I ran.

But he wasn't a normal human. He was an Otherworlder.

Taking a deep breath and ignoring the shaking in my legs, I tried desperately to remember what we were taught to do as kids if we were ever approached by an Otherworlder. It had been a few years since a teacher from the Crown had come to our village to give a seminar on the topic, but it wasn't too difficult to remember.

Be friendly. Be uninteresting. Be naïve.

Whoever decided that FUN would be the acronym to use in the event of an Otherworlder attack was messed up in the head.

"H-Hey there," I said, giving the boy a friendly smile that hid how close I was to soiling myself. Hopefully. "You alright?"

The boy didn't react to my question, unless staring and blinking occasionally was a form of communication that I couldn't understand.

Did he hear me? Was he dead? I knew that Otherworlders were supposed to be similar to humans superficially, but I also knew there were supposed to be some differences. Was it possible that he could be dead and still blinking? Chickens could run around with their heads chopped off, and it was totally possible that a similar rule could apply here. As I desperately held on to the little hope I had, the boy's head swiveled around before he stood up and looked at his own hands.

I still held on to my hope. Maybe Otherworlders could also move and breathe while being dead.

"I'm alive?" the boy said slowly.

Maybe Otherworlders could still ponder their existence while being dead?

As my hope silently slipped away, his head swiveled toward me, and we locked eyes once again.

"Excuse me," he said. "Are we on Earth?"

Naïve. I had to be naïve.

"Earth?" I asked, trying to keep my voice from stuttering. "I've never heard of that country before. Are you a foreigner?"

He stared at me for a few seconds before looking at his hands and grinning madly.

"Oh man, that settles it," he said. "I've really been *isekai'd*."

I didn't understand whatever that word he'd just said was, so I pretended I didn't hear it. I didn't know if the smile that I kept plastered on my face was convincing at all, but it seemed like he wasn't paying much attention to me. It was a small miracle that I hoped would be followed by a bigger one. Clasping my hands together, I made a silent prayer that the boy would simply die.

When the boy dropped to his knees, a little hope rose in me, but it faded instantly when he let out a victorious cheer.

"Hell yeah!" he shouted. "I've been isekai'd!"

I had no idea what he was talking about, so I kept smiling until he turned back to me.

"Excuse me, miss. Can you understand me?"

Deciding not to point out the fact that it should've already been obvious that I could, I nodded. "Yes, I can. Is something wrong, sir?"

The boy paused for a long moment, thoughts obviously running through his mind while I stayed still, trying my hardest to pretend that the silence he left me in wasn't the most terrifyingly awkward one I'd ever felt in my life.

"Ah, yes," he said eventually, giving me a smile. I assumed he thought it looked sincere. "Actually, I have to admit that I am in a bit of trouble. I'm a traveling adventurer, but I accidentally misplaced my map and I've been lost in these woods for quite a while. Could you possibly guide me to the nearest village?"

"Of course!" I nodded, hopefully not too enthusiastically. "I can show you to my village. We have maps there, if you want to buy one to replace the one you lost."

"Oh. But I don't have money."

My eyes widened as I realized my mistake. One of the other rules of interacting with Otherworlders was to make their lives as easy and convenient as possible, but it was harder to remember than the three main rules. Possibly because somebody liked the FUN acronym a little too much to change it. "I can lend you some," I said quickly.

"Really?" he asked, looking more surprised than I would have expected. "You'd do that for me? A stranger you just met?"

He'd just traveled to another world, and this was what surprised him the most? Basic human decency? Okay, maybe a bit more than I would typically offer to a stranger, but still.

"Sure!" I said, hoping he didn't notice my voice cracking. "Every night before I fell asleep, my mom told me to be good to those in need. I made it my personal motto."

I have no idea why I lied for no reason like that. I'd like to think my mom had raised me well, but she hadn't done anything dramatic like that. I blamed the fear and panic for making me speak before thinking.

"Wow," the boy said. "She must have been a good mom."

"Yeah," I said. "I guess she is."

"Is?" he asked. "Don't you mean was?"

For the first time since I saw him, the smile dropped from my face.

"My mom's not dead," I said.

The boy stared at me for a few seconds.

"Are you sure?" he asked.

"Yeah."

"Oh." There was a long pause before he spoke again. "I just thought that was like... your tragic backstory or something. The way you talked about her seemed pretty emotional, y'know."

I had no idea how to deal with the awkward silence that had spawned between us. So I chose not to.

"Should we start heading over to my village?" I asked, plastering a smile on my face again and pointing in the general direction of where it was.

"Uh, sure," he said, seeming just as eager to forget his misunderstanding as I was.

I expected him to follow me when I started to walk away, but I prayed he wouldn't. Unfortunately, judging by the sound of crunching twigs that followed me, my prayers had gone unanswered.

"So, what's your name?" the boy asked.

"You know, it's only polite to give your name first when you're introducing yourself to someone."

I froze, unable to believe that I'd just lectured an Otherworlder on manners. I knew I was terrible under pressure, but I couldn't help but curse my lack of survival instinct. The Otherworlder looked somewhat surprised at my comment, but before he could say anything, I let out a laugh to try and play it off as a joke.

"Ha!" I said, unable to summon a genuine laugh on command. "Ha, ha! I am joking!"

The Otherworlder's face softened somewhat as he looked away from me, his mouth curling into a smile and a quiet chuckle escaping his lips. I had no idea how, but it seemed like I'd convinced him. I didn't know why he was blushing slightly, but I decided to ignore it.

"No, you're right," the Otherworlder said. "I'm sorry for being so rude."

"It's no problem!" I said, speaking quickly so he wouldn't have enough time to take back his apology. Miraculously, speaking quickly didn't screw me over again. "So, what's your name?"

The Otherworlder looked back up at me. Our eyes locked, and I was taken aback by how unremarkable he was. He had fair skin, dark brown hair, and light brown eyes, but I had trouble picking out any other ways to describe him. His clothing was strange, I suppose—I'd never seen a hood attached to a shirt before, only cloaks—but nothing else stood out to me. It would be difficult to describe him when I eventually gave my witness report to the Mediators.

He turned his head away from me, and the quick movement shocked me out of my focus. My eyes widened when I saw an angry red glow growing on his cheeks. Had I offended him in some way? I knew that Otherworlders were somewhat similar to humans, but it was possible that I had done something culturally strange to him by maintaining eye contact. I panicked, opening my mouth to make some sort of excuse for my offensive behavior, but thankfully, he spoke before I could dig an even deeper grave for myself.

"My name is Jam—" He cut himself off, pausing for a long moment. I wasn't sure why, so I simply tried my best to smile and wait. He shook his head, making me think I'd done something wrong again, but then he spoke.

"My name is Ryuji," he said. "Ryuji Nightblade."

I clapped my hands together. "That's a wonderful name! Ree-yoo-ji. Am I pronouncing it right?" The name sounded foreign, but I tried to match his pronunciation as best as I could.

"Y-Yeah," he said, looking back at me.

My eyes widened when I saw the angry red glow on his cheeks was still there. What had I done wrong? I turned away from him and hid my face. I wasn't confident enough in my fake smile to hide the horror I felt.

"It really is a wonderful name," I repeated, hoping he would forgive me if I praised him some more. "Ryuji Nightblade. It sounds beautiful."

"T-Thanks," he said.

The pause that followed was the most nerve-wracking experience I'd ever had in my life. He'd thanked me, but I had no idea if he was still mad or not. I was too afraid to turn to check, in case the movement triggered the Otherworlder to pulverize me with whatever magic he possessed.

"What's your name?" he asked. "I'm sure it's just as beautiful."

I made a silent prayer of thanks to the gods.

"Lena," I said.

"Lena, huh?" he repeated. "That's a pretty name."

"Thanks." I gave him a genuine smile, more from relief than gratitude.

"So, Lena. Not that I'm not grateful, but what were you doing wandering around in the forest? I don't know much about the area, but I can't help but assume that it might be dangerous for a young girl to be alone in a place like this."

I had no idea why he would assume such a thing, but I saw no reason to call him out on it, nor did I see a reason to lie to him.

"I was just practicing my magic," I said.

"Really?!" Ryuji shouted, nearly making me jump in surprise. "You can do magic?!"

I turned around cautiously to see Ryuji's mouth stretched into a mad grin. I wasn't sure how exactly I managed not to break down into tears.

"Yeah," I forced out.

"Can I see?"

I knew some Otherworlders supposedly didn't have magic in their original worlds, so I could understand his excitement at the idea of seeing magic for the first time. I was just slightly below average at best, so I wasn't sure if I could satisfy his excitement, but it wasn't like I could say no.

"If you insist." I reached out, with my palms facing up. "I'm pretty bad at it, though, so don't laugh if I fail, okay?"

Ryuji nodded violently, staring down at my hands with an intensity that made me sweat. Ignoring the feeling, I closed my eyes to better focus on the flow of mana within me, begging it to work so I could entertain the Otherworlder for a few seconds.

I wasn't a sorcerer of any sort. I'd only picked up the practice to make life a little more convenient for myself, and though I ended up enjoying it, it was more like an occasional hobby for me than anything else.

I was a novice magic user, so my mana control wasn't too great. I typically kept my mana within my body, but the whole reason I was out in the forest in the first place was to practice externalizing my mana in the form of fire without risking my house burning down. Thankfully, I hadn't been practicing for long enough for my mana to have burned away, so I still had more than enough inside me for another attempt.

"Here I go," I said, with my eyes still closed.

Summoning my mana to my hands, I imagined a thin needle puncturing the skin of my hands, just enough for mana to escape from my body and into the air. I imagined the mana being combustible, igniting as soon as it exited my body.

I opened my eyes as my hands grew hot. A small fireball floated lazily above my hands, about the size of a cherry.

"Fireball," I said, holding it out so Ryuji could see.

"Damn," he said, the fire reflecting in his wide eyes.

I was glad to see it worked so cleanly and to see such a positive reaction from him. His mouth gaped open, and I swore I could see some drool threatening to drip from it. He reached out to it as if to grab the floating ball of flame, but I felt my mana quickly evaporating, so I was forced to clasp my palms together, imagining the hole in my hands sealing shut and stopping the flow of mana from escaping.

I let out a slow breath, ignoring the sheen of sweat that had suddenly covered my body. It was tiring stuff manipulating mana, especially for a ball of fire so big. I'd really pushed myself to the limit for that.

"That was so cool," Ryuji said, whispering as if he were in the presence of something sacred.

I smiled, and for the first time since I'd found him, I found that my smile was at least somewhat genuine. Regardless of who was praising me, it felt good to be recognized for my efforts.

"Thanks."

Ryuji's face broke out into a grin, and once more, I realized that he looked just like a normal guy. I could almost pretend that he was just a kid from the neighboring village or something. The way he was smiling, as if he were just a giddy child who had found a new toy, was admittedly a bit infectious.

"That was seriously the coolest thing I've ever seen in my life, Lena," he said.

"It really wasn't that great," I said, even as my lips threatened to twitch upward into a genuine smile. While I was one of the few people in my village who ever bothered with trying to learn magic, I wasn't particularly talented in it. I wasn't used to being praised for my magic.

"You think I could do that someday?" he asked.

"Yeah, everybody has the latent ability to sense and use mana," I said. "It's just a matter of training it."

Ryuji nodded. "Mana, huh," he said, furrowing his brow and staring off into space. His eyes widened before he grinned madly.

"God, I hope this works," he said. "Status."

I was about to ask why he just blurted out a random word like that, but I recovered from my tired daze fast enough to remember who exactly I was talking to. I froze in place, returning to my default response of ignoring something whenever I didn't understand what was happening. For some reason, Ryuji started to poke at the air and focus on something I couldn't see. I had no idea what he was doing, but I had no desire to find out, so I simply smiled and waited.

"Okay," he said suddenly. "I think I got it."

"Hmm?" I had no idea what he was suddenly talking about. "Got what?"

Ryuji grinned at me and held out his palms.

"Fireball."

It was a small miracle that I managed to survive. The intense smell of sulfur and singed hair hit my nose and assaulted my senses before I registered what was happening. I felt the fluid in my eyes threaten to boil from the heat, and I was blinded by the light of the large gout of endless fire that burst from Ryuji's hands and into the sky, incinerating a hole in the canopy on the way. Without any sort of conscious thought, my eyes followed the great gout of fire as it escaped into the sky, refusing to fade even as it soared into the heavens and evaporated clouds along the way. I wasn't sure it ever truly died out, only disappearing as it grew too far to actually see.

I blinked twice, wondering if I was dead or hallucinating. My skin felt flushed, and the scent of burning foliage and wood surrounded me. A perfect circle had been carved into the canopy, blackened on the edges but not catching fire in the slightest. It didn't make much sense. Simply being exposed to that kind of heat should have made the forest burst into flames, but it wasn't nearly the strangest thing about the whole experience.

I looked down at Ryuji, who turned away sheepishly.

"Sorry," he said. "I guess I'm not used to controlling my mana."

I stared at him for a few seconds, then clapped my hands together.

"Wow. You are very, very talented." My voice came out in chattered staccato notes.

"I have a lot to work on," Ryuji said, chuckling quietly.

I stared at him some more.

I questioned myself how I could think he was a normal person, even for a second. He was an Otherworlder. I had no idea how I'd forgotten that.

I turned around right before my frozen mask fell, my smile dissolving into a wild look as I clenched my teeth together to keep them from chattering in fear. I wasn't confident I could look at him without crying.

"Let's go," I somehow managed to say.

"Okay," Ryuji replied.

Chapter 2

Damsel in Distress. So Much Distress

As we walked back to my village, Ryuji kept relatively quiet as he trailed behind me. The silence between us was occasionally broken whenever he asked questions about my life or the village, but I tried to keep my answers as short and direct as possible, without seeming unfriendly.

Even though it seemed like a normal conversation on the surface, it was exhausting to keep my emotions hidden and not break out into tears. I didn't practice my magic too far away from my village, barely at the edge of the forest, but it felt like we'd been walking for hours, even though I logically knew that it was only about ten minutes away.

When I finally saw the familiar buildings against the horizon, I nearly cried out in relief.

"There's the village, Ryuji," I said, still getting used to the unfamiliar pronunciation of his name.

It took a second for him to reply.

"Oh yeah," he said. "I'm Ryuji."

I turned around to face him, deciding not to comment on the giddy smile plastered on his face.

"That's my village," I tried again. "It might not look like much, but we have all the essential businesses to cater to anybody who might travel to our village. There's a tavern you can eat and drink at and a general goods store that can sell you maps, like I mentioned."

"Hmm. Does the tavern also have rooms I can stay in?"

I paled at the thought of an Otherworlder staying in my village, but I nodded. Be friendly. "It does," I said. "But not many people actually stay there. I've heard that it's pretty expensive while being pretty cheap in quality."

I apologized internally to Alec, whose family owned that tavern. I knew they worked hard to deliver the highest quality service they could, but I was doing them a favor, really.

"Then is there anywhere else I could stay?" he asked. "What about your house?"

It was a testament to my survival instincts that I didn't burst into tears.

"Excuse me?" I said instead, hoping I'd heard wrong.

"I'll need a place to stay," he said. "At least until I can get an idea of where I want to head next. As long as it's not a bother."

It was a bother. More than that, actually.

"As much as I'd love for you to stay, I'm sorry. My dad wouldn't approve of me bringing a boy over."

Once again, my quick mouth spouted out the first thing it could think of, but I was surprised by how reasonable this claim was. My dad wasn't the controlling type, but I doubted he would be happy if I tried to convince him to have a boy stay over, especially if it was a stranger. Though I hadn't checked with him, I could only assume that was doubly true if it was an Otherworlder who could annihilate the village with a single thought.

"Oh," Ryuji said. "That makes sense. I guess it would be hard to trust your daughter with some guy you've never met. At least not until he's proven himself."

I'm not entirely sure Ryuji meant for me to hear that. From the way he was mumbling, it seemed like he was talking more to himself than anything. So like always, I ignored him.

"And here we are! Welcome to the wonderful village of Plainswood!" I said, raising my arms and pointing at the array of small buildings that crowded the main road. We were still far enough from the village that the people milling around the main street didn't seem to notice us, but we were close enough that I could recognize their faces.

I desperately glared at them, hoping that some of them would hear my silent cry for help and look my way.

None did. I'd never felt so betrayed before.

"So," I said. "What do you think?"

"Weird name, but it looks nice," he said. "Very medieval."

Once again, I ignored the word I didn't recognize. "I'm glad you like it," I said, assuming it was a compliment. "The name's just because we live right between the forest and plains lands. Nobody really cared to be creative when they were building the village. I've been living here my whole life, so it's just normal for me."

"Is that so?" Ryuji asked. I couldn't tell what expression he had on his face, but I could tell he was thinking hard about something, from the inflection of his voice. "I can see how you'd get tired of living in such a small community after a while."

I didn't know how he came to that conclusion from what I said, but I just smiled and nodded, not wanting to disagree with a boy who could potentially kill me in the blink of an eye. "Yeah, I guess so," I said. "Lots of people my age do end up going to the city to get better jobs."

"The city, huh?" Ryuji mused. "What's it like over there?"

My eyes widened, sensing a way out. I was already trying to figure out a way to get Ryuji to go to the city to meet with a government official who was trained to deal with Otherworlder arrivals. If Ryuji wanted to go to the city naturally, that would be the best possible outcome I could hope for.

"Oh, it's wonderful! There's so much to do in the city! Good food, good entertainment, and... lots of things to do." I was slowly realizing that I didn't actually know much about what it was like. I hadn't strayed too far from home and had no real interest in leaving, so I'd never bothered to try to figure out what it was like outside of it. "I've always wanted to go there. In fact, it's been my lifelong dream!" I said instead, trying to make up for my lack of knowledge with enthusiastic lying.

"I see," he said.

The comment was so casual that I had trouble understanding why it sent a shiver down my spine.

There was another one of those long pauses I was becoming so accustomed to. I knew that I should say something to stop Ryuji from thinking I was being rude to him, but I couldn't stop myself from grinding my teeth together in dread for some reason.

Once I'd managed to relax my jaw enough to open my mouth to say something, a miracle happened.

"Hey Lena!"

I look up to see a familiar face staring at me. Bran, the sheriff's son and my current guardian angel, was leaning against a small post in the ground meant for hitching donkeys to. He gave me a casual wave and a smile, though it seemed to falter the closer I walked. I watched his eyes search my face, and with a start, I realized that I wasn't smiling anymore. As quickly as possible, I gave him a shaky grin and a smile.

"Hey Bran," I said, waving back at him. "How's it going?"

By now, Bran was frowning. Pushing himself up, he walked over to me.

"Hey, Lena," he said cautiously. "You doing alright? You look like shit."

I winced, but I was suddenly grateful that I'd had my back to Ryuji for our entire walk. Bran was a good friend, but he was also really dense.

If a guy like him could tell how close I was to pissing myself with fear, I was glad that I had hidden my face from Ryuji.

"I'm fine," I said, hoping that at least my voice wouldn't betray me.

"Who's your friend?" he asked, cocking his chin toward Ryuji. I paled quickly at his casual disrespect for the Otherworlder but quickly realized he had no idea what he was dealing with.

"Oh, that's Ryuji. Ryuji, this is Bran, my childhood friend," I said, walking forward to grab Bran's shoulder in a vice grip. He winced, but I quickly put a finger to my lips, hiding the motion from Ryuji with my body. "I'll introduce you two some more in a second, but I got to talk to you about something I saw in the forest. Ryuji, could you wait here a second while I talk to Bran?"

I smiled at Ryuji but paled when I saw a deep frown on his face.

"Alright," he said.

I nodded at him and tried to drag Bran away quickly, but he held firm. Not wanting to waste any time, I discreetly punched him in the side as hard as I could.

Bran winced at the blow and glared down at me, though he seemed more annoyed than injured. "Hey, what's wrong with—"

I cut him off with a violent yank on the arm before he could continue.

We still weren't close enough to the village to have any buildings to hide behind, so I just dragged him far away enough for us to be out of earshot.

"Lena," Bran immediately said once we stopped. "Is that guy bothering you? You want me to chase him off?"

I gripped his other arm and looked up at him. He was about a foot taller than I was and probably about twice my weight, but the look in my eyes must have put him on edge because he tried to lean away from me.

"Lena," he said. "What the hell—"

"Bran," I said, cutting him off and gripping him even tighter. "I need you to shut up and listen to me. That guy is not bothering me. And he isn't bothering you. In fact, he shits rainbows and sunshine as far as anyone in this town is concerned, because if we don't treat him like a king, we die."

My voice was getting raspy from the hissed whispering, and the next breath I took felt harsh against my throat, but I spoke anyway.

"That guy," I said, motioning my head toward Ryuji. "Is an Otherworlder."

Bran didn't have the reaction I was hoping for. I was hoping for him to suddenly pale with the realization of what he'd done but still be calm enough to nod and listen to what I had to say. I was hoping for him to do his job as the deputy sheriff and help me help him get us through the biggest crisis our village had ever faced.

What I didn't hope for was for his lips to flatten into a thin line before he let out a weary sigh.

"Dammit, Lena," he said. "I can't be doing this now that my dad's actually been treating me seriously. Who is that guy, anyway? Some bored kid from Oakwood you suckered into pranking me?"

I paled. At this point, I would have been surprised if my skin wasn't completely transparent. "I'm not joking, Bran," I said. "I've never been this serious in my life."

"Yeah, yeah," he said, reaching over and peeling my fingers off his arms with a surprising amount of ease. I tried to grab him again, but he was a warrior. Even though his father only started to seriously train him for the deputy sheriff position last year, Bran had been training his swordsmanship ever since he could walk. With his superior strength, he was easily able to grab my wrists and stop me from grabbing at him.

"You're gonna really scare someone if you keep acting like this," he said, giving me an almost pitying look. "We've already got Old Faran running her mouth about the supposed demon she saw in the forest. We don't need another baseless rumor floating around and scaring the kids, so why don't we just drop it, okay?"

My mind flashed with panic at the idea that he wouldn't take me seriously. "Please, Bran," I begged. "You have to believe me."

He looked at me, his eyes narrowing.

"Gods, Lena," he said. "Are you crying?"

I blinked, suddenly aware of the fact that my cheeks felt a little cold. I recoiled in surprise, trying to retreat so I could discreetly wipe them away, but Bran still had a grip on my wrists and wasn't letting go.

"You're serious?" he said, the casual annoyance in his expression slowly melting away to one of neutrality.

I nodded frantically, allowing myself to feel some hope. I wasn't sure if he believed me completely yet, but I was getting to him. I couldn't even be mad at myself for crying like a child if it got results.

"Yes!" I hissed. "I'm telling you I saw him fall from the—"

It was something in Bran's expression that made me stop talking. The way his eyes darted up and widened in shock. He let go of my wrists and took a step back, his hand falling to his side where a short sword rested in a scabbard at his waist. I don't know if he intended to draw it or if it was just a reflexive action, but he never got the chance as Ryuji suddenly appeared in front of him, faster than my eyes could register.

Bran froze. He was slightly taller than Ryuji and twice as thick, but he stood in place, unable to move.

Ryuji casually stepped sideways to put himself directly between me and Bran.

"I will never allow a beautiful girl to be hurt in front of me."

I blinked twice, unable to believe what I was hearing.

Before I could gather my thoughts, Ryuji turned around to face me.

"Lena," he said. "Are you alright?"

As his eyes scanned my face, I suddenly became aware of the fact that I wasn't smiling. I quickly fixed that, but a brisk wind chilled my damp face, reminding me of the tears that were still there.

"Y-Yeah," I said, quickly wiping my eyes. "I'm good."

Ryuji's eyes softened, and he reached out a hand. I froze, unable to draw away as his finger approached my face. When he touched my cheek and smeared my tears messily across my face, I just wanted to cry even harder.

"It's okay," he said. "He can't hurt you anymore."

I had no idea what was going on. So I smiled.

"Um!" Bran shouted, a little too loud and panicked than what could be considered normal, and about an octave or two higher than usual. "Excuse me! I just want to make it clear that I wasn't doing anything bad."

Ryuji's head whipped around to stare back at Bran. Bran's eyes shifted down to meet mine, and I could see from the panic in his eyes that he believed me now. Seeing Ryuji teleport so casually probably made it easier to believe my story than my tears did.

"Really?" Ryuji asked. "So you're telling me you didn't make Lena cry?"

"No!" Bran shouted, then winced when he realized that the evidence seemed to be stacked against him. "I mean, yes! But that isn't because I'm a bad guy or anything. I'm a good, friendly guy! I'm also very uninteresting! And naïve!"

"Would a good guy harass a girl and make her cry?" Ryuji asked.

"No!" Bran shouted. I think he meant to deny the fact that he made me cry, but his shout was just kind of nonsensical instead.

I internally screamed when I saw Bran still had his hand on his sword. I assumed he believed that Ryuji was an Otherworlder at this point, but the placement of his hand might have been a subconscious attempt at reassuring himself, like a weapon-shaped security blanket. Unfortunately, if Ryuji saw that as a threat, I was afraid of what might happen.

Ryuji wasn't looking at me, so I tried to motion to Bran to take his hand off his sword. It was very crude sign language, but even if he could have interpreted it, Bran was unfortunately too focused on his potentially impending death to actually notice my movements.

Ryuji stepped forward. Bran stepped back.

Ryuji stepped forward and lifted a hand into the air. While Bran flinched at the movement, he didn't immediately piss his pants, so I had to assume he didn't understand it for the threat that it was. As someone who had witnessed him casually shoot a pillar of fire into the sky without even trying, I was glad that my bladder wasn't full.

I motioned to Bran again but gave up, seeing his eyes locked with the Otherworlder's. Bran's hand twitched, possibly as a nervous tick or as a reflex, and Ryuji noticed, shifting forward slightly and extending his arm.

Bran was annoying at times, but he was my friend. Honestly, if I were being rational, I wouldn't say I liked him enough to give up my life for him, but it seemed that my mind worked strangely under stress.

I tried to grab Ryuji's arm to point it to the sky, but my legs buckled underneath me as I lunged forward, making me crash into his back instead. On instinct, I grabbed on to whatever I could to stop myself from falling but froze when I realized exactly what I was grabbing.

I was grappling an Otherworlder, and I was so dead.

Chapter 3

What's an Anime?

Ryuji didn't move for a moment, his body going stiff in my arms. I desperately wanted to pull away, but for now, he was standing still, and I didn't want to do anything that might change that. Maybe if I never moved from that spot for the rest of my life, he would be permanently frozen too.

When I felt him shift under my arms, I winced and closed my eyes, turning away from him. Whatever horrible things he was going to do to me, I didn't want to watch. I only prayed that my death would be quick.

Nothing happened.

"Um, L-Lena," Ryuji said. I couldn't tell if he was stuttering out of rage, but for some reason, his voice sounded a bit timid to me. Perhaps it was an auditory hallucination. Maybe I was already dead.

"I..." He paused, taking a deep breath. "I can feel something soft," he said. "On my back."

I had no idea what he was talking about, but he sounded nervous for some reason. I opened my eyes, daring to peek up at my death.

I was shocked to see Ryuji staring down at me, a heavy blush on his face, so red that it looked like... No, wait. Was that actual blood?

"You're bleeding?" I said, the comment coming out as a question. I knew Otherworlders were technically mortal, but I'd never heard of an Otherworlder that was so fragile that he'd start to bleed randomly. Did he have some magic that was related to blood?

It didn't seem likely. Ryuji seemed as confused as I was.

"I am?" he asked. He seemed to think for a moment before reaching up to touch his face.

As his finger wiped the blood from underneath his nose, his eyes widened and his mouth fell agape.

"Status," he said. "Current status effects."

As Ryuji swept his finger randomly in thin air, I noticed Bran slowly creeping away from the scene, walking backward step by step. I had no idea how he had the fortitude to keep his knees from going weak, but I was jealous.

"Help me," I mouthed silently to him, not trusting my own legs to sneak away fast enough.

Bran nodded slightly at me but continued to walk away, doing nothing to help me do the same. Apparently, lip reading wasn't a skill of his.

"Oh, are you kidding me?!" Ryuji suddenly shouted. "Anime character constitution? Am I going to keep getting nosebleeds every time this happens?!"

I heard a pattering of footsteps and looked around to see that Bran had used the outburst as an opportunity to run away. Bastard. I was so holding this over his head for the rest of his life if we got out of this alive.

Ryuji seemed to be finished with yelling up into the sky and turned around to me, mumbling something about shitty tropes, whatever that was. He still had a thick blood smear on his lips, but I wasn't about to point it out to him.

"Sorry about that," he said.

"Are you okay?" I asked, hoping the answer would be, "No, I have a terminal illness called Anime Character Constitution, a non-contagious disease native to my world. I will die soon and will no longer be a danger to you."

"Yeah," he said instead. "Hey, where did that bastard go?"

"Oh, Bran?" I asked, internally agreeing with the bastard sentiment. "He just left. But he won't be bothering us anymore, thanks to you."

"Oh," Ryuji said, blushing and turning to the side. "You're welcome."

I had no idea why my spiteful comment pleased him, but I donned a smile and ignored the reaction in a routine that was slowly starting to get more and more familiar to me.

"So," I said, changing subjects away from Bran with the subtlety of a sledgehammer. "I suppose I should show you around the town, huh?"

"Show me around town?" Ryuji repeated, blushing again for some reason. "You mean like a..."

He trailed off, and I had no idea why.

"Like a what?" I asked.

"Never mind," he said.

I liked to think that by now, I'd gotten used to the awkward silences to the point where I no longer even bothered to acknowledge them.

"I'll take you to the mayor." I waited for a response but continued when I didn't get one immediately. "Anybody visiting our village has to report to him or the sheriff, just so they know that you're not a sketchy person or anything."

Although few people bothered to make those reports—it was usually only family members of villagers who ever came to visit Plainswood, and the odd merchants who visited our town usually didn't know of the rule—it was still technically the truth.

I paused for a long while. I'd hoped that Ryuji would comment on it or ask any sort of follow-up questions, but when he stayed silent, I started to feel more and more uncomfortable. I hadn't gotten used to the awkward silences like I'd hoped. It was especially bad since I kept walking in front of Ryuji. While it helped ease my worries, knowing that I wouldn't have to constantly keep my expression friendly, it was hard not being able to see Ryuji's face and get a gauge for how he was feeling at any given moment.

Looking around me, I saw my fellow villagers either smiling woodenly at Ryuji or quickly picking up their children and scurrying away as fast as they could without looking like they were running. To his credit, Bran really knew how to get people to listen to him. I knew he and his family were popular in the village, but it took real charisma to get these people not to run away screaming.

Unfortunately, even if Bran had done his job perfectly, it didn't seem like any of my fellow villagers were born actors, with most of them being much worse than I imagined myself. I could even see some of them crying through their smiles.

"So!" I said, drawing Ryuji's attention to me as his eyes wandered to the people edging away from him. "Anime! What's that?"

I wondered if it would be dangerous to poke the Otherworlder for knowledge that was clearly unique to his world, especially if it was somehow related to a syndrome that could cause him to bleed spontaneously. As soon as the question came out of my mouth, I worried that it would seem like I was trying to pry into his weaknesses, but it was hard to think of another topic.

"Huh?" he said. "Wait, you've heard of anime? You guys have anime in this world?" he asked, clearly excited.

"N-No," I stuttered, a little scared to disappoint him. "You said it a few seconds ago. I've never heard that word before, and I was just wondering what that was."

"Oh," he said, clearly disappointed, but much less than I feared. "Well, it might be a bit difficult to explain."

"I don't mind," I said. "It's a bit of a walk to the mayor's house." And I needed something to distract him on the way there.

Ryuji looked surprised for a second, then his eyebrows scrunched together in concentration. "Well," he said. "It might be difficult to explain it without a frame of reference. Do you guys have stuff like moving pictures in this wor— I mean, country?"

I ignored the slip-up and the poor attempt to cover it. "Moving pictures?" I asked. "I can't say I have."

"I guess that means they don't have TVs here, either," he said, mumbling more to himself than to me. "I wonder how hard it would be to make one."

He grumbled to himself for a few more seconds before shaking his head and turning his attention back to me.

"You guys have plays here, right?" he asked. "Like with actors and stuff?"

I nodded, already having lost the thread of conversation but not willing to admit it.

"Well, anime's kind of like that, except instead of actors on a stage, it's pictures in a box..."

By the time I regained my senses, I realized we were standing outside the door to the mayor's house. My hand was raised, like I was prepared to knock, but I had no idea what had happened in the past twenty minutes or so it would've taken us to walk here, somehow having zoned out completely despite the situation I was in.

"But when Hirito gets to the hospital, he's ambushed by the bad guy, but this time he has a knife and he's prepared to kill him and Nasuna in the real world, since, you know, he couldn't do it in the virtual world. But since Hirito's been fighting so long in the virtual world, all that fighting data is ingrained in his instinct, and he's able to beat the bad guy up, even without his game stats. Man. That scene was so cool."

Oh yeah. That.

For the past twenty minutes, Ryuji had been trying and failing to explain what anime was to me, but even if I hadn't zoned out completely, I doubted I would have understood what he was talking about. Maybe if I were a smarter person, I would've been able to piece together the literally otherworldly knowledge that he was giving me to gain a better understanding of the world beyond my own, but the seemingly random rambling was beyond my abilities to interpret.

"I hate to interrupt you, Ryuji," I said, interrupting him eagerly. "But we're here."

"Oh," he said. "Okay. I guess talking to the mayor is more important for now. Maybe I can tell you more later?"

"Sure!" I hoped my laugh didn't sound too manic. "Maybe later. But let's not keep the mayor waiting, shall we?"

I knocked on the door, possibly a bit louder than was normal.

"You may enter!" came a response, much louder and higher pitched than was normal from the mayor.

It seemed like Bran had managed to warn him.

I opened the door, eager to deposit the problem into the lap of a responsible adult.

Chapter 4

Responsible Adults

I'd been in the mayor's home before. Since our village wasn't big enough to have a town hall or community center, the mayor and his wife often liked to host dinner parties and festivals for important days and occasions at their home instead. Though the parties would mostly be held outside, his house was always open to anyone who wanted to escape the sun or the cold, depending on what time of year it was.

I hadn't gone inside too often, but I at least remembered the mayor's house well enough to know that he'd changed some things.

For one, there was a plush red carpet that extended all the way from the entrance to the living room, where the mayor was standing. If that wasn't strange enough, inside what should have been the living room was a long dining table that the mayor usually only took out during his parties for seating the pregnant, elderly, or whoever else couldn't stand for long times for whatever reason. It could seat twenty comfortably and looked ridiculous being set up indoors.

"Oh?" he said. "I wasn't expecting guests. Please, do come in!"

I had to hand it to him, though. As ridiculous as his setup was, the mayor was a pretty good actor. If I didn't know that his voice was usually an octave lower, I would've never guessed that something was wrong.

The mayor had set up an assortment of pastries and drinks along the table, and he motioned to Ryuji to sit down.

"Come now, Lena and friend. I wouldn't be a good host if I didn't at least offer a drink or a snack. Feel free to eat as much as you want."

Looking down at the assortment, unless Otherworlders could somehow consume ten times the amount that an average human could, it was impossible that we would make a dent in the feast of pastries laid out before us. It was like a feast meant for a king—if feasts were made exclusively of tea snacks and cookies.

It was at that moment that I realized what the mayor was doing. Was he literally trying to treat Ryuji like a king? Was it because of what I said to Bran?

"Uh, it's okay," Ryuji said. "I'm not actually that hungry."

"Oh," the mayor said. "Then is there anything else I could do for you? Anything at all?"

"Actually, there is!" Ryuji said. "Is there anything like an adventurer's guild here in this village?"

The mayor smiled. After I counted about ten seconds of him staring blankly at Ryuji, I realized he was employing the same tactic I'd been using until now—ignoring anything he didn't understand. Unfortunately, it didn't seem like it worked when he tried to ignore a question that was asked directly to him.

"Umm," Ryuji said, breaking the silence. "Did you hear me?"

"Oh?" The mayor shoved his pinky in his ears. "I'm sorry, sir. It seems like my hearing's been going recently. Old age. What did you say?"

"I asked if there's anything like an adventurer's guild in the village."

It didn't seem like the mayor understood completely that ignoring the question wouldn't work a second time.

With the mayor's uselessness becoming clearer to me with each passing second, I didn't hesitate to jump in before the silence became stale.

"A guild? Like a worker's guild? I wasn't aware that being an adventurer was considered a profession, but I guess it might be a bit different in the country you're from," I added quickly, once I saw the slightest hints of surprise entering Ryuji's face.

"Ah, yeah. Yeah, adventurers' guilds are pretty common where I'm from," he said, accepting the excuse I handed him. "You guys really don't have them?"

From how disappointed he sounded, I wished I could say we did, but it would just be too difficult a lie to keep up long-term.

"No, sorry," I said, wincing internally and bracing myself for magical destruction, in case he decided to shoot the messenger, who in this case was me. After a moment of thought, I inched toward the mayor, deciding I could use him as a distraction if necessary. Unfortunately, he noticed and slowly inched away from me at the same pace.

"Maybe it's called something different?" Ryuji asked. "In my country, adventurers were brave people who were willing to do any task, no matter how dangerous or difficult it was."

Surprisingly, the description did happen to match a lifestyle that was somewhat common in this world. Unfortunately, "homeless vagrant who does odd jobs for cash" was probably a much less glamorous title than the one he was searching for. I supposed "mercenary" was an alternative name for that, but those were just homeless vagrants who happened to be more murderous in nature, and I preferred if we didn't plant the idea of killing for a living into a man who was more than capable of it.

Now that the mayor was standing across the table, having had ample time to scoot as far away from me as possible, I could see his face clearly. I saw the gears turning in his mind, and his eyes widened as he realized the same thing I did. Except he seemed to be a lot happier about it.

"Actually, we do have something—"

"To go!" I said quickly, cutting him off as fast as possible. Though I had no way of knowing, I had a gut feeling that the mayor was about to suggest that Ryuji's dream job in his world was the equivalent of a homeless murderer in ours, and I didn't want to be here when it happened.

"Something to go to!" I repeated, clarifying myself.

Ryuji and the mayor stared blankly at me.

"I have something that I need to do! I should go," I said, clarifying myself properly on the third attempt. I hoped.

From the horrified look on the mayor's face as he realized I was about to leave him alone with Ryuji, I felt like I'd done a pretty good job of making myself clear. I let out an internal sigh of relief, mouthing a silent thank you to the mayor. Though Ryuji was looking at me, I was surprised he didn't notice the sound of the mayor's clothes flapping frantically as he shook his head violently.

"Ah, is that so?" Ryuji said, sighing out loud.

"Oh no, no," the mayor said. "I'm sure you can stay for just a few more moments, Lena."

"Sorry," I said, suddenly aware of the fact that I didn't know his name, even though he apparently remembered mine. It reminded me of the fact that the mayor wasn't usually a bumbling idiot and that he deserved to be honored after he inevitably committed accidental suicide via Ryuji. "Thanks for having me, but I've got to go."

The mayor looked to be near tears. The person causing his tears smiled awkwardly, not noticing the mayor's distress whatsoever as he rubbed the back of his head.

"Ah, that's a shame," he said. "Well, it's been a pleasure, Mayor, but I guess we have to be heading out now."

It took me a few seconds to realize what Ryuji had said.

"You're going too?" the mayor asked, his tears of despair slowly turning into hope.

"Yeah," Ryuji said, rubbing his head. "It's dangerous out there for a lady like her to walk alone."

The mayor opened his mouth, as if to protest out of pride, knowing that our village was one of the safest in the county, but for the first time since we'd come by, his common sense prevailed.

"Well, it was a pleasure to meet you, Mr..." He trailed off when he realized he didn't actually know Ryuji's name.

"The name's Ryuji Nightblade. Remember the name. I'll be the best adventurer in the world one day."

Ignoring the fact that I still wasn't completely sure what an adventurer was, I walked outside, hoping he wouldn't follow me.

But he did.

"So," Ryuji said, oblivious to my suffering. "What did you want to do again?"

I wanted to cry. I wanted to shove him to the mayor and force him to take responsibility for Ryuji. I wanted to tell him that he didn't need to come along, or at least ask him why he automatically assumed he was invited, but more than anything, I didn't want to risk upsetting him.

"I have to do something at home," I lied. "My dad needed help moving some meat." A part of me was horrified that I'd just doomed my parents into interacting with Ryuji, but I was starting to realize just how bad I was under pressure.

Plus, the childish part of me just wanted to see my parents. Have them deal with the terrifying Otherworlder for me while I buried myself under the covers like I was five again, trying to hide from thunder and lightning.

"Moving meat?" Ryuji asked. "Why would you do that?"

"My dad's a butcher," I said. "The village isn't big enough that he needs more than just himself working the shop most times, but I help out whenever he needs me."

"Oh," he said. "That's cool."

Once again, I made sure to walk ahead of Ryuji, both to lead the way and to give my face a break from having to fake a smile constantly. With Ryuji outside of my field of vision, the fact that I couldn't see his reaction made me constantly on edge. Just judging from his voice, he sounded a little distracted.

Looking around, I noticed on the way that the streets of my village were oddly empty, with a distinct lack of open windows and children playing underfoot. It seemed that news had already reached this far, but I was a little annoyed that they were making it so obvious. Was this the reason he sounded distracted?

I opened my mouth. I wanted to say something, anything to draw his attention back to me, so he wouldn't notice the strange emptiness of the streets, but the words died in my throat. I couldn't help it. Even if it was just pure bad luck, I knew the responsibility had been given to me to keep Ryuji from snapping and killing us all. Even so, I couldn't help but want to pretend like I didn't exist, in the wild hope that he'd somehow forget about me.

So I kept quiet. We didn't have much further to walk anyway.

My house was a bit separated from the other houses since my grandparents had built the house, knowing that it would be used as a butchery. Animal blood was a scent that I no longer noticed, but that didn't mean the neighbors would think the same way, after all. There was a large stretch of road where there weren't any more empty houses to look at, but Ryuji still kept silent.

By the time we reached my house, I was sweating, prepared to cry from how tense the silence between us had gotten. I was still too scared to look back at Ryuji, afraid to see an angry scowl on his face after I'd unknowingly offended him in some way, so I just didn't look back. The only thing I could do was to silently pray that everything was alright.

The front door to my house was the customer's entrance, which I rarely used, but I didn't want to lead Ryuji into the part of my home where I slept, for obvious reasons. It led to a small foyer, where a large counter separated the room from the rest of the house.

Sitting at the other side of the counter was Dad.

Though he was well-liked in the village by the adults, Dad was a big guy, and the sight of him usually scared the more skittish of the village kids. I didn't blame them, knowing that the combination of his resting scowl and the permanent animal blood stains smeared on a majority of his clothes made his appearance a bit intimidating to anyone who wasn't used to him. I could tell he was nervous. He only ever crossed his arms when he was uncomfortable.

Even so, his face didn't betray anything, his naturally stiff expression working out in his favor.

"Hi Dad!" I yelled a bit too loudly and waved a bit too wildly.

"Daughter," he said. "How are you?"

Terrified and scared out of my mind.

"Great!" I said instead.

He locked eyes with me and nodded.

In that moment, I couldn't help but feel real hope. My dad always had my back, and I knew that if anyone could get me out of this situation, it was him.

Growing up with him, I had learned that even though most people assumed he was stoic from how monotone his voice was and how little his face moved, my dad was far from expressionless. It was in the minor details, and most importantly his eyes, where I'd learned to read his emotions. Staring into them now, I could tell that he was scared and that all he wanted to do was to run away from the monster stalking me, but that he wouldn't. His eyes promised to keep me safe.

I couldn't help it. I cried.

Thankfully, it wasn't loud. I felt the tears running down my cheeks, but I also felt a genuine smile spread across my lips.

"Hello, sir," Ryuji said from behind me. My smile fell somewhat as I was reminded of why I was so scared in the first place. He was still trailing behind me, so I was confident that he hadn't seen my tears, but I wiped them away as quickly as I could.

My dad broke eye contact with me to face the threat.

"Hello, young man," he said.

"It's nice to meet you, sir. My name is Ryuji Nightblade."

"I am Hal," my dad replied. "Would you like to purchase some meat?"

"Umm, no. I was just here to help Lena. She said she had some chores to do," Ryuji said, sounding uncertain.

My dad raised an eyebrow, an intentional gesture since he usually wasn't expressive enough to let his surprise show so obviously. "Why would you want to do that? No. You're here to purchase some meat. You look like a traveler of sorts. Come in. I'll show you some jerky you can purchase for cheap. Good for the road."

"I don't—"

"I insist. Even if you have no money, I'm not so cruel hearted to let you leave without at least a sample. As I tell all my customers, the first purchase comes free."

I wasn't sure whether it was a good idea to be so pushy, especially with such a nonsensical claim. I was about to lose faith in my dad's abilities until Ryuji spoke up.

"O-Oh. That's nice of you. I guess it wouldn't hurt."

My dad nodded, as if expecting nothing else. In reality, I could see the bright flash of relief in his eyes as he turned to me. "As for you, young lady. Your mother has been searching for you all day. Why don't you go into the house and see what she wants?"

For a second, I wanted to stay. I knew how stressful it was to be in the presence of an Otherworlder, and a part of me just didn't want to subject my dad to dealing with it on his own. The larger part of me just wanted out.

"Alright. I'll go see what Mom wants," I said, practically running forward, a bounce in my step. I still felt bad about leaving my dad to deal with this on his own, but I was too relieved to care.

But when my dad's eyes widened almost imperceptibly, with a flash of anger and fear, I couldn't help but freeze in place. With how stoic he usually was, the slight motion of his brow was the equivalent of a normal man letting out a sharp gasp.

I stayed in place and watched his eyes dart wildly between me and Ryuji, who was still standing behind me, but he said nothing.

Eventually, I tried to move again, but the look on his face gave me pause. He looked like he was about to cry. Thankfully, Ryuji didn't seem to notice, which made sense since my dad had only slightly furrowed his brow. I searched my dad's face, asking for any sort of explanation, and he seemed to register my silent question because he nodded.

"Excuse me for one second."

By the time he disappeared into the door leading into the rest of our house, I couldn't wipe the shock from my face. The betrayal from Bran and the mayor had hurt a little, but the fact that my own father had abandoned me to deal with this monster on my own was like a solid punch in the gut.

Before I could consider shouting at him, Ryuji spoke up.

"Well. He seemed nice."

I quickly wiped my sleeve across my eyes in case there were still tears there before I turned back around to face him.

"Yeah, I guess."

Before I could actually badmouth him like I'd planned, my dad popped back out from behind the door, making me take back all of the nasty things I was about to say about his receding hairline.

"I am back," he said, sounding slightly out of breath for some reason. "Lena, your mother is waiting. She wishes to speak to you."

Something about the way he said that put my teeth on edge, but I was so eager to leave the room that I didn't think twice about it. I nodded and almost ran toward the door, not even bothering to say bye to Ryuji. It probably wasn't the best idea to be rude for no reason, but I could feel myself nearing the breaking point, and I didn't want to interact with him for a second longer than I had to.

Bending over to duck underneath the counter, I saw my dad wince at the action for some reason, but he said nothing as I pushed my way into our house, and I wasn't eager to stop and ask him about it.

I jumped when I pushed open the door to see my mom hiding right behind it, tears flowing freely as she held her hand over her mouth, as if she were physically holding back a scream. At the sight of me, her knees buckled from underneath her, and she sank slowly to the ground.

I rushed over to her side to help her up before her words made me pause.

"I'm sorry," she said. "This is all my fault."

Chapter 5

A Blessing and a Curse

I had no idea what my mom was talking about, but whatever she wanted to say, I knew this wasn't the place to say it. While my dad was an outwardly stoic man, Mom was the exact opposite, wearing her heart on her sleeve and being unable to hold anything back to save her life. Unfortunately, that saying could prove to be more literal if she wasn't careful.

"Come on, Mom," I said, hooking my arm under hers and dragging her deeper into the house. "Let's get out of here first."

I could hear my dad talking a lot louder than he usually did and could only assume he was trying to drown out our voices. Maybe he was just being overly cautious, and my mom wasn't loud enough to be heard, but I couldn't be too careful.

Mom seemed to agree with my unsaid assessment and let me drag her to the opposite end of the house. As soon as she deemed it safe enough to make some noise, however, she launched herself at me. While I was bigger than her by a fair margin, I still struggled to keep my balance.

"Oh, Lena. I heard everything from your father. I'm so sorry you have to deal with this. This is all my fault," she said, her voice shuddering with every word.

I wanted to console her, but I was a bit emotionally burned out by this point. Before I could figure out a question to ask her, she shook her head.

"No, we mustn't give up hope just yet. Surely there must be a way to fix this. It doesn't have to be you. Maybe I could go in your place. Your father would be devastated, but he would understand."

I looked at her as if analyzing her would somehow make it easier to make sense of what she was saying. It didn't help. My mom was more disheveled than I'd ever seen her before, with her usually neat hair messy and wild like she'd been grabbing it and trying to tear it out. Her eyes were unfocused and wild, and she seemed to be on the verge of hyperventilating.

"Mom?" I asked, hating how pathetic I sounded but not caring enough to stop myself. "What are you talking about? You're scaring me."

Her eyes snapped to me, as if she'd just realized I was there. I almost flinched back from the intensity of the motion, even though I knew my mom would never hurt me.

"Mom," I called again, growing more anxious by the second. The fact that I had no idea what she was worried about made it worse. "What's going on? What are you talking about?"

My mom looked at me as if I'd asked her something absurd. "I thought you would've figured out by now," she said, a little cautiously. "Your father told me what happened out there."

"What are you talking about?" I asked. "Dad only saw Ryuji for about ten seconds before he ran back here to talk to you."

My mom mumbled to herself for a second before looking at me. "Lena. Can you tell me how the Otherworlder's been acting around you?"

"Mom." I was growing a bit frustrated by the lack of communication. "Can you just tell me what's going on?"

She shook her head violently, flinging some tears from her eyes into the air.

"It's possible that your father was simply mistaken, dear. I don't want to scare you for potentially no reason. Please. Tell me how the Otherworlder's been acting around you."

I wanted to protest, but the way my mom was acting was uncharacteristic of her, and frankly, she was already scaring me enough that I didn't want to argue with her. Unfortunately, I had no idea what to say. I hadn't really been paying attention to Ryuji. I'd been much more focused on keeping my own emotions in check.

"He's been..." I paused, struggling to find the right words to describe Ryuji. "Pretty normal," I said, surprising myself when I realized it was the truth. Mostly. "Aside from the fact that he cast a fireball big enough to burn a city to ashes without breaking a sweat, he's been acting surprisingly normal."

Somehow, my mom didn't seem to care about my description of Ryuji's abilities.

"Normal, how?" she asked instead. "How exactly has he been interacting with you?"

"I don't know," I said.

"That's not helpful," my mom said, grabbing my shoulders and shaking them. "Lena, honey. Please try to think."

I felt my fear slipping away and slowly being replaced by irritation. "I don't know," I said, stressing each word as I peeled my mom's hands away. "It's been more than a bit stressful for me, Mom. If you'd just stop talking in riddles and just tell me what's going on, maybe I could tell you what you want to know."

My mom flinched back, as if just realizing that she was treating me so roughly. "I-I'm sorry, dear," she said, biting her lip nervously. She opened her mouth and closed it, as if thinking about what to say, before she stared me in the eyes. "Just tell me. You must have been walking around with him. How were you walking? Side by side? Was he leading the way while you followed? Were you leading the way?"

Of all the options she suggested, the last one was easily the one she seemed most nervous about. I hesitated to answer, since it was clearly the one answer she wouldn't be happy about, but I still had no idea why such a thing could even matter.

"I was walking in front of him."

My mom gasped and stumbled backward onto the floor. Normally, I might have lunged forward to catch her before she fell, but her reaction was so unexpected and nonsensical that I remained frozen in place.

"Lena," she said, apparently unfazed by the hard fall. "Please tell me, were the two of you making good conversation? Or did the Otherworlder seem silent or distracted in any way?"

Again, the way my mom's voice shuddered as she described the second option made it obvious that it was the wrong one, but unfortunately, that was what had happened. Though we'd made a little bit of small talk, I couldn't honestly say that we'd talked all that much. I hadn't been in the mood to complain either. If Ryuji didn't want to talk, then there was less of a chance for me to screw up.

"He was pretty quiet."

My mom let out a low moan. "It's just as I feared."

I couldn't remember the last time I'd yelled at my mom, but I was seriously considering it. The only thing that stopped me was the fact that a volatile mage was standing at the other end of the house. I still had no idea how similar an Otherworlder's anatomy was to ours, but I wasn't discarding the possibility that he had enhanced hearing. "What's just as you feared?" I hissed instead. "You still haven't told me anything, Mom."

"I'm sorry," she said. "This is all my fault."

I felt my eyelid twitch at the non-answer. I leaned down and grabbed her shoulders, hard enough that I might've been worried about it hurting her if I wasn't so panicked myself.

"Mom. What is it? If it involves me, I deserve to know," I said. Though I had intended to say it with conviction, the shakiness behind my voice took away some of the power behind my request.

Even so, my mom looked me in the eyes, tears flowing down her cheeks, and nodded hesitantly.

"You." She paused, taking a shaky breath to gather her composure. She didn't seem to find it, but she spoke anyway. "You've got a lovely ass."

I wasn't surprised that I'd somehow misheard her, with how badly her teeth were chattering as she said it. Maybe if we were in any other situation, I would've laughed at the absurdity of what I'd misheard, but I was just too stressed to find any sort of humor in it.

"Sorry, Mom," I said. "I didn't hear you properly. What did you say?"

My mom looked up at me, took another deep breath, and spoke again, this time with a bit more clarity.

"You've got a lovely ass. Breasts too. It's likely he hasn't noticed yet, since he's been trailing behind you. But when he does..." My mom trailed off, choking on her words as she sniffled.

Even though I definitely hadn't misheard her the second time, there was no way I hadn't misheard her.

"What?" I asked again.

"You got it from me," she said, completely misunderstanding my confusion. "We come from a long line of women blessed with immaculate genes."

I opened my mouth as if to respond, but no words came out. My mom held her face in her hands as a low, gasping sob escaped between her fingers.

"I'm sorry. Ryuji's infatuated with you, Lena. But don't worry. We'll get you out of this somehow. I wouldn't be able to live if you became a Follower."

"Mom," I said, finally finding my voice. "What are you talking about? There's no way Ryuji would fall in love with me after a few minutes."

"It happened to your father," my mom said, her voice taking a wistful lilt to it. She gazed at me, but her eyes didn't seem to register me properly.

"It was eighteen years ago during the midsummer festival, at the peak of the celebration. I'd had my eye on your father for some time at this point, but he never seemed to notice me until that night. I was wearing a dress that my mother had woven for me, but I had taken the liberty of modifying it to show off a bit more than she'd hoped. She was so angry at me."

I grabbed her shoulders, intending to shake them and snap her back into reality when I realized something strange about what she said. Whenever I'd asked them about it before, I'd never gotten a clear answer about how my parents had met. Though it was a relatively minor thing I shouldn't have taken notice of in the context of my current situation, the truth of my parents' marriage had evaded me for so long that I couldn't help but notice.

Eighteen years ago? Wasn't I seventeen?

I was pretty terrible at math, so a liberal shake of my head was enough to stop my attempts to calculate how many months separated my birthday and the midsummer festival. Unfortunately, learning the circumstances of my birth was the least of my problems. I would process that potential trauma once I was more certain of my upcoming survival.

"Okay, fine. Whatever," I said, pushing through the topic as bluntly as I could. "But you at least knew Dad and he knew you. Ryuji is a stranger. There's no way he'd fall in love with me so easily?"

I'd meant for that to be a statement, but a moment of weakness turned it into a nervous question, the smell of hellfire still too fresh in my memory to completely ignore the possibility, despite how ridiculous it was.

My mom stared at me, a look of pity in her eyes.

"Oh, my sweet child," she said. "You never did understand the hearts of boys."

My fear had slowly been melting away for a while now, gradually replaced with exasperation at my mom's ridiculous theory, but I refused to completely dismiss it since it could potentially mean my survival. It was this casual insult that finally tipped me over the edge, as a wave of heat blossomed over my face.

Ever since I was a kid, I'd always hung out with boys more than I did with the other girls. Even if I had been interested in dating, the dating pool in the village was non-existent. I knew the boys in the village well enough that I would either feel too disgusted or too awkward to ever consider it. I knew my mom disapproved, constantly telling me that she was afraid I would never end up getting married, but I hadn't expected her paranoia to extend to the point where she was acting so rashly when there was a very real threat to our village standing at the other end of the house.

"Mom," I said, my voice coming out without stuttering for the first time in a while. "This isn't the time."

"Isn't the time for what?" my mom asked.

I felt my brow furrow in frustration. I couldn't tell if she was pretending to be innocent or if she genuinely believed that she had no idea why I was so frustrated with her. First, the mayor, and now my mom. I could only hope that my dad wasn't somehow signing the village's death warrant while he was unsupervised.

"We need to make sure the village is safe," I said, wincing when I realized that I'd said "we." It seemed that I'd accepted the idea that I had some sort of responsibility in containing the threat that was Ryuji. Before today, I had no idea the adults in the village could be so unreliable. "Then we need to make sure the Mediators know that an Otherworlder's here. Ryuji already seems to be interested in staying in the village for a bit, so that's more than enough time to get someone to ride toward Redstone with the news."

My mom, who hadn't bothered getting up from where she'd fallen, stared up at me, a look of confusion in her eyes. "Yes, of course," she said.

I nodded, glad we were finally in agreement on something. "I already promised Ryuji to 'lend' him some money for the trip, but he doesn't seem to be in a rush to leave, and I think it would be safer to keep him in the village for at least a day, just so he doesn't feel like we're kicking him out," I said, immediately hating the suggestion.

"Lena," my mom said, slowly pushing herself up off the floor. "Why don't you leave all that to the adults?"

"I would. If I hadn't seen firsthand how useless you adults could be." At that moment, my panic was too strong to maintain any sense of politeness. Thankfully, my mom didn't seem to notice or care about the casual insult. "If Dad seems to be handling Ryuji well, I'll let him take the reins, but from what I've seen, I seem to be the only one in this village who doesn't feel like committing suicide via Otherworlder."

My mom shook her head violently, grabbing my shoulders again. "You mustn't get yourself any more involved with this. The more you expose yourself to Ryuji, the more he will come to fall for you." She paused, letting go and biting her lip nervously. "Although we shouldn't keep you away for too long. Distance does make the heart grow fonder."

I threw my hands up in frustration.

"Mom! I get it! I'm not good with boys. I know I've never had a boyfriend before. You've been drilling that into my head my entire life!"

It wasn't as bad as I might have implied, but the way that my mom brought my non-existent love life up in random conversations did get on my nerves. I hadn't thought it would be bad enough to interrupt in a life-or-death situation like the one we found ourselves in, but today had been full of surprises.

"Lena—"

From the look in her eyes, I knew she was just going to say the same thing. I cut her off with a frustrated groan as I pulled at my hair.

"Mom! This is serious," I said. "We need to focus on making sure the village isn't burned to the ground by the end of the day."

"I care about you more than I do this village," she snapped.

"I live in this village, Mom! We all do! I'm not in any more danger than anyone else here. Ryuji doesn't care at all about me."

I turned around before my mom could even open her mouth to reply. "I'll prove it."

I vaguely heard my name being whimpered by my mom as I stalked down the hallway. I ignored her and walked across the house, approaching the door that led to the storefront where my dad and Ryuji were talking.

When I opened the door, I was surprised to see my dad trying to kill Ryuji with his meat.

Or at least that was what it looked like at first.

The amount of free goods my dad had piled into Ryuji's arms was absurd. It looked like Dad had taken a large canvas bag that was typically used to transport large carcasses and had stuffed it with anything and everything he could find in his inventory. But even though the bag looked like it should've crushed a man of Ryuji's stature, with it looking like it weighed about three times as much as he did, the Otherworlder was casually lifting the mass with one hand.

My dad's face was mostly expressionless, but his slightly wider eyes suggested that he was on the verge of passing out from fear. Ryuji, on the other hand, was looking up at his feat of strength with a sense of childish wonder.

Neither of them had noticed me entering the room, but in my shock at Ryuji's display of strength, I hadn't had the sense to close the door gently. It was a heavy door, designed to keep the smells of the butchery and the house separate, so when it slammed shut behind me, my dad and Ryuji both looked toward me.

My dad didn't seem to recognize me for a split second, but his eyes widened in fear at the sight of me, even more so than they already had been. Ryuji almost dropped the goods that my dad had given him, but he caught then when he saw me.

And he smiled.

"Hi Lena," he said.

It was at that moment that I internally apologized to my mom and said a silent prayer to the gods, asking them to treat me well in the Aether when I died.

I recognized that smile.

It was the same smile my dad got on his face when my mom snuck up behind him to give him a hug after a long day of work, the only time his expression didn't seem so stiff. It was the same smile that Bran got when Polly waved at him from across the road, giggling whenever he would trip over himself and fall flat on his face. It was the same smile that my old dog would get before he started humping anything that moved, until one traumatizing day, he tried to hump a moving cart and got caught underneath its wheels.

"I forgot something," I said, before running back through the door I came in from and racing down the hallway.

It wasn't long before I crashed into my mother's arms, shivering as I pushed myself into her chest. I didn't cry, even though I desperately wanted to; my eyes were too dry to summon any tears.

"I'm sorry I yelled at you."

"Shh, shh. I know."

"I don't want to go."

"You won't," she said. "We won't let him take you."

I shuddered in my mom's arms, recalling the gout of fire that Ryuji had so easily conjured from his palms. The way he could lift a horse's weight in meat without even straining. I tried to imagine my mom picking up a sword and trying to protect me, and although I trusted her, I wasn't blind to the truth of the situation.

Chapter 6

A FATHER'S WORRIES

When the sheriff's boy first came by to the butcher shop to tell Hal and Arina that an Otherworlder was in Plainswood, being guided around by their daughter, Hal's first instinct was to dismiss the claim as a prank. It was a difficult thing to do, with how badly the boy shivered as he spoke, looking like he'd just stared death in the eye, but Hal simply didn't want to let himself believe it.

Once he realized that denial wasn't a viable way for him to protect his daughter, his second instinct was to go out and find Lena and protect her himself. While he was more than willing to ignore the fact that he had no idea how he planned to protect her from an Otherworlder, his logical side was able to stop him before he went and got the entire village destroyed.

While his parental instincts screamed in protest, more than willing to sacrifice the entire world if it meant keeping his daughter safe, his logic prevailed in the internal debate once he reminded himself that Lena lived in the world too.

So he sat and waited, sending Arina back into the house, hoping that his daughter would do the right thing and push the Otherworlder onto the nearest authority figure in the interest of her own self-preservation.

With his eyes glued to the window, it didn't take too long for him to see Lena walking back home with an unfamiliar boy trailing behind her. Hal couldn't help but feel a surge of disappointment and pride in equal measure at the idea that his daughter had taken it upon herself to shoulder such a huge responsibility in order to protect the village. If that was what she wanted, he would play along.

Hal braced himself, ready to act as a friendly butcher who just wanted to help a weary traveler, but when Lena got close enough, his heart almost stopped when he saw the strained expression of pure terror on her face, barely mitigated by the stiff and unnatural smile that clashed horribly with the fear in her eyes.

And then his heart started to pound in his ears when he noticed where the boy was looking.

His parental instincts were roused once more, sending him into a righteous fury. How dare a boy look at his daughter in that way? Hal felt his fingers gripping his counter, regretting deeply that it wasn't the handle of a cleaver instead, even as his logical side screamed at him not to antagonize the all-powerful Otherworlder.

What stopped him from leaping over the counter and giving the boy a piece of his mind wasn't the idea that he would die pointlessly for it but a surge of fear once he remembered something about Otherworlders.

Otherworlders were notorious for many things, including their tendency to adopt Followers. Of course, this was one of the tamer things that an Otherworlder could do, considering the large-scale actions of an Otherworlder could mean the toppling of governments, the destruction of cities, and the murder of hundreds or even thousands. In that moment, the only thought on Hal's mind was that he would rather die if it meant sparing his daughter from the fate of becoming a Follower.

A child becoming a Follower was technically a path for great success and riches. Not only did Followers boast an exponential rate of growth in their talents and skills when "partying up" with an Otherworlder, but they were also given a handsome reward by the Crown if they helped mitigate the Otherworlder's destructive actions.

While Hal knew that his own parents would've been thrilled by the idea—at least if they weren't rotting in their cold, forsaken graves—he couldn't say the same.

In his youth, Hal had read "The Chronicles of a Witness." It was a book written by a woman named Eti who had been a Follower of the Plague King since she was twelve—an autobiography.

The first-hand experiences recorded in that book made Hal shudder, and the Plague King had been known to be one of the less temperamental Otherworlders that had spawned in Astranta. Eti, as well as two other Followers, had been made to witness a number of disturbing acts that the Otherworlder had committed.

The Plague King was dead now, and Eti was still alive and ridiculously rich. She'd been paid out by the Crown for her help in mitigating the damage done by the Plague King and had the royalties from the book that she'd written based on her experiences, but she had been quick to retreat into isolation afterward, making her riches useless.

After bearing the responsibility of handling an Otherworlder since she was only twelve years old, her sense of reality had been severely twisted, and she'd never been able to properly reintegrate herself into society. Hal didn't blame her. After seeing the aftereffects of the Plague King's actions on society, it wasn't surprising to think that she would want to hide away from it, if only to avoid the misplaced guilt of what she could have prevented.

Hal shuddered to think that that could be the fate of his daughter. He would do anything in his power to prevent it.

As Hal watched Ryuji's reaction to Lena bursting awkwardly into the room and leaving just as quickly, Hal grimaced as the lovestruck expression on the powerful being refused to fade.

"I apologize for my daughter," he said. "She can be quite rude at times."

Ryuji frowned at that. "Really? She seemed pretty nice to me. Are you sure you should be talking about your daughter like that?"

Hal felt sweat drop down his brow. He wasn't sure whether the Otherworlder was threatening him, but it seemed like he was already infatuated to the point where he would defend her honor. That wasn't good.

"She is my daughter," Hal said, with a shrug. He wasn't sure whether his attempts at being nonchalant were succeeding. "I love her, but I am not blind to her flaws."

"Well, I didn't notice anything bad about her," Ryuji insisted. "She just seems a bit shy."

Hal was surprised the gritting of his teeth wasn't more audible in the quiet room. "Perhaps," he said. "Say, traveller. May I ask you a question?"

Unfortunately, Hal wasn't a subtle man. Ryuji raised an eyebrow, not oblivious to the sudden change in topic away from his daughter but seeming willing to play along.

"Sure," he said.

"What is your goal here?"

Ryuji's narrowed eyes softened, taken aback in confusion.

"Huh? What do you mean?"

"What is it that you want to do in this world?" Hal asked, wondering if that was too direct. Though a normal person would probably interpret "in this world" a little more generally, he was dealing with an Otherworlder who could take that in a more literal sense. Hal hadn't realized that until he'd said it out loud, but thankfully, Ryuji didn't seem to take notice, focusing more on the question itself.

"Well, I want to become an adventurer for sure," he said. "Bit disappointing to find out that guilds don't really exist in this wo— country, but I guess that's not too big of a deal."

"I see," Hal lied. "And what exactly does an adventurer do?"

"They... do adventurer things," Ryuji said, seeming both confused and disappointed by the questions. "Dungeons, monster hunting, questing. You start off with killing goblins and eventually escalate to hunting dragons and demon kings. Isn't that normal here?"

Hal paled.

"That's a good dream," Hal lied, too stunned by the proclamation to even dream of disagreeing with the Otherworlder.

Though he had to admit that Ryuji seemed quite docile at first glance, it appeared that the Otherworlder had a murderous streak. While he had no idea what a demon king was supposed to be or whether the Otherworlder's world had dragons in it or if he still believed in fairy tales at his age, Hal knew what a goblin was. While Hal couldn't claim to have a goblin best friend or to have even interacted with particularly many of them, he wasn't a man who subscribed to any amount of prejudice toward other races either.

Even though he had grown up around racist parents, who were eager to shout profanities at any non-humans who would pass through their small village of Plainswood, the casual way that Ryuji declared that killing goblins was a part of his ideal lifestyle would've made even his parents wince.

Hal wondered if he should send a messenger to the nearby villages to warn them of the racist Otherworlder. He could only assume that there weren't any non-humans in the area, but he did know of one butcher in Oakwood who was half-goblin and had noticed a retired couple who had moved into Plainswood from Redstone who were either gnomes or just particularly short and strange-looking humans.

He hadn't been rude enough to ask.

Hal realized with a start that he'd been lost in thought for a few seconds, plunging his store into an awkward silence. Fortunately, Ryuji didn't seem to notice. He was gazing off into space instead.

"Yeah," he said. "I'm going to have so much fun here. It won't be anything like it was back home."

Hal had no idea what to say to that, so he stayed quiet. He had planned to try and dig into Ryuji's motives a bit more, to try to figure out if he could have any possible reason to drag Lena into them, but the Otherworlder had fallen into a trance-like state, and it was the closest thing he'd had to a reprieve since the Otherworlder had arrived in his shop. He still felt uncomfortable about having the Otherworlder inside his store, so close to his wife and child, but he would take any small victories he could get.

At the very least, it seemed like Ryuji was no longer thinking about his daughter.

"Goblins, huh?" Ryuji said wistfully. "That would be a pretty good start. I wonder if this village has a goblin problem."

Hal opened his mouth, as if to deny the idea, but shut it quickly, not wanting to disturb him. For some reason, it felt like a bad decision not to say something, but his survival instinct told him not to draw any more attention to himself than was necessary.

Hal felt his legs shaking underneath him.

Chapter 7

TUTORIAL: FIGHT THE (???)

When I felt the ground shaking underneath me, I immediately knew that Ryuji had caused it somehow, but I was willing to pretend I didn't know that.

With my head still buried in my mom's chest, I felt her tense slightly, no doubt thinking the same thing that I was.

"Shh," she said, muffling my words with a gentle squeeze, despite me not saying anything. "I'm sure it's just a little earthquake. It's not so bad."

I decided to put my trust in her, just because I desperately wanted it to be true. To be fair, it wasn't all blind faith. She was right that it wasn't so bad. We'd definitely had worse earthquakes before. If I weren't lying down on the floor, I wasn't even sure I would've noticed the tremors, just barely strong enough that I couldn't delude myself into pretending that it was just my imagination. Still, they were weak. It wasn't so bad.

I let out a quiet sigh of relief.

I let out another quiet sigh of relief.

And another.

Eventually, I became vaguely aware that I was hyperventilating, as if sighing rapidly could somehow summon relief through brute force.

Why weren't the tremors fading?

Was that screaming I heard in the distance?

"Mom?" I didn't want to ask any questions, dreading what the answers would be.

My mom nervously looked between me and the door that Dad was standing behind. Thankfully, I could still hear his voice. Although muffled by the door, it was clear enough that I could vaguely understand that he was trying to push more meat onto Ryuji. I wasn't sure if it was working, but at the very least, he was alive.

When I heard Ryuji's muffled response to something that my dad said, I couldn't help but furrow my brow.

"He's still talking to Dad," I whispered.

"Your father has this under control, Lena," my mom said, stroking my hair as she whispered back. I wasn't sure if she did it to comfort me or herself. "He'll deal with the Otherworlder, don't you worry."

"I'm not talking about that," I said. "Ryuji's still talking to Dad, but that rumbling seems like it's coming from far away."

My mom looked down at me, apparently not understanding what I was talking about.

"Ryuji might not be causing it," I said, though I didn't know whether that was a good thing or not.

"Should we check to see what's going on?" I asked, hating the question as soon as it left my mouth.

My mom bit her lip, glancing between the door to the storefront and the back door leading outside toward the village and the source of the suddenly audible distant screams. "Maybe we should let the others deal with it," my mom said, gripping me tighter.

I wanted to agree with her, and I didn't know whether it was arrogance that made me disagree, but thinking back to how Bran had abandoned me and how useless the mayor had been, I didn't have enough faith in my fellow villagers to put my life solely in their hands.

"I'm going to take a look," I said, not wanting to get caught unaware if possible.

"Lena," my mom hissed, trying to keep me from getting up. Fortunately, her arms were too shaky and weak to hold me down properly. "It could be dangerous."

"I just want to check out what's going on," I said, easily brushing her hands away and standing up. "I'll be safe. I promise."

I didn't wait for her response. I went to the back door and opened it.

Thankfully, the scene I saw outside wasn't nearly as bad as my paranoia would have expected. The village seemed mostly untouched, and even though the rumbling wasn't getting any weaker, the screaming seemed to be quieting down. At first, I couldn't help but assume the worst, that the screaming was fading because people were dying, but I could still hear a few voices shouting across the village. While they didn't sound happy, it didn't seem like the village was devolving into a full-fledged panic.

I looked around for any sort of explanation as to what was going on, and it seemed that many of my neighbors were doing the same. The street that had been so empty while I was leading Ryuji through it was slowly filling up with curious faces, peeking out of their barred windows to see what was going on. I saw more than a few rucksacks on their backs, stuffed with whatever they could have packed in the short time they'd heard of Ryuji's arrival.

With more people becoming emboldened enough to explore the area, I stepped out of my doorway, ignoring my mom's protests not to leave.

I didn't need to go far to see what was causing all the commotion. A large, ethereal panel hung in the air, like a pane of blue glass floating impossibly high in the sky. On it was a sentence written in a language I shouldn't have recognized.

But somehow, I could understand it.

Event on standby.

Event will proceed after the Hero has accepted the relevant quest.

Even though I could recognize what was written on it, I still had no idea what that meant. Regardless, I could only assume that Ryuji was involved in this. It was easy to blame him for anything I didn't understand at this point. But why could I understand what those words meant?

My thoughts were interrupted when I realized someone was calling my name.

I looked up to see Bran waving nervously at me. He stopped yelling when he noticed me staring at him and jogged up to me.

"Bran. What's going on?" I asked.

"I was hoping you could tell me," he replied.

"Why me?" I asked. Just because I'd seen the Otherworlder first didn't mean I was an expert on him. I had no idea why Bran seemed to assume I did.

"Because it obviously has something to do with the Otherworlder," he said without missing a beat. "Do you happen to know if he's had any interactions with goblins?"

Whatever I'd been expecting, it hadn't been that. A traveling group with a few goblins in it had dropped by Plainswood and stayed for a few days about a month ago, but I doubted that had any relevance to what was happening here.

"No?" I said, feeling too uncertain to give a confident answer. "I pretty much stumbled across him as soon as he fell from the sky. I don't know if there were any goblins in the forest, but we didn't stop to talk to anyone until we got back to Plainswood."

"I see," Bran said, obviously unhappy about the answer. "Then why is there a group of armed goblins stomping around outside the village?"

I stared at him blankly, not exactly knowing how to respond. While I might've panicked at the idea of an armed group of people acting aggressively toward our village on a regular day, it was a lot less intimidating than an Otherworlder.

That being said, I couldn't help but be at least a little surprised by Bran's complete nonchalance.

"Bandits?" I asked.

Bran shrugged. "Maybe?" he said, completely uncertain. "They just look like regular folk with weapons, and they haven't made any demands or anything. They didn't even say anything when we asked what they wanted. They're just stomping around. It's kind of creepy. I thought it might have something to do with the Otherworlder."

It wasn't too big of an assumption, I supposed. Our village having bad enough luck to have an Otherworlder land right beside it was one thing, but having a random group of goblins threatening our village on the same day was just too unlucky to be written off as a coincidence, and it was easy to blame the Otherworlder for everything bad that would happen beyond this point.

That being said, that wasn't the only reason I assumed they were connected.

"I'm pretty sure you're right," I said, my voice deadpan. "You think that freaky blue panel in the sky is just for show? No way the Otherworlder doesn't have something to do with this."

Bran just stared at me, his brow knitting together in confusion. "What blue panel?"

Before I could judge whether Bran was just fucking with me or not, I saw the panel twitch in the corner of my eye. The foreign letters twisted around into another indecipherable combination of unfamiliar symbols, but once again, I could somehow understand what they meant.

Quest accepted.

Initiating event in 10...

My eyes widened as the symbol shifted.

9...

It was a countdown.

"Bran," I said.

8...

"We need to get everyone to safety."

7...

"Why? What's going on?"

6...

"We don't have time!"

5...

"All I know is that something bad is going to happen."

As I said that, the panel disappeared. I looked around frantically, trying to figure out where it could have gone.

"What's going to happen?" Bran asked, looking like he was about ready to run.

"I'm not sure," I said.

As if summoned by my statement, I heard the faint sound of a door slamming open behind me.

"Oh hey, Lena," Ryuji said. His smile instantly vanished when he noticed who was standing beside me. "Hey, is this guy bothering you ag—"

He was cut off by a bloodcurdling scream from the other edge of town.

That scream cut through the air, silencing everything. But it was only for a second. A loud howl sounded out in the air, echoed by a dozen voices. It was a miracle that I could even hear the sheriff's voice shouting over the sound.

"We're under attack!"

"What?" Bran said, echoing my thoughts.

I'd never witnessed an actual battle before. I didn't think that was a very uncommon sentiment. Sure, I'd seen an odd fight or two when there was a dispute between villagers, but nothing that could be described as anything more than a scuffle.

But even though I'd never heard it before, the sound of battle was unmistakable.

The harsh sounds of steel hitting stone echoed in the air, accompanied by war cries and screams of pain. The sheriff tried to shout orders over it all, but the noise drowned out his voice.

"Dad," Bran whispered, seemingly frozen in place. I wasn't sure whether it was shock that kept him rooted in place or fear.

Ryuji, on the other hand, seemed to have no problem with running toward the source of the noise. When I glanced at his face, I saw a giddy and childlike expression, before a shockwave of air followed in his wake as he dashed forward impossibly fast, forcing me to shut my eyes so I wouldn't get dust in them.

When I opened my eyes again, I noticed him fading quickly in the distance, but just barely. Moving faster than my eyes could keep up with, it was easier for me to track the large clouds of dust that he kicked up in his wake as he sprinted down the single road that cut through the village. Rafters and entire houses shook in his wake, but thankfully, he wasn't as destructive as I knew he could be.

"Should we stop him?" Bran asked.

The sheer absurdity of the question made me think I'd imagined it for a moment.

"How do you suggest we do that?" I asked, staring at the spot where Ryuji stood moments ago.

Bran bit his lower lip nervously. "I don't know," he said. "But don't you think we should at least try something?"

We? Why was it that Bran automatically included me in that suggestion? Did the situation really need me to attend to it?

"Leave Lena's home alone, you monsters!"

Ryuji's voice was somehow audible through all the noise, ringing loudly through the air.

I closed my eyes and took a deep breath. When I opened them, I tried to ignore the stares from my neighbors and Bran.

"Fine," I said, too used to the now constant state of dread I found myself in to give a stronger reaction. "Let's go."

As I approached the scene of the battle, I didn't expect that I would be able to do anything. Though a small part of that assumption was because I knew I knew next to nothing about fighting, the main reason I assumed I would be useless was because I didn't think there would be a battle by the time I arrived.

I'd seen firsthand what Ryuji could do, and with the memory of his "fireball" spell still fresh in my mind, I didn't expect there to even be a battlefield anymore—just a hole in the ground where the enemies had once stood.

It was why I was confused by the sight of Ryuji retreating as he dodged a strike from a creature that was most definitely not a goblin.

At first glance, the creature that Ryuji was fighting did have similar features to a goblin, but its skin was a void of darkness that seemed to warp the light into it. The way that it refused to reflect any light made it difficult to even recognize it as a three-dimensional creature, giving off the illusion that Ryuji and the villagers were fighting nothing more than moving silhouettes. Though I'd never seen one take the shape of a goblin before, it was obvious what it was.

A creature of pure Aether. A demon.

I didn't believe my eyes at first. I'd never seen a demon with such a strong outline. Most of them were nearly see-through, looking more like clouds of fine black mist without any mass.

I'd also never seen so many demons in one spot before. I knew that it was technically possible, but we didn't live near any rips in the Aether that would be big enough for so many demons to appear.

My eyes widened when I saw another faux-goblin swipe at Ryuji with a shadowy club. Were these demons working together? Were they sentient?

"Dad!" Bran said, more concerned with making sure his dad was safe than he was with watching Ryuji's fight.

I turned to where Bran was staring and was surprised to see the sheriff standing at the sidelines, with his sword gripped in his hands and a deep frown on his face, his eyes locked onto the fight that Ryuji was having with the demons. I followed Bran as he jogged toward his father.

"Dad!" Bran said. "Are you alright?"

The sheriff didn't even turn to Bran as he spoke. "I'm fine. Just confused," he said, keeping his eyes fixed on the fight. Even if he seemed content not to join in, his body was tense, poised for a potential fight. Looking around, I couldn't help but notice that he wasn't the only one. Our village's small volunteer militia watched the fight carefully with their weapons raised at the ready but otherwise stayed out of it and let Ryuji fight by himself.

"What's going on?" Bran asked. "Why are those goblins randomly attacking the village?"

I raised an eyebrow. Goblins?

"I know just as much as you do," the sheriff said, not correcting Bran's mistake. "I'm just hoping that the Otherworlder doesn't brutalize them too badly before they can explain what's going on."

I opened my mouth, about to ask them what they were talking about, when an eerie, inhuman screech sounded out from the battlefield.

As if they were growing frustrated with the way that Ryuji was casually dodging away from their attacks, two of the six demons fighting Ryuji let out a shrill battle cry before rushing forward with their shadowy weapons raised. Before they could hit him, Ryuji held out a palm toward them.

"Enough playing around. Time to get serious," he whispered, his words somehow clearly audible despite his low tone. "Flame blade!"

A crimson flame erupted from his hands, and my first instinct was to flinch away, expecting another pillar of flame to incinerate the area around him, but it was more contained this time. In an impossible feat, the flame morphed, defying the laws of nature and condensing into the unwavering shape of a blade.

Though I was awestruck by the sight, the demons didn't seem to care at all. They continued their charge forward, their blank faces giving nothing away.

Ryuji gave them a lopsided smirk.

"Heh, too slow."

I didn't know why he was talking in a fight, but he was clearly powerful enough to get away with it. With a casual sweep of his magic, he cut through both of the demons charging at him. For a moment, the world seemed to freeze. The two demons stood there mid swing, stopped in their tracks. Then Ryuji flicked his magical blade to the side, and the upper halves of the demons slid to the side and fell to the floor.

"Who's next?" Ryuji asked.

I didn't know why I felt the sudden urge to close my eyes and bury my face in my hands, but I did anyway.

"Shit," the sheriff said, his face twisting at the sight.

Bran, for some reason, bent over and threw up.

I yelped and jumped away as his vomit splashed against the floor, almost hitting my shoes.

The sheriff winced and stepped forward to place himself between Bran and the fight.

"I'm sorry you had to see that, kids," the sheriff said. "Shouldn't be something that anyone has to see."

I stared at him, confused about what exactly he was talking about. I understood that Ryuji's abilities were frightening and disturbing, but I got the feeling that the sheriff was talking about something else. His body was wide enough that it blocked my entire view from the battlefield unless I walked around him, but I could still see the sparks and flashes of magic as Ryuji yelled.

"Fireball! Flame barrage! Ember storm!"

"What are you talking about, Sheriff?" It was a little difficult to ignore Ryuji shouting out the names of his attacks like a kid, but I managed to ignore it. I was infinitely more curious about why the sheriff seemed to care so much about the demons dying. "He's just exterminating some demons, right?"

The sheriff stared blankly back at me, and I had no idea why he looked so confused, but before he could speak, his eyes widened imperceptibly as he seemed to notice something appearing behind me.

"Watch out!" he yelled, reaching out to grab me.

I wasn't a warrior. I was decently active for a girl my age, but that didn't mean I had the reflexes or the survival instincts to know how to handle myself in a fight. That was especially true when I didn't even realize I was in a fight in the first place.

I turned around, following the sheriff's eyes to see why he looked so worried, and was met with the sight of a demon standing over me. I had no idea how it had gotten there without me or the sheriff noticing, but I could only stare wide-eyed as its shadowy club swung toward my head.

Chapter 8

A Hero Comes to the Rescue

I stared at the club swinging for my head.

I stared for about three seconds before my body and mind were able to agree on an appropriate response.

"Argh!" I screamed. I stumbled backward and bumped into the sheriff's chest before falling to the ground. My hand slipped on something slick on the ground as I tried to scramble away, but I paid it no mind. I was more interested in surviving.

It was only after a few seconds that I realized that the demon didn't actually seem to be interested in hurting me.

Though my heart was still pounding wildly in my chest, I couldn't help but feel a little curious about the demon's actions. Born of pure Aether, I knew that demons had an alien thought process or no thought process at all. It was already strange enough to see a group of demons seemingly working toward a goal rather than simply milling around aimlessly, but this was even stranger. It was simply frozen in place, its weapon mere inches away from where my head had been a second ago.

"What the hell?" I muttered to myself. I looked to the sheriff as if to ask for an explanation.

"What the hell?" I repeated.

The sheriff's arm was outstretched as he reached—no, dove—toward the spot where I'd been. His entire body was somehow balanced on his toes, looking more like he was floating than anything else.

I didn't think it was appropriate for me to do, but I poked him in the shoulder to see if he would fall.

He didn't.

I looked around and saw the rest of the world similarly frozen in place. A few feet away, Bran was leaning against a wall, stuck in a pose where he was trying to wipe the residual vomit from his lips. He seemed unaware of what was going on, even though I could see some of the braver villagers frozen in gasps of horror, with half of them looking at the demon that was about to attack me and the rest looking at Ryuji fighting further in the distance.

"Am I dead?" I wasn't sure why I asked that out loud. Maybe I hoped someone would respond and prove me wrong.

No one did.

I looked again at the silhouette of the demon attacking me. It was difficult to decipher from this angle, but the shadowy weapon it was holding appeared to be a malicious-looking axe. I couldn't tell how sharp it was, nor how heavy something like a weapon made purely of Aether would be, but I knew it was probably more than dangerous enough to kill me if I touched it.

So why was I still alive? What was going on?

"Am I dead?" I asked again, a little louder this time.

Again, nobody responded.

It felt strange. It felt like I should probably be having a stronger reaction to seeing my entire village inexplicably frozen in time right before my near death, but I just felt too exhausted to do anything but sigh. I was about to put my face in my hands, just to see if any tears would come out, when I finally noticed what I'd slipped on during my initial scramble away from the demon.

I scrunched my face in disgust and walked a few feet over to wipe my hand on Bran's shirt, returning his vomit to him.

I felt bad about it immediately after, but finally being able to release some of my pent-up frustration was such a good feeling that I didn't care. Sorry, Bran.

It was difficult not to assume that I was dead. There wasn't much of anything else this could be. Didn't a lot of people say that time seems to slow down when you're about to die? Well, those stories all came from people who'd clearly survived their near-death experiences, so maybe actually dying made it so time stopped altogether.

But it all felt too real.

I tried not to look at the other obvious answer. It was reasonable for me to assume that Ryuji had somehow caused all of this to happen, but somehow, the thought that Ryuji had the power to freeze time so easily was more terrifying than the possibility that I was dead.

I looked anyway.

Ryuji was frozen in place too.

I blinked a few times, unsure if my eyes were working properly. I rubbed them too, wincing when I realized that my hands were still sticky with Bran's vomit. I ignored it in favor of confirming whether my eyes were working properly or not.

They were, but before I could start to hyperventilate, I noticed the blue panel floating in front of Ryuji's face. It was translucent enough for me to see the strange symbols shining through from the other side. The message was backward from my perspective, and though it didn't matter much when I couldn't read the symbols in the first place, the meaning of the words were still somehow translated perfectly in my mind.

Valiant White Knight

By partying with your love interest, you have unlocked the skill [Valiant White Knight]! Under certain conditions, this skill allows the Hero to rush to protect bonded party members from certain death.

Whenever a bonded party member shouts, "Save me!" the Hero may activate this ability to instantly teleport to their side.

MP Cost: 0

Cooldown: 30 days

I felt my mind go blank. There was just a bit too much to process in that one panel that I couldn't help but sit down and press my face into my hands. I didn't even care about Bran's vomit at this point.

No tears came out, no matter how much I wanted them to.

Love interest? Party member? Certain death?

I had no idea where to even begin.

So I didn't.

I went home.

Chapter 9
A Hero Comes to the Rescue... Eventually

The walk didn't give me as much time to calm down as I'd hoped, with my house being only about ten minutes away from the battle. Regardless, it gave me some much-needed alone time. It had only been about an hour since I'd stumbled upon Ryuji, but it felt like it had been forever since I'd had a moment of peace.

Although it wasn't really that peaceful, considering I was stuck in some sort of weird time spell, it was the best I'd gotten in a while, so I couldn't afford to be too picky.

"Mom, I'm back," I said, casually opening the door as if I was just returning from a normal day.

I flinched when I realized she was standing right behind the door, and I'd slammed it in her face. Frozen in time, she didn't react.

"Shit. Sorry, Mom," I said, even though I had no idea if she would feel it when time unfroze.

The sudden thought of whether time would ever unfreeze crept into my mind, but I brushed it aside; I wasn't prepared to deal with a potential existential crisis just yet.

I closed my eyes and sighed heavily as if hoping the thought would latch onto my breath and leave my body with it.

When I opened my eyes again, I yelped at the sight of a blue panel that had inexplicably appeared right in front of my face.

Valiant White Knight

By partying with his love interest,the Hero has unlocked the skill [Valiant White Knight]! Under certain conditions, this skill allows the Hero to rush to protect bonded party members from certain death.

Whenever a bonded party member shouts, "Save me!" the Hero may activate this ability to instantly teleport to their side.

MP Cost: 0

Cooldown: 30 days

I looked around nervously. Even after a few seconds passed, I was still a little paranoid that the panel would burst into flames and incinerate both me and my mom, but nothing happened. Eventually, I mustered the courage to move away from the panel.

Thankfully, it didn't set me ablaze out of protest.

I walked toward my room, intent on taking a quick nap. Maybe if I fell asleep, I'd wake up and realize this was all a dream. It was a long shot but one I was willing to try.

As I crawled into bed, I realized that it would be difficult. Though I was definitely tired, my heart was pounding with anxiety and my mind kept turning back to the day's events.

I wasn't sure I could ignore everything well enough to fall asleep, but when the blue panel appeared in front of me, floating just above my head where I lay in my bed, I could tell my anxiety would be the least of my worries.

Valiant White Knight

The Hero has unlocked a skill that allows them to protect bonded party members from certain death.

Whenever a bonded party member shouts, "Save me!" the Hero may activate this ability to instantly teleport to their side.

This skill is currently available for use.

Did the text change? I wasn't sure. Technically, I couldn't actually read what was on the panel. Maybe it was just my interpretation of the text that had changed. After all, who was to say that I wasn't just imagining that I could read these strange symbols? Who could say whether I wasn't just hallucinating? Who could say I wasn't just imagining all of this or that this wasn't all just a dream?

I ignored the way the blue panel pulsed with light, as if reacting to my thoughts. Unfortunately for the panel, that only supported the idea that it was just a figment of my imagination. The alternative was that it could somehow see into my mind, and wasn't that just horrifying?

So I did what I could.

I closed my eyes and willed myself to sleep.

After less than a minute of silence, I gave up, though not for lack of trying. I managed to make it close to unconsciousness a few times, using my will to ignore my intrusive thoughts and my eyelids to shut out the light of the mid-afternoon sun and the glow of the blue panel. Unfortunately, I was rudely pulled from my sleep each time by the chatter of the birds outside.

I grumbled as I stuffed my fingers in my ears, but I knew it was futile. There was a reason I never took afternoon naps during the springtime. The birds were always especially loud at this time of day, and only the most determined of people could sleep through their noise.

Maybe on a normal day, I would've been able to ignore them, but the combination of things that demanded my attention was just too much, and I lurched forward and out of bed, recognizing that I wouldn't be getting any real sleep.

I tried to ignore the blue panels of light that had spawned in front of me, trying to keep my eyes unfocused enough that I wouldn't focus on the symbols, but it wasn't like I was actually reading the symbols in the first place. Apparently, whatever magic was injecting the meaning of the words directly into my brain didn't seem to care if I was focused on the lettering or not—a glance was enough.

Tip: Following Instructions

Not all instructions have to be directly stated. Sometimes, instructions can be implied!

Valiant White Knight

By partying with your love interest, you have unlocked the skill [Valiant White Knight]! Under certain conditions, this skill allows the Hero to rush to protect bonded party members from certain death.
Whenever a bonded party member shouts, "Save me!" the Hero may activate this ability to instantly teleport to their side.

This skill is currently available for use.

I kept my face as neutral as I possibly could. I think I managed to succeed, but it was pointless if the panel could read my thoughts.

Honestly, I didn't know what to think. I was so stressed at this point that I didn't have the energy to react, so I was surprised when I felt a surge of annoyance at whatever the hell the blue panel was. Was it a good idea to get annoyed at the possibly omniscient object that seemingly had the power to subdue an Otherworlder like Ryuji? Probably not, but it was pure spite that drove me to punch the panel.

Without resistance, my fist went right through it.

I grumbled in response, half disappointed that I wasn't able to touch it, half glad that it hadn't incinerated me on contact. Thankfully, now that I knew it was incorporeal and seemingly harmless, I closed my eyes.

Unfortunately, those birds were still singing.

Usually, I wouldn't really care about something as benign as birds just being birds, but I was at my breaking point.

"Shut up!" I shouted. "Shut up, shut up, shut up!"

I thought I heard a few startled squawks, but I knew that must have been my imagination. My voice wasn't all that loud, and the birds were used to humans to the point where nothing but thrown rocks would bother them. Even so, my outburst alone was a great relief.

I didn't think I'd ever shouted like that before in my life. It felt surprisingly good to yell at the top of my lungs—not that I'd ever do that normally. If it weren't for the fact that time was frozen, I would probably have felt too embarrassed to shout at those damn birds.

It took me a second to figure out why that thought bothered me so much. When I finally did, I rushed out of my room and toward the back of the house.

"Mom?" I shouted.

My mom had her back turned to me, but I could easily tell that she was still frozen in place. Even though there were birds chirping outside.

The blue panels reappeared in front of me.

Tip: Tutorial Events

While Tutorial Events may temporarily pause the actions of any Players and NPCs, the in-game clock will still progress. Any time-based status effects such as hunger and thirst will progress as normal while the Tutorial Event occurs.

Valiant White Knight

A bonded party member may shout, "Save me!" to activate the effects of [Valiant White Knight].

Even if I hadn't realized it a few seconds before, the blue panels made it obvious. I couldn't stay in this frozen state forever, and I somehow had the power to end it, but the specific wording the panel used worried me. Was it trying to threaten me by holding the lives of the villagers hostage?

My eyes narrowed as the symbols on the first blue panel shifted imperceptibly, subtly enough that I might not have noticed if it weren't for the fact that I wasn't actually reading the words on the panel. I was just understanding them, and the spontaneous shift of my understanding was a lot more jarring than seeing the symbols merge quietly into each other.

Tip: Tutorial Events

While Tutorial Events may temporarily pause the actions of any Players and NPCs, the in-game clock will still progress. Any time-based status effects will progress as normal while the Tutorial Event occurs.

I didn't know why exactly the mentions of hunger and thirst had disappeared, but I assumed the panels hadn't meant to threaten me and that they were trying to pretend like it had never happened. It also pretty much confirmed that the panels could read my thoughts, but that wasn't as much of a shock as I assumed it would be. The fact that it could easily freeze the people in this village, one of them being an all-powerful Otherworlder, was a feat of much greater power.

While the idea of my most personal thoughts being invaded should've terrified me regardless, the deep emotional exhaustion I felt dulled that feeling of terror, letting my spite shine through instead.

Fuck you.

I hoped it read that thought loud and clear.

The blue panels didn't change, though they appeared to waver slightly. Probably my imagination.

Staring at the lower panel, I let out a deep sigh and walked out of the house, making my way back to the site of the battle.

I knew what would happen after this. Once I did what the damn panels wanted me to, Ryuji would save me and defeat the rest of the demons. The mayor would dip into the village's emergency funds to give him a reward for saving the village—the demons being a convenient excuse to give him the funds necessary for basic survival—and send him off on his way to the nearest city, where a trained Crown official would take Ryuji in and contact the Mediators to deal with him.

But before Ryuji left, he would ask me to come with him.

It was a common theme in many horror stories told by parents to keep their children in line. Do your chores, or a big bad Otherworlder will take you as his Follower. Eat your vegetables, or the Otherworlder will want to be your friend. Stuff like that.

While many Otherworlders were notorious for "taking" Followers, the reason they were called Followers instead of Abductees was because most Followers often had a "choice" in whether they would follow the Otherworlder or not.

In practice, it was incredibly difficult to turn down an offer from a person who could easily kill you and destroy your entire country on a whim, but there were ways to get around it, with the most common ones being to fake your own death. Claiming that you had an illness or family obligations wasn't recommended in most cases, since an Otherworlder might be inclined to insert themselves into your life with an even stronger persistence, but it could sometimes work.

However, I wasn't sure if I had a choice in the matter. Ryuji had a power that he obviously didn't have complete control over, and even if he did, it could clearly be influenced by outside parties, AKA me.

I had the power to unfreeze my village and save them from slow death by starvation. Would Ryuji's power have frozen the village if I wasn't there in the first place? Possibly not. Would it happen in the future if I didn't follow him? Again, possibly not, but I didn't think I would be able to live with myself if I didn't follow Ryuji to keep an eye on him, knowing that I had the ability to dampen his destruction for some reason.

I'm not ashamed to admit that the thought of leaving the villagers to die did cross my mind at one point. Unfortunately, just like how it had caused me to get stuck in this damn situation in the first place, my conscience couldn't let me kill my friends and family.

I sighed. I wondered if there was a way to get my conscience surgically removed.

Arriving back at the battlefield, I stood in the exact same spot that I'd been in before time froze. I spared a glance at the sheriff, still with his arms outstretched toward me, and at the shadowy weapon hovering a few inches from my head. If I managed to unfreeze everyone but the panels were lying and Ryuji didn't save me, the weapon hitting my head was guaranteed to kill me.

I wasn't sure whether I would prefer that fate to becoming Ryuji's Follower, so I shrugged.

After a harrowing day, my voice was hoarse and I had no more energy in me to spare, but the blue panels never said anything about emotion.

With my voice flat and my expression flatter, I muttered under my breath.

"Save me."

Chapter 10

The Final Stage of Acceptance

The burst of sound was what surprised me the most. Though the world hadn't been silent while everyone else had been frozen, the amount of screaming, shouting, and howling that erupted in an instant was enough to make me flinch.

The second thing that surprised me almost as much was the shadow that fell over me as soon as time resumed. Looking up, I was no longer staring at a swinging weapon as it hurtled down at my face. Instead, my vision was blocked by the strange clothes that the Otherworlder wore.

His flame blade was locked against the demon's own, which made no sense since I'd seen him cut through the other two demons already, and their "weapons" were made of the same Aether as their bodies. He looked back at me with an awkward grin.

"Are you alright, Lena?"

I stared at him. For the first time since I'd met him, I realized that he looked a lot younger than I'd first thought. Though he was pretty tall, rivaling the sheriff in height, he was a lot lankier. His figure was mostly hidden by the baggy hooded shirt he wore, but with how close he was standing to me, I could tell that his proportions looked slightly off—the hallmarks of a boy who was still being ravaged by the worst of puberty.

The demon growled angrily at Ryuji as it tried to force its way through the stalemate of their locked blades, but Ryuji didn't seem to be bothered. He gave one last grin, an awkward-looking smile might've been an attempt at looking cool, and slashed behind him without looking.

The demon fell to the floor, bisected like its fellows.

"Don't worry," he said. "I'll protect you."

Without waiting for a response from me, he launched himself forward at the remaining demons.

I watched out of the corner of my eye as Ryuji flourished his blade and shouted some other nonsensical words each time he cast a magic spell. I mostly ignored the display as the light of his flaming blade threatened to blind me. I focused instead on the reaction of the sheriff and the rest of the villagers who had gathered around to watch. A majority of them had turned pale and ducked away to the side of the road, bending over and retching just like Bran had as Ryuji split more demons in half. The sheriff and a few more of the older villagers didn't have as bad a reaction, but even they seemed to grimace in disgust.

"Hey Sheriff," I said. "Those are goblins, right? Made of flesh and blood? Not demons made of Aether?"

The sheriff looked confused by my question. "Yes," he said. "Lena, are you alright? My son told me you've had quite a stressful day."

I laughed. That was putting it mildly. The fact that the sheriff had confirmed that the villagers were somehow seeing something different than what I was only made it even worse. Maybe I was going crazy. Somehow, that thought was more comforting.

"I'm fine," I lied. Not so convincingly if the sheriff's expression was any indication, but an ear-piercing screech drew our attention back to the fight.

"That'll teach you to attack innocent people," said the Otherworlder to the demon impaled on his flaming sword, as if he expected it to somehow retain the lesson he was trying to teach it. Ryuji flicked his sword to the side, sending the demon's body sliding off and tumbling a few times on the floor from the momentum.

A few more villagers lost their stomachs at that.

Ryuji locked eyes with me, gave me a smile, and turned to the villagers before raising his sword.

"You are safe now!" he said.

I could tell that nobody in the village believed him. I looked around to see if anyone looked like they weren't about to soil themselves, but even the sheriff looked like he was considering laying down his sword and begging for mercy.

I sighed, finally accepting that I, little old Lena, amateur magic user, apprentice butcher, whose only noticeable qualities were a nice ass that I'd just learned about today, was somehow the most reliable person here under pressure. Maybe that was unfair, since the rest of the onlookers probably saw Ryuji standing proudly in a pile of goblin guts and gore rather than the quickly fading Aether that made up the demons' bodies, but I didn't care.

"Three cheers for the adventurer!" I said, further cementing my fate as his Follower. "Hip, hip, hurray!"

Judging from Ryuji's wide smile, he didn't seem to notice that I was the only one cheering.

"Hip, hip, hurray!"

The sheriff joined in with me on the second cheer, for which I was grateful.

"Hip, hip, hurray!"

A small handful of adults accompanied me on the final cheer, though they'd spoken in almost a whisper, as if trying not to draw any attention to themselves.

Ryuji smiled and lowered his sword. He opened his mouth as if to say something when a blue panel appeared in front of him.

"Hip, hip, hurray!"

I frowned when I heard the fourth cheer, now with more people joining in. The crowd sounded nervous, and they must've been if they'd lost their ability to count. Ryuji didn't seem to notice, too focused on the blue panel to pay attention to anything else. It was written backward from my perspective, but once again, I had no problem understanding it.

Quest: Defend the Village [COMPLETE]

By defending the village, you have cemented yourself as a Hero and a true adventurer in their eyes.

[GOBLINS] defeated: 7/7

Casualties: 0

Grade: S+

Rewards:

+200 EXP

+20 Stat Points

+20 Skill Points

"Hip, hip, hurray!"

Were they still going? At this point, most of the villagers who weren't still recovering from puking their guts out were shouting, creating a dissonant cheer from the onlookers who sounded like they didn't want to be there.

Ryuji didn't seem to notice. He was more engrossed with doing a little shake of excitement before tapping the blue panel with his finger. It disappeared instantly and was quickly replaced by another.

Secret Objective: Save the Girl! [COMPLETE]

By saving your love interest from certain death, she surely must be grateful. This gratitude could undoubtedly blossom into something more in the future.

+15 [AFFECTION] (Lena)

Why the hell did the panel sound so uncertain? And what the hell did [AFFECTION] mean? I saw Ryuji glance up at me, and I quickly pretended I was looking somewhere else, cold sweat dripping down my brow.

"Hip, hip, hurray!"

I looked around to see a few new faces that hadn't actually been around to see what Ryuji had done but had been attracted to the site by the commotion, their curiosity somehow overwhelming their desire to stay away. I was sure that half the people cheering at this point had no idea what they were cheering for.

Ryuji walked up to me, and the nearby villagers stepped back to clear a path, despite being nowhere close to him. Thankfully, he didn't seem to notice the villagers avoiding him like the second coming of the Plague, but unfortunately, that was mostly because he had his eyes locked onto me.

Seeing no way to pretend that he wasn't walking straight for me, I turned to him and gave him a smile, regretting every single decision in my life that had led up to this point.

"Are you alright?" he asked, scanning my body, hopefully just looking for any wounds.

Remembering what my mom told me, I struggled to resist the urge to hide my body with my hands.

"Yeah," I replied.

Ryuji smiled. "I'm glad."

I don't know if I expected him to say anything else, but we just stared at each other for a few seconds, the awkward silence only being broken up by the occasional "hip, hip, hurray." By the time I realized that I should've said something, the silence had gone on for too long.

Fortunately, the panels finally decided to work in my favor for once.

Tutorial: Leveling Up

Congratulations! By completing your first quest, you've earned enough EXP to advance to the next level! You can now allocate your newly acquired Stat Points by using the [Status] command to access your status window.
You may also allocate your Skill Points in the skill menu by using the [Skills] command.

Why don't you try it out?

As Ryuji let out a loud cheer of his own, interrupting the villagers in the middle of yet another "hip, hip, hurray," I couldn't help but notice the insistent tone that the panels had. Though it was obvious that the panels had some form of sentience to them, I still wasn't sure what their goals were. I knew I would be watching them closely in the coming future.

"Status!" Ryuji shouted. "Skills!"

As the blue panel disappeared, I expected to see more panels pop up to replace them, but nothing happened—at least not from my point of view. However, the way Ryuji was poking at the air made it obvious that he was seeing something that the rest of us couldn't.

I didn't know why I could only see some panels and not others, but I felt like I wasn't going to get my answers just by watching Ryuji awkwardly pawing at the air, oblivious to the world around him.

"Hey, Sheriff," I whispered, motioning to the man who had backed off nearly five feet since Ryuji had moved closer to me.

The sheriff flinched when he heard me call him, but when Ryuji didn't seem to notice, too engrossed in whatever he was doing, he nodded at me to show me he was listening.

"I think you should get most of these people out of here," I said. "Ryuji seems to be distracted for now, but I'm not sure how long that's going to be the case."

The sheriff nodded immediately. "Right," he whispered. "I'll get right on that, ma'am."

My first reaction was to want to laugh at the amount of respect the sheriff was showing me. It felt strange to see the tough man avoid my gaze like I was royalty. But before I could feel any sort of humor in the situation, I realized that he was right.

I wasn't strictly royalty, but Followers were considered to be powerful people in their own right. While the outright manipulation of an Otherworlder was forbidden, the position of being a Follower did have an inevitable amount of influence on an Otherworlder's actions, which demanded a certain amount of responsibility and respect on its own.

While I wasn't officially a Follower yet, the sheriff seemed to think I was a Follower in every way that mattered.

And he was probably right.

I sighed, watching the sheriff follow my suggestion like it had been a command and round up the villagers. On the other hand, Ryuji stood in the center of the road, mumbling to himself while the demons slowly disintegrated around him. I wondered how that looked to the rest of the villagers, who might still be seeing them as goblins, but I didn't want to ask them and risk sounding crazier than I already felt.

Before long, there were only a few of the braver villagers left behind to convince Ryuji that he hadn't been rudely forgotten about while he was in his trance. As we waited for Ryuji to stop scrutinizing the air so intensely, they stood around in silence, too nervous to make any noise. Though they all stole quick peeks at Ryuji, curious about what he was doing, none of them were brave enough to stare at him directly or for too long.

Only after a few minutes did I realize they were looking at me the same way.

Chapter 11

TO BE A FOLLOWER

Everything ended up happening in pretty much the exact way that I'd predicted.

Ryuji asked me to come along with him on his adventures, and I said yes, partially because I was too scared to say no and partially because I knew I was the only one who could interact with the blue panels that seemed to be even more powerful than he was. If there was nothing keeping Ryuji and the panels in check, there was no telling what sort of destruction they could cause.

My mom crying and begging me to stay was something I'd expected too, but when my dad placed his hands on Ryuji's shoulders and threatened to kill him if he didn't keep me safe, I almost passed out. Thankfully, Ryuji had either taken it as a joke or simply didn't feel threatened enough to do anything in retaliation, so he just laughed it off and agreed to keep me safe.

It was the first time I'd seen my dad cry. It was an odd thing to see tears dripping down his face despite there being no changes in his expression.

Not a single villager was willing to take us on the five-day ride by horseback to the nearest city, but thankfully, Ryuji seemed excited about walking. It would only take us eight days, since we could use the path that led through the forest to make up some of the time that we would've otherwise lost by traveling on horseback. However, the three-day difference would still be enough time for a messenger to reach the city before us and tell them of the incoming Otherworlder.

We could have stayed in the village to ensure that the message would arrive before we did, but the way the entire village seemed on edge in Ryuji's presence made me worried that someone would do something to reveal to Ryuji that we were all scared of him. Though I wasn't sure how he would react to that, I didn't want to find out.

The villagers provided us with the best camping and traveling materials that they had in the village. Though most of it came from the general goods store run by Old Tom, Polly gave me a matching set of a green cloak and boots, which she had apparently bought during her recent visit to the city. They seemed to be more suitable for fashion than travel, but Polly swore up and down that they'd serve me well before wrapping me in a hug.

Though we weren't particularly close, I thanked her and put them on. They were admittedly very comfortable—better than my own travel clothes.

Now, as I stood at the edge of the very forest I'd found Ryuji in, I couldn't help but wonder one last time whether I was having a nightmare or not. It didn't feel like a nightmare. It was a perfect day. The sun against my skin was just warm enough to be pleasant, and a gentle breeze wove around us, occasionally blowing my hair against my face.

I subtly scratched myself and hissed in pain when it didn't wake me.

"You ready to go?" Ryuji asked.

I turned to look at him, and he smiled back at me.

"I like your new cloak," he said. "It really brings out your eyes."

"Thanks," I said, cursing Polly internally. I briefly searched for anything I could compliment on in return. "I like your shirt. I've never seen anything like it before."

Thankfully, the lame excuse for a compliment seemed to be good enough for him. His eyes lit up and his smile grew wider.

"Thanks! It's my favorite hoodie!" he exclaimed. "I'm glad you like it."

I stared at him for a few seconds before readjusting my bag and nodding.

"Yeah," I said. "Now we should get going. We only have a few hours of sun before we'll need to start setting up camp and cooking dinner."

As the words left my mouth, I couldn't help but worry that I came off as standoffish. Ryuji didn't reply, and the silence between us stretched out longer than I was comfortable with. I opened my mouth, as if to say something, but I couldn't find anything to talk about.

This time, when the blue panel appeared in front of Ryuji's face, I couldn't help but feel almost grateful for its intervention.

Quest: Travel to the City

Your adventure takes you outside the sleepy village of Plainswood and toward the mighty city of Redstone, where further excitement surely awaits.

Objective: Enter Redstone

Rewards:

+50 EXP

+5 [ENDURANCE]

I let out a sigh of relief when Ryuji's attention was immediately captured by the blue panel, but I couldn't help but feel a pit of worry in my stomach.

While the blue panels clearly wanted to help me out for some reason, the way they helped was quite jarring and pretty obvious. Though Ryuji seemed to be more than enthusiastic in his interactions with them, I wondered how many times the blue panels could pop up to break any awkward silences between us without Ryuji becoming bored of their presence.

Even if the blue boxes could entertain him indefinitely, I knew that we'd eventually have to talk. Even if I was able to hand him off to someone actually qualified for the job as soon as we got to the city, we would still be traveling together for eight days.

When Ryuji tapped the blue panel, making it disappear, he glanced at me and immediately looked away, his face burning a bright red. It was a strange feeling, knowing that Ryuji was somehow in love with me. Even with what my mom had told me and the blue panel confirming that I was his love interest, I still couldn't quite believe it. At that moment, Ryuji just looked like a kid with a bad crush.

But regardless of how childlike he looked, he was still the most powerful being currently alive.

"Let's go?" I asked, trying not to sound annoyed.

Ryuji nodded, and we started our journey.

I made sure we were walking side by side this time.

We made it about thirty minutes before we were attacked. It was a small group of not-goblins again, and though I had no weapon and no way to defend myself, Ryuji alone was able to defeat them all handily without any problems. I was a bit nervous about the excessive amount of fire spells he used in his combat, but luckily, he didn't start any forest fires.

Quick Event: Goblin Ambush [COMPLETE]
Defeat the [GOBLINS]: 5/5
+100 EXP

After tapping the panel, Ryuji pumped his fist. "Sweet! Level up!" he said, his eyes scanning another panel I couldn't see.

I was still confused as to why I could see some of the panels but not others. What was on that panel that I couldn't see? It was a shame that I didn't know. The more I understood Ryuji, the better I'd be equipped to handle him.

Tutorial: Leveling up

Remember to apply any Stat Points and Skill Points you've acquired through leveling up! A personal notice will be available each time you level up, so don't forget to apply them through your personal menus whenever you get the chance! Using the Status and Skill commands will allow you to view your personal Status and Skill menus whenever you wish.

I wondered if the panels were purposefully being as helpful as possible, or if they were just easy to trick into giving me the information I wanted. Either way, it didn't seem like it intended to ever talk to me directly, only speaking through implications. Thankfully, it didn't seem to care about subtlety whatsoever. The fact that it repeated the word "personal" so many times seemed to confirm why I couldn't see what Ryuji was seeing, but did that imply that the panels I'd been seeing so far were for public viewing? Why couldn't anyone else see them then? Would there be anyone else that could see them, or was it just me?

No panels popped up to answer my unspoken question. Was it withholding information?

"Why am I getting a tutorial now?" Ryuji mused before tapping the panel and dismissing it. "I've been leveling up for a while now. What a shitty system."

"What did you say?" I asked. The fact that Ryuji had a name for the panels was surprising to me, though in hindsight it shouldn't have been. He'd been eagerly interacting with them and with ease. Maybe it was something from his old world?

Ryuji turned to me like he'd only just remembered I existed. His face turned crimson red, and he turned away.

"Nothing," he said. "It's dumb."

I was surprised by how unconfident he seemed. Here was a guy who'd just casually bisected eleven demons in the span of a few minutes and had enough power to destroy the country, and though I'd been careful not to let him know that, I couldn't see why he sounded so embarrassed. Maybe it was a secretive thing, or maybe he was too shy to talk to his crush.

I winced when I remembered who exactly his crush was.

"It's just..." Ryuji started again, staring at the floor. "You ever heard of video games?"

He answered for me by slapping a palm against his forehead.

"Of course, you haven't," he said. "Those probably don't exist here."

"I'm interested in learning," I said, hoping it wouldn't be anything like the time he tried to explain what anime was to me. At the very least, this seemed to be related to his powers.

"Really?" he said, turning to me with genuine surprise on his face. "Why?"

Why indeed? I struggled to think of a reason. I was tempted to reuse the same excuse that I'd used to get him to start talking about anime, but the way he was seriously scrutinizing me made me think he wouldn't accept that I just found it interesting, especially since this was the first time he'd mentioned them. While I could guess that these video games were somehow connected to these blue panels and not something he'd randomly blurted out, I wasn't sure I wanted Ryuji to know that I could see the panels at all.

I shrugged, buying myself a few seconds to think of an answer. I searched his face briefly for anything I could use, but he quickly turned away to look sheepishly back at the floor. It was so uncharacteristic of him that it made me realize what I could say as an excuse.

"I'm not sure," I started. "But it has something to do with why you randomly stare into space, right?"

"Oh, do I do that?" Ryuji asked nervously, scratching the back of his head. "Sorry."

Though I was going to follow up what I said with my excuse, Ryuji's behavior threw me off a bit.

"What are you apologizing for?" I asked.

Ryuji winced. "Well, it's annoying, right? People generally don't like it when others don't pay attention to what's going on around them."

Well, I supposed that was true, but I didn't want to suggest to the Otherworlder that I was annoyed at him.

"No," I said, shaking my head quickly. "I was just about to say that you look really happy when you stare into space. If these video games have something to do with that, they're obviously important to you. I'd be happy to learn more about them."

When Ryuji's only reply was to stare wide-eyed at me, I was worried that I'd said something wrong. Though I didn't tense up in fear like I usually did, it was only because I'd accepted the fact that there would be no possibility of me surviving if Ryuji did decide to kill me. I didn't have the energy to run, and even if I did, I knew he could catch up to me in an instant.

"Oh," he said simply. "Thanks."

I nodded. I didn't know why he thanked me, but I wasn't about to let any gratitude go unclaimed. "You're welcome."

There was a long stretch of silence between us, interrupted only by our footsteps and the leaves fluttering with the occasional gust of wind. I didn't know what to say, so I just pretended I was comfortable with the silence between us—at least until another panel appeared in front of us.

+85 [AFFECTION] (Lena)

Ryuji grumbled and covered his reddening face before punching the panel and making it dissipate. I was glad I managed to hold back the urge to try the same.

Chapter 12
It's My First Time

After Ryuji had calmed down somewhat, he started to talk about video games and how they related to his power. I was surprised by how open he was about the basis of his power, even though he tried to veil his Otherworlder nature with some excuse that he had an inherent bloodline ability of sorts—whatever that meant.

All in all, I learned some interesting things.

Most of what he said confused me, especially the concept of video games, which he described as a play where the audience could control the actors' every move. Throughout the play, the actors would grow stronger to defeat whatever conflict was present in the story at the time, gaining levels, stats, and skills.

I didn't understand the minute details that Ryuji spouted out in great length. Still, I at least understood that Ryuji grew in power by "leveling up," which was achieved by gathering "experience points."

What did concern me was when he mentioned that actors would usually get experience points for killing things. Though it seemed like the same logic didn't apply perfectly here, since I knew he could get experience points through completing benign tasks, I hoped that Ryuji wouldn't go on a killing spree to test it further.

Honestly, the fact that Ryuji had revealed to me that he would be getting stronger as he leveled up was the most terrifying thing I got out of his explanation. He seemed to imply that his power was in its infancy. Given that he was already powerful enough to burn down a city on a whim, I wasn't eager to see what it looked like when he progressed even further.

"So I usually go for Dex or Int builds in video games, so they'd probably be the most comfortable for me, but I'm not sure how much they would apply to real life," he said, already forgetting about the cover story he'd made up that he'd had this ability all his life. "Still, Assassin and Mage builds are just too cool to pass up, you know?"

I, in fact, did not know, but rather than clamming up and trying to figure out a way to answer his question without getting myself killed for saying the wrong thing, I was surprised that I was calm enough to recognize the question as a rhetorical one.

Though it might have been my hysteria talking, it was getting difficult not to see him as just a normal, excitable boy. While I still wasn't completely comfortable with him, I no longer felt like the slightest misstep would result in my quick incineration.

"Why don't you just do a little bit of everything if you're not sure?" I asked, genuinely curious as to why he didn't take the obvious solution.

"Eh, that'd be suboptimal." He blushed and stammered less the more he spoke, though I wasn't sure if that was because he was getting more comfortable with me or he was too focused on the subject of our discussion. "The higher your stats are, the more access you have to better abilities, so a specialist would have a more exponential growth in power."

"I see," I said. The fact that he would have slower growth only supported the reasons I would want him not to specialize in a single stat, but I assumed that's something he wouldn't want to hear. "So what are Dex and Int then, if you don't mind me asking?"

"Oh," he said, rubbing his head in embarrassment. "Right. Sorry."

"It's alright."

Once again, I was confused about why he was apologizing, but he'd done enough at this point that I'd accepted it as a personality quirk of his.

Again, he seemed to appreciate that I'd pardoned him for whatever faux pas he thought he'd committed. Perhaps he had done something that was considered rude in his culture.

It was a little worrying how easily I was starting to forget that Ryuji wasn't human. He was an Otherworlder who likely had his own mindset and culture that were foreign to my own way of thinking, even if he did act somewhat how a human would.

"So," I said. "What were you saying about Dex and—"

I paused when I heard the hoot of an owl. Though the sun was still shining through the forest canopy, the reddening hue of the light suggested that nightfall was fast approaching.

"Maybe we should continue this conversation some other time?" I said, motioning toward the vague direction of the sun. "We should start setting up camp."

"Really?" Ryuji asked. "It's still so bright out."

"It's easier to set up camp when there's still light out. And it's been a long day. I know we have rations ready, but I'd rather cook something up if possible."

"Oh. I guess that makes sense."

With nothing else to say, I stopped talking and scanned the area around us for a suitable clearing to camp on. I didn't have to look hard. The path through the forest was lined with small patches of flat, dry ground, either natural or artificially flattened by larger groups of travelers who had built their own camping grounds there. I chose a spot that would accommodate two tents comfortably without them being too close to each other.

Setting up the camp was relatively simple, something I'd done many times in my life whenever I went to the forest to practice my magic.

Once I doffed my travel bag and survival kit, it was a simple process to unroll and set up. I was done with my tent in a matter of minutes.

Ryuji, on the other hand, wasn't having such an easy time. He was grumbling and griping as he struggled to put together the tent. I wasn't sure he even knew what each part was used for, other than the general idea that the tarp should go on top.

When I heard a laugh, I couldn't help but feel like I imagined it, especially since it sounded like my own. But when Ryuji looked at me with shock and utter mortification, I realized that the laugh had come from me.

I knew that Ryuji liked me on some level, but that had never given me the confidence to truly be comfortable around him, in case he changed his mind. I knew he could still kill me, but tangled up in a mess of ropes, poles, and tarps, Ryuji looked almost helpless.

A giggle escaped me, and I felt a vague flash of panic when I realized I was laughing openly at an Otherworlder, but that panic only made me find the situation even funnier somehow. I slapped a hand over my mouth, as if that could stop the laughter from escaping it, but a torrent of giggles flowed freely until it devolved into full-blown laughter. A small handful of birds flew away with indignant squawks at the sound.

I honestly had no idea why I was laughing so hard. It wasn't even that funny. Maybe my mind had finally snapped under the pressure it had been under. Maybe I was delirious. Who knew? Certainly not me.

Though tears of laughter flowed freely down my cheeks, my hands were too busy clutched around my aching stomach to wipe them away. Eventually, my laughter petered out, and I managed to catch my breath again and wipe the tears from the corners of my eyes.

I might have burst into laughter again when I saw Ryuji's indignant expression, if it weren't for the fact that I was completely spent already. He was red-faced and had trouble looking directly at me, but at least he wasn't setting me on fire.

"It's not that funny," he said.

"Sure," I said. "C'mon. Let's get you set up."

It took about three minutes to set Ryuji's tent up, which seemed to humiliate him even more, but I held back my laughter this time, deciding I didn't need to push my luck any further. Squashing down the amusement I had, I focused on gathering wood for a fire and digging a small pit for a makeshift washroom far enough that we wouldn't smell it. Ryuji didn't do much, choosing instead to watch me work as he calmed down from his embarrassment. I didn't mind. I was used to camping out alone, and an extra person didn't add too much work.

He did offer to start the campfire, which was nice, but he only ended up embarrassing himself again when he cast a spell that was too strong and incinerated the firewood I'd gathered.

I wasn't going to make him gather more firewood with me to replace the pile of ash that he'd made, but I was grateful when he insisted. He wasn't too good at it, but he seemed to know that and didn't mind me telling him what to do.

"Don't do that," I said. "It's not good to break off branches from young trees."

"Sorry," he said, letting go of the branch he was about to snap off. "Is it because of the circle of life or something? We should use the older trees, so the young ones have room to grow?"

"No?" I said, unsure of what he was talking about. "The young ones are supple and full of water. They don't burn as easily. Try searching on the ground for drier twigs."

"Oh."

It was a funny image to see an Otherworlder squinting as he pushed around the forest debris with his foot. While the sun was still up, it was quickly setting, and it was getting increasingly difficult to see in the dim light. I wasn't surprised when Ryuji failed to gather any more sticks after that point. Thankfully, I had gotten enough that starting a fire wouldn't be a problem.

"How are you so good at this?" Ryuji asked as we walked back to our tents.

"Practice," I said simply.

Ryuji nodded, but that seemed to be the end of his questioning.

"How about you?" I asked.

"Me?" Ryuji asked, as if there was anyone else I could possibly be talking to.

"Yeah," I said. "You seem to be new to this. Do adventurers from where you're from not need to travel long distances?"

Ryuji looked at me and shifted his eyes away. "No, they do," he said. He sounded nervous for some reason, and though he fell silent, I could tell he wanted to keep talking. "I actually wasn't an adventurer back at home. This is my first time doing something like this."

Though that meant nothing to me, since I still wasn't too sure what an adventurer was exactly, nor what his home was like, he seemed a little ashamed by the admission.

"Well, that's fine," I said. "You're what, fifteen? Sixteen?"

I was surprised by how low my guess was. I hadn't thought about how young he was until this point, and I wasn't too shocked when Ryuji nodded.

"Fifteen," he answered.

"Then you've got time," I said. "You're still young. You've got a dream. You'll be a great adventurer soon."

Ryuji stared at me like I'd spontaneously spoken a foreign language. I suddenly felt embarrassed by how much I sounded like my parents when I was only two years older than him.

"Nobody's ever said that to me before," he mumbled.

"Said what?" I asked.

"That they believed in me."

I had no idea how to reply to that. Though I had just confirmed that he was young—only fifteen—in that instant, he looked even younger than that, like a child. I coughed to hide my discomfort and unloaded the sticks we'd gathered into the small fire pit I'd dug out beforehand.

"Well, that's dumb. I'm sure you can do whatever you put your mind to. Like starting a fire! Ready to redeem yourself?"

Ryuji looked at the pile of firewood and the pile of ash just underneath it, a reminder of his previous failure.

"Are you sure?" he asked.

"I believe in you. Just try to make it weaker this time."

Even if he did fail, we didn't necessarily need the fire. I mostly wanted it to cook our food and keep the bugs away, but we had rations, and I was no stranger to bites. Still, I didn't feel like he needed to know that.

Ryuji, once again, looked shocked by my statement, but his shock quickly morphed into determination as he placed his hands directly over the firewood.

I hoped he didn't notice me subtly backing away.

"Spark."

What looked like a tiny red lightning bolt arced out of Ryuji's fingers and disappeared into the pile of wood. At first, it didn't look like anything had happened until I noticed a tiny ember in the tinder at the center of the pile. Ryuji looked torn between excitement and not knowing what to do, so I bent down and started to blow on the fire to keep it alive. It was a substantial flame already, so I didn't need to do much to make it catch on to the thicker branches.

"See?" I said. "I knew you could do it."

Ryuji seemed too distracted by the fire to hear me, so I let him be, taking a moment to appreciate it with him for a few seconds before starting to unpack our food.

Chapter 13

The Boring Parts of Traveling

We didn't talk much after that. Ryuji seemed to fall into a state of deep thought, and I was fine with letting him think about whatever he wanted while I cooked something up.

The firewood gathering had taken a little bit longer than I thought, but it was still early enough in the night to make a decently sized meal consisting of roasted yams, fresh bread, and some of the barely frozen meat that my dad had given Ryuji for some reason. It wouldn't keep well, so I roasted most of it over the fire. We could eat the leftovers for breakfast and leave whatever we couldn't eat for the critters.

"It's... pretty good," Ryuji said after his first bite.

"It's fine to think it's bad," I said, waving off the obvious lie. "I'm no cook, especially not without a proper kitchen. Takes too much time to care about making it tasty when all you have is a fire and some pots. As long as it's edible and doesn't make me sick, it's good enough for me."

Ryuji nodded, accepting the answer as he took another bite. Though he didn't look offended by the food, he didn't look happy about it either.

"That's fair," he said, sounding comically disappointed.

I let out a small laugh. "Not what you expected?"

Ryuji shrugged. "I guess," he said. "I mean it makes sense when you think about it, but all the stories I've read just skipped over the boring parts of traveling."

I nodded, understanding what he was talking about. "Not much point in a story going into detail about the mundane parts of life where nothing exciting happens. But it does happen," I added a little uselessly.

Ryuji nodded. I wasn't sure whether he was agreeing with me or if he was just acknowledging that he'd heard me, but I didn't think it mattered enough to ask.

The rest of the meal passed by quietly. It was dark by the time we finished it, but the light of the fire was bright enough for me to clean up by it. Gathering the pots and pans, I placed my palms above them and started to summon my mana.

A slow and steady stream of mana leaked from my hands, turning into water as it escaped my body. I struggled to keep my eyes open from the strain of the spell but managed to keep the flow steady until I felt like there was enough.

I let out a deep sigh when I finally closed off the mana inside my body, feeling the strain of its depletion.

"Why don't you use more water?" Ryuji asked.

I wasn't aware that he'd been watching. "I only need a little bit," I replied. "And besides, I don't have enough mana to make more."

"You don't?" he asked.

The amount of surprise in his voice made me laugh. "I hope you're not comparing me to yourself. It's frankly crazy how strong your magic is, especially as a beginner."

He stayed silent for a few seconds before muttering something to himself. I couldn't quite catch what he said, but I didn't ask him to clarify. Even in the dim light, I could tell that he wasn't looking at me, even though he was facing my direction. The panels again?

He raised his finger and poked at the air, confirming my suspicions.

"I guess I am pretty OP," he said.

I wasn't sure I'd heard him right. "OP? What's that?"

"Oh. Right. It means I'm super strong," he said with a smile, as if it weren't the understatement of the century. "Do you want me to make more water for you? I've never tried it before, but it should be simple enough."

I hadn't forgotten the last time he'd tried something for the first time. The image of the pillar of fire he'd made flashed through my mind.

"No, I'm fine, thank you," I said, hopefully not too quickly. "I'm used to this amount. I don't need any more."

Ryuji stared at me, and I wondered for a second whether he would try anyway. He certainly didn't need my permission to do anything. Thankfully, he didn't offer again and simply watched as I cleaned the pots.

After I finished cleaning, I wrapped up all the utensils and leftover food in a small tarp and slung it over a high branch to keep the larger forest animals from trying to get at it.

"You're really good at this," Ryuji suddenly said.

I was surprised by the compliment but not enough to be startled by it. "Thank you," I said. "I spend a lot of time in the forest, though. It only makes sense I'd get better at it eventually."

Ryuji nodded, but he seemed to be distracted by his thoughts. "You mentioned that. Why do you camp so much? Do you just enjoy nature?"

"I guess," I said, with a shrug. "But that's not the reason. I started camping out away from the village to practice my magic, but I guess the camping itself became a hobby at some point."

"You learned magic here? Like from the forest itself?"

I laughed, and from the sound of it, I couldn't help but think that I was either an even better actor than I'd thought, or I was actually starting to get a little comfortable in Ryuji's presence.

"I learned the usual way from instructional books and random tips that the other magic users in the village taught me," I said. "As for why I practiced in the forest specifically, I just didn't want to cause any property damage. After the second mattress I burned a hole through by accident, my parents suggested I take up camping."

"And you started camping alone?" Ryuji asked.

"Went with a hunting group a few times, but I'm a light sleeper and they snored too much," I said with a shrug. "I found it easier to just be on my own."

Ryuji stared at me for a few seconds. I half-expected him to ask another question, but he broke eye contact instead, turning to look directly into the smoldering fire.

"I don't know if I snore or not," he said. "Sorry."

Once again, the random apology confused me more than anything else.

"I'm sure you'll be fine," I said, shrugging again. "Loud snoring is reserved for dads, and you look too young to have had children."

Ryuji replied with a noncommittal hum but gave no other indication that he'd even heard me, simply staring into the fire instead. Not taking enough pride in my bad joke to be offended at his lack of laughter, I said nothing, staring into the fire alongside him. Staring at the fading flames and tracing the red lines scored into the firewood with my eyes, I fell into a comfortable and familiar trance as I sat there, almost forgetting that I was sitting next to the most dangerous person in the world.

"I've decided," Ryuji said suddenly. "I'm going for a Dex build."

Not knowing what he was talking about, I was tempted to ignore him.

"What was that?" I said instead.

"A Dex build," he replied. "You remember? We were talking about what I should put my stat points into before we started making food."

"Oh," I said, trying to remember what he was talking about. The words he was using were familiar, but I hadn't quite grasped the Otherworlder terms well enough to instantly recall their meaning. "Yeah, I remember. I don't think you ever explained what a Dex was, though."

Ryuji looked at me for a few seconds before slapping a hand against his head. "Right," he said. His hand cast a shadow that covered his face, making it difficult to see his expression in the dim light of the fading campfire, but it was easy enough to guess from his voice that he was embarrassed. "Sorry."

"Don't be," I said. "You can explain it to me now."

Ryuji paused for a moment before slowly lowering his hand from his face.

"Dex is short for Dexterity. The more Dexterity I have, the faster I am," he said.

"Okay, makes sense," I lied. While I acknowledged that being more dexterous could lead to increased speed, it wasn't the first benefit that came to mind. I also couldn't quite fathom why Ryuji wanted to be faster. I'd seen him move at speeds that made him seem like he was teleporting. I couldn't imagine anything faster than that.

"What about Int?" I asked, instead of trying to wrap my head around his reasoning. "Does that stand for something too?"

He nodded. "Int stands for Intelligence. The more I have, the better I am at magic."

Again, intelligence didn't really have much correlation with magical talent. I nodded anyway.

Ryuji sighed. "You think I'll regret not choosing Int?" he asked. "I mean, I'll still have basic magic, but I might be cut off from the flashier spells."

"I'm not sure," I admitted, trying not to imagine what could possibly be flashier than what he'd already shown off. "It seems like you're not entirely sure either."

"Well..." He trailed off while looking at me. "I thought it might throw off our party balance if there were two mages in a team. Besides, Dex builds are really fun."

I didn't know what a party balance was, but was he implying that I was an actual mage? The thought was ridiculous. I was a hobbyist at best, but before I could say anything, Ryuji threw up his hands and let out a groan.

"Augh. Screw this. I'm doing it," he shouted, causing a few distant bushes to rustle as their residents retreated from the sudden sound in a panic. "Status!"

He poked his finger in the air multiple times. In his frenzy, I noticed that his finger was bending back slightly every time it reached a certain spot. I'd assumed up until this point that him touching the panels could only cause them to dissipate, but it seemed like they were corporeal to him. I was surprised by the revelation, even though I was sure it was an ultimately useless piece of information.

After about half a minute of poking, Ryuji left his finger hovering in the air before swinging it down with an air of finality. He had his eyes closed and his face tensed like the act would physically hurt him, but a few seconds passed, and he lowered his finger, passing through where the invisible panel had been a few seconds before.

He let out a sigh as he slid down the log he was seated on until he was sitting on the floor.

"Welp, that's that. No turning back now," he said, an arm draped over his eyes.

I didn't know what he wanted me to say in response, or if he was even looking for one. I glanced at the dying campfire instead.

"Seems like it's getting late," I said. "We should get some sleep."

Ryuji stayed motionless for a few more seconds before taking his arm off his face. I didn't know if he acknowledged what I said at all, especially since his eyes were still closed, but he nodded.

I walked over to the small bucket of dirty water that I'd saved from cleaning the pots and threw it over the campfire. The flames died down with a quiet hiss, but when I looked over to Ryuji, he was still sitting down on the floor with his head on a log, tilted up to the sky.

Once again, I wondered if I was misunderstanding Otherworlder physiology. Was this how Otherworlders slept? Had we packed a second tent for no reason?

When I saw the light of the night sky reflected in Ryuji's eyes, I wondered if Otherworlders slept with their eyes open too.

"Wow," he said, disproving my theory for now.

"What is it?" I asked.

"The stars," he said, pointing upward.

"What about them?" I asked.

"I've never seen the night sky like this," he said with a naked sense of wonder in his voice. "It's awesome."

The sentiment confused me. I looked up, trying to see if there was any strange Otherworlder magic interfering with the view, but I saw nothing other than the usual sea of stars in the night sky.

"Hey Lena?" Ryuji said.

"Yeah?"

"Remember when I said all the stories I've read about adventurers always skipped describing the traveling part of their adventures? Because it would be boring?"

"Yeah."

"Well, this is the most fun I've had in my life."

I looked up, trying to find out why he was so enamored with the stars. I supposed they were beautiful like always, but nothing special. I looked back down at Ryuji to see him staring at me.

"Thank you," he said. "I'm glad we didn't skip this part of my story. I don't want to skip anything ever."

I didn't know what he was talking about, but I did know that he was thanking me, and I wasn't about to refuse his gratitude.

"No problem," I said, giving him a thumbs up.

We went to our tents soon after, and after seven more days of traveling, mostly occupied by a surprisingly comfortable silence, we finally made it to the road leading up to the city.

Chapter 14

A Friendly Stranger

Redstone was a city that looked too grand to be a mere eight days of foot travel away from a small village like mine. Despite its relative isolation from the other Astrantan cities, it was an important source of one of Astranta's main exports, redstone.

It wasn't a very creatively named city, but I couldn't say much, being from a village called Plainswood.

I didn't know much about Redstone, only having been there a handful of times when I was much younger, but one thing I did know about it was that it was a booming metropolis. Redstone wasn't just one of the most important cities for Astranta's economy as a whole; it was the only city in the entire eastern quarter that had a significant impact on the national economy.

That meant that the entirety of the eastern quarter of Astranta was driven by the mining industry in Redstone. The redstone miners, refiners, and exporters still needed to eat, drink, and be entertained.

The land around Redstone wasn't too arable, so food and other essentials were usually imported. A constant stream of imports was needed to keep the city supplied, and a constant stream of exports was needed to maintain the city's revenue. Redstone City was a metropolis that stopped for no one.

"Excuse me," a man's voice droned behind me. "Carts coming through."

He was at the head of a large convoy, and with how much noise the horses and carts were making as they caught up to us, I hadn't needed the warning, but I figured he was just being polite. I nodded at the driver and walked off the road.

Ryuji followed me dutifully, openly staring at the carts passing by us.

The trade convoy was a pretty impressive one, consisting of a few dozen carts and two horses for each. Most of the carts were built in a way that it seemed that they could just settle down in any marketplace and act as a portable kiosk to sell the trinkets and accessories that dangled inside them. Other carts were closed off, either to act as mobile homes for the merchants' families or as general storage for their goods. Likely both.

Each cart in the convoy had at least one driver. Several armed guards walked alongside the convoy, looking bored and weary but relieved to finally be reaching their destination. I wondered how long they'd been traveling for, passively staring at none of them in particular until I noticed one of them glancing at me.

Our eyes locked for a moment, but instead of looking away, he gave me a smile and a wink. I turned away, embarrassed to have been caught staring.

"Do you know that guy?"

The sudden question surprised me, but though it was easy enough to answer in theory, the automatic answer on my lips died when I looked up at Ryuji. It took me a moment to realize that his teeth were showing, not in a smile, but in a grimace.

The sight of it sent a sudden chill running down my spine. Spending a week with Ryuji had been less stressful than I had assumed it would be, but mostly because we'd barely talked throughout it. Most of our communication had been done through quiet nods and polite smiles.

Not having a reason to suspect Ryuji would use his terrifying power against me made it easy to forget that he had it in the first place, but as he glared angrily at the caravan guard, I was hit with the sudden reminder of who, or rather what, I was dealing with.

"N-No," I said, barely even remembering his question. "I've never seen him in my life."

Thankfully, though his eyes were still narrowed, they weren't directed toward me.

"I don't like him," Ryuji said. "He's leering at you."

I looked back at the guard but couldn't quite agree with Ryuji's assessment. The guard's eyes were narrowed, but though it was difficult to tell from this distance, it felt like he was staring at Ryuji more than he was at me. At the very least, he was looking at both of us together.

"No, no. He's not," I said quickly, remembering how eager Ryuji had been to "protect" me from Bran in a similar way. "Let's just let them pass, and we can forget about him, okay?"

"He doesn't seem too interested in letting that happen," Ryuji said, narrowing his eyes even further.

Though it was difficult to will myself to take my eyes off Ryuji, even for a second, I spotted movement in the corner of my eye and was too on edge to ignore it.

The man had left his original spot by the convoy and was walking toward us with an easy smile on his face. For a moment, I thought I saw a slight furrow in his brow before he shot a casual grin and an equally casual wave toward us.

"Ho, fellow travelers," he said in a voice that was way too loud for how close he was to us. "You seem like you've had a few long days' worth of travel. Would you like to tag along with us for a while? Rest your legs until we get to Redstone?"

It wasn't a surprising offer to receive. Ryuji and I were young travellers, and I could only assume we looked at least a little worse for wear after spending a week in the forest. Or at least I probably did. Ryuji looked just like he had when I first met him, probably due to some Otherworlder magic.

"How'd you know we're going to Redstone?" Ryuji asked. He took a step forward, not quite stepping in front of me completely but still in a way that conveyed his defensive intent.

The man laughed. "Where else would you be going?" he asked. "No need to be so tense, my friend. I wish you and your sister no harm."

Ryuji frowned despite the man's friendly tone.

"We're not siblings," I said quickly, before Ryuji could say anything else. "And we're fine. We wouldn't want to trouble you, sir. We'll get to Redstone at our own pace."

The man just laughed, clearly oblivious of the danger he could be in if he wasn't careful.

"Nonsense!" he said. I was afraid he would reach over and clap me or Ryuji on the shoulder, but at the very least, he didn't seem oblivious to the fact that he wasn't entirely liked. He just didn't seem to care. "Rest your legs. It's only a few more hours until we reach our destination. No point in tiring yourselves out when you don't need to."

I was about to decline his offer again when Ryuji spoke up.

"We'd be glad to," he said, a bit of an edge to his voice. When I looked up to see him smiling, I couldn't help but shiver even more. For some reason, the sight scared me more than him frowning.

"Excellent!" the man said loudly. "It'll be wonderful to have new faces to talk to, even if it's only for a little bit. My name's Medric," he said, extending a hand.

Ryuji smiled again, and I couldn't help but wonder if I imagined the eager flash in his eyes. "My name's Ryuji, and this is Lena," he said, reaching out to grab Medric's offered hand. "It'll be a pleasure getting to know you."

I wanted to stop Ryuji from taking Medric's hand, but I was too slow to react. When Medric grabbed Ryuji's hand, he winced slightly before Ryuji let him go.

"That's one hell of a grip you have, son," he said, shaking his hand once before flashing a smile at Ryuji and laughing once more. I couldn't remember if he'd said a sentence yet that hadn't been punctuated by his laugh. "You're a lot stronger than you look! Have you ever thought about becoming a hired guard?"

Over the past few days of talking and walking with Ryuji, I had gotten to know some of his strange quirks. One of them was that he was incredibly weak to anything resembling praise. The shift between Ryuji's veiled anger and his confusion was surprising but relieving at the same time.

"Oh," he said, scratching the back of his head in embarrassment. "No, not really. I've always wanted to be more of an adventurer."

"Oh really?" Medric said. "That's a noble thought, son. I've always regretted not exploring the world more at your age. So much to see in the world, and I've only seen the tiniest portion of it!" He shook his head and chuckled under his breath, as if he were telling some sort of inside joke. "It's a good dream to have when you're young."

It sounded a bit patronizing to me, but I was glad Ryuji didn't seem to think so, beaming as he took the praise at face value.

"Now." Medric clapped his hands together. "Why don't we stop standing around? I'm sure your friend wouldn't mind giving her tired legs a rest. We all benefit, don't we? I like my coworkers, but they're harder on the eyes. Having the company of a beautiful girl like you would definitely be a nice change of pace," he said, directing his attention back at me.

Even if my mom was right in that I'd never been interested in romance, it didn't mean I was completely clueless about it. I knew enough to know that Medric wasn't seriously flirting with me. He looked about twice my age and was smiling in a way that made it feel more like a friendly joke than anything else. I almost smiled at the compliment until I noticed Ryuji's face out of the corner of my eye.

Though his mouth was still smiling, his eyes were not. Narrowed and sharp, I could see renewed anger in them. Why? What happened? It was all going so well!

"Uh, yeah," I said, a little too panicked to accept Medric's compliment with any sort of grace, while I struggled to figure out the cause of Ryuji's anger so I could fix it. "Thanks."

There was a long, awkward pause between the three of us before Medric coughed into his hand.

"Well, shall we?" he asked, gesturing to the carts.

I followed behind him with Ryuji, taking subtle side glances to see whether he was still angry. When I saw that he still was, I panicked, but I didn't know what I could do or say to fix it when I didn't even know what was wrong.

Medric led us to the head of the convoy and nodded at the cart driver, who waved at me and Ryuji but didn't say anything before turning his attention back to the road. He didn't stop, so I was a little confused as to how I was supposed to get inside. My confusion quickly morphed to surprise when I felt someone tap my shoulder.

"May I?" Medric asked, gesturing to the cart.

I nodded, assuming he wanted to help me up.

I yelped when I felt my feet getting swept out from underneath me. Feeling myself falling, I grabbed on to the closest thing I could, which happened to be Medric's neck. The older guard chuckled as he lifted me up in his arms.

"Sorry for that," he said as he casually jumped into the cart with me still in his arms. My eyes widened in surprise at the casual display of his strength, which he clearly enjoyed as he laughed at my expression.

"Show off," the driver of the cart mumbled without turning back to look.

"Bah, everyone's a critic," Medric said as he laid me down on a sack of what felt like potatoes. Looking around me, I could see the cart was filled with similar-looking sacks. This had to be the cart for the convoy's food supply. It made sense that they wouldn't want me sitting in a cart with their wares.

As I looked at my surroundings, I didn't notice Medric's face coming closer to me until he was close enough to kiss my forehead. I froze at the sudden proximity, but he continued to lean closer until his mouth was right next to my ear.

"Is he hurting you?" he whispered.

What?

"What?" I whispered back, voicing my thoughts out loud.

"I'm not blind, girl," Medric said, his voice serious. It was a stark contrast from the jovial tone he'd had not a few seconds ago. "I see the way your face goes pale whenever he so much as twitches. You want me to send him away?"

If my face went pale every time Ryuji moved, I was glad that Medric was too close to see my face now. I couldn't imagine what I looked like while imagining him starting a fight with Ryuji. When I was twelve, I accidentally set my own hair on fire when I first started to practice magic. The memory resurfaced suddenly, and I remembered the acrid scent of human hair being burned to a crisp.

"No, no," I said, a bit louder than I'd wanted. "Ryuji's good to me! It's fine!"

Medric stood up, looking down at me as I sat in the cart. I'd only known him for a few minutes, and the sight of a deep frown on his face already looked odd to me. He stared at me for a few more seconds before he clicked his tongue.

"I won't get involved in your business if you don't want, girl. But you should ask yourself if your boyfriend truly makes you happy. If you ever need help getting out of whatever your situation is, ask around for me. Hopefully, I'll still be in Redstone by the time you realize."

Before I could say anything, he hopped off the cart.

"Oh, sorry, son," he said. His voice had shifted back into its usual loud and jovial state so fast that I couldn't help but wonder if I'd imagined our entire conversation. "Turns out there isn't as much space in that cart as I thought. The little lady took up the last spot, so you'll still have to walk. But you're a strong guy. I'm sure you can handle it."

"Oh, that's fine," Ryuji said. I was still sprawled out over a sack of potatoes, so I couldn't see what he looked like, but his voice held a familiar tone to it that I couldn't quite place. "I actually wanted to talk to you a bit."

"Oh, really?" Medric asked. I wasn't sure if I'd imagined it, but it sounded like his voice had taken on a bit of an edge. "What for?"

"You mentioned that you thought I could be a guard, right?"

"Yeah?"

"Well, since you mentioned it, I started to get a little curious about how I'd do as one. You think we'd be able to spar a bit, just to see how I stand against someone already in the business?"

My eyes widened in fear, and I scrambled off my ass and crawled over to the edge of the cart. When I peered over, Medric glanced at me, locking eyes with me for a moment. Before I could nonverbally convince him not to commit suicide via Otherworlder, he shook his head and turned back to Ryuji.

"Well, son. While normally I would refuse to start any unnecessary fights while I'm on the clock, I'm feeling pretty generous today. You probably think you're a scary guy, right?" he said, his eyes flicking toward me for a moment.

I tried to send him a nonverbal signal that he should immediately stop talking and beg for forgiveness. Unfortunately, it seemed like my strategy of standing still, frozen in fear, wasn't as effective at conveying the message as I'd hoped.

"Word of advice. The most important thing I've learned during my career as a guard is that, at some point, you're gonna have to realize that you're not that scary after all. You may think you're the strongest, most dangerous person to walk this earth, but one day you'll learn that's just not true."

I could tell Medric was a good guy. The look in his eyes was telling me that everything was going to be okay. He wasn't actually talking to Ryuji. He was talking to me. Unfortunately, everything he was saying was completely and utterly wrong.

I made one last final attempt. I willed myself to move, to mouth the word "Otherworlder" to him before he burst into flames.

Medric nodded as if he understood but turned to face Ryuji with his fists raised in a fighting stance.

"Maybe I'll be the one to humble you today, maybe not. Either way, let's make this a friendly little match, shall we?"

The eager smile that spread across Ryuji's face made me shiver, so unlike the quiet ones that he'd shown me in the forest. I'd seen that face before. It was the same face he had when he sliced a small army of demons in two.

But the sudden realization hit me. I don't know if it's because I genuinely hadn't realized it before, or if I simply didn't want to acknowledge it while I was stuck alone with him in a forest for more than a week, but even though I'd seen the demons for what they were, that wasn't true for anyone else.

Just like the villagers, Ryuji had seen them as goblins.

In his mind, he'd been murdering people.

"Yeah. Let's."

Chapter 15

A Friendly Stranger Dies

I watched in horror as Medric and Ryuji stared each other down. Medric had his fists raised while Ryuji's arms were casually hanging down at his sides. Both of them seemed too relaxed to suggest they were about to fight, though I could only assume that was because each assumed that the other was no threat to them.

I wanted to shout at them and stop the massacre before it began, but I didn't think Medric would listen to me, too deep in his misunderstanding to believe anything I said.

"Ryuji!" I shouted instead. The thought of trying to command an Otherworlder was terrifying to me, but so was the possibility of witnessing the murder of an innocent man. "Don't do this! You don't need to fight!"

Ryuji seemed to be taken aback by my outburst and looked like he was actually going to listen to me for a second until Medric intervened in my attempt to save him.

"Aw, don't worry, missy," the unintentionally suicidal man said, cracking his knuckles. "I'll make sure he comes out in one piece."

Any hesitation in Ryuji's eyes completely disappeared as he glared at Medric. I tried to wave to catch his attention again, but he refused to look at me. Cursing Medric under my breath, I panicked as my brain worked overtime to figure out a solution.

Ryuji wouldn't listen to me. Medric wouldn't listen to me. But would he listen to his boss?

I scrambled to the front of the cart I was in. I had no idea if this particular driver was the leader of the trading group, but he was the one that Medric had talked to before offering to give us a ride. At the very least, Medric would listen to him.

"Hey!" I said, my voice a harsh whisper. I leaned as close as I could to the driver without falling out of the cart. "You have to stop them from fighting. Medric is going to die if you don't."

"You've no need to worry, child," the driver said, not bothering to lower his voice in the slightest. "Medric is a kind man, but he's also very strong. Look how the rest of the convoy is acting. We all know that he is capable enough to humble your friend without hurting him."

The driver didn't bother turning around. He had a thin shawl draped over his head to protect him from the sun, so I couldn't see his expression, but from his voice, I imagined him as a kind-looking man. The way he talked about Ryuji with a little bit of bile made it obvious that Medric had shared his theories that Ryuji was somehow hurting me. Fortunately, unlike Medric, I could talk to the driver without having to shout.

"No, Medric can't stand up to Ryuji. Nobody can," I said.

I looked around to confirm that Medric and Ryuji weren't close enough to hear me. They had wandered off somewhere to the side, a bit further away from the carts, and were slowly being left behind as none of the cart drivers bothered to stop and accommodate the fight. True to the driver's word, none of the convoy members seemed too interested in watching the fight, only glancing at it with mild curiosity.

None of them seemed focused enough on me that I was afraid of causing a panic with what I said next.

"Ryuji's an Otherworlder," I whispered.

That managed to get the man's attention. He finally turned back to look at me, relying on his horses to guide themselves for the moment. He looked more or less how I'd expected him, though I'd assumed he would be a little bit younger based on his voice.

"That's not a claim one makes lightly. You could get into some serious trouble if the wrong people heard you saying that," he said. "Is that what the boy told you?"

Unfortunately, his expression was a lot different from what I wanted. Rather than a look of abject horror, he gave me a stare filled with pity.

At a loss for words, I could only stare back until I realized what he was suggesting.

"I'm not lying. I'm not dumb either." I was too panicked to feel offended, but I felt like I had to make it clear for him to even begin to believe me. "Please believe me. I know you probably think I'm some sort of naïve girl and he's just some random thug or an abusive boyfriend. I've seen how strong he is. He's not human."

He looked a little surprised by how I'd called him out on his implied insults on my intelligence, yet he still didn't seem to believe me.

"Look, child. It will be alright. Medric—"

The sound of gasping and cheers interrupted whatever the driver was about to say. I looked to the side, worried that I would see Ryuji standing over a corpse. To my surprise, Medric was still alive. In hindsight, the members of the convoy wouldn't be cheering if they saw Medric being murdered.

Medric's movements were sharp and precise to the point where even I could tell that he was incredibly skilled. The way he bobbed and weaved, throwing out punches and feints at dizzying speeds, was impressive to watch, and I had trouble keeping up with what he was doing.

Ryuji, on the other hand, didn't seem to have the same problem.

Watching Ryuji dodge Medric's attacks so casually was a strange experience because it didn't look like it made sense. I might not have noticed if I didn't have Medric to compare him to, but Ryuji looked like a complete amateur. While Medric's fighting style spoke of experience and skill, Ryuji's simply lacked any sort of substance, his movements looking random and improvised.

Despite that, none of Medric's attacks even got close to hitting Ryuji. Every time an expertly aimed punch was thrown at him, Ryuji would simply move out of the way, faster than I could follow. I'd lose track of Ryuji every time he moved, and it seemed like Medric did too, pausing after every punch before he chased down Ryuji in his new spot.

Oddly enough, it seemed like Ryuji hadn't attacked Medric at all, which was obvious from the fact that Medric hadn't inexplicably turned into a fine mist of blood and flesh. I didn't know why he chose to keep Medric alive when he was obviously so much stronger.

My eyes widened in realization at the simple answer that had been so obvious in hindsight.

Did Ryuji have morals?

Though I'd gotten more comfortable with Ryuji over our travels, the relish he had when killing the goblins and/or demons had made me assume that his mindset was too alien for such a thing.

Seeing Ryuji dealing with Medric without harming him gave me hope.

"Well, he's good, I'll admit that much," the driver said, interrupting my thoughts. "But that ain't an Otherworlder. We wouldn't be alive if he were."

I was a little disappointed that he still didn't believe me, but now that I'd seen evidence that Ryuji wouldn't turn into a murderer at the slightest inconvenience, I no longer needed him to. The driver gave me a strange look.

"You're crying," he said with a frown.

I blinked twice and realized he was right. The world was turning blurry from the moisture in my eyes, and I could already feel large streams of tears dribbling down my face. I was a little surprised at how much I was crying. I'd thought I was all cried out after the first day I met Ryuji, but I realized that these tears were special. These were tears of relief.

I simply smiled at the driver, not bothering to wipe my tears away, finding myself a little amused at how confused he looked. Now that it was clear that there wasn't a danger of Ryuji murdering someone, I could finally relax.

I turned to look at the fight as a simple spectator. I didn't usually enjoy watching fights, but with the lack of any landed blows and the threat of violence gone, I could appreciate the fight as an impressive display of acrobatics.

The convoy had stopped moving a while ago, with the drivers and guards becoming interested enough in the fight to stop and watch, so we were still close enough that we could see most of the action. As Medric continued to attack and Ryuji continued to dodge, I was almost tempted to join in the cheering and jeering of the convoy guards as they teased their captain for losing against a teenage boy. I didn't end up doing that, simply being content with watching and crying sweet tears of joy.

Medric didn't seem to notice the crowd's taunts, his eyes focused on trying to hit Ryuji, but at some point, the endless assault seemed to tire him out. He attempted one last punch, which Ryuji dodged casually, not breathing any harder than he had been at the start of the fight. Instead of following up with another attack, like he had been for the entirety of the fight so far, Medric stepped back, putting as much distance as he could between himself and Ryuji.

Even from the distance we were at, I could tell that Medric was buying time to catch his breath. He held his hands up in a defensive stance while he regained his energy, but Ryuji didn't seem interested in taking advantage of the situation. He simply stood there, still standing in the same casual pose that he'd started the fight in, and gave Medric a cocky grin.

As the convoy guards continued to throw friendly jeers at their captain, Medric finally seemed to notice their presence. His eyes darted back, and his mouth opened in a snarl, as if he were about to tell his men off, but for a split second, he locked eyes with me.

He stood there, with his mouth still open for about half a second before snapping it shut. He had a firm look in his eyes, and his strength seemed to suddenly return to him in a moment of resolution. He nodded at me, sending me a nonverbal message that I didn't quite catch. My eyes were still watering, and I didn't think they would stop any time soon.

I smiled at him, silently thanking him for getting Ryuji to reveal his humane side.

For some reason, my smile made Medric frown even harder. He turned back to Ryuji.

In a move that surprised me, Medric lowered his hands and sighed.

"Fine, you got me," he said, raising his hands in surrender. The convoy guards gave him a few playful boos as he approached Ryuji with his hands up, but he ignored them. "It was a good match. You clearly beat me, in everything but age," he said with a friendly smile and a laugh.

Ryuji seemed surprised, and he might've lowered his guard if he had one up in the first place. He said nothing as Medric slowly walked closer to him.

Once he was close enough, Medric slowly reached out to Ryuji. Ryuji seemed confused but didn't hesitate to reach out and shake the outstretched hand.

In a move that was too fast for me to follow, Medric lashed out with a high kick, creating a spray of embers that spewed out from the burned-out soles of his boots. Ryuji dodged the surprise attack, stepping back just enough that he wasn't hit by the flames, but Medric reacted as if expecting the dodge. Reaching for his side, his hand grabbed the hilt of a dagger that he had strapped to his belt.

And with a resounding crack, Medric fell to the ground.

The jeering immediately stopped.

Ryuji, standing directly behind Medric's fallen body, stared disdainfully down at him, with his hand raised in a chopping position. "That was very dishonorable of you. Consider yourself lucky that I stopped here," he said.

Leaning down, Ryuji picked Medric up by the waistband and slung him over his shoulder like he weighed nothing. He walked over to the cart I was in and smiled at the driver.

"Medric might be unconscious for a few hours," he said, shaking the body on his shoulder. "Mind if I toss him in the back? I could carry him the rest of the way, but he might wake up with a sore back."

The driver said nothing. I empathized with him. I didn't know what to say either.

Ryuji seemed to take the silence as confirmation, jumping up and into the cart. He glanced at me.

"Hey, Lena," he said. "Don't worry. He won't be able to bother you for a while now. Hopefully, by the time he wakes up, we'll be in the city already. Can't guarantee he'll stay out for the rest of the ride, but if he wakes up, I can—" Ryuji swung his free hand down in a chopping motion. "—just do that again."

"What?" I croaked.

"Oh, this?" Ryuji asked, chopping the air again. "It's something that people do all the time in my w—country. Just a solid chop to the neck." Ryuji swung his hand once more. "And they're knocked out. First time I've tried it out, though, so I don't know how long it'll last."

What? This time, the question died on my lips. What was he talking about? Could a chop to the back of the neck just knock someone out so conveniently? Maybe he was right. Maybe he had some secret Otherworlder technique to safely disable an opponent peacefully and it just happened to make a horrifying noise that sounded exactly like Medric's bones had exploded from the force.

Yeah, that must have been what had happened. It had to be. If it wasn't, then that meant that I was wrong and Ryuji did have the capability to be an unrepentant killer. Yeah. No way I'd been wrong about that.

I stared Ryuji in the eyes, as if begging him to confirm my internal monologue.

He didn't seem to understand what I wanted from him and simply smiled.

I looked at Medric instead, silently begging him to give me any sort of sign that Ryuji wasn't a murderer.

He stared back at me, his neck twisting at an impossible angle. Impossible for a living human, at least. Unless Medric was secretly the world's most talented contortionist?

The corpse stared back at me, the whites of its eyes exposed as it hung upside down off Ryuji's back and gave me the blankest expression that could ever exist on a human face.

I screamed.

Chapter 16
Life and Death

As if triggered by my scream, the silent world around me burst into a cacophony of sound. The confused shouts of the convoy men and the screams and stamps of startled horses filled the air as I stared into Medric's dead eyes.

Ryuji stared at me like a confused dog, tilting his head to one side.

"What's wrong, Lena?" he asked.

I still hadn't stopped screaming, so I couldn't answer him.

"Are you alright?" he asked, dropping Medric unceremoniously on the floor. His body tumbled awkwardly against the cart, eventually settling face down on a sack of vegetables. With my eye contact broken, I noticed Ryuji walking slowly toward me. My first instinct was to scramble away, to run from the murderer, but I remained frozen.

There wouldn't have been any point in running anyway.

As Ryuji leaned over, my eyes watched his hand getting closer to me. The same hands that had just killed a man seconds ago. I closed my eyes, too afraid to stare at my death so openly.

I kept my eyes closed, even as I felt a hand lightly touching my shoulder.

I stayed still, not wanting to give him any reason to kill me. I didn't cry, though not out of any level of bravery. They'd either run dry, or I was just too tired to cry anymore.

"Lena?" Ryuji asked. "Are you okay?"

He sounded uncomfortable, and I almost laughed at the idea.

"No," I croaked. I was surprised at how flat my voice sounded, and I wondered how I'd managed to keep my emotions from bubbling to the surface until I realized that I didn't need to hide them. I'd already accepted that I was going to die.

"Why?" Ryuji asked, sounding shocked. "What happened?"

This time, I did let out a laugh, though I wasn't sure if it could be counted as one. It was an odd sound, more of a cross between a croak and a hiccup, devoid of any humor.

"What happened?!" I said, punctuating the words with another croak. I could sense the hysteria creeping into my voice and my mind. "You killed someone. That's what happened. I don't know how people from your world feel about that, but over here, that's generally considered to be a rude thing to do."

I laughed again. It was probably a bad idea to scold an Otherworlder, but I simply didn't care anymore. If I was going to die, I might as well be a little petty about it.

I had my head down, staring at my lap as I curled up into as tight a ball as possible. My eyes were still closed, but I could imagine Ryuji's confused look as he struggled to fathom why that was a bad thing.

"What?" he asked instead, his hand retreating quickly from my shoulder as if he'd been shocked. "What are you talking about? I'm not a murderer."

I looked up at Ryuji. He was standing a few steps away from me. The genuine offense he seemed to take at my suggestion was enough for me to doubt what I'd seen. I glanced at the place where Medric had been discarded and half-expected him to get up and stretch, confused as to why he'd been knocked out for a few minutes.

Nope. He was still dead. Ryuji noticed where I was looking and turned around to examine his handiwork. His eyes widened in surprise and... fear?

"No. No. I'm not. I can't be," he said, backing away from the body slowly.

As if responding to what he'd said, a voice shouted out from somewhere I couldn't see.

"Come out with your weapons dropped and your hands up, murderer!"

I had been too focused on Medric's corpse to remember that we weren't alone. I couldn't see them, with the walls of the cart being too high to see over the edge while sitting down, but it sounded like a few men had surrounded the cart.

"I'm not a murderer," Ryuji said weakly, too quiet for anyone besides me to possibly hear him.

It seemed like he hadn't meant to kill Medric, but that didn't change anything. I didn't know if he thought Medric was stronger than he was or if Otherworlders had an anatomy that allowed them to snap each other's necks and still live, but that didn't change the fact that Medric was still dead.

"You are," I said bitterly. "You killed him."

Maybe it was wrong of me to be petty here, but I'd built up too much momentum to even bother trying to stop myself. A moment ago, I'd stopped caring about what I said because I thought Ryuji would kill me regardless, but now I couldn't help but think he was just clueless. It should've given me at least some level of hope that he wasn't actually a murderous psychopath, but every time I had tried to anticipate his next move or simply understand him, I had been blindsided by something completely unexpected. I was exhausted.

"No! I didn't!" Ryuji said, turning around to shout at me. He'd backed up far enough from Medric's body that he was close to me, almost shouting into my face, but I barely reacted to it. "He's not dead yet! I can fix this!"

It took a few seconds for me to process what he'd just said, but when I did, my eyes widened in realization. That was right. I wasn't just dealing with a random kid who'd accidentally killed someone in a freak accident. It was absurd to think that anyone could bring someone back from the dead, but if anyone could do it, it was an Otherworlder.

"You can?" I asked.

"Well..." Ryuji said, suddenly hesitant.

No. He wasn't backing out of this now. I'd gained and lost so much hope in the past few minutes that I refused to let go of the little faith I still had in him. In a moment of madness, I stood up and grabbed Ryuji's face.

I had meant to pull him down toward me, but he was so stable on his feet that I just ended up lunging forward until our noses almost touched. He looked uncomfortable. I could imagine why.

Though I hadn't seen my reflection in days, I could only guess how I looked: wide-eyed and disheveled, bloodshot eyes from crying, manic, desperate eyes. I must have looked like death, but I didn't really care. If anything, I was glad that my appearance was helping me inflict on Ryuji even a fraction of the discomfort that he'd made me feel, in a small act of petty revenge.

"Fix this," I said.

Ryuji gulped and stepped back. I followed him, keeping my eyes locked on his the entire time.

"Heal him," I repeated.

"I'll try," he said hesitantly.

I wasn't too happy with the lack of confidence in his voice, but I would take what I could get. I let go of him and stumbled backward, unsteady on my feet. When Ryuji tried to step forward to help me, I fixed him with a glare and pointed to Medric's body.

Someone on the ground yelled something, not that I could understand it. Now that I was standing, I could look around to see who it was, but before I could identify the shouter, I noticed the driver that I had talked to. He was standing a few feet away from the ring of guards that had surrounded us. From the look on his face, I could only assume that he'd changed his mind about Ryuji not being an Otherworlder. He was raising his hand as if he wanted to tap one of the guards on the shoulder to tell him something but didn't seem to have the courage to try.

I could empathize with him, but I was too annoyed at him to care. If he had believed me from the start, none of this would have happened. I could admit that if I'd been in his shoes, I probably wouldn't have believed some random girl's claims that her travel companion was an Otherworlder either, but that didn't stop the spite I felt.

"Don't make us climb up th—"

A flash of bright light interrupted the guard, forcing him to cover his eyes in reaction. I turned around to see Ryuji standing over Medric's body.

There was only a brief moment of silence before the guards started to yell at us again. I ignored them as I examined Medric. Though his neck looked much less crooked than it had been a moment ago, he was still unmoving. Despite not wanting to get my hopes up, I watched the body with bated breath.

When Medric opened his eyes, I let out a sigh of relief, but with my lungs empty, all that came out was a cough.

"Ferra!" Medric screamed, sitting up and grabbing at the air. When he managed to grab nothing, he blinked slowly and looked at his hands, his mouth gaping open at the sight.

The rest of the guards suddenly quieted down at the voice of their leader. The air was silent, save for Medric's heavy breathing.

"I'm alive?" Medric asked no one. His voice was barely a whisper, but in the relative silence, I could just barely hear him. "But I saw her. I was—"

"Never dead in the first place," Ryuji said with a nervous laugh. "Just a little tired after our spar. No harm done?"

Medric looked up at Ryuji with fear and awe in his eyes. Ryuji's hands were still glowing with the residual mana that he'd gathered to cast the spell. Though it was fading quickly, I had no doubt that Medric understood how powerful Ryuji had to be to summon that much mana without dying. Unfortunately, it didn't seem like he'd come to any conclusions yet and was just trying to recover from having been brought back from death.

I could have been sympathetic to his situation, but I was just too irritated to care.

"You should've listened to me," I spat out. "But you know what? I hope you had *FUN*."

Though Medric barely seemed to register my voice at first, the way I stressed the last word made him turn toward me so fast that I thought he would break his neck again. I fixed him with a flat stare, narrowing my eyes as if daring him to not understand what I was trying to say.

When his eyes widened, I knew that he finally understood.

"O-Oh," he said, still staring at me and not at the Otherworlder standing over him. "I suppose accidents can happen. It was a pleasure to be humbled by you, my friend. My uninteresting ways have left me naïve over the years."

I somehow managed to resist the urge to slap my face in frustration.

"Huh?" Ryuji asked, clearly confused.

All around me, I could hear the confused mumbling of the guards and drivers who were gathered around our cart, their weapons still brandished. After hearing the voice of their supposedly dead captain, it seemed like they had no idea what to do.

"Medric," I barked. "Call your men off before they do something stupid." I thought it was obvious enough without specifying what might happen if they tried.

Medric seemed like he didn't understand, but thankfully, not for lack of trying. His eyes darted around nervously, trying to find any clues about what was going on. I wasn't sure if he could even hear his travel companions yelling at us or if he even knew where he was.

"Your men," I said, not willing to give him however much time he would need to figure it out on his own. "Who think that you died and are clearly mistaken."

Medric still didn't seem to clue in to what I was saying, but the men who were listening in seemed to understand a little better. Most of them were starting to look embarrassed, and even the ones who weren't completely convinced—whether it was because they hadn't heard Medric speaking or they were still angry that their captain had been injured in the first place—still lowered their weapons in response to the awkward atmosphere.

I glared down at Medric, who still hadn't said anything, but before I finished considering whether I should physically kick him into action, his already bulging eyes somehow widened even further.

"O-Oh!" he said, standing up.

The last remnants of mumbled dissidents died down completely at the sight of their very much alive captain. While most of the convoy looked away awkwardly, as if not acknowledging their perceived misunderstanding would make it go away, some of them looked expectantly at Medric.

He took a moment to survey the scene around him, his eyes wide and unfocused, before he started on the spot, as if he had woken up abruptly from a daydream.

"Uh, it's okay, guys," he said, his voice shaky as he waved them down. "I'm fine. Go back to your station and let's get a move on, shall we? No reason to delay our journey to Redstone just because of a little fun accident, right?"

The rest of the convoy men, aside from the driver of my cart, seemed to be confused about what had just happened. However, with their leader clearly still alive, the small mob quickly dispersed, eager to forget about the silly little misunderstanding that had just happened. Medric looked back at me, as if silently asking for my approval.

"Good," I said begrudgingly. "Now get out of here and do your job."

Not needing any more encouragement than that, Medric launched himself out of the cart, leaping as far as he could and taking guard at the furthest cart he could possibly go to. Our cart didn't move for a while, since our driver refused to come back, but after he'd traded places with a younger and more confused driver, we continued our journey to Redstone.

Ryuji was still standing in the cart with me, and he looked at me nervously. He opened his mouth multiple times but said nothing. I was content with letting him stew in his own discomfort and was willing to let the rest of the journey play out in silence until it showed up.

Secret Objective: Safe Travels [COMPLETE]

An adventurer's journey is never truly safe, with danger being a constant companion to any adventurer worth their salt. But despite a few accidents, you managed to keep everyone safe. All's well that ends well, right?

+100 EXP

"Get out," I said.

Ryuji opened his mouth one more time, as if to protest, but quickly thought better of it and hopped off the cart, bringing the blue panel with him.

A few seconds after he left, I kneeled on the floor and started rummaging through my travel sack, cursing and grumbling the entire time. I shoved my hand into my bag until I finally found what I was looking for.

Any embarrassment I felt about stripping underneath the open sky was overshadowed by the humiliation of having wet myself in fear. At the very least, the cart walls were high enough that I was hidden from view from everyone on the ground.

Clad in a fresh set of underwear and pants, I felt a little better about myself, but marginally so. I felt tempted to burn my discarded clothes, more for the catharsis than to destroy the evidence, but I refrained, not wanting to draw any more attention to myself. I felt I would snap at anyone who even looked at me right now.

Throwing my pants to the furthest corner of the cart after deciding that they were no longer my problem, I sat down against the wall, thinking up strategies on how I could abandon Ryuji as fast as possible once I managed to hand him off to some Crown official in Redstone.

Chapter 17
LOVERS' SPAT

I wasn't sure whether I'd been awake or in a daze, but when the cart stopped and I looked up to see what was happening, I was startled to see that we were already very close to Redstone.

My cart had arrived at the end of a long queue of travelers, most with large carts just like the one I was sitting in. At the other end of the line, there was a massive gate that led into the city, wide enough to let at least five or six carts through comfortably at a time. While the line was moving steadily, it was still a slow process, since it seemed like the guards spoke with every group that rolled through.

"Umm, excuse me." I turned to the source of the voice. The younger driver who'd been roped into driving my cart glanced between me and Medric, who was standing a few feet away from the cart, looking nervously back at me while pretending like he wasn't. "Medric wanted me to tell you that you can leave now."

Medric's eyes widened. He shuffled closer to the driver, motioning to him to come closer. The driver sighed and leaned down to Medric, who whispered into his ear.

"He also wanted me to tell you that I didn't mean to sound disrespectful," the driver said, with a roll of the eyes. "But there's no real reason for you two to stick around. You're just visiting, right? This queue's mostly for people who're coming on business. Unless you want to sell something or buy wholesale, you can pretty much just walk right in."

The driver glanced down at Medric, who was trying very hard not to look at me.

"Thanks," I said. An hour hadn't been nearly enough time to calm down completely, but I was able to control my emotions to the point where I wouldn't snap at someone for no reason. "Can you help me down?"

The driver sighed and moved to get off his seat, but before he could do anything, Medric had already jumped onto the cart, kneeling in a deep bow like I was royalty. Wordlessly, he extended a hand.

I sighed and took the offered hand, ignoring the strange look that the driver was giving me.

Medric kept his head down the entire time he helped me off, and even after I had both feet on solid ground. I considered thanking him, but I got the feeling that he didn't want any of my attention whatsoever, so I spared him the trouble.

Ignoring the stares and whispers of the other convoymen, I walked toward Ryuji, who was standing a few feet ahead of the convoy with a deep slouch in his posture. I don't know if he heard me approaching, but he kept his eyes firmly on the ground in front of him.

It pissed me off. While the cart ride had given me enough time to cool off somewhat, the sight of Ryuji sulking around like he was somehow the victim in all of this was enough for me to get angry all over again. A small part of me screamed in agony as I threw away all sense of self-preservation and roughly grabbed Ryuji by the sleeve.

Ryuji looked up and seemed surprised to see me.

"Lena?"

"We're leaving," I said, speaking as little as possible as I pulled at his sleeve some more.

Though I knew Ryuji wouldn't have budged if he didn't want to, he came along with me dutifully. I saw more than a few onlookers watching us with a glint of humor in their eyes and vaguely heard the words "lovers' spat" being thrown around by more than a few people, but I was far past the point of caring.

"Are you angry at me?" Ryuji asked quietly.

I didn't bother giving him an answer.

When we reached the gate, a friendly-looking guard by the side noticed us and waved us over. He gave us a smile when we reached him.

"Hello, hello, and welcome! You folks here for trade or for pleasure?" he asked.

I might have thought the man's attitude to be pleasant at any other time, but I was too haggard to appreciate it at the moment.

"Pleasure," I lied, not seeing a third option available. I doubted a random gate guard would be the person to talk about Otherworlders to anyway.

"A fine choice our city is, then," he said with a wink. "Just because it's a mining town don't mean it hasn't got its own character. In fact, I'd say it means the opposite! Just a few quick questions for you folks before I let you in, though. Whereabouts are you folks from?"

I tried not to sigh. I just wanted to get inside and find the nearest Crown office. "Plainswood," I replied.

"Oh!" the guard said, his smile growing even wider somehow. "Plainswood, huh? I've actually got a cousin from Oakwood. You wouldn't happen to know a Roren, would you?"

"No," I said, as bluntly as I could.

Though the guard's eyebrows furrowed slightly at my reply, the smile didn't fade from his lips.

"Alright, then. I can see you're in a hurry to get inside our lovely city," he said with a laugh. "Just one more question, and I'll let you folks get to your sightseeing."

When it became obvious that he was waiting for me to say something in response, I nodded, hoping that would be enough for him to continue.

It was difficult to tell if he was happy about that or not, with how wide his smile stayed, but I could only assume that at this point that he was more than eager to get us into the city as I was to enter it.

"Don't worry, it's an easy one," he said. "Do either of you have a criminal record?"

I couldn't stop myself from frowning, but I hoped that my frown was already deep enough that there wouldn't be much of a difference in what he saw.

"No," I said. "Can we go now?"

Though the guard didn't answer immediately, scanning my face for a brief second and looking behind me at Ryuji's, he eventually nodded and smiled again.

"I don't see why not," he said, motioning toward the city with both hands. "Welcome to Redstone. I promise you'll enjoy your stay."

I nodded and walked off, with Ryuji's sleeve still in my hands. The guard gave him an amused smirk but didn't stop us from passing by.

We made it about twenty steps before Ryuji suddenly stopped. The sudden stop almost made me stumble backward, but I was able to barely hang on and right myself, using Ryuji's shirt as support.

I turned around, as if to yell at him, but when I saw the deep frown on his face, I was reminded that no matter how docile he seemed, he was still an Otherworlder. Somehow, my exhaustion and anger were strong enough that my fear didn't overtake me, but not enough for me to want to completely disrespect Ryuji and risk angering him just because I was feeling spiteful.

He stared down at me, and I could tell he wanted to say something, so I waited.

"Are you mad at me?" he asked.

Yes. No. Maybe? The possible answers ran through my head, but none of them seemed right.

"No," I said, surprised by my own answer. "I'm just a little upset. Terrified. Angry, yes. But not at you."

Just what he was. Thankfully, I was able to hold that particular comment back.

"You're really not angry?" he asked.

"Didn't I just say I am?" I asked, poking him in the chest. "I am angry. You killed a man, Ryuji."

Ryuji winced. "I healed him, though." He chuckled nervously. "All's well that ends well, right?"

A painful throb of anger coursed through my head as I remembered the audacity of that stupid blue panel to even suggest such a thing. I poked Ryuji in the chest, not trusting myself to say something coherent. Thankfully, Ryuji seemed to understand what I meant. He shrunk back, as if my finger could possibly hurt him.

"I didn't mean to," he said weakly.

"I know," I replied. For all of his faults, I could tell that much was true. I still didn't know what to think of his lust for battling with demons, but it was clear that he was truly remorseful about killing Medric. "It's why I'm still here and not running away as fast as I can."

It probably wasn't a good idea to admit that, but I was letting my mouth run more than I expected to. It was true that while I felt an obligation to make sure that I brought Ryuji to the Crown, it was only because I had at least some faith that he wouldn't kill me on the way there. If he'd been an unrepentant murderer from the start, I simply wouldn't have tried.

Thankfully, my admission didn't seem to make Ryuji feel worse. In fact, a slow smile started to spread on his face.

"Really?" he said. "Then we're fine?"

I had no idea what he meant by that, but I sighed and nodded. "I guess," I said. "As long as you try to learn how to control yourself so you don't kill anyone else. I don't know what your country is like, but someone has to teach you what common sense is here."

That someone wouldn't be me, but Ryuji didn't have to know that.

I looked back up at him, hoping that I hadn't accidentally said that out loud. Thankfully, he was still smiling at me.

Sensing the conversation was over, I grabbed his shirt and started to walk down the road once more but was immediately stopped in my tracks. Ryuji wasn't resisting my pull anymore, but it wasn't him that stopped me. Rather, it was the sight of the friendly guard standing just behind Ryuji, frowning at me with his arms crossed. And this time, he wasn't alone.

Though he hadn't drawn the sword that hung on his hip, the two guards by his flanks held their spears casually by their sides. They weren't pointed at us yet, though the look in the guards' eyes promised that could quickly change. The once friendly guard in the center wore a frown as he scanned my and Jamie's bodies for threats. Looking around, I noticed that a crowd had gathered around us in a large circle, whispering about murderers.

Oh. I guess we weren't being very quiet.

"So," the friendly guard said. "No criminal record, huh? What's this I'm hearing about a murder, then?"

"It was nothing, sir," I said, trying to give him the best smile I could. I wonder how it looked to him. An unkempt girl, who'd just spent eight days in a forest, and a tall boy in strange clothes, talking about how he'd just murdered a man. I didn't like my chances.

"Sure, sure," he said. Using the hilt of his sword, still sheathed for now, he pointed at my shoulders and my feet. "You know, I didn't really notice until now, but that's a nice cloak. Your boots too. Where'd you get them?"

I could feel my smile becoming crooked. What the hell, Polly? "I'm not sure," I said. "A friend gave them to me, sir."

"A friend gave you a matching set of designer clothes, huh? Straight from Pollor's? My wife's been hounding me to buy her a set just like that. Not something you can buy so easily off a senior officer's salary, so I was just curious about what your boyfriend does. But if it was a friend who gave you those clothes, now I'm even more curious. You mind coming with me for a bit so I can ask you a few questions?"

My eye started to twitch uncontrollably. "No chance we could attend to our business first, is there, sir?"

"Not sure there is," he said. "Not that you mind, I'm sure."

Ryuji stepped forward as if to say something, but I quickly grabbed him, afraid of what he would do.

"We'll go," I said. "I'm sure we'll be able to clear up this misunderstanding in no time."

The man raised an eyebrow and let out a sigh. "I sure hope so," he said. "I suppose not even murderers would be dumb enough to talk about their crimes within earshot of the guard they'd just finished talking to."

I let out a laugh that sounded a lot more nervous than I had meant it to be.

About half an hour later, a young girl around my age opened the door to my holding cell, casually spinning a set of keys around as they dangled from her finger. Though most of my focus was directed at figuring out whoever the hell this was, since she was in no way dressed like a city guard, I couldn't help but be distracted by how short she was. She wasn't even tall enough for her head to reach my shoulders if I were standing.

She gave me a grin that I didn't quite understand and stared down at me, a feat that was only barely possible since I was sitting down.

"You know," the girl said. "There are a lot more comfortable places to have a conversation than a prison."

"I didn't choose to be here," I replied gruffly. "Who are you anyway?"

The girl seemed genuinely surprised by my question.

"Isn't it obvious?" she asked, pulling back her sleeve to show me a tattoo of an eye on her forearm. "We need to talk about the Otherworlder."

Chapter 18
GIRL TALK

"Oh, thank the gods."

"You're welcome, but I'm just a normal girl. No need for the flattery," the girl said, smiling at her own joke even if she didn't laugh. "Call me Sera. It's a pleasure to meet you, Lena."

"You know my name," I said, a bit lamely.

"Your village sent a messenger to Redstone, and the Crown officials told me about you. Well, not me, but someone told my director, who told me. You get the point."

"Are you a Mediator?" I asked, as she hadn't actually confirmed it yet. I hadn't expected to speak directly to someone from the international peace-keeping group, but the eye tattoo on her forearm was a dead giveaway. The punishment for impersonating a Mediator was harsh, often ending up in execution, so I didn't think she would've strolled into a prison if she was afraid of being outed as a fraud.

I would admit that Sera didn't exactly fit the image I would've thought a Mediator might look like, but she exuded a sense of utter confidence that didn't match her outer appearance whatsoever. It was quite possibly the only reason I had assumed she was around my age, despite being more than a head shorter than me.

"Yup! And I'm here to help you out with your little Otherworlder problem," she said casually, as if she was offering to help me clean up my room. "We could have a quick chat here or—if you don't mind—we could head over to the head warden's office? It's not particularly comfortable, but it can't be worse than a literal prison cell, right?"

I nodded slowly, not quite able to keep up with the pace of the conversation, especially given how tired I was.

Sera grinned and twirled her ring of keys around her finger once more before catching it and casually dropping it into her pocket without looking.

"Let's get out of here," she said, with a wink and an offered hand.

When I took it, the amount of strength that Sera had in her tiny body surprised me, being strong enough to easily pull me off my seat. She smirked at me, as if knowing exactly how surprised I was, but didn't say anything.

It was only when I walked out of the cell that I realized something.

"Is it really fine to leave Ryuji in jail?"

"Hmm?" Sera said. "Is that your boyfriend's name? The messenger didn't mention it."

I shivered. "He's not my boyfriend."

Sera's smirk fell off her face, and a look of horror appeared on her face for a brief second before she managed to force it into a more controlled grimace. "Shit, sorry," she said. "The guard who took you in told me that you were a couple, so I thought that was the cover story you were using. I didn't mean anything by it; I'm just not too used to dealing with amateurs."

I was surprised by the admission and surprisingly grateful. It had been too long since someone had taken me seriously so quickly. A ghost of a smile fluttered on my face. "It's fine."

"It's okay to admit it's not," Sera said, squeezing my hand and making me realize that she had never let go of it. "But we'll have someone talk to you about that later. And to answer your original question, no, we shouldn't bring him. After all, it would be rude to gossip about him to his face. Better to do it behind his back."

I wasn't sure whether the casual way she was talking was putting me at ease or making me more nervous. Was she being confident or arrogant?

"But won't it be dangerous to leave him on his own?" I asked.

"Maybe," Sera admitted. "But there really isn't a better way to do this, Lena. I need to talk to you alone, and he's been sitting alone in a cell for a while now. I'm sure a few more minutes won't make a huge difference. And I do have people watching over him too, y'know."

"Not that anyone can stop Ryuji if he wants to leave," I said.

"True," Sera said with an easy laugh that didn't quite match what she'd just admitted to. "Which is why we should hurry up, shouldn't we?"

I nodded. Sera started to move again, dragging me by the hand to the warden's office, which wasn't particularly far, given that the prison wasn't particularly large.

We passed by a few offices until Sera stopped at a door that looked identical to most of the ones we'd passed by already. Without knocking, she finally let go of my hand to push it open and beckon me inside.

The room was sparsely decorated, not looking too much different from the prison cell, aside from the difference in furniture. Everything was colored in a drab grey or brown, except for the large mountain of colorful snacks that sat on the large desk at the center of the room. Most of the snacks were of a variety that I'd never seen before, and from the overly fanciful boxes, I could tell they were probably expensive.

"The perks of being important enough for people to want to impress you," Sera said, closing the door behind me. "We don't have all day, so we might as well get to it."

I heard a heavy *thunk* and turned to see Sera locking the door. She raised a single eyebrow at me that made me wonder if I'd reacted a little more violently than I'd thought.

"Do you want me to keep it unlocked?" she asked.

"No, it's fine," I said.

"You sure?" Sera asked, unlocking the bolt before I could answer. "I don't mind."

"Either way's fine," I said.

Sera stared at me for a second and shrugged. I couldn't help but feel like I was the one in the wrong for wanting to get this over with quickly so I could just leave Ryuji in their hands and go home to sleep for a week. Thankfully, Sera left the door unlocked and walked behind the desk, falling back comfortably in the chair that was designed to seat a man twice her size.

The fact that her shoulders barely seemed to reach the table didn't seem to bother her in the slightest, even when she had to lean over to grab a cookie from the center of the table. The action looked so childlike that it probably should've been funny, though I wasn't in any mood to laugh.

"Cookie?" she asked, offering me the one she'd just picked up.

"No thanks," I said. "Can we just talk about Ryuji now?"

"You sure?" she asked before tossing the cookie into her mouth. She chewed maybe twice before she swallowed and reached for another. "These are seriously good. The head warden knows his sweets."

"Positive."

She shrugged before she swallowed her second cookie and reached for a pastry. "I can appreciate a girl who gets down and dirty as fast as possible," she said. "So, you want to be a Follower?"

With how casually she asked it, it took me a second to react to the question. I paled at the thought. "No," I said, the image of Medric's corpse still fresh in my mind. "No way."

"Really?" Sera asked. "Then why did you tag along with him, if you don't mind my asking? Normally, folks just send Otherworlders on their merry way when they find them. Not too many go above and beyond like you did."

Unless they wanted to be Followers. I heard the unspoken suggestion loudly. I shook my head.

"I just wanted to make sure he got to where he needed to be, and I didn't trust anyone else to do it properly."

Sera gave me an analytical stare.

"So, just to be clear, you don't want to continue being his Follower? Are you aware that if you choose to remain as a Follower to an Otherworlder, you will be paid a minimum of eight gold on a monthly basis, potentially rising up to ten times that amount depending on how dangerous the Otherworlder proves to be?"

I hadn't known that. I was technically aware that Followers were paid generously for their services, but the exact amount was mind-boggling to me. My parents made maybe the equivalent of two gold coins per year, so the fact that I could potentially earn eighty in a month put the whole Follower thing into a completely new perspective.

Even so, I shook my head.

"No way," I said. "Not for all the money in the world."

Sera stared at me for a few more seconds before she smiled.

"Good. I assumed as much, but I had to make sure," she said. "I am glad to let you know that you'll be rewarded for your services up until this point regardless, but we'll have to figure out the details on that later. I'm sure you're not in the mood for paperwork right now."

I nodded before fully processing what she had said.

"Wait, does that mean that's it?" I asked. "I'm free?"

"So eager to leave just after we've met?" Sera asked with a laugh.

I was surprised that I laughed too, more due to my quickly rising mood than the joke itself.

"You're free to go," Sera said, answering my previous question. "I would prefer if you could stick around to answer a few questions about the Otherworlder, just to help us understand how to handle him better, but I won't stop you if you want to get up and leave the room right now."

"No, that's okay," I said, nodding quickly despite my urge to take Sera up on her offer. I could only imagine Plainswood was still within his blast radius, after all. "I'll help as best as I can."

"I'm happy to hear that," Sera said, with a wide smile. "You ready for your first question, then?"

I couldn't help but smile with her as I nodded.

"What do you think is the Otherworlder's dream?"

I don't know what sort of expression I had on my face in reaction to that question, but Sera didn't make any indication that she was joking, still wearing the same kind smile that she'd had a moment before.

"Excuse me?" I asked, just in case I'd misheard.

"You didn't mishear me," Sera said, instead of repeating her question. "It's not a trick question or anything. We're just trying to understand the nuances of his powers, outside of the whole 'skilled at everything' package that all Otherworlders seem to come with. There's a theory that an Otherworlder's powers are shaped by their deepest desires."

"That sounds ridiculous," I couldn't help saying.

Sera shrugged.

"It's about as ridiculous as a teenage boy having the power to destroy the country we're in with the snap of a finger, isn't it?" she said, giving me a smile. The effect was somewhat ruined by the cream filling that stained her cheek from the last pastry she'd shoved in her mouth. I had already lost count by now, more focused on the conversation than her voracious eating, but I guessed she'd shoved seven snacks down her throat. "But if you want an example, you know about the Plague King, right?"

If I were in a brighter mood, I might have laughed at the question.

"Do I know the Otherworlder that was responsible for killing half of the world's population?" I asked, not knowing how else Sera expected me to answer.

"It's actually a little closer to forty percent, but yeah. That would be the one," Sera said, ignoring the sarcasm in my question and nodding. "His dream was to be a healer and rid the world of all disease. It gave him the ability to manipulate living material on a whim."

"The Plague King wanted to rid the world of all disease?" I couldn't help but ask, incredulity replacing my previous sarcasm this time around. It would be a strangely ironic dream for the Plague King to have, given the pox he'd unleashed upon the world before his disappearance.

"Yes. Ironic, I know," Sera said, shaking her head. "But before we become too side-tracked, we should go back to the more relevant Otherworlder at hand. We're not on a tight schedule, but we shouldn't waste time gossiping either."

"Sorry," I said.

"It's okay," Sera said. "I'm the one who brought it up anyway. So, any ideas on what this one's dream might be?"

"Well, it's obvious that he wants to become an adventurer—whatever that means," I said. "But if you want to hear about Ryuji's powers, then I can just tell you about them."

For the first time since she'd sat down, Sera's mouth snapped close over the cookie instead of swallowing it whole. Half a cookie remained dangling in her hand.

"Oh?" she asked. "What do you mean by that?"

She was still smiling, but her eyes were narrowing, rapidly losing their playful edge. I couldn't help but think I'd made a mistake.

"Umm," I said, suddenly a lot less confident in what I was going to say. "I'm not sure."

"Do you see things that other people can't see?" My eyes widened when she set the half-eaten cookie on the counter, discarded and forgotten. "Things that the Otherworlder can obviously see as well? Panels floating in the air? Glowing labels floating above people's heads? Random music playing in the air that nobody else seems to hear?"

"Yes?" I said cautiously. "Not all of those things, though. Just the panels."

Sera stared at me for a few more seconds before gently placing her head in her hands and letting out a heavy sigh.

"Why? What's wrong?" I asked, a little afraid of her reaction.

Sera shook her head and hopped off her chair. At first, I wondered if that meant I should get up too, but she walked over to me too fast for me to decide whether I wanted to stand or not.

The look in Sera's eyes scared me. She should've been barely taller than me while I was sitting, but when I was forced to crane my neck to look up at her, I vaguely realized I was curled up in fear, my arms wrapped around my knees as if I could somehow escape Sera's apologetic, pitying expression if I made myself small enough.

"I'm sorry, Lena," Sera said, wrapping me up in a hug. "You're a Chosen Follower."

I didn't know what that meant exactly, but I could tell it wasn't good.

Chapter 19
Serious Talk

It took me about five seconds before I couldn't take it anymore. I pushed Sera away from me, a little more violently than I intended, but she didn't seem bothered by it, catching herself before she could crash into the wall or any furniture.

"You said I could leave, right?" I said, trying to push myself up. Before I could stand up, however, Sera moved in front of me and placed a hand on my shoulder, keeping me in place.

I looked up at her. "Please let me go," I begged, hating the way my voice shook as I spoke.

"Lena," Sera said, the pitying look in her eyes returning. "You need to know what you are. Denying the truth isn't going to help anyone, especially not yourself."

I shook my head. "You must be mistaken. I'm just a normal girl from a small town in the middle of nowhere. I'm no one special."

Sera sighed and leaned down to give me another hug. When she pulled away, the resolute confidence she held in her eyes gave me a moment of clarity. In the relative silence of the room, I suddenly became very aware of how heavily I was panting.

"I know it's scary, but I promise I can help. You need to know more about the situation you're in so you can better understand how to handle it and how to get away from it."

I perked up at that. The only sound that filled the room was the frantic pounding of my heart as I stared Sera in the eyes, searching for any hint of a lie. She held my stare easily, and the ghost of a smirk reappeared on her face.

"Breathe, Lena," she said. "It won't do us any good if you pass out."

I hadn't realized I was holding my breath as if subconsciously trying to overcompensate after I realized that I had been heavily panting a moment before. After Sera mentioned it, I couldn't help but gasp and greedily suck in the air I hadn't known I was missing. The sudden intake of air was rough on my dry throat, but I managed not to devolve into a coughing fit. Sera backed away from me and sat back down in her seat across the desk, confident that I wouldn't try to get up and leave again, no matter how much I wanted to.

"You're a Chosen Follower," she said.

"Care to explain what that is?" I asked.

"We don't have too much time," Sera said. "I'll explain in more detail later, but for now you'll have to be satisfied with the short version."

"Okay," I said. It didn't seem like she was asking for my approval, but I gave it anyway, if only to trick myself into believing I had more control over the situation than I did.

"Before I explain what a Follower really is, I need you to understand something, Lena. Being a Follower isn't as rare as you might think. There are at least a few hundred Followers or ex-Followers alive in the world today. Just like you, they started their journey afraid and unconfident, but the Mediators put a lot of resources into making sure they lead normal lives as much as possible, just like how we'll make sure you feel as comfortable as you possibly can throughout your life. Do you understand?"

I didn't. "A few hundred?" I asked. "Didn't the Plague King die over fifty years ago? Wasn't he the last Otherworlder to come here?"

"He was the last Otherworlder to have had more than significant effects on an international scale. It doesn't mean he's the only Otherworlder to have arrived since then. Dozens of Otherworlders were alive during the Plague King's rampage, and dozens more are alive today." Sera smiled and reached over the table to place a comforting hand gently over mine. "Do you understand what that means, Lena?"

I looked down at Sera's hand, a little confused. Though the idea that there were more than a few potential copies of the Plague King alive and running around should have terrified me out of my wits, the way that Sera was talking and how she was trying to comfort me while talking about such a horrifying concept didn't seem to match up. I was actually feeling a lot better, which surprised me, and it took me a second to guess why.

"Not all Otherworlders are as bad as the Plague King," I suggested.

Sera nodded, pleased at my revelation. "Exactly," she said, letting go of my hand and tossing another snack into her mouth. "Though the world is filled with these terrifying creatures, most of the world is unaware simply because the situation is under control. The Mediators have the situation under control, and we're right here, ready to help. Does that make you feel any better?"

I wasn't surprised to realize that it did. I felt a few tears of relief streaming down my cheeks and sniffled before wiping my nose on my sleeve.

"Cookie?" Sera asked. I didn't look up at her, but she slid one into my view. I nodded in thanks and took it.

It felt a bit childlike to indulge in such a sugary thing, but with Sera having already eaten about half her weight in snacks, I felt a little less bad about it. I expected my shaky emotional state to make it difficult to taste food properly, but if anything, the cookie almost tasted sweeter by being the only good thing to happen in my life for the past week and a bit.

"Told you it was good," Sera said with a laugh. Evidently, my expression told a story on its own. I didn't care. I devoured that cookie and immediately reached for another.

Seeing that I was too busy to reply, Sera continued to talk.

"I'm glad you feel better, even if it's just a little bit," she said. "I do want to clarify something, though. The Mediators are here to help, and I promise that we will do our best to get you through this as undamaged as possible, but it's not going to be easy. The important thing to keep in mind is that it is possible."

She was repeating the conclusion I'd already come to, but hearing it said out loud did make me feel better. After being stuck without hope for so long, the mere idea that I wasn't stuck forever was a huge relief.

"Unfortunately, I will admit that the process is very vague and difficult, especially for a Chosen Follower," she said, holding up a hand to stop me from speaking up before I could even consider it. "And just like I promised, I'll explain what a Chosen Follower is.

"I can't explain to you all the methods that the Mediators use to categorize Followers. There's a literal book on that topic that I could potentially lend to you in the future, but one of the categories that Followers fall into depends on whether they're connected to their Otherworlder's power or not. You ever read 'The Chronicles of a Witness'?"

"Umm," I said slowly, giving myself some time to think of why it sounded familiar. "Is that the book that the Plague King's Follower wrote?"

"Yup," Sera said. "You read it, then?"

"No, but my dad did. He didn't talk too much about it."

"Good. It's a horrifying book. I only brought it up because I wanted to give you an example of a Follower who wasn't Chosen. I won't go into the details, but the entire book was written from the point of view of a helpless observer who was just there as… well, an observer. There was nothing she could really do to change the course of the Plague King's path. Even if she was Chosen, it might not have mattered, but it certainly didn't help that she wasn't."

The implication wasn't lost on me. "So you're saying that a Follower can influence their Otherworlder more if they're Chosen? Why?"

"It's because a Chosen Follower has access to their Otherworlder's power," Sera said, pointing at me.

I suddenly felt uncomfortable again. "What?" I asked. "What are you talking about? I'm not nearly as powerful as Ryuji is."

"I didn't mean power in that sense," Sera said. "Otherworlders may possess godlike powers, but that doesn't mean that they are gods themselves. Simply put, the panels that you see are a necessary management system of sorts that allows the Otherworlder to access their power without their bodies spontaneously exploding and taking a country or two down with them. It manifests in every Otherworlder slightly differently, but the fact that you can see it means that you have access to it, to an extent."

"Why? Why me?" I asked.

I hated the apologetic grimace that Sera gave me.

"There isn't one catch-all reason why a Follower becomes a Chosen, since it does require the Otherworlder to actively want a Follower as their companion," she explained. "I haven't had the opportunity to talk to him yet, so you would know better than me. Why did this one choose you?"

"I—" I paused, not wanting to say it out loud, as if admitting it would solidify it as being true. I was tempted to say I didn't know, but I had the feeling that lying would only make it harder for me in the long run. "Ryuji's in love with me."

Sera's smirk disappeared instantly as she shot up. Her chair clattered to the floor violently, the sound echoing through the small room.

It was only the fact that I was afraid of that exact reaction that I didn't jump out of my own seat in surprise.

Sera stared at me in silence before bending down to pick up her chair and sit back down. She folded her hands together in front of her, returning to her more professional pose, but the smile she wore was strained.

"Sorry," she said. "I might've overreacted."

No, she hadn't.

"That's bad, I assume," I said.

Sera kept the smile for a few more seconds before it fell. "It is," she admitted. "Still manageable, but it does make it more challenging. How did you figure it out? Did he tell you explicitly? Is it just a feeling you have, or is there some other reason you might assume this?"

I didn't like how she almost hesitated as she gave me that last option.

"The panels described me as his love interest," I said. "They also keep telling him that the numbers related to my Affection keep going up, whatever that means. Is that bad?"

Sera grimaced and stood up again. It wasn't violent enough to send her chair flying again, but her movements were still sharp and intense.

"Yes. It is. We should go," she said. "Your situation is still salvageable, but I don't want to waste any more time."

"What's going to happen to me?" I asked. I heard my voice as if it were an outsider's. It was eerily calm, almost bored of the constant twists and turns that seemed to send my life spiraling down further and further, my mind-numbing panic doing exactly that, dulling my thoughts into indifference. "I'd like to know."

I couldn't tell why Sera was grimacing. There were simply too many possibilities for me to guess just one.

"I shouldn't have reacted like that," Sera said. "I was just surprised. I promise you'll still be safe, Lena. I'm more afraid of the overtime I'll have to pull, if anything."

I wasn't sure I believed her words or the little smile she had on her face as if she actually thought her little joke was funny. It must have shown on my face because Sera walked over to me and stood directly in front of me. Even with her short height, I found myself looking up at her with how low I was slouching in my seat.

"I'm being serious, Lena," she said, reaching down and grabbing my hand in both of hers. While it might've been a sweet gesture in any other scenario, I was just too numb to feel it. "It doesn't do me much good to sugarcoat anything for you. In fact, it just makes me harder in the long run if I lie just to make you feel better. Like it or not, you're a Chosen Follower. You don't deserve what's happened to you, and I and the rest of the Mediators will do everything in our power to fix things. It may take some time, but with a bit of hard work, I know that we can break the connection you have with the Otherworlder."

I looked down at my hand, held up by Sera's gentle grip. I really wanted to believe her, but the past couple of days had cultivated my level of cynicism to a level that I'd never experienced before. Having hope only meant I could lose it.

"Yeah?" I said, scoffing at the idea. "Care to share how without being super vague about it?"

Instead of answering my question with another vague promise, Sera did something that I would never have expected.

I was only vaguely aware of her lifting my arm but didn't realize what she was doing until I felt her hands overlapping with mine, gently pressing my fingers into something warm and soft. When I realized what was happening, I looked up, not knowing how to react to Sera using my hand to grope her own boob.

"That's how," she said.

"Huh?" My brain was too numb to decide on an appropriate reaction. When I felt my fingers twitch and gently squeeze Sera's chest, the more primal part of my brain finally woke up and I yanked my hand away as fast as I could, my face flushing a crimson red.

Sera laughed and stepped away from me to give me space.

"I'm going to seduce the Otherworlder away from you," she said.

Chapter 20
Sera's Plan

Sera knew she was a good liar.

While a small part of her couldn't help but think that wasn't something to be proud of, that opinion was a lingering remnant of her life as a civilian. Lying was nothing more than a tool, and while it was often used with less than pure intentions, Sera was a Mediator who had saved countless people with her lies.

It was quite literally her job.

"You didn't have to give me a demo," Lena said, grumbling quietly and cutting through Sera's thoughts. "Mediator or not, I should report you for sexual harassment."

One thing that Sera hadn't mentioned to Lena was that while the Mediators did have tabs on several dozen Followers around the world, all of them were trained professionals. Sera herself had come to the city to become a Follower but had apparently been beaten to the punch by a civilian from the middle of nowhere. However, after meeting the girl in question, Sera found herself unsurprised by the revelation. Lena was objectively beautiful, and with the Otherworlder reportedly being a young boy, it wasn't a huge stretch to think that he could fall in love with her so quickly. Sera couldn't help but think that if Lena were uglier, she might not have become so entangled in this mess.

Sera laughed loudly as she put a finger to her lips in a shushing motion.

Sera had to focus on two things: keeping Lena unaware of the danger she was in and fixing it before it became worse. While she'd already failed on that front, uncharacteristically letting her true reactions to Lena's plight show, she knew she couldn't dwell on the mistake.

"Sorry about that," Sera said with another laugh. "I wouldn't blame you if you reported me, but I'll ask that you don't. I wouldn't get arrested, but if my superiors heard about what I did, I'd probably get a huge scolding, a hefty fine, and about a year of overtime with no pay. I know I'm not really setting a good example for the organization, but believe it or not, sexually assaulting civilians is a big no-no for us."

"Then why'd you do it?" Lena asked, shaking her hand violently, as if that would remove the memory of what it had touched.

"I had to do something to put a smile on your face," Sera said, smiling despite the scowl that appeared on Lena's face. "Or a frown. Anything was better than that dead-inside look you had."

In response, Lena's frown flattened out into a thin line as she gave Sera a blank stare, as if she was trying to deny Sera the satisfaction of succeeding.

Sera was surprised by the genuine chuckle that the petty reaction drew out of her. She'd only known Lena for a couple of minutes, so she was surprised that she'd become so attached to the girl already. The girl was smarter than the average civilian, at least enough to realize what was going on with minimal explanation despite the obvious panic she was in. It was an admirable quality, even if it made Sera's job more difficult. She had to be more cautious about what she said to Lena, lest she accidentally gave away something that would only send her into a panic.

"Cute," she said, reaching up to pat Lena's shoulder and giving it a brief squeeze.

Sera wondered if Lena was even aware that she was leaning into the touch. Sera's hand lingered for a few more seconds than it needed to before she eventually let go. Lena scowled at the brief contact, but Sera didn't miss the way that she stepped closer, as if subconsciously seeking more. Lena's expression was becoming increasingly complicated too. She could see hope there, but she could also see that Lena was desperately quashing it as best as she could, expecting to be let down once more if she dared to believe that she would be saved.

Poor girl.

Sera hummed happily as they made their way to the Otherworlder's jail cell. It had been popular in the region a few years ago, and though her humming was off-key, it was close enough to the original song that it would be subconsciously recognizable. The subconscious nostalgia would soothe Lena a little, though Sera regretted that it was the only comfort she could give her for now.

When she was five years old and had first joined the Mediators, she had made a vow to herself that nobody would ever die to an Otherworlder in front of her ever again. It was a foolhardy goal and Sera knew it, but it didn't stop her from dedicating her entire life to the study of Otherworlders.

The Mediators knew that this particular Otherworlder had the potential to be a difficult case. Though that could admittedly be said quite often in her line of work, where every Otherworlder had the power to potentially destroy Materia if they went unchecked, what was concerning about this one were his actions.

Within the first day of his arrival, he had reportedly slain a small group of goblins, forced the villagers of Plainswood to cheer for him while he did it, and kidnapped a girl from her home. Sera had only heard second-hand details of these events. Protocol would have had her interrogate Lena for more details as a primary witness before taking action against the Otherworlder, but Lena seemed so hurt and traumatized that Sera couldn't bring herself to force her to relive those moments.

Lena was just a normal girl, and while it had honestly been amazing to hear that a civilian had taken charge of an Otherworlder case with no training whatsoever, there was no doubt that she had suffered permanent mental damage from the experience.

Sera could only hope that she would be able to prevent Lena from suffering any more, but it was undeniable that at that very moment, Lena was in a much more dangerous situation than she could have possibly guessed.

One of the most horrific Otherworlders that the world had ever seen had existed about a few centuries before, given the moniker of "The Harem Lord." He wasn't known to the public, since his actions didn't have a widespread effect and the Mediators of the time had been able to stop any news from spreading, but that didn't make him any less terrifying.

He was the reason why the term Bland Love Interest Syndrome had been coined. Sera shivered to think of those poor women who had been stripped of their personalities, transformed into mindless automatons that lived purely to stroke the Otherworlder's ego.

BLIS wasn't a universal factor when it came to dealing with all Otherworlders, since every Otherworlder was unique and not all of them had access to a BLIS factor. While Sera couldn't be sure if this Affection rating that Lena saw was anything similar, she didn't want to gamble on the chance that it wasn't.

"Lena," Sera started as they approached the door to Ryuji's holding cell. "I wish I could give you more time to brief you on what's about to happen, but it's better to do this as fast as possible. You won't have to do anything difficult. Just agree with whatever I say in there and try not to speak up unless you're directly spoken to."

"Okay." Despite her protective mask of grumbling and cynicism, Lena was quick to nod. The frown on her face was strained as if she was purposefully keeping herself upset so she wouldn't be disappointed when things ultimately failed. Sera had the urge to tell her to stop and remind her that she needed to smile in front of the Otherworlder, but she didn't want to stop her from doing what she needed to do to cope. Lena had survived this long without any help. Sera decided to trust that she knew what to do.

"Oh, and one more thing," Sera said, her false smile finally cracking as she grimaced at what was to come. "Please don't think badly of me for how I'm about to act."

Sera's plan to replace herself as the Otherworlder's love interest wasn't a suicide mission. There were proven ways to avoid falling to BLIS.

The most common way that Mediators did this was to become a slave.

While slavery was illegal in all civilizations across Materia, the Mediators would occasionally fabricate entire slave economies with paid actors to falsify their own identities as slaves and establish themselves as Followers.

The slave method was a proven method for convincing the Otherworlder that there was no intrinsic need to strip a Follower's personality down if a falsified "slave contract" guaranteed a Follower's loyalty without it. It was unsavory and sickening, but so many Otherworlders had a preference for slave Followers for some unknown reason that this method was used whenever possible.

Unfortunately, false slavery wasn't a viable option for Sera to take since this method needed time to set up. While the Mediators had a near-infinite pool of resources to draw from, at this point, it was too late to set up anything substantial in Redstone at least. There was the option of waiting until Ryuji arrived in a false city where "slavery" was much more common, but she didn't have the time. Lena needed help now.

With slavery not being an option, another reliable method was to adopt a false personality to match the Otherworlder's ideal type. This would achieve two things.

Firstly, by presenting herself as the Otherworlder's ideal type, she could convince him that she was a much better option than Lena and outright replace her. Even if this Otherworlder was the type to take multiple Followers, she hoped to cement herself as the main love interest and eventually wean Lena off the Otherworlder's influence slowly without destroying her.

Secondly, she would be protecting herself. As long as she presented a false identity that was already perfect, there would be no risk of her succumbing to BLIS, as there would be no reason for the Otherworlder to want to mold her mind to be any different.

Unfortunately, the method wasn't as reliable as the slavery tactic. Not only was it more difficult to maintain, even for the most experienced of Mediators, but it was also difficult to get right. Oftentimes, it needed at least a few days of intense study of the Otherworlder's psychological profile to accurately determine their ideal personality type, making it no less resource-intensive than the slavery method, but Lena didn't have that time. For all Sera knew, Lena was already affected by BLIS and would only deteriorate further if she didn't do anything to fix it immediately.

She would have to forge a personality off the little that she knew. It was dangerous, but she didn't have much of a choice. Fortunately, she had all the important pieces. Regardless of whether she had the finer details or not, one thing was obvious.

This Otherworlder was a murderous sociopath.

It was both fortunate and unfortunate that it wasn't an uncommon psychological profile that was shared amongst many Otherworlders. Unfortunate, because it was obviously more troublesome to cater to the desires of someone with unlimited power if they weren't a murderous sociopath. Fortunate because it gave Sera and every other Mediator a whole archive of past examples to draw experience from.

While every Otherworlder was unique, a psychological profile was still a useful tool in predicting an Otherworlder's preference in Followers. Aside from the universal requirement for a Follower to be conventionally attractive, Otherworlders who were murderous sociopaths often preferred their travel companions to be incompetent, mindless, submissive. Oddly enough, many also enjoyed their Followers having a faux-aggressive personality while paradoxically maintaining their weak-willed nature, possibly due to their desire to "earn" their Follower's affections through a challenge in a twisted way.

Sera closed her eyes for a second, taking the brief moment to center herself, imagining the ideal personality that the Otherworlder just beyond the door might prefer.

Incompetence, mindlessness, submission, and aggression. The personality was easy enough to conjure in her mind.

Steeling herself, Sera took one last deep breath before she put a wide smile on her face, opened the door, and stepped toward the Otherworlder.

She immediately tripped over her own feet.

"Wahwahwah," she yelled, waving her arms like a windmill as if trying to catch herself before falling forward.

Sera saw the Otherworlder's eyes widen as she barreled toward him but made no moves to stop her. That was good. He was receptive at the very least.

Sera let out a loud, high-pitched cry as she gave into her momentum and tackled the Otherworlder off his seat. As she flipped head over heels, tumbling to the floor with the Otherworlder, she caught a glance of Lena's face, which was a perfect mixture of horror and confusion. Sera shot her an apologetic smile that she was sure the girl wouldn't see before focusing on her tumble.

Sera and the Otherworlder rolled over twice more, with Sera subtly controlling their momentum as they tumbled, manipulating his position to suit her purposes. Once they came to a stop, Sera sat up and pretended not to notice the situation she'd put herself in.

"Ouchie," she whined, rubbing her head to soothe the non-existent injury. "I'm such a klutz. Teehee."

She then looked around the room in an exaggerated manner. "Huh?" she said. "Where'd that cute boy go?"

After a moment of silence, she looked down to see the Otherworlder on the floor, directly beneath her. His face was a bright red, and his eyes were fixed forward, nearly bulging out of his head. Her skirt had been flipped up during the tumble, and if it weren't for her underwear, his nose would've been touching her crotch directly. Sera tried not to gag at the idea and, letting the anger she felt at the Otherworlder's existence serve as inspiration, she summoned a deep flush to her cheeks that would hopefully look like a blush of embarrassment.

"Kyaa!" she cried, slapping the Otherworlder in the face. "Pervert!"

Chapter 21

A New Rival Approaches

No matter what I do, don't act surprised.

Sera's words echoed through my head as I watched the scene unfold before me, but I didn't know if I could follow her request. I don't know exactly what I had expected, but I certainly hadn't expected her to literally throw herself at the Otherworlder and physically assault him.

I didn't know if I was more afraid for her or of her, if she thought that provoking Ryuji with violence was the best thing to do to endear herself to him. My mom had been right when she said I didn't understand boys, but I knew enough to know that whatever this was probably wasn't the best way to try to seduce one. It was only shock that kept me from running away in fear of Ryuji's retaliation.

"Pervert!" Sera cried out again as she smacked the top of Ryuji's head, driving his face deeper into her crotch at the same time.

An explosion happened. When I saw the spray of blood erupt from under Sera's skirt, my first thought was to assume that she'd stabbed him with a hidden weapon of some sort.

"Shit!" Ryuji cried out, easily crawling out from underneath Sera and forcing her to roll off of him. "I'm so sorry," he said, clutching at his face to cover the steady spray of blood shooting out from his nose. "Goddamn Anime Character Constitution!"

I still didn't understand what anime was, but Sera either seemed to know what Ryuji was talking about or was just skilled enough to adapt to the situation instantly. Her expression, though slightly confused, showed a naked concern that looked genuine enough that I almost forgot that she was putting on an act.

Ryuji looked up and my first reaction was shock. The flow of nose blood had stopped just as quickly as it had started, and his face and chest were painted red, but that wasn't the only thing that stood out. The palm-shaped welt on his face was horrifying to look at. It didn't look like Sera had put too much force into her swing—certainly not enough to inflict damage on an Otherworlder.

"A-Are you alright?" The question had been automatic, and I winced when Sera glanced back at me with a shocked expression, reminding me that I didn't want to draw any attention to myself.

"Did I hurt you?" Sera asked quickly, as if trying to hide the fact that I'd spoken out of turn. "I'm so sorry, I didn't mean to. I was just surprised."

"Yeah," Ryuji said. "I'm fine. It's nothing to worry about."

"Are you sure?" Sera said, crawling up to Ryuji and cupping a hand under his chin. It was a good thing he was sitting down, or she probably would've had to stand on her tiptoes to reach him. With her on her knees and him sitting down against the wall, she stared deep into his eyes, close enough that their noses were almost touching.

There was a moment of silence before Ryuji's face turned a bright crimson. The speed of the change was fast enough to make me recoil, but Sera paid no mind to it. A blush emerged on her face as she pushed Ryuji's face to the side, diverting his gaze away from her.

"D-Don't get the wrong idea. I don't care if you're hurt or not. I just didn't want to feel guilty about hurting you. Idiot."

I had no idea what that meant, but I was getting more and more uncomfortable watching this play out. Our previous conversation had left a good enough impression on me that I had some amount of trust in her, but the character that Sera was playing to "seduce" Ryuji was clearly skating on the brink of mental instability.

I didn't know whether I wanted to intervene. While she was an alleged professional, the last time Ryuji had become irritated in any way had resulted in a man's death. Sure, Medric had gotten better and Ryuji hadn't meant to kill him in the first place, but it didn't mean I enjoyed the experience overall.

I lifted a hand as I debated with myself whether I should stop Sera or not.

??? has joined your party!

I stared at the panel for a few seconds before I actually registered its existence. Rubbing my eyes once to make sure I wasn't hallucinating, a complex stew of emotions swirled inside of me.

On one hand, I was relieved to see that Sera was as good at her job as she claimed to be. On the other hand, I couldn't help but be a little disappointed at the fact that it had been so easy for her. I knew I should've been ecstatic to know that I could trust her a little more, but a part of me thought that Sera's ability to deal with Ryuji so easily kind of cheapened how hard it had been for me for the past week.

The panel was hovering right in front of Ryuji's face, interposing itself between him and Sera. Though it was somewhat translucent, Sera's face was probably obscured enough from Ryuji that he wouldn't see her blank expression as she stared at the panel. Though she usually hid her emotions well, I could only guess that she was experiencing similar feelings to mine.

When Ryuji tapped a finger on the panel, dismissing it, the room fell into an awkward silence for a few long seconds.

"My name's Sera, by the way," Sera said eventually, and though her voice held a perfect mixture of bubbly cheer and lingering concern, I couldn't help but imagine an imperceptible passive-aggressive tone beneath it all.

"Oh," Ryuji said, still blushing heavily. "My name's Ryuji. Ryuji Nightblade."

Sera didn't respond immediately. Though I wasn't sure if I imagined it or not, I noticed a subtle rise in her shoulders as she took a deep breath, as if to refocus her thoughts before she spoke again.

"Ryuji. That's an interesting name," she said, placing a finger on her chin in a thinking pose that was way too exaggerated to be natural.

Ryuji didn't seem to agree with the assessment. He blushed and turned away, scratching his head in embarrassment.

"Thanks," he said.

As the conversation died immediately, Sera stared at Ryuji for a few more seconds before giving him a natural-looking smile.

"I'm sure you're wondering why I'm here. Right, Ryuji?" she asked.

"Oh, yeah," he said, looking up at her with a new sense of confusion in his eyes, as if he'd just noticed that he was talking to a stranger. "Why are you here?"

"I heard you're an adventurer," Sera said. "Someone that does dangerous jobs on request?"

Ryuji's eyes lit up at that.

"Yeah!" he shouted, his voice bouncing against the stone walls.

Sera let out a relieved sigh. "You don't know how happy I am to hear that," she said, giving him a smile as she took his hands in hers. I was impressed by how easily she could summon fake tears as she stared into Ryuji's eyes. The mood in the room instantly shifted as she took on the role of a young, distraught girl. "I need your help, Ryuji."

Though he was still blushing, Ryuji grinned and nodded quickly. "What do you need me to do?" he asked. "I would do anything for a fair maiden like you."

"Thank you, Ryuji," she said, sniffling as she wiped a tear away from her eyes. "It's my grandmother. She was supposed to come visit me in

Redstone a week ago, but I haven't heard from her. I was hoping you could accompany me to find her. The road is far too dangerous for a young girl like me to travel alone. Word is that a tribe of bandits has recently formed and is roaming out there."

Ryuji's eyes lit up in a look of childlike delight that I might've described as innocent if I hadn't seen the exact same expression on his face when he had been slaughtering demons back in the village and the forest. I felt a shiver run down my spine.

"Bandits?" he asked excitedly.

"Yes, terrible ones," Sera said, unbothered by his sudden enthusiasm. She smiled and nodded, as if just remembering something. "I just remembered! The bandits have a bounty too! If we come across them, you might be able to get a reward for their heads!"

Instantly, Ryuji's smile disappeared, and for the second time since I'd entered the room, he glanced at me with an uncomfortable expression on his face before turning back to Sera.

"Their heads?" he asked hesitantly.

Sera seemed to recognize that something was wrong, glancing back to flash me a questioning look before turning back to Ryuji. A smile instantly reappeared on her face as she nodded happily, pretending not to have sensed the sudden shift in Ryuji's mood.

"These bandits are ones that have escaped the executioner's block. You would be rewarded for hunting them down. Is something the matter?" she asked.

"Yeah," Ryuji said, scratching his head awkwardly. "I'm actually not that happy about the idea of killing people. It just doesn't sit right with me. Could we just capture them or something?"

Though Sera's smile remained unchanged, I could see the slightest hint of her brow furrowing. She opened her mouth and closed it as she struggled to think of something. Though I wasn't sure what exactly was wrong, it was clear that her original plan had been compromised in some way.

I felt the urge to jump in to cover for her, but unlike the villagers of Plainswood, she was professional enough not to freeze up completely.

"Well, we could, but they would be executed regardless," she said, pausing to think for a moment. "Astranta isn't kind to goblin bandits."

Ryuji's eyes lit up again. "Wait, they're goblins?" he said, his voice full of relief. "Why didn't you say so?"

I was glad that Ryuji wasn't focused on me because I was sure my expression was filled with a level of disgust that I wouldn't be able to hide. Even knowing that Ryuji had only killed demons so far, the fact still remained that he at least thought he had killed several goblins already. Watching him be this happy about it was enough to draw a scowl to my face. If Sera shared even a fraction of the emotions I felt, she was a good enough actor to hide it from Ryuji.

"Oh, so you're okay if it's goblins you're killing?" she asked as casually as if she were asking his preference in colors.

"Well, duh," Ryuji replied, smacking his forehead and laughing. "They're just monsters. You really had me going there for a second, Sera. I thought you were suggesting that I should kill people."

I couldn't help but grind my teeth at that. It certainly wasn't the worst thing that Ryuji had done, but the casual social injustice was terrible to listen to regardless.

"I see," she said, thinking for a moment before clapping her hands and standing up. "Then in that case, we should leave as soon as possible. I've already posted bail for you. It wasn't much since they only had you in for a public disturbance misdemeanor."

"Oh, really?" Ryuji asked. "Thanks."

Sera blinked a few times, fluttering her eyelashes a little more than might've been necessary, before crossing her arms and turning her head to the side in a pout. "It's not like I did it for you or anything, idiot," she grumbled.

Ryuji's expression turned strangely giddy for a second, but it quickly shifted into a look of concern as something in the corner of his eye seemed to catch his attention.

"Lena? Is everything okay?"

Even with him calling my name, it took me a moment to realize that he was looking directly at me, and I felt a flash of panic run through me as I remembered that I wasn't a passive observer, nor was I an invisible one. I didn't even know what sort of face I should be putting on at this point, but as I struggled for a moment to regain control over my expression, Sera quickly stepped between me and Ryuji, blocking me from his view.

"Oh yeah. Lena, was it?" she said. "May I have a quick word with you?"

Though she had her shoulders taut and her arms crossed over her chest, the barely concealed aggression in her voice clashed heavily with the apologetic smile on her face, hidden from view from Ryuji. Without giving me time to respond, Sera walked forward, hooked an arm casually around mine as she walked past me, and dragged me out of the room with enough force that I stumbled to catch my footing.

It was only when Sera dragged me out of the room completely that she placed her hands on my shoulders to steady me, right before putting a finger to my lips.

"You're a saint to have dealt with that for a week," she whispered, grabbing and pulling the door handle with her other hand to make sure it was completely closed.

I wanted to say thanks, but before I could even form the words, Sera shifted her hand to cover my mouth and shook her head silently.

"I don't care that you saw him first," Sera hissed, loudly enough that I assumed she wanted to be heard, before dropping her voice to a whisper again. "Just nod or shake your head. That went better than I expected, but I doubt I was able to free you yet. You still see the panels?"

I nodded.

"I was hoping you wouldn't say that," Sera said loudly, following it with a sigh that sounded like it had been whispered. "I'm not going to go back on my promise to get you out of this, but I won't lie, you scared me a little when you chimed in earlier. You do still want to get out of this, right?"

My eyes widened. I nodded.

"Good. I'm glad to hear it," Sera said, with a loud huff, before dropping her voice again. "He seems receptive to me, but that doesn't necessarily mean he'll immediately lose interest in you unless he has a reason to. We'll work on that. Don't ignore him if he tries to talk to you, but don't talk unless he initiates. I'll also make it clear that I don't like you, so he'll be forced to choose between us instead of trying to keep both of us. Hope you don't take it personally."

A small smile formed on my lips at the idea that Sera actually seemed concerned that I might be put off by the act she was putting on. Though she couldn't see it, she seemed to feel the shift in my expression under her hand, and she matched it with her own.

"Good to hear it," she said, finally taking her hand off my mouth but raising a finger to her own lips to signal that I should still be quiet. "Alright, we don't have much time to discuss any further before the Otherworlder starts to wonder what's going on, so I'll quickly explain. We're going to leave Redstone as soon as we possibly can, but I'll send a signal to my team to clear out the goblin civilians from the roads leading out of the city without causing a panic. There are enough goblins living in Redstone that it's already a miracle that the two of you managed not to see one before you were arrested, and I'm not in enough of a gambling mood to hope that it'll happen again."

I wanted to nod, but I had already guessed what she was going to say next.

"We'll have to go back in," Sera whispered, and from the way that she winced as she said it, I could only assume that she knew just how much I had been dreading those exact words. "My people are good at what they do, but they'll still need a few minutes. Just pretend you don't like me, talk as little as you possibly can, and try not to judge me for what I'm about to say to get in the Otherworlder's good books."

Sera stared up at me, and I got the feeling she was waiting for a response.

I nodded.

A look of relief came across her face.

"Thanks," she said before nodding to the door. "You ready?"

The answer was no, but I didn't think that mattered in the slightest.

I nodded.

Chapter 22
Goblin Killer

"So... What did you guys talk about out there?"

"Just some girl stuff," Sera answered easily, giggling as if Ryuji had said something funny. "Nothing you need to worry about, Ryuji."

"Are you sure?" Ryuji asked, ignoring Sera to stare directly at me. "You seemed pretty upset, Lena. Are you sure you're okay?"

I froze, unprepared for Ryuji's sudden attempt to talk to me. Thankfully, Sera seemed to notice my moment of indecision.

"Ryuji," she said with a sigh, putting her hands on her hips. "She's fine. Isn't that right, Lena?"

"Yeah," I said, finally able to gather my voice. "Just feeling a little under the weather, I guess."

"Oh, are you feeling sick?" Ryuji asked. "Do you want me to heal you?"

I couldn't stop myself from wincing when he raised his hands, his fingertips already glowing with the faint glow of ambient mana in the same green tint from when he'd healed Medric. Regardless of Ryuji's intentions, the casual display of power was too overwhelming for me, and I couldn't stop myself from glancing at Sera in a silent plea for help.

If I were being honest, I hadn't had the chance to properly form an opinion on Sera yet. Logically, I knew she probably wasn't lying about a

Mediator, but with how many people had already disappointed me when it came to handling Ryuji, I hadn't allowed myself to trust in her completely, not wanting to raise my hopes just to see them crushed again. However, when I saw her glance back at me for just a split second, I couldn't help but be a little hopeful.

The complete nonchalance in her reaction to Ryuji's magic and the barely imperceptible wink she sent in my direction before turning back to Ryuji made me realize that, for the first time since I'd gotten into this situation, I didn't have to be the responsible one.

I felt the urge to say something, to give an excuse about why I probably looked as haggard as I felt, without letting Ryuji know that it was his fault, but I held myself back, looking at Sera instead. Whether she noticed my silent request or not, with her back turned to me, she still sighed and shook her head on my behalf.

"Ryuji," she said, "period cramps can't be healed with magic."

Before I could renounce my faith in her, Ryuji's mouth turned into a perfect O shape as his eyes widened.

"O-Oh," he stammered, his face turning red from embarrassment. He tore his eyes away from mine so fast that it was dizzying.

It was convenient too, since I wasn't sure exactly what expression I was wearing, but I was certain that it wasn't anything flattering.

"It's okay, Ryuji. I know you were just concerned, but if you're not careful, you'll come off as being pushy, and girls usually don't like that." Sera sighed and shook her head. "You're lucky you're cute," she mumbled.

Once again, Ryuji's head spun so quickly that I was sure he might have snapped his neck if it weren't for his Otherworlder physiology. Thankfully, this time, he wasn't looking at me. I still hadn't gathered my wits enough to wipe the baffled expression from my face, and I doubted that I would be able to gather them any time soon.

"C-Cute?!" he stammered out.

Though it wasn't quite as intense as Ryuji's, the speed of the blush that rose to Sera's cheeks was equally impressive when I considered the fact that she was just a regular human.

"W-What?!" Sera stammered back.

"You called me... cute," Ryuji said, sounding almost accusatory at first but losing confidence quickly until his voice fell into a near whisper by the end of the sentence.

Sera didn't seem to notice as she crossed her arms and looked away.

"W-Well, don't get a big head about it," she said.

Somehow, Ryuji's eyes widened even more until I was almost afraid they would pop out of his skull from utter shock. I placed my face gently in my hands and let out a sigh filled with an emotion that I didn't quite have the energy to identify.

Thankfully, even though the room was quiet enough that my sigh echoed, nobody else acknowledged it, letting it echo unanswered.

I didn't know how long the three of us stood there for, but eventually, Sera cleared her throat.

"A-Anyway," she said, clearing her throat once more before continuing. "Did you want to talk about my job offer?"

"Oh," Ryuji said, clearing his throat in turn. "Yeah. We should do that."

"Yeah," Sera replied.

In the silence that followed, I took a chance at lifting my face from my hands to glance back at the scene. Noticing my gaze, Sera glanced up at me, letting her eyes linger on mine for long enough to shoot me a confident grin that contrasted oddly with the lingering blush on her cheeks before reverting to an embarrassed pout.

"Maybe we should talk outside," she said. "You wouldn't believe how tight I am, Ryuji."

Ryuji looked up at her with a strange expression on his face.

"Oh, sorry," Sera said. "I meant cramped. This room's tiny."

Even though Ryuji nodded quickly and looked away in embarrassment, I resisted the urge to slap my hand against my face, not wanting to risk drawing attention to myself. Sera had reduced my role in the scene from a participant to a mere spectator, and though I would've preferred not to even be that, I wouldn't be ungrateful for what she'd done.

So when Sera leaned over to grab Ryuji's hand and drag him out of the room, I didn't complain as she let the door swing shut behind them, leaving me forgotten inside. For a moment, I wondered what I would do if the door magically locked behind them, or if that would even be preferable if it meant that I wouldn't have to witness what was going on outside.

Unfortunately, the more reasonable part of me knew that I might just draw more attention to myself if I suddenly disappeared from sight, so no matter how much it pained me, I pushed open the unfortunately unlocked door easily enough and followed a few steps behind them.

"So you hate goblins too?" Sera asked.

I frowned at the conversation opener but reminded myself that she was playing a character.

"I don't particularly hate them," Ryuji replied, surprising me, given the fact that he seemed to think that he'd murdered entire groups of them in my village and on the way to Redstone.

"Really?" Sera asked, likely just as confused as I was underneath the facade of innocent curiosity she put on. "Then why did you kill so many of them?"

"Why wouldn't I?" Ryuji asked, as if the alternative was unthinkable. "They're just goblins. Aren't they kind of like pests?"

I felt my frown return in full force, and I couldn't help but notice how Sera twitched at the words, even if the smile on her face didn't budge.

"The worst kind," Sera said, nodding as she spoke. "At least normal pests just dig holes in your gardens. But goblins..."

Sera shuddered in lieu of stating an actual opinion, and Ryuji nodded along with her non-existent input.

"They murder, rape, and steal," he said casually like it was an irrefutable fact. I was glad that he wasn't looking in my direction at all, letting me scowl freely at the back of his head.

At this point, I thought I had all but given up on trying to understand Ryuji, but I was surprised at how disappointed I felt in him.

As someone who lived in a small town in the mostly human country of Astranta, I was no stranger to people who firmly believed it should stay that way. However, even the worst of them didn't go any further than accusing the occasional goblin merchants who passed into the village of being scam artists or loudly suggesting that goblins didn't practice hygiene whenever one would stay at the local inn.

I doubted that even the most racist of them would echo Jamie's prejudices so easily.

"Really?" Sera asked, sounding more intrigued than offended. "Most people around here don't think that way."

"Oh," Ryuji said, wincing and rubbing his head. "Sorry."

"No, no. I don't mind!" Sera said with a happy smile. "I'm just happy that I've found a person who thinks the same way that I do."

"Really?" Ryuji asked. His eyes practically lit up as his excitement quickly returned.

"Of course," Sera said with a smile. "Do most people from where you come from hate goblins?"

"What? You mean Americ—" Ryuji's eyes widened as he caught his mistake, coughing into his fist quickly as if that would help. "I mean, yeah. Kind of. To be honest, goblins are becoming a lot more popular nowadays, so a bunch of people in my country do like them, but one of my favorite recent animes is 'Goblin Killer.' The only good goblin is a deceased goblin, right?"

Ryuji's words, along with the giddy smile he had on his face after he said them, should have left me utterly horrified. It should've left me wondering why I was still following close behind him instead of taking the chance to run away while he was preoccupied with talking to Sera. I knew that trying to run wouldn't be a good idea, but I should have been scared enough to try it anyway, or alternatively, I should've been too stunned by the realization of how psychopathic Ryuji was that I should've been rooted to the spot with fear.

While I did stop moving, my steps slowing down as Sera and Ryuji continued to walk and talk, it wasn't because I was afraid.

I was just confused.

"What's an anime?"

I didn't realize I had asked the question out loud until I noticed Sera glancing back at me, her eyes wide with a mixture of confusion and fear.

"What was that?" Ryuji asked, tilting his head as he looked back curiously at me. "And why are you so far away? Should we slow down for you, Lena?"

I stared into Ryuji's eyes, and even from so far away, I couldn't detect any malice in them. I tried not to draw any conclusions from what I saw, too tired of having my assumptions proven wrong yet another time, but I couldn't believe that Ryuji would be the type of person to kill so callously, regardless of what he thought of the other person. Or at least, I couldn't see him killing another person on purpose.

"An anime. You said it was a box of light?" I asked, struggling to remember the details from when I'd last heard him try to describe it.

"And why does that matter?" Sera cut in, stepping in front of Ryuji and crossing her arms. While it didn't do anything to block me from his vision, given how much shorter Sera was than him, it did allow her to send me a look that silently screamed at me to stop drawing attention to myself.

"I—"

"Listen, Lena," Sera cut in before I could get another word in. Though she said it with a resigned sigh, she sent me a look of concern that almost made me reel back from guilt. "I get that you're trying to help, but don't butt in where it doesn't concern you. Unless you happen to agree that all goblins deserve to die?"

My mouth snapped shut, almost in reflex at what Sera was suggesting and the angry tone that she was saying it in. Her expression begged me to let myself be shut down by the aggressively racist persona that she had adopted, but something still bothered me.

"Yeah, yeah, I get it," Sera said quickly, interrupting me before I could even start to speak. "I know what your type is like. Soft-hearted little progressives who think that everyone deserves a chance. Astranta used to be a proud human country, but now we're infested with dwarves, nymphs, and now goblins just because our government is full of people like you who don't have the sense to keep them out. They're taking our jobs and our land already, but what's next? Our lives? Well, I'm not interested in finding out just how much these immigrants will take given the chance, and neither is Ryuji, so unless you want to help us keep Astranta clean instead of letting it rot from the inside, I suggest keeping your mouth shut."

I did exactly that, snapping my mouth shut so quickly that I was afraid that my lips might bruise, but it wasn't because of what Sera said.

It took Sera a second to realize that I wasn't looking at her anymore, and out of the corner of my vision, I saw her slowly following my eyes upward, turning around to look at the boy standing behind her.

Ryuji didn't seem to notice, even as his wide eyes darted between both me and Sera, his mouth agape in horror.

"Ryuji," I began. "Is anime real?"

I might have assumed he was frozen in time again if it weren't for the barely imperceptible motion in his head as he slowly shook it from side to side.

"Goblins are people?" he asked, the question so quiet that I almost convinced myself that I'd imagined it.

Though I didn't answer immediately, the look on my face must have been an answer by itself, or Ryuji simply drew his own conclusions.

"Oh God."

Suddenly hunching over, he held his hand against his mouth as a horrible retching sound escaped from his throat. Nothing came out, but after a few seconds, he stood, panting as he stared down at his hands in horror and disgust, like they were covered in something that only he could see. Tears started to stream down his face before he covered it with his hands and ran.

Sera raised her hand as if to stop him, but he was too fast, turning into a blur as he ran past me, back into the cell that we had just left.

The loud bang of the door slamming behind him echoed like cannon fire in the small hallway.

Chapter 23
QUEST

There was a moment of silence before Sera let out a long sigh and walked over to me.

"It seems like I've made a bit of a mistake," she said.

"A bit of a mistake?" I repeated, surprised by the nonchalance with which she admitted it.

Sera sighed again and shook her head. "I guess it's more than a little bit. That's what I get for breaking protocol and making too many assumptions."

"How bad is it?" I asked.

"I have no idea," Sera said with a sad smile. "Well, we're still alive and the building's still standing, so it's not anywhere close to the worst result that could've happened."

"But it's not good either," I guessed.

Sera shrugged and gave me an awkward smile.

"No," she admitted. "I can't imagine it is. In the worst-case scenario, Astranta might be leveled to the ground in a few hours."

I didn't know whether it was the casual way that she said it, or if it was because I had already made the same assumption myself, but I didn't feel particularly surprised.

"What can we do?" I asked.

Sera shook her head and patted my shoulder.

"What I can do is try to fix the mess I made because that's my job, not yours," Sera said. "You haven't changed your mind about being a Follower, have you?"

"No," I said quickly. "But a lot of people might die if I do nothing."

"Well, as true as that is, you shouldn't worry too much about it." Sera laughed. "I'll ask for your help if that's what you want, but you should prioritize getting rid of your Follower status first and foremost. Be a little selfish, will you?"

I tried to laugh, to match Sera's, but all that came out was a quiet huff. I had no idea how Sera was so calm when there was an Otherworlder crying his eyes out down the hall, but I had to admit it was easy to be swept up in her easy-going confidence.

But unfortunately, before I could respond, a familiar blue panel appeared in front of my eyes.

NPC Quest: Begin the Main Story

The Hero has just learned the terrible truth that he has slain another living being with his own hands. But that's not quite true, is it?

Objective: Tell the Hero the truth behind the [CORRUPTED Goblins] that he slew.

Rewards: ???

[Accept]

Before I could process the information fully, Sera asked, "The Otherworlder's power is communicating directly with us?"

"Yeah," I said. "It's happened a few times to me. Is that not normal?"

"Not really," Sera admitted. "An Otherworlder's power management system is subconsciously created to stop the Otherworlder from having their minds implode under the strain of their godlike powers. There typically wouldn't be a reason for the system to interact with any Chosen Followers directly."

"If it's a part of Ryuji's subconscious, doesn't that mean he wants our help?"

Sera gave me a strained smile. "You really can't help yourself, can you?"

"What do you mean?" I asked.

"Never mind," Sera said, shaking her head before pointing up at the panel between us. "So, do you have any idea what that means?"

I looked where she was pointing, directly at the text that translated into my mind as [CORRUPTED Goblins]. I shook my head.

"I have a pretty good guess, but I don't know for sure..." I blinked in surprise as the text flickered, changing from CORRUPTED to DEMON in a split second. Sera seemed to notice my surprise and turned to look at the panel. "Okay, now it's a better guess."

Sera stayed quiet as I explained how Ryuji had slain a group of demons in the village and in the forest that seemed to appear as goblins to everybody else but me. Saying it out loud, I grew increasingly aware of how crazy I sounded when I claimed that I only saw them as masses of shadowy Aether, when the entirety of my village would have testified otherwise, but Sera didn't seem to think so. She nodded along with my story seriously.

After I finished, Sera stayed silent for a few long seconds before holding her face in her hands and letting out a slow, low hiss.

"Shit, I knew something didn't add up," she said.

"What do you mean?" I asked.

"The bodies," Sera said, shaking her head angrily. "My supports couldn't find any. The graves your village dug for them were empty. They saw traces of ash, so they assumed the bodies had just burned up from the Otherworlder's magic. I should've known. Was the trader he killed just outside of Redstone a demon too?"

"No," I said, surprised by how much Sera already knew. She never told me that she'd sent people to my village, nor had she mentioned knowing about Medric. "But he's alive. Ryuji healed him afterward."

Sera lowered her hands and gave me a blank stare. "Of course, he did. Fuck me for being considerate, I guess. Should've just followed protocol and done some proper research before trying to help you out." Shaking her head, she let out a deep sigh. "Sorry. Not your fault. Just a little frustrated at the moment."

She inhaled slowly, letting the breath pass through her teeth. She let it out just as slowly before regaining her composure and turning to me.

"It's become clear to me that I've been operating on some false assumptions here. Nothing I can do to fix that, but what I can do is to make sure I don't make the same mistake here. If I'm going to complete this task, I'm going to need your full..." Sera's speech slowed down to a halt as she read the updated text in the panel floating in front of me.

Lena's Quest: Begin the Main Story

The Hero has just learned of the terrible truth that he has slain another living being with his own hands. But that's not quite true, is it?

Objective: Tell the Hero the truth behind the [DEMON Goblins] that he slew.

Conditions: Lena must complete this quest without the assistance of any other party members and/or NPCs. No individuals not including Lena or the Hero may be present during the completion of the Quest.

Rewards: ???

[Accept]

"Are you fucking kidding me?" Sera asked.

"They do that," I replied, on behalf of the panels. Though I knew they could technically respond to her on their own, I doubted Sera would appreciate the vague way that they communicated. She seemed on the verge of having an aneurysm from frustration, and though my preferred stress response was to have several mental breakdowns rather than getting angry, I could still empathize with how she felt.

"You mean updating in response to things you say?" Sera asked. "Even if the Otherworlder in question isn't around to hear it?"

I frowned. "Yeah," I said hesitantly, even as I slowly realized that it didn't make much sense.

"Well, I guess the Otherworlder's listening in on us, though I can only make the assumption that he doesn't realize it. I know I haven't had a good track record with those recently, but it also doesn't make sense that he would freak out over killing real people if he knew that he only killed demons in the first place," Sera said, jerking a thumb at the text. "We can only assume this panel operates purely off his subconscious thoughts and that he's not actively controlling it."

"So he subconsciously wants me to talk to him?" I asked.

Sera's expression twisted in a myriad of emotions before settling on a sympathetic grimace.

"That might also be partially my fault," Sera said, scratching the back of her head awkwardly. "Might've come on a bit too strong with the racism, so I'm automatically not an option anymore. Though I can't take all the credit. You seem like a nice girl with a good head on your shoulders. Maybe he would've trusted you more, regardless."

Sera sighed again.

"Looks like you're going to have to do this on your own."

It was depressing to think that I wasn't very surprised at this turn of events. "Got any tips for me?"

Sera smiled at me and extended a hand toward me. It took me a moment to realize that she'd grabbed both of my hands hanging limply by my sides. I imagined she was giving them a gentle squeeze as well, and I might have felt a little reassured by it if I could feel anything right now.

"Too much to tell you right now." She had an easy grin that looked too casual and too contrasting with the furious grimace she had on her face a few seconds ago. "I might just overwhelm you if I tried, and no number of tips would turn you into a trained Mediator. Besides, I wouldn't want to change what you've been doing so far. You're the most remarkable person I've ever met."

"Really?" I asked a bit indignantly. If she didn't sound so genuine, I would've assumed she was mocking me. "What makes you think that?"

"We're still alive. Despite that," Sera said, gesturing to the hallway with her eyes. "You've done well, Lena. I'm proud of you."

I didn't know what to say to that. I was a bit too tired to care, but a small part of me couldn't help but try to smile at the genuine praise.

I don't know what kind of expression I actually made, but Sera seemed to like it, smiling brightly up at me.

"Thanks," I said.

Sera let go of my hands and patted me on the shoulder.

"Ready to save everyone's lives again?" she asked.

I stared at her. With the panel floating right in front of my face, I could only vaguely see her smile through the translucent blue. I sighed.

"No," I said.

"But you'll do it anyway."

"Yeah."

I turned around and started to walk down the hallway to where Ryuji was. The panel floated along with me, slightly obscuring my view but not enough for me to be afraid of bumping into anything.

I gave it one last glance before I pushed my finger against the panel.

Rather than passing through it harmlessly like it usually did, I felt my finger push up against something solid. The "Accept" text flashed a dull gold before the panel disappeared entirely.

I continued walking.

Chapter 24
Let's Chat

The doors to each holding cell were identical, but it wasn't hard to guess which one Ryuji had run into. Spiderweb cracks blossomed out the doorframe and the door itself was slightly ajar, with the handle crushed into an unrecognizable shape. I stood at the door for a few seconds, not really thinking, just waiting.

Nothing prompted me to go inside. Nothing would.

Taking a deep breath, I grabbed what was left of the handle, taking care not to cut my fingers on the jagged metal, and opened the door.

Ryuji didn't acknowledge me as I stepped inside, not even when the door creaked on its hinges as I let it swing shut behind me. Rather than the bench, he was sitting on the floor in the far corner of the room, hugging his knees to his chest. In the dim lighting of the single redstone lamp that was embedded in the walls of the cell and with his hood drawn over his head, I couldn't see his face at all.

He made no indication that he knew I was there, even when I walked forward and stood directly in front of him. I squatted down to bring myself closer to him.

"You're not a killer, Ryuji," I said. "Those goblins weren't real. They were creatures made purely from Aether. We call them demons here."

Lena's Quest: Begin the Main Story [COMPLETE]

By telling the Hero the truth behind the [DEMON Gob-

lins] that he slew, you've opened the path to further adventure as he delves to learn about the truth behind [DEMONS] and the [AETHER].

Rewards: 1 EXP

Despite what the panels seemed to think, my job wasn't done. Just because I'd told Ryuji the truth didn't automatically mean he would believe me. Anyone or anything that thought otherwise was either profoundly naïve or utterly stupid.

I waited to see if the panels would respond to my thoughts. They didn't.

I quickly reminded myself that hurting the panels' feelings was probably the last thing I wanted to do here, since apparently, they were just creations of Ryuji's subconscious mind. Still, I'd spent so long antagonizing them that it was difficult to shift my mindset.

"Liar," Ryuji said, his voice muffled. "You don't really think that. You think I'm a monster."

I frowned. "Ryuji, I..."

I stopped. I was too stressed, too exhausted, and too agitated to deal with this. I let out a low hiss of a sigh, slowly letting out all the air in my lungs, and along with it, my last dredges of common sense.

"Yeah," I said. "I am. I'm a liar. I've been lying to you the entire fucking time I've been traveling with you. And you know what? I'm sick of it. I'm sick of having to dance around you because I'm too scared of being killed by you to do anything that could possibly upset you. I'm sick of pretending that everything's fine while you're having the time of your life, prancing around, talking about how your dream is to become a homeless wanderer that kills for a living."

Ryuji looked up at me, a shocked expression on his face. Admittedly, I was just as surprised at what I'd said as he was, but my frustration had burst out of me like a river through a dam. I considered—just for a split-second—pretending like I hadn't spoken, blaming my words on a strange whistle on the wind, but I had built too much momentum to stop.

"Ever since the moment I met you, you've been acting like this world was tailor-made for you. You go around doing whatever you please because everyone's too scared to stop you. And you don't even notice! You don't care enough to stop and think about the effects of your actions on other people. You just go around, showing off your absurd power and telling people in the same sentence that you'll be the greatest wandering murderer in the world. You really think people won't be afraid of you?

"You know why Medric decided he wanted to fight you? He wanted to fight you because he saw how afraid I was of you. We'd been traveling together for more than a week, and a random stranger could pick up on how I felt better than you could. And then you killed him. You killed him and dangled his corpse in front of me like you were a cat showing off the mouse you managed to catch and bite the head off of."

I gasped when I stopped, surprised by how out of breath I was. The sound of my heavy breathing echoed around the small empty room.

"I didn't mean to." Ryuji's small voice was barely audible. I had to strain to hear him. "I didn't know."

He sounded so small.

"Yeah," I said, once I caught my breath. "I know. But at the time I thought you did. Do you remember how I reacted?"

Ryuji sank his head into his knees. "You screamed at me," he said. "And then you told me to fix it. And then I did."

I frowned. It wasn't the exact conclusion I wanted him to come to, but it was close enough.

"I did scream," I said. "Because I was scared. Whether you meant it or not, whether you fixed it later or not, you killed a man in front of me. I was terrified out of my mind, Ryuji. I pissed myself. I'm a fully grown woman and I pissed myself."

I hadn't meant to reveal that. I'd wanted to take that to my grave but it just spilled out.

"Sorry," Ryuji said a bit sheepishly.

"Don't apologize for that. Just forget I said it." I felt a blush rise to my cheeks. "Please."

Ryuji didn't say anything.

I coughed into my fist, as if clearing my throat.

"Anyway," I said. "The point I wanted to make is that when I saw you killing a person in front of me, I freaked out. I couldn't control my emotions, even though I desperately wanted to pretend that everything was fine. You see where I'm going with this?"

Ryuji looked up at me. His eyes were bloodshot and swollen, but he'd already wiped his tears away, leaving them dry. He locked eyes with me for a few seconds before shaking his head slightly.

I wanted to give him a smile, but I didn't feel good enough to form a genuine one. I was sick of the fake smiles I'd been forced to keep up for the past week, and I didn't want to summon one again. I sighed and turned to sit down against the wall. With Ryuji backed into the corner, I couldn't quite sit beside him, but I didn't care about that.

"You're not a killer, Ryuji," I said. "If you had really killed some goblins back in Plainswood, I wouldn't have been as calm about it as I was. I don't know what you saw, but all I saw you do was slash through a bunch of demons and scatter their Aether to the wind. That's the only reason I didn't run away screaming. I wouldn't have traveled through the forest alone with someone who I thought was a murderer. I would've just taken my chances and tried to run away from you."

I turned to face Ryuji and met his eyes again.

"You believe me now?" I asked.

He didn't answer.

"Oh," he finally said, looking away from me.

It was a quiet thing. With his gaze locked forward, staring at nothing, a slow and steady stream of tears flowed gently out of the corners of his eyes, crawling down his cheek and converging at his chin, steady drops falling to the floor. He made no indication that he noticed, not moving as the sound of his heaving breath echoed through the otherwise silent cell.

And then he sniffled.

He sunk his head into his knees again, hiding his face, not from me, but from the world around him. As he struggled unsuccessfully to hold back his sobs, they caught on his throat, coming out in quiet croaks. It was a strange sound, almost amusing if it weren't for how pitiable it was.

I watched for a few seconds before scooting closer to him. His body was too awkwardly placed, backed up too deep into the corner of the room for me to hug him, but I felt like a simple hand on his back would be enough.

The moment my hand touched his back, Ryuji's shoulders started to heave. His croaking cries stopped, replaced with a low, consistent moan instead, shuddering whenever he took in a shaky breath.

We stayed like that for a few minutes before Ryuji calmed down somewhat. With his face still hidden in his knees, he reached down and wiped at his nose with his sleeve. He sniffled a few more times before his breathing evened out.

"You okay?" I asked.

He took a deep breath before he answered. "Yeah."

I could tell he was lying.

"You want to talk about it?" I asked, not knowing exactly what *it* was.

Ryuji's heavy breathing stopped immediately. He looked up at me, his eyes completely swollen and his face covered in tears and snot. He opened his mouth, and then closed it.

"I want to see," he said.

"Want to see what?" I asked.

"I want to know for sure that I didn't kill anyone for real," he said. "I want to go back to your village."

"You don't believe me?" I asked. I wasn't offended, and I hoped it didn't come off that way.

"I... I want to," Ryuji said, with a sniffle and a swipe of his shirt sleeve against his nose. "But I need to make sure."

I nodded. "Okay," I said, standing up. "We can go."

Ryuji looked up at me. I extended a hand to him to help him up. He took it.

Knowing how sturdy he could be on his feet, I was surprised how light his body actually was. Unfortunately, I was also surprised by how slimy his hands were.

"Sorry," he said, wincing when I wiped my hands against my pants, smearing them with snot.

"Don't worry about it," I said. "Let's go?"

Ryuji nodded, but when I pushed open the door to the cell and stepped outside, I noticed that he hadn't moved from his spot.

"Something wrong?" I asked, holding the door open.

"I—" Ryuji said. "I'm a hypocrite."

I waited for him to continue.

"I've been lying to you too," he said, looking away sheepishly. "I've been hiding a pretty big secret from you this entire time."

He looked up at me from the corner of his eye.

"My name isn't really Ryuji. It's Jamie. And... I'm not from this world."

I waited to see if he was going to say anything else. When it was clear he was done, I nodded.

"Nice name," I said. "I like it much better than your fake one."

Ryuji, or rather, Jamie, blinked a few times at me, clearly stunned.

"Umm," he said. "I wasn't joking. I really am from another world."

"I guess I forgot to mention it, but I knew you were an Otherworlder from the moment we met," I said, jerking a thumb behind me. "Now let's go. Might as well head out early while there's still daylight. Maybe we can hire a cart to take us instead of having to walk again."

"An Otherworlder?" Jamie asked.

"Sera will explain," I said, more than happy to throw the responsibility at someone else for once.

I half expected another panel to pop again, to tell me that it would be my job once again to explain to Jamie what exactly an Otherworlder was, but nothing happened. I let out a small sigh of relief.

"You ready?" I asked Jamie.

Jamie looked at me. His eyes were still puffy, and he looked like he wanted to say something more, but after a few seconds of deliberation, he stepped forward. Once he walked through the door, I let it close and walked beside him, back through the dim hallway, toward the light coming from the open door to the station lobby.

Chapter 25
Full Disclosure

Telling Otherworlders that there was a whole system implemented in our world to deal with their arrival was generally something you didn't do. The "N" in FUN stood for Naïve for a reason, and though it was arguably the least important part of the acronym, it was still an important aspect of interacting with Otherworlders.

When I told Jamie that I knew he was an Otherworlder, I'd been vaguely aware that I was breaking this rule, but I chose to do it anyway because I was sick of hiding how I felt. Maybe if I'd really tried, I might have been able to squeeze out another lie, but I had been too emotionally charged to hold myself back.

When I saw Sera's face again, smiling at Jamie and me, pretending as if nothing was wrong, I was almost worried about what sort of reaction she would have when I told her how our conversation went.

I hadn't expected her to smile and brush it off like it was nothing. I hadn't expected her to be fully frank with Jamie either, freely explaining her identity as a Mediator and her role in containing Otherworlders like him.

Sure, she phrased it more delicately, telling him that the Mediators had a goal to "guide" Otherworlders toward their dreams, rather than to minimize the amount of damage they could do, but the subtext was clear—at least to me.

With her identity as a Mediator revealed, Sera took the opportunity to use her power and influence more openly. Once Jamie admitted his desire to return to Plainswood, Sera supported the idea and pushed for us to leave as soon as possible, instantly leading us out of the jail. The streets were a lot emptier than they had been when we first arrived in Redstone, but with how Jamie had his head hanging down as we walked, I doubted he noticed anything.

Two horse-drawn carriages were waiting for us at the gates with a driver—a male and a female—sitting in front of each. They weren't Astrantan, and I quickly assumed from their ash-grey skin and white hair that they were Timurans. I'd never met anybody from Timur before, as most of the people who had a reason to cross the large desert that bordered our countries were probably either too important or too busy to visit a small town like mine. With Jamie's arrival, however, Plainswood was suddenly becoming a lot more important than it had ever been before.

When the drivers smiled and waved at us, I suddenly realized that I'd been staring, but I was too tired to feel embarrassed at my lack of manners. I nodded back at them, and from the corner of my eye, I could see Sera doing the same. She made no motion to introduce them and instead opened the door to one of the carriages, beckoning Jamie and me inside.

Jamie climbed in first. When I followed him, I was a little surprised to see that it was already occupied by a tall man with a friendly smile. I didn't have much time to figure him out, as Sera climbed into the carriage right behind me, ushering me to sit beside Jamie and across from the tall man. Right when she closed the door behind her and sat beside the tall man, the carriage started to move.

"Jamie, Lena. Let me introduce you to Oren," she said, pointing to the other occupant of the carriage. He gave us a friendly wave. "Driving the cart we're in currently is Laush. Tenna is driving the other cart."

"It's nice to meet you," Jamie said. His greeting was a little subdued, but it made sense given how tired he looked. "You're all Mediators, then?"

"Aside from Lena, yes," Oren said, pulling down his sleeve to reveal the eye tattoo on his forearm. "Sorry for deceiving you like this. I hope you're not too offended?"

"No, it's fine," Jamie said, glancing sideways at me. "It makes sense why you would lie. Sorry for scaring you."

"No need to apologize, Jamie," Oren said, with a laugh. "You can't help being an Otherworlder."

Jamie frowned at that. Sera cocked her head to the side in confusion.

"Is there something wrong, Jamie?" she asked.

"No, it's just..." Jamie paused to gather his thoughts before speaking. "Sorry, I'm still not getting this whole Otherworlder thing. Are there a lot of other people like me?"

Oren nodded. "Several. Approximately two Otherworlders drop into Materia from Earth every year, though most people are not aware of that," he said, smiling at me. "Regular civilians, such as Lena, are told that it's a lot rarer than that."

"Otherworlders are really that common?" I couldn't help but ask. While Sera had mentioned this to me already, two per year felt excessive.

"Yup," Sera said. "And the Mediators are well equipped to help every single one."

"Help?" Jamie asked before I could.

"We help you integrate into our world in a safe way," Oren explained. "It is our duty to ensure the transition between yours and ours is as seamless as possible. In your case, we tried to cater to your desire to be an adventurer by offering you a bounty to pursue, but it seems we were mistaken in our approach. For that, we apologize."

Oren bowed his head deeply, and Sera sent Jamie an apologetic grimace, bowing her head as well after a moment of hesitation.

"I'm sorry. It was my fault," Sera admitted, mumbling into her lap before she raised her head to stare up at Jamie with remorseful tears in her eyes. "I just wanted to help."

Jamie drew back at the sight, as if physically shocked by it.

"It's okay," he said quickly, almost shouting as his eyes darted around everywhere except on Sera's tearful expression. It looked like he glanced at me a few times, as if silently asking for my help, but he quickly pursed his lips together and shook his head.

"It's okay," he repeated. "You were just trying to help."

Sera beamed up at Jamie but winced and shook her head a second later.

"Well, it didn't work, did it?" she growled before standing up. She looked like she wasn't quite done with what she wanted to say, but before she could continue, the carriage suddenly lurched violently as one of the wheels hit something.

I heard a curse hissed out in a foreign language from the front of the carriage.

"Sorry!" Laush, if I remembered Sera's introductions correctly, shouted out. "There was a rock on the road. Getting a little too dark to see."

A series of low moans echoed throughout the cabin in response, and I couldn't help but agree. A dull lance of pain traveled up my lower back, and I rubbed at it to relieve the pain, grateful for the luxurious seating cushioning the impact and stopping it from being any worse. Oren didn't seem like he'd been so lucky, rubbing the top of his head from where he'd bumped it against the roof of the carriage, and Sera...

"Ouchie," Sera grumbled. She seemed confused and rattled by the impact, enough that she didn't seem to realize that she had lost her footing and had fallen directly onto Jamie, with her face pressed against his crotch.

While a small part of me couldn't help but feel a sense of secondhand embarrassment for her, I couldn't help but feel like I'd seen this before.

For a moment, I was afraid that she might hit him again, but she simply shook her head and looked up at Jamie with the same tearful look that she'd had before she'd fallen over. If it weren't for the absurdity of the idea, I might have believed she simply didn't realize the position she was in.

"I still need to make it up to you," Sera said in a voice that practically begged him not to disagree. "If there's anything, anything at all, that I could do for you..."

She trailed off and blinked rapidly as she stared up at Jamie, conveniently fluttering her long eyelashes at him in a way that was almost artistic, with the thin coating of tears making them glimmer in the soft lamplight.

"Jamie," she said in almost a whisper. "Tell me what you want me to do."

Jamie didn't respond in any way. His expression was so stiff that I might've assumed he was frozen in time again if it weren't for the way that every inch of his skin quickly flushed a deep shade of crimson as a thin line of blood slowly seeped from his nostril.

"U-Um," he stammered out.

"Jamie?" Sera asked. "What's... wrong?"

She looked down and let out a little squeak before quickly standing up, hiding her face behind her hands. Between her fingers, her cheeks reddened in a faint yet obvious blush.

She stared at Jamie wide-eyed, her gaze darting from his face to his crotch.

"W-What were you thinking about?" she stammered.

"N-Nothing!" Jamie stammered back, his voice echoing in the small carriage.

Sera stared at Jamie for a few more seconds before she fell back into her seat, hiding her face completely behind her hands.

"Pervert," she said, her voice muffled. "Though if that's what you really want—"

Oren coughed loudly, making Sera and Jamie both jump in surprise.

"Might I suggest that the two of you discuss this later? And in private?" he asked, his voice tinged with an equal amount of annoyance and amusement. "As much as I enjoy watching Sera embarrass herself, there's such a thing as seeing too much. For Lena's sake, as well as my own, perhaps we should stop here for the night. I'm afraid of what might happen the next time we hit a rock in the road."

"Oren!" Sera shouted, punching the other Mediator in the shoulder, while Jamie turned a shade of red that I was certain wouldn't be humanly possible for anybody else.

Though he winced at the hit, Oren threw his head back and let out a loud laugh before placing his hand on Sera's head and roughly ruffling her hair. Sera slapped his hand away with an annoyed growl, but the damage had already been done.

"I hate you so much," she growled as she ran her fingers through her hair, trying and failing to straighten it back out.

"Yeah, yeah," Oren said, grabbing Sera's head one more time. He ignored her yelped protest before calling out, "Laush, Tenna. We're stopping here for the night."

The carriage we were in slowed down immediately, and once we slowed down to a full stop, Oren reached over to the door to push it open.

"Finally, some fresh air," he said, letting out a relieved sigh as he climbed out.

Being the closest to the door, I stood up to follow him before I felt something grab my wrist and pull me down before I could leave.

"Lena." Sera smiled awkwardly at me, with the remnants of her blush still painting her cheeks. "Could you stay behind for a moment?"

I was more surprised than I should've been at the reminder that I wasn't just an invisible spectator to whatever was going on here, but I recovered quickly enough.

"Yeah." I nodded. "Sure."

"Do you want me to stay behind too?" Jamie asked, voicing the exact same question that I had in my mind.

Sera blinked a few times before shyly turning away from him. "I was going to ask Lena if she could help me change..." she said, gripping the hem of her skirt nervously.

After Sera trailed off, it took a moment for Jamie to react.

"O-Oh, sorry. I'll give you your privacy," he said, before hastily rushing to join Oren outside.

Sera gave him a shy wave before she leaned over to grab the door. She closed it, bolted it shut, and immediately turned to give me a sheepish grin with no trace of the embarrassed girl she'd been pretending to be.

"Sorry you had to see that," she said, her voice returning to the same confident tone that she had when she first introduced herself to me. "If it's any consolation, it was probably more uncomfortable for me to act like that than it was for you to watch it."

"So it was an act," I said, more as a statement than a question.

"Frankly, I'm a little upset you need to ask," Sera said with a laugh. "Or maybe I should be proud of myself."

"For lying to a kid?"

When I saw Sera wince, I couldn't help but feel a little guilty that I'd even asked.

"I prefer to think of it as performing for him," Sera said, not quite meeting my eyes as she brushed her fingers along her hair in an attempt to straighten out the mess that Oren had left it in. "And it's not like I want to act like I am, but I've already established a character for him to expect from me. Just because you revealed our identity as Mediators to him doesn't mean we're comfortable playing with an open hand. He's still more than capable of killing us all, Lena."

I winced, surprised by the sudden reminder. Or that I even needed a reminder in the first place.

"I'm sorry," I said.

"You're just a civilian." Sera sighed. "Ideally, you would never have been in the position to spill those secrets in the first place, but you somehow bonded closely enough with the Otherworlder that he specifically called for you and no one else."

"Sorry," I said again.

"You shouldn't apologize for being nice," she said.

"I'm still sorry that I told him everything. I was just so tired of lying," I said, feeling a little embarrassed at how much that sounded like an excuse once it came out of my mouth.

"And honesty would be an admirable quality to have in any other situation," Sera said, with more than a little amusement tinging her voice. "But if you're that insistent on earning my forgiveness, you could help me fix my hair."

I nodded, eager to take the chance to redeem myself, even in such a small way. I took the seat beside Sera, and when she turned to back me, I started to run my fingers through her hair, trying my best to straighten it out.

She let out a small, content sigh.

"It killed me to send you to face the Otherworlder alone," she said. "And I'm glad you're safe. That's all I wanted to say."

Another pang of guilt hit me, and I winced.

"Sorry," I said.

"Again?" Sera chuckled quietly. "What is it this time?"

"I shouldn't have accused you like that. You're just doing this because you're trying to protect everyone," I said. "I just didn't like seeing you lie to Jamie like that. I know he's an Otherworlder, but he was genuinely scared of the idea that he'd hurt anyone. He's not a bad person. He's just a kid."

Sera didn't respond immediately, and for a moment, we sat there in silence, the only sound in the carriage coming from the silent brushing of hair against my fingers.

Eventually, Sera let out a deep sigh and pulled away from me, sitting on the other side of the carriage and reaching into a hidden compartment that I hadn't noticed underneath the seat. She pulled out a brush and ran it through her hair a few times before putting it away and folding her hands in her lap.

"Lena," she said, her voice suddenly grave. "What I'm about to tell you is strictly confidential. Repeating what I'm about to tell you to a non-Mediator would see you arrested on the charges of grand treason, with no trial, and the likely punishment being execution. Both yours and mine."

She gave me a soft smile.

"I'm not saying this to threaten you, and I'm not eager to trust my life with just anyone, Lena," she continued. "I'm offering this to you because I think you have a right to understand why we treat the Otherworlders the way they do. This case is already a bit of a shitshow, so hey, what's one more break in protocol?"

Sera said that last bit with a grin. It felt like an attempt to bring the mood back to normal, but I couldn't quite ignore the fact that she'd just told me I could be executed if I wasn't careful.

But I needed to know. Not for any reason other than selfishness. I hated the pang of guilt I felt at not speaking up as the Mediators lied to Jamie, and I knew that I wouldn't be able to sleep at night unless I knew I was staying silent for a good reason.

"I want to know," I said.

Sera didn't respond for several seconds, staring up at me as she waited for me to change my mind.

Eventually, it became too late.

"The goal of the Mediators as an organization is to kill every Otherworlder that arrives in Materia."

Chapter 26

Death of an Otherworlder

The revelation wasn't as surprising as I might have expected, but that didn't make it any better. I tried to remind myself that Jamie was an Otherworlder, capable of murdering everyone I knew and loved within the blink of an eye. However, no matter how much I tried to imagine Jamie raining hellfire upon my world, I could only summon the memory of him crying in relief at the realization that he wasn't a murderer.

"I think I knew that already," I said, trying to distract myself.

"You did?" Sera asked, more in curiosity than surprise.

"I assumed," I clarified. "I can't imagine an Otherworlder dying of natural causes, so I assumed you had some way to get rid of them."

"You'd be right," Sera said. "While you can never kill an Otherworlder through conventional means, the Mediators have known how to purge Otherworlders from Materia since the organization's inception."

I frowned but didn't say anything, folding my arms across my chest and waiting for her to continue.

"The method for purging an Otherworlder is surprisingly simple, at least on paper. To purge an Otherworlder, the Mediators need to know their dream. I've already told you that their dreams are the source of their powers, but it's also what powers their very existence. The Otherworlders, for whatever reason, arrive in our world because they had a dream they couldn't fulfill while they were on theirs."

I waited for Sera to keep going, but she didn't make any indication that she had anything else to say.

"Are you serious?" I couldn't help asking. "That sounds like a fairy tale."

"It's the truth, as fantastical as it may sound." Sera shrugged. "Not even the Mediators know why or how they're powered by something as abstract as their dreams, but the connection is undeniably there. We can sever that connection by granting their dreams or by getting them to give up on them. Their existence slowly fades after that."

Sera got up from her seat and sat down next to me. She gave me a serious look as she turned her head to lock eyes with me.

"Unfortunately, that's where the problem is," she said. "They fade slowly. We call the final moments of an Otherworlder a Finale Event, but it's far from a single moment. It might take anywhere from a single hour to several days for an Otherworlder's existence to fade completely, but to an Otherworlder, that's no time at all. In that hour, they can lash out and kill millions of people if they want to."

It was obvious what she was talking about. "The Plague," I said.

Sera nodded. "The personality of the Plague King and his dreams were especially complicated. Unfortunately, we had no way of knowing that, and a novice Mediator was given the lead for that case." Sighing, she leaned over to the side and placed her head gently on my shoulder. "It was a disaster in every sense of the word. The worst mark on the Mediators' history in five hundred years."

I looked down at Sera. Leaning on my shoulder, she was the picture-perfect image of a young, vulnerable girl looking for comfort. I could've sworn I saw her eyes giving off the watery sheen of unshed tears. My eyes narrowed.

"Any reason why you're putting up this act?" I asked. "Does it have anything to do with the fact that you haven't mentioned that the Plague King had a civilian Follower? I haven't forgotten you mentioning that."

Sera looked up at me and gave me a sheepish smile, any traces of sadness instantly gone. If it weren't for the fact that I already suspected she was putting up an act for me like she was doing for Jamie, I might have been shocked by the sudden change. She sat up, leaving her spot on my shoulder, and looked forward, avoiding my eyes.

"Sorry," she said. "I thought it might make you more comfortable."

I sighed, leaning away from her, resting my head on the wall of the carriage. "It doesn't," I said. "I'd prefer if you were just honest with me. You think I'm a liability."

"No," Sera said immediately. "You've more than proven to be able to handle yourself, and you never wanted to be a Follower in the first place. Although I won't deny that you have the potential to become a liability."

"That's the same thing."

"It really isn't. You're a smart girl. You pick up on things quite naturally, and you work well under pressure despite being a civilian. The only concerning thing about you is that you're untrained and you don't have the same knowledge that a Mediator typically would. But we're fixing that right now, aren't we?"

I thought about it for a moment before sighing again.

"Fine," I said. "But from now on, be honest with me. No more bullshit."

"Promise," Sera said.

I didn't believe her, but I didn't blame her either. If I were in her position, I didn't think I would trust me either. I was just a random country girl who had no real talents or skills. If it weren't for the fact that I was a Chosen Follower, I doubted that she would've bothered to keep me here.

But I was here. I didn't know how much she would tell me, but if she was offering to arm me with the knowledge to keep myself from accidentally getting Jamie to destroy the world, I wasn't going to say no.

"Fine, I believe you," I lied. "You can continue your explanations."

Sera smiled at me. I don't know whether she could tell I didn't believe her, but if she could, she didn't seem to mind.

"Well, in that case, let's continue."

Sera stood up again and took her original seat across from me. She held up two fingers.

"There are two major goals that the Mediators have when dealing with Otherworlders. The first one is to determine the exact dreams that the Otherworlder gave to the Guide when they first arrived in Materia. Whether we decide to go the route of fulfilling them or forcing them to renounce them, this is important to determine as soon as possible."

She put a finger down.

"Then we need to determine their personality. Even though the Otherworlder's dreams are technically the most important thing to know if you want to trigger a Finale Event in the first place, their personalities are much more important to figure out if we want to ensure that our world is still standing at the end of it.

"While some are more than happy to trade their lives to complete their dreams, many of them are too afraid of death to take it gracefully and decide to throw a temper tantrum in their final moments, if they're not satisfied with what preceded it. It's our job to determine how exactly we can force an Otherworlder to be satisfied before their passing. Sometimes it takes years for us to be fully confident in the psychological profile we make for them, but a majority of Otherworlders are simple-minded enough that they only take a few weeks to figure out. That being said, even in these edge cases, the Mediators will typically spend at least a few months before we even think of initiating a Finale Event. Tell me, what do you know about elves?"

The question felt like a random non sequitur, but a sinking feeling fell in my gut at the suspicion that it wasn't.

"Not much," I said.

"Tell me what you do know," Sera said.

"They're a race of people that lived thousands of years ago," I said, numbly repeating the words I'd read in history books back when I was a child. "They're extinct."

I didn't like the conclusions that my mind was making.

"Elves were mythical, nigh-immortal people that ruled Materia long ago," Sera said, continuing on with the history lesson. "They had their own system of managing Otherworlders, but it was unrefined. It was effective enough for them to prevent a majority of the tragedy that might've occurred as a result of free-roaming Otherworlders, but it only took one mistake to result in the worst Finale Event in known history, remembered by a single surviving elf who went on to found the Mediators in hopes that a similar tragedy would never happen again."

Sera smiled. She stood up and reached over to where I was sitting to push her thumbs against the corners of my mouth, forcing my lips up into a grotesque smile. If I wasn't so shocked, I might have moved away, but learning that I could possibly destroy the entire world if I said the wrong thing was... a lot.

"Come on, Lena," Sera said. "Get your smile on. We should get going. We can only pretend we're fixing up my skirt for so long. I just wanted to make sure you knew what the stakes were before we continued any further. I'll make sure you learn more when we have the time, but we can only stay in here for so long before the Otherworlder starts to wonder what's going on."

Sera took her thumbs off my mouth, and I felt my lips snap down from the forced smile into the horrified, gaping expression that expressed my emotions better. Sera laughed and shook her head as she reached down and easily slipped out of her skirt and shirt in one quick motion. I didn't have the emotional capacity to blush or look away, frozen in my horrified state.

"Be honest, she says," Sera said, chuckling to herself as she reached under her seat into a hidden compartment to grab a spare change of clothes. "No more bullshit, she says."

I felt a slight tinge of regret that I'd said that. Maybe I would've been happier if I had chosen to remain ignorant.

"Well, you can't un-know it anymore," Sera said, as if responding to my thoughts directly. She was clad in a pair of tight pants now and was just adjusting her belt to fit it properly. "You're cursed with the knowledge forever."

She paused, as if giving me the opportunity to answer. When I didn't, she gave me an apologetic half-smile and patted my shoulder twice.

"It's a lot, I know, but you'll get through it. It's honestly astonishing that you're not having a panic attack. I know I sure as hell did when I met my first Otherworlder. Unfortunately, even though I understand how you must feel, you've got responsibility now. You have to put on a smile, Lena, or the Otherworlder will know something's wrong. You'll have the opportunity to vent during your therapy sessions. Try to hold on until then."

"Therapy sessions?" I asked. I wasn't sure if it was a joke or not, but the idea was so nonsensical that I couldn't help but react.

Sera seemed amused at what I'd chosen to react to, but she made no comment on it.

"Yeah, therapy," she said. "All Mediators regularly attend therapy and are trained therapists themselves. It's a requirement."

"You're going to be my therapist?"

Sera laughed out loud.

"Oh, hell no," she said. "You and I have way too much going on between us. No. Oren will be your therapist."

A couple of days ago, I might have considered the idea strange. Oren was not the type of person I would have imagined as a therapist.

Even though he'd been nothing but nice and polite, he was a huge, hulking figure that oozed intimidation simply by existing due to his sheer size and bulk.

But over the past few days, I'd experienced so many more terrifying things to be afraid of just a particularly large man.

"Fine," I said.

Sera laughed, though I couldn't guess what she found so funny.

"Oh, don't sound so disappointed, Lena," she said. "Don't worry, there's no need to be lonely. I'm not going to abandon you."

"Who says I'm lonely?" I asked incredulously.

Sera laughed again and reached up to poke at my face with her fingers. I grimaced and pulled back from her before she could force my lips up into a smile again.

"That's seriously annoying, you know," I said.

Sera smiled at me and lowered her hands.

"I had to do something to put a smile on your face," she said, unfazed by the scowl I gave her. "Or a frown. Anything was better than that dead-inside look you had. At least you've got some life in you now."

I did my best to deaden my face in response. It might have been a petty way to get revenge, but it was better than nothing. Annoyingly, it only seemed to make her laugh.

"You did the same thing back in Redstone," Sera said. "It's cute."

I scowled at her again and turned to open the carriage door, if only to force her to stop. Sera's laugh bubbled out of her anyway, echoing into the night.

Chapter 27

To Make a New Friend

I was a bit surprised to see that nobody noticed us exiting the carriage. Jamie and Oren were occupied with cooking something in a large pot over a roaring fire, chatting idly with each other, while a man and a woman were setting up the tents a fair distance away.

Though I thought they hadn't noticed us, they gave us a brief wave before returning to their work.

"Mediators work in teams of five," Sera said. "You'll meet the last member once we return to Plainswood."

"There's already someone there?" I asked.

"He's been there for a while," Sera said. "He arrived there the day after we got the report of a new Otherworlder and has been staying there ever since."

"Really?" I asked, making a few mental calculations in my head. "How?"

"How what?" Sera asked.

"How did he get there so fast?" I asked. "I'm guessing you guys were stationed at Redstone, so how did he make the trip in a day?"

Sera smiled. "He teleported," she said. "We all did, actually. None of us were even in Astranta when we got the report."

"How?" I asked. I'd gotten used to ridiculous feats of magical prowess, but only from Jamie, who was an Otherworlder. The idea that whole groups of people could be teleported over large distances without the power of an Otherworlder was an absurd claim. I didn't think Sera was lying, but it was a little hard to believe.

"Magic," Sera said smugly. "And by that, I mean the Founder's magic. There are a couple of perks that come with having a nigh-immortal elf as your boss."

"Convenient," I said, still unsure of how to feel, knowing that a literal legend was still alive.

When it became clear that I had nothing else to say, Sera laughed and grabbed my wrist, dragging me to the fire that Oren and Jamie were tending to. When Jamie noticed us approaching, he tensed up briefly before relaxing and giving us a smile and a wave. I smiled and waved back, trying not to think of how I could potentially destroy the world if I said the wrong thing.

"Hi," Sera said, waving shyly. "Sorry for taking so long. The zipper was jammed, and I needed Lena's help to slip me out without tearing my skirt. What's cooking?"

"Just some stew," Oren responded, staring into the pot and stirring the contents with a long ladle.

Now that I was closer, I realized it smelled heavenly. I hadn't had an actual decent meal in over a week. Judging by the way Jamie was staring intently at the pot with a hint of drool peeking out the side of his lips, I could tell he was thinking the same thing.

"How long until it's done?" Sera asked.

"Around forty-five minutes," Oren answered.

My stomach gurgled quietly in disappointment. I clutched at it, hoping that nobody heard. Sera glanced at me and smirked before looking back toward the pot.

"It's been a long day," Sera said. "Can't we just eat it sooner?"

"Hush, you. As I was telling Jamie, good stew takes time," Oren replied, giving the pot another slow stir. "You can't just throw vegetables and meat in a pot and scoop it out once it starts boiling. You've got to give the stew time to soak and infuse the ingredients with each flavor; otherwise you'll just have an uncomfortable jumble of clashing tastes. It takes time, effort, and care to turn it into a harmonious dish."

Sera made a vague sound of distaste. "You sound like my mother, Oren. Are you going to say that the secret ingredient to any dish is love, too?"

Oren let out a quiet and gentle chuckle that clashed heavily with his brutish appearance. "Something like that," he said. "They do say that if you have a conversation with a friend around the pot, it'll taste better."

"Oh yeah?" Sera asked. "Who's they? What are their credentials? Have they published their research to the proper review boards?"

Oren rolled his eyes and gently tapped Jamie's shoulder with his elbow. "Can you believe this girl, Jamie?"

Jamie jolted in his seat, not expecting to be called upon. "Hmm?" he said absentmindedly. "Oh, yeah. I can believe her."

Sera laughed.

Oren just sighed and shook his head.

"Huh?" Jamie said. "Did I say something weird? Sorry. I wasn't paying attention."

"No need to apologize, Jamie," Oren said, patting him gently on the back. "It's not your fault Sera is insufferable. Just ignore what she's saying."

Sera responded by sticking out her tongue.

"To catch you up," Oren continued, "I told Sera and Lena that talking with a friend while you're cooking stew makes it taste better once it's finished. It's an old wives' tale, but Sera decided to be an annoying brat and challenge the validity of the statement."

"And challenge it, I will!" Sera said. "I still think we should try staying silent for the next hour. I'm all for busting dumb superstitions."

Oren shook his head. "Sorry, Sera. Jamie and I were already talking before you girls came along. We've already contaminated the stew."

"Oh, boo! When did you two become so close?" Sera complained.

Ah. I finally understood what they were trying to do.

Jamie didn't seem to realize what Oren was trying to imply immediately. He stared at the pot for a few seconds before turning his head to look at Oren so fast that I swore I heard his neck snapping.

"Huh?" he said, as if he couldn't believe what he had figured out.

"Damn boys," Sera said, shaking her head and pretending like she hadn't noticed Jamie's reaction. "Always making friends with each other so easily. You don't have any idea how hard it was to convince Lena to like me." Sighing dramatically, she leaned toward me until her head fell gently into my lap. "She's always playing so hard to get."

"I'm not even sure I like you yet," I said. Casual sexism aside, I was already unhappy enough that I was being dragged into this manipulative act that I was being somewhat truthful. "And I'm not playing 'hard to get.'"

"See?" Sera said, turning to Jamie and pointing up at me, while still lying across my lap. "Boys have it so easy."

I pushed her off my lap. Sera sputtered and flailed wildly as she fell to the floor, but I had no doubt she had expected it.

"Hey, watch it!" Oren said. "You'll knock the stew over. You know how much work Jamie and I put into this? A conversation between friends is a priceless ingredient, you know. I'll have you compensate us if you ruin it."

When Jamie spoke, his voice was soft, almost too soft to make out in the clamour of Oren and Sera's raised voices.

"We're... friends?"

Oren turned to Jamie and raised his eyebrow, pretending like this wasn't what he and Sera were trying to achieve in the first place.

"What are you saying, Jamie? Of course, we're friends. Well, if you want to be," Oren said, turning away and looking into the fire instead. "I don't want to be presumptuous."

"O-Of course I want to be!" Jamie said, standing up suddenly. He immediately sat down and turned away, looking slightly embarrassed at his own reaction. "I mean, if that's alright with you."

Oren blinked a few times as if he couldn't believe what was going on. He was an excellent actor, even better than Sera was. The beaming smile on his face looked completely genuine as he extended a hand to Jamie.

Jamie turned to Oren, his eyes darting between the offered hand and his beaming smile. He carefully extended his own and grabbed it.

"Friends?" Jamie said hesitantly, as if the offer would suddenly disappear if he seemed too eager.

"Friends," Oren said, pulling Jamie in and thumping his back twice.

Oren has joined your party!

I glanced up at the panel, not letting my gaze linger on it for too long. I couldn't stop a grimace from rising to my lips. Even though I had been given the knowledge that Jamie was even more of a danger to the world around him than I'd originally thought, I still couldn't quite shake the memory of him crying his heart out in front of me.

He was still just a kid. The fact that the Mediators were using Jamie's obvious desperation for friendship to endear themselves to him left a bad taste in my mouth, even more than Sera's strange approach to seduction did.

I understood that it might be necessary, that it was something that needed to be done to ensure the safety of the world, but that didn't mean I liked it. The blatant emotional manipulation was difficult to watch.

I stood up.

"I'm feeling restless from sitting down for so long," I said. "I'm going to walk around for a bit."

Without waiting for a response, I wandered off.

I didn't go too far. The night sky was covered mostly in clouds, and without the light of the fireplace, it was difficult to see much of anything. I didn't trust myself not to trip over something if I wandered too far into the plains. I just didn't want to hear any more of whatever act Oren and Sera were cooking up to endear themselves to Jamie even further.

It didn't take long for me to hear footsteps coming up behind me.

"I can imagine how distasteful it must look from the outside," Sera said.

"He's just a kid," I said.

Sera didn't respond right away. She stood behind me for about a minute before walking up to stand beside me. Out of the corner of my eye, I could see her looking up into the cloudy night sky.

"Sometimes I forget you're not a Mediator," Sera said. "I keep catching myself thinking that you'll see the things in the same light that we do and think about them in the same way."

I didn't respond. I didn't want to criticize her and tell her that the Mediators were messed up in the head if they could casually fuck with a kid's head like this. I knew that they were just doing their job to make sure our world was safe from the monstrous power that each Otherworlder held. But again, he was just a kid.

"To be clear, I'm glad you don't think like us. I hope after all this is over, you'll go home and never think about Otherworlders or Mediators ever again. Just live a peaceful life off the copious amounts of money your government will give you. It's a good thing you feel sympathy for the Otherworlder. It means you're normal."

In the edges of my vision, I saw her turn toward me, but I kept staring forward into the night.

"You never use his name," I said. "You keep calling him 'the Otherworlder.'"

Sera turned away from me and sighed. It took her a few seconds to say anything, though I wasn't sure if that was because she had to gather her thoughts first or if she was just letting the silence run its course for the sake of it.

"Otherworlders aren't typically happy people. Otherworlders who have similar or identical personalities to Jamie's aren't uncommon in the slightest," she said. "Even so, Mediators are taught not to sympathize with them, regardless of what they were like back in their home world. Power corrupts, and they all have the potential to become monsters when they arrive here. Some do. Some don't.

"It's harder to deal with the ones that don't. On a personal level, at least. Our job is to get rid of them, to protect the world from their influence. Even if the way we do it is by fulfilling their greatest desires, at the end of the day, we're still killing them. It's not as soul-crushing if we don't think of them as being like us."

"So you act like Jamie's a monster, just to make it easier to kill him?" I asked.

"Yes," Sera replied, surprising me with her blunt answer. "Because I might not be able to if I didn't. And he needs to die, Lena. He's too dangerous to be kept alive."

I didn't know what to say to that, so I said nothing.

"He's by far the most sympathetic and stable Otherworlder I've met. But he's still too dangerous. All Otherworlders are. If it makes it any better, I'll mourn him when he dies."

I sighed.

"It doesn't make it any better," I said.

"I'm sorry."

"You're saying that to the wrong person."

"I know."

Chapter 28

Second-in-Command

Oren felt something tickle his forearm, a signal from Grunt Laush. She had been using magic to create small breezes and quiet popping sounds to see if the Otherworlder would wake up at the minor annoyances.

The Otherworlder was asleep. He had been for the past ten minutes or so, but Oren didn't move until he was absolutely sure of the fact. He wouldn't risk the fate of millions of lives over a simple mistake.

Oren got up silently and made his way to the carriages.

While Grunt Laush and Grunt Tenna had set up enough tents that each member of the group could take one, Sera and the civilian had chosen to sleep in the carriages, being small enough to comfortably lie across the seats.

Oren made sure to activate the small, pocket-sized redstone lantern he had in his hands. He didn't need the dim light it provided, but it was important for appearances.

He knocked on the door to the carriage that the civilian was sleeping in. It took two seconds before the latch clicked open and the civilian warily peered out at him.

Oren smiled and waved.

The civilian gave him a frown in response but let the door swing open. Oren stepped inside, closing the door behind him.

He expected the civilian might feel uncomfortable sitting in a dark, enclosed space with a man of his size, so when he sat down, Oren made sure to shrink in on himself as much as possible and give her a gentle smile that clashed with his otherwise brutish appearance. The light of his lantern was weak, but he positioned it in a way that she could vaguely see his expression.

"You don't trust me," he said.

It wasn't the standard way to start a conversation, but by acknowledging her distrust in him and validating it, he hoped that it would paradoxically get her to reconsider it.

"It's fine that you don't. I haven't given you any reason to trust me, unless you count the fact that I'm a Mediator," he continued. "Though judging by your conversation with Sera, I assume that's hardly a positive point to you at the moment."

"She told you about that?" the civilian asked.

"She did," Oren said. "It was a difficult conversation, from what I've heard."

"And now you're here to give me another one?"

The civilian came off as antagonistic, which made sense given that she'd been witness to how he manipulated the Otherworlder earlier in the night.

"Therapy is rarely easy," Oren said.

"This hardly feels like a therapy session," she replied, crossing her arms in defiance.

"Therapy is mostly about having difficult conversations. Though I will admit this may not be the ideal setting for it. Is there anything I could do to make you feel more comfortable? Perhaps Laush or Tenna could take over if you feel especially uncomfortable with me."

Oren knew that even if the idea might appeal to her, she would refuse it. The civilian was intelligent enough to recognize that she didn't actually have an issue with him. Even though he'd been the one to manipulate the Otherworlder directly, she knew that it was a consequence of his role as a Mediator, rather than his personal doctrine. She wouldn't feel any more comfortable with another Mediator.

"No, that's fine," she said. "But I would feel more comfortable if we could turn on a few more lamps. I'm not afraid of the dark or anything, but this is a bit too much. I'm starting to feel a little claustrophobic."

"I'm sure you recognize the need for secrecy here," Oren said. "Jamie's a deeply insecure boy, and he would react negatively to the idea that his love interest and his new best friend are meeting in secret, regardless of whatever explanation we give him. I would prefer if we didn't have to deal with whatever would happen if we were discovered, so we won't be using any more lanterns than necessary."

She sighed, no doubt a reaction to the reminder of her status as the Otherworlder's object of affection.

"Great," she said. Sarcasm.

"I apologize," Oren replied, bowing his head deep enough that the back of his neck was visible to her—a sign of submission.

She didn't say anything. She wouldn't want to say anything. If there had been any moment where she might have seen their "therapy session" in a positive light, it had long since passed. Still, Oren waited, trusting that she would break the silence before he would.

"You can leave," she said.

"I apologize," Oren repeated, still with his head bowed low. "As I have already offered, another Mediator can take over in my stead if I have personally offended you in any way."

"It's not you specifically," the civilian said. "I just don't want to be involved anymore."

"May I ask what specifically you are referring to?"

"This Otherworlder-Mediator business."

There were many angles he could approach this from, all with their own advantages and disadvantages.

"And why is that?" Oren asked. "Many civilians would be enthused to become a Follower if they had the opportunity."

She narrowed her eyes, glaring at where she must have thought his eyes were. She ended up staring at his chin instead.

"That sounds like bullshit."

"It's the truth," Oren said, unoffended by her words. "Being a Follower comes with many benefits. Monetary compensation and access to an Otherworlder's power can make any ordinary civilian into a powerful person in a few weeks."

"Most people I know would be too scared to even consider all of that stuff. Myself included."

"I never said most. I said many. I apologize if there was any confusion."

"That sounds like bullshit too."

"What specifically?"

"Are you asking because you're genuinely confused or because you're looking for feedback so you can lie better next time?"

Oren sighed.

"The former," he said. "I will admit that this is new ground for me. It has been some time since I've conducted a therapy session for a civilian, and Mediators are a sort that appreciate any sort of questioning that helps them analyze their own psyche."

The civilian said nothing, crossing her arms as a complicated emotion crossed her face, even when she thought he couldn't see her. She was performing for no one, yet her emotions spilled out of her liberally. It was the type of thing that Oren would never see in another Mediator, and he couldn't help but think of the last time an emotion had appeared on his face unprompted.

"You're not sorry," the civilian said. "Don't apologize for something that you don't actually care about."

Although Oren could see where she was coming from, he didn't agree with it. He didn't care about much, but apologies were too powerful a tool not to use. He would follow along if it made her more agreeable, but it wasn't a binding agreement in the slightest.

"Okay, I won't," Oren said. "But I sincerely didn't mean to confuse you. It's true there are benefits to taking a Follower role as a civilian, and I was curious about why you personally didn't care for them, regardless of the majority opinion."

"I'm not crazy enough to want to risk my life by even being near an Otherworlder," the civilian said, seemingly content to go along with Oren's quick change of subject.

"But Jamie isn't just an Otherworlder. You've become a companion to him. Do you truly believe he will harm you?"

The civilian frowned.

"No. Not on purpose, at least."

"Then why do you push away the role of a Follower, if your main concern is addressed by Jamie's personality?"

The frown deepened.

"I said I didn't want to talk about Otherworlder stuff," she said.

She hadn't, at least not explicitly, but Oren nodded.

"Understood," he said.

The civilian said nothing in response, and Oren decided it was time to go to his next topic.

"What's your opinion on Sera?" Oren asked.

"Huh?" the civilian said, starting in surprise. "What brought this on?"

Oren smiled innocently in hopes that the civilian would at least be able to see the vague shape of it in the low light.

"I won't push you to talk about things you aren't ready for, Lena," he said. "But I'd rather not sit in silence for a whole hour if we don't have to. I suppose Sera would fall under the category of 'Otherworlder stuff' given her profession, but quite frankly, I don't know you well enough to suggest another topic."

Oren hadn't thought he would bring up this topic so early, but he had put Lena off balance enough that he was confident with advancing to the main topic he wanted to explore that night.

While the beginning of the mission had started in a controlled manner, as soon as they made contact with the Otherworlder, the Leader had started to make many large and unnecessary breaches of standard protocol, the chief of them being her attempts to forcefully pry apart the bonds that the Otherworlder had made with its Chosen civilian.

Standard Operating Procedures stated that if an Otherworlder bonded with a civilian and gave them Chosen status before the assigned Mediator group's first contact, several weeks of observation and reconnaissance would be necessary to analyze how best to sever the bond with the least amount of risk. The Leader's approach had ignored this SOP entirely, and when he confronted her about it, she could not give him an explanation as to why she had accelerated the usual timelines without caution.

As a second , it was not his place to defy orders, but it was within the scope of his work to question them retrospectively after executing them. If the Leader would not provide the answers to his questions, he would simply adapt and acquire them elsewhere.

"It's a safe enough topic, don't you think, Lena?" Oren asked with a friendly smile. "If the more bizarre events that have entered your recent life are too difficult to talk about, we could talk about the more mundane parts instead—not that I would call our little leader mundane in any sense of the word." Oren chuckled at the premeditated joke. "I would prefer if you didn't mention that I said that, even in jest. She can be surprisingly petty, and I'd rather not get my pay docked."

"She controls your pay?" the civilian asked.

It wasn't the direction he wanted the conversation to flow toward, but Oren played along. "Not directly, but as the leader of the team, she's responsible for each member's performance reviews, which can influence my salary. But enough about me," he said, not willing to let the deflection last for long. "What about you? What's your opinion on our venerable leader?"

The civilian frowned. "You know my opinion on you Mediators already."

That opinion was an issue Oren planned to address later, but it was still deflection. "I'm not asking about the Mediators, Lena," he said, giving her a gentle and patient smile. "I just want to talk about Sera as a person. She's clearly the person that you're closest to within our group. Do you truly see her as nothing beyond her title? I was under the impression that the two of you were becoming genuine friends."

The civilian opened her mouth but closed it before anything came out. Scrunching her face in concentration, she thought for a few seconds before giving up, letting out a loud sigh.

"I don't know about that," she said. "I mean, yeah, she's nice. But she's a bit much."

"A bit much?" Oren asked. "How so?"

"Well, she's a little too physical, for one," the civilian said, sighing into her hand. "I mean, I guess some people are like that, but I'm not really comfortable with it. Especially not at the level that she does it. Is she just usually like this? Have you touched her boob before?"

Oren smiled through his confusion. "I can't say I have."

"I guess it's different since you're a guy," the civilian said, letting out a quiet huff, apparently disappointed by his answer.

"D-Do you mean to imply that you've touched the Leader's breast?" Oren asked, surprised at how naturally the stutter came to him. "In a sexual manner?"

There was a short pause before, to his surprise, the civilian let out a bark of a laugh.

"What? No," she said, her voice conveying an equal amount of disbelief and amusement. "That's absurd."

"Then why did you imply that it happened?" Oren asked.

"Well, it did happen, but it's not like she meant anything sexual about it," the civilian said, shaking her head quickly. "I was going into a panic attack, and she just did it to distract me. I mean, it's not the way I would do it, but I guess you're the professionals, right?"

"I'm sure she had your best interests at heart," Oren said with a smile.

The civilian let out a sigh before leaning to the side and facing the wall, looking away from him for the first time since he'd entered the carriage. It was an unintentional success on his part. He hadn't expected the topic to get the civilian to let her guard down so effectively, but it was difficult to focus on the civilian with the information she had divulged.

"I guess you're right," the civilian said. "Maybe I've been too harsh on you guys. I don't mean to be. I know how dangerous Jamie can be, and it's not like I don't understand why the Mediators are doing what they do. It's just hard to watch, I guess."

Oren nodded. "For what it's worth, we do appreciate the understanding," he said, hoping that his automatic reply would be enough for her, with a majority of his mind distracted with figuring out the Leader's actions.

"I mean, I know it's not on the same scale, but my dad's a butcher, so I know that everyone loves buying and eating meat, but nobody wants to watch it being processed," the civilian continued, not even acknowledging his response, which was fine for him.

Oren nodded along as the civilian launched into some inane story of the first time she'd helped her father cut open a pig, barely paying attention as he thought about what she'd said about the Leader. It was all highly disturbing. Not the fact that she'd sexually harassed a civilian, but the fact that she'd done it for seemingly no purpose.

The civilian had been correct when she assumed that the idea of distracting someone out of a panic attack was strange. While it wasn't nearly as effective as one might assume from its popularity in dramatic plays, it had a low enough success rate that Oren was certain it hadn't been the Leader's main intention, but if that was the case, what was the point of her actions?

The obvious answer was seduction, but Oren doubted that was the case. According to the personality profile they had created for the civilian, as minimal as it was, there was no indication that she had a sexual attraction to women. While that in itself did not completely close off the avenue for sexual seduction, it meant that further investigation would be needed in order to determine and tailor the methods of operation for the target.

But even if the Leader had felt that she could bypass those steps, Oren could not understand why she might think it was necessary. There was no need to coerce the civilian toward a specific mindset, since the civilian's goals already aligned with the Mediators'.

Frankly speaking, Oren could not see how the Leader's actions benefited the mission. It was irrational behavior.

And in a similarly irrational thought, Oren wondered if seduction was indeed at play here.

Oren was an expert on the matters of love and attraction, as he'd done extensive reading and studies on the subject throughout his career. He knew that attraction to another person was characterized by many things, including irrational behavior.

Though he wanted to dismiss the idea that Sera could risk the whole operation for a chance to get closer to her object of attraction, to his horror, he couldn't deny the possibility.

Sera was famous among the Mediators. She was among the few young Mediators in the organization's active ranks and the youngest team leader by a large margin. She had spent her entire life surrounded by hardened agents decades older than herself. Meeting the civilian was likely the first time that she had spent more than a few hours interacting with someone close to her own age.

In the middle of the civilian's inane story of how she had fought with her childhood friend after his attitude toward her had shifted during puberty, she paused, staring up at Oren.

Though he hadn't been paying enough attention to what she'd been saying to provide an opinion on it, he didn't know if she was seeking one. She stared at him for a moment before grimacing.

"Sorry," she said. "Did I say something wrong?"

Oren couldn't help but be surprised by the question.

"No, not at all," he said, in the most reassuring voice he could summon. "Have I done something to make you think that, Lena?"

"Well, you're frowning," she said.

In the darkness of the carriage, Oren's first reaction was to assume that she was mistaken. He was wearing a perfectly affable smile, after all. There was no reason he wouldn't be, as he wanted the civilian to be able to think of him as someone she could be candid with. A frown would only hurt the chances of that happening.

However, Oren knew his body too well not to realize that he'd lost control of it. He didn't need to do anything as inane as reaching up to touch his lips to know that they were twisted downward, but he was tempted to check anyway. For the first time in years, his true emotions had slipped through the mask he wore.

"I apologize," he said, quickly quirking his lips up in a strained smile, hoping that it would convey a sense of embarrassment rather than any sort of frustration. "You reminded me of an embarrassing time in my past."

Thankfully, the civilian seemed to accept that excuse, letting out a quiet laugh.

"Yeah," she said. "I guess we were all dumb kids at some point, right?"

Oren was not sure that had ever been the case for him.

"I suppose so," he said.

Chapter 29
Changes in Management

Talking with Oren had been surprisingly nice. Contrary to what he had claimed at the beginning of our talk, saying that therapy consisted mostly of difficult conversations, most of the night had consisted of me talking away at him about whatever came to my mind. He had been surprisingly compliant with all of it too, not even trying to steer us back to talking about Otherworlder business, just nodding along as I vented my frustrations at him.

By the time Oren announced that our hour together was up, I had practically forgotten about my previous animosity toward him. It was only after he left that I realized I should've probably apologized to him for how antagonistic I'd been at the beginning of the session. However, I was too tired to go outside and try to find him, so I decided I would go to sleep and apologize to him the next day.

After a good night of sleep, I ended up feeling relaxed for the first time in a while. The morning sun shining through the fabric of the curtains, the chirping of birds muted by the thick walls of the carriage, the softness of the plush cushion that I'd slept on. It was comfortable enough that I didn't want to get up.

So, I laid there, deciding that Oren's apology could wait a few more hours. It had been too long since I'd had more than four or so hours of sleep in a night, on account of the fact that I'd been traveling alone with Jamie for more than a week.

Though I'd never thought that Jamie would attack me, even back when I was still scared of him, I was still nervous enough around him to not want to be asleep near him. Now that I was less afraid of Jamie and had an entire team of Mediators to watch over him in my stead, I felt I could finally take the time to clear my sleep debt after a week of surviving on only a handful of hours of sleep each day.

Unfortunately, a knock on the door interrupted that idea.

I sighed, swinging my legs off the side of the carriage seats and standing up. When I opened the door, I was surprised by who was standing behind it.

"Tenna, right?" I said.

"Right!" he said, giving me a wide smile. He had a slight accent but spoke Astrantan with the confidence of a local. "Pleasure to finally meet you, Ms. Lena. Officially, that is."

It was an overly friendly greeting for someone I'd never spoken to before, but the default persona that each of these Mediators held seemed to be one of overwhelming friendliness.

"Pleasure to meet you too," I replied.

"May we talk inside?" he asked.

I wondered how many more times I would be cornered in this carriage. I nodded and stepped back, not seeing much of a reason to deny him nor any possibility that he would simply leave me alone if I did.

Not needing any further prompting, Tenna gave me a polite smile and a slight bow before stepping up into the carriage. I sat down as he pulled the door closed behind him. Despite how comfortable I'd thought the seat was a moment ago, I was starting to get sick of it.

He sat down across from me. With him being slightly shorter than I was, the carriage wasn't as claustrophobic as it had been last night with Oren's size taking up most of the space. Still, I was painfully aware that the Timuran man sitting across from me was likely strong enough to kill me if he wanted to. I wasn't too bothered by that fact, though; I had become numb to it by this point.

"I'll get straight to the point, Ms. Lena," Tenna said, folding his hands over his lap. "I'm here to let you know that Leader Sera has stepped down from her position and has appointed me as leader."

"What? Why?"

It didn't seem like Tenna had finished talking. He still had his mouth open as I spoke up, but he didn't seem upset by the interruption.

"I was just about to get to that, Ms. Lena," he said, with a hint of amusement in his voice. "I would ask you to be patient and hold your questions until I am finished."

I shut my mouth. He nodded in satisfaction and continued.

"This position will be temporary, and though Leader Sera still holds complete authority over this mission, after a discussion with Second Oren, she has deemed herself unfit to make any decisions in the capacity of her role and will defer to me. While I am trained in the responsibilities of a leader, I will admit that this would be my first time adopting the position outside of training sessions."

He bowed his head to me.

"I apologize, but I do not have the experience nor the confidence to allow the flexibility and lenience that Leader Sera has shown you," he said. "As a result, I would be more comfortable if we could stick to standard practices."

His sudden deference surprised me, but not enough that I didn't recognize the deliberately vague way that he was speaking. It seemed like that trait of Mediators was universal.

"What does that mean?" I asked.

"I am not confident that I can properly monitor your interactions with the Otherworlder," he said with his head still bowed. "I understand that the two of you have had isolated interactions under Leader

Sera's supervision, but standard practices say that civilian Followers should not be allowed to freely interact with Otherworlders in an uncontrolled environment."

I frowned. Was this because of my talk with Sera last night? I guess it made sense. I had shown compassion for someone that they planned to kill, maybe too much if they thought they needed to isolate me from him.

When millions of lives were hanging on the balance of a young boy's mental state, it made sense to think that they wanted to control every factor that could potentially set him off, up until the moment they killed him.

I shook my head, not wanting to think of it.

"Why did Sera make you leader, again?" I asked instead.

Tenna looked up, finally raising his head. "Second Oren had a talk with Leader Sera, which led to her making the decision to step down."

"And what was that talk about?" I asked.

"I was not told," Tenna said. "And it was not my business to ask."

I couldn't tell if he was lying or not, but I'd grown to learn that that was a standard sentiment when it came to dealing with Mediators. I had no idea what was going on regardless, and it didn't really matter in the end. I was still determined to distance myself from this entire situation, and what Tenna was asking of me didn't actually differ from what I wanted in the first place.

"Thanks for telling me all this," I said. "Was there anything else you wanted to say?"

"No, there is not," Tenna said, bowing again. "Thank you for your time, Ms. Lena. If there is anything you need of me, please do not hesitate to ask."

"Sure," I said.

Taking my lazy answer as a dismissal, Tenna bowed once more before leaving the carriage and closing the door behind him.

I sighed and let my head rest against the wall for a few seconds before getting up and opening the door. I wanted nothing more than to fall back asleep and pretend that everything was okay, but I couldn't stand the idea of another Mediator possibly cornering me in the carriage for more conversations. I needed to leave.

Outside, I wasn't surprised to see that all the Mediators were already up. They were scattered around the campsite, and though they all pretended that they hadn't noticed my exiting from the carriage, I wasn't naïve enough to actually think that was the case.

Oren and Tenna were talking to each other in muted voices under the shade of a distant tree, while Laush was stowing away a pile of bags into a storage compartment on the side of the second carriage. Sera was sitting alone at the fire pit, staring at a pile of embers that housed a few baking potatoes in its center.

Jamie was absent from the scene, though judging from the one tent that was still standing and the fact that it was only barely past dawn, I assumed he was still sleeping.

With Oren apparently busy, I made my way to Sera. She didn't look at me even as I sat down beside her.

"So, you're no longer Leader," I said.

Sera kept her eyes locked forward, fixed on the fire. "I'm sorry," she said.

"What for?" I asked, more confused by the sudden apology than anything else. "Is this about Jamie?"

Sera glanced toward me with an odd expression on her face before turning back to the fire. I waited for her to say something, but for the first time since we'd met, she stayed completely silent, staring at the potatoes with a blank expression on her face.

I sighed and shook my head.

"Look," I said. "I actually wanted to apologize to you about that. I realized something while I was having my therapy session with Oren last night."

Sera's eyes widened as her head turned to me. She returned her attention to the potatoes quickly, her eyes softening back into a look of nonchalance.

"And what was that?" she asked.

I paused for a moment, confused by her reaction, but continued before I could lose my resolve and crawl back to the carriage.

"I've been too hard on you," I said, sighing deeply. "I don't mean to be. I know that you're just doing what's best for the world, but it's just hard to see it happening in front of me. I've been taking it out on you, treating you like some kind of cruel monster, even though I know it's unfair to you. I'm sorry."

Sera stared at her potatoes in silence, and the only sound that filled the air between us was the quiet crackling and popping of fire.

"You shouldn't be," Sera said.

"Excuse me?"

"I might be a monster," Sera said, staring forward in what seemed like a resolute determination not to look in my direction. "I don't think you should speak to me anymore."

I felt my brow furrow in confusion and frustration at the vague response. Staring at Sera, her gaze flickered toward my face, but she managed to stop herself each time just before making eye contact with me. Eventually, she seemed to tire of it and just closed her eyes instead, blocking me off completely.

"Please return to your carriage," she said, her voice completely flat. "Someone will bring you your breakfast when it's ready."

I thought of saying something in response, but quite frankly, I was tired of not understanding what was going on and even more tired of trying to figure it out.

I stood up. Sera twitched at the sound, but though I stayed long enough to give her an opportunity to respond, she said nothing, keeping her eyes closed and keeping her face pointed toward the fire.

I walked off, and after seeing that Oren was still talking with Tenna, I headed to my carriage.

For the rest of the day, nobody bothered me. When we started to travel again, we rode with different seating arrangements. Jamie and Oren rode in the same carriage, with Laush as their driver, and Sera drove my carriage, while I sat inside with Tenna. I didn't talk at all, and Tenna seemed content to let the silence sit, taking the time to cross his legs and meditate for the entire day. I busied myself with watching the passing scenery out the window. With us riding through a road that cut across the plainlands, it made for a very boring pastime.

We stopped at night to have dinner and set up camp. Though I joined the group for dinner, I remained silent the entire time, having nothing to say. Jamie, Sera, and Oren all talked to one another, telling jokes and stories while the rest of us ate in relative silence.

Once everyone finished eating and turned in for the night, I stayed up, waiting for Oren to come to my carriage for our next therapy session. I don't know how long it took for me to fall asleep, but eventually, I woke up to the morning light with a sore back and neck from sleeping against the wall in a sitting position. It seemed that our therapy sessions were over.

The rest of the days were more or less the same. The seating arrangements occasionally switched around so Jamie wouldn't always be sitting with the same person, but I was never assigned to sit with him. Whoever I sat with, I didn't talk to, spending my time either gazing out the window or practicing my magic if I got too bored. With most of our time spent traveling on the road, that meant that the only time I saw him was when we woke up and had breakfast and when we set up camp and ate dinner.

More than a few times, I noticed Jamie looking in my direction, acting like he wanted to say something to me or at least involve me in the conversation somehow, but before he could, one of the Mediators would always do or say something to distract him away from me. He probably never noticed.

On the fourth night, Sera made an announcement that we would be back in Plainswood by noon the next day.

I was glad that the trip was ending, and with one more night to go, I was eager to fall asleep and get to the next day as soon as I could. After we ate dinner and said our goodnights, I went to my carriage and threw myself into bed immediately.

It was difficult to fall asleep. I wasn't used to sitting around all day like this, and after so much inactivity, I was too restless to want to stay still for even longer. Despite my desperate desire to sleep, it seemed like my body was fighting that urge to the best of its abilities.

I sighed but stayed lying down, recognizing that the only thing I could do was wait and hope that sleep took me anyway.

A few minutes later, I heard a knock on my door. I was nowhere near falling asleep, but I was in a bad enough mood that I wanted to blame the knock for interrupting my sleep anyway.

For a second, I wondered who it was and what they wanted, before I quickly decided I didn't care.

It was only after the fifth knock that I got annoyed enough to get up and swing the door open with the full intent of kicking whoever was on the other side in the face.

The door did that for me, swinging open and smacking my visitor with a meaty thwack. I considered closing the door just so I could do it again, but I noticed who was standing outside it.

"Jamie?" I asked.

The boy sheepishly grinned at me, peeking his head out from behind the very door that had smacked him in the face.

"Umm, hi," he said.

What was he doing here?

"Hi?" I said hesitantly.

Jamie's smile faltered a bit as he looked nervously around him, though it seemed like he was avoiding my gaze more than he was trying to actually look at anything in particular.

"Sorry, were you sleeping?" he asked, scratching the back of his head. "Sorry."

"Stop apologizing," I said automatically, then winced when I realized how harsh I had sounded. "Sorry, I'm a bit on edge."

Jamie's smile returned, though it was skewed awkwardly in a hesitant grin. "Yeah, I kind of noticed," he said.

A long silence stretched between us. A ridiculous feeling of nostalgia came over me, as I remembered how these silences would be commonplace between us, back when I was still afraid of him killing me.

Jamie coughed into his hand.

"I feel like we haven't talked in ages," he said, still awkwardly refusing to meet my eyes. "If you're not sleepy, I was thinking we could just talk for a bit. If you want to, of course."

I stared at him for a few seconds, wondering what brought this on, before I noticed movement in the corner of my eye. Oren's figure was hard to miss as he crawled out of his tent and stretched his body in an exaggerated manner. Jamie followed my gaze and noticed Oren, just as Oren pretended to notice us.

"Oh," Oren said, acting surprised. "Are you two having trouble falling asleep as well?"

"Kind of, yeah," Jamie replied.

"I get how you feel, my brother," Oren said, stretching again and walking toward us. "Being cooped up all day is making me restless. It's nice that we've got good company, but I'll be glad when this is over."

"Uh, yeah. Same," Jamie said.

"You want to go for a walk?" Oren said, jerking a thumb down the road. "Might be good to shake some of the restlessness off."

"Yeah, that sounds good," Jamie said, looking back at me. "You want to come too, Lena?"

Though I was making eye contact with Jamie, at the corner of my vision, I could see Oren giving me a pointed stare.

"No, I'm fine, thanks," I said, taking the hint. "I'm a little tired."

Jamie frowned. "Are you still... under the weather?" he asked. "I know Sera said I can't heal you, but maybe I can help with some of the symptoms."

I wondered what I looked like for him to act so worried. I smiled as best as I could manage, though I wasn't sure it would be anywhere near enough to be convincing.

"No, just tired," I said. "I'll be fine. Go on your walk."

"Oh," Jamie said. "I did wake you up, didn't I? Sorry."

I shook my head.

"You didn't," I said. "I'll talk to you later, okay?"

"If the lady says she's tired, you shouldn't push her, Jamie," Oren said, gently chastising him. "Come, my brother. Let me teach you the proper way to talk to girls."

Jamie spun around to blush and sputter at Oren, insisting that that wasn't what he was trying to do. I didn't hear most of it, since I quickly stepped back into my carriage and closed the door, blocking any and all sound from coming in.

I sat down and let out a weary sigh.

Chapter 30

A Friendly Chat

The next morning, Jamie tried to talk to me again. He was pulled away from me at the last second by Oren, who conveniently wanted to try sparring with an Otherworlder. Jamie seemed anxious at the idea at first, but after a bit of gentle goading by the rest of the Mediators, he reluctantly agreed to a friendly spar.

Oren started the fight by firing off a salvo of small rocks at Jamie before rushing him, using all of his limbs to trap Jamie in a whirlwind of flying strikes.

It was an awe-inspiring display. Oren's sheer speed was a sure sign that he was using magic to enhance his body beyond its natural limits, but the fact that he could cast body-enhancing magic while simultaneously launching magically controlled rocks was something I could never have imagined witnessing.

I wouldn't have been surprised if Oren was considered one of the strongest magic users in the world.

Even so, it didn't make a difference against Jamie.

Jamie evaded every single attack with ease. Though he had a small grimace on his face throughout the fight, it didn't seem like he was worrying about Oren's assault. I could imagine that he was remembering the same thing I was. His fight with Medric. How he had killed someone.

Though Oren was much stronger than Medric had been, I doubted it made a difference to Jamie. At any point, if he wanted to, he could have smacked Oren on the neck, easily breaking it like he had with Medric.

After about five minutes, Oren collapsed on the floor, sweating profusely and bleeding out of his nose despite the fact that Jamie hadn't retaliated at all. Drool began dripping from his mouth, quickly forming a puddle as he lay panting on the floor.

Mana depletion. While it could have been acting, for all I knew, I also didn't doubt that Oren would go as far as to actually deplete his mana just to make it more convincing to Jamie.

Whether it was faked or not, it worked to Oren's advantage.

Even though Jamie never touched him, he still felt guilty enough for Oren's plight that he was easily convinced to spend the rest of the morning helping Oren as he fought against the symptoms of mana depletion. I had experienced mana depletion once before, and I could sympathize with how Oren struggled to even eat his food, forcing him to ask Jamie to physically tilt his head back so he could at least swallow some stew.

Although Oren was getting better by the time we finished breakfast, he was still woozy and needed help getting into the carriage. Obviously, the perfect person to take care of him was Jamie.

I ended up sharing a carriage with Sera, with Laush driving. We hadn't spoken since I had apologized to her a few days ago, and with how poorly it had gone, I had no intention of trying again. Unfortunately, a few hours into our journey, Sera took that choice out of my hands.

"We're getting close to Plainswood," Sera said.

Though she paused, giving me the opportunity to speak, I stayed silent, not knowing what sort of response she expected from me.

"We think we're close to being able to cut you off as the Otherworlder's Follower. Oren and I have been working to make him feel an ample amount of companionship with us, and we're hoping that with one final push, he'll be willing to release you from your role as a Chosen Follower. If all goes well, you'll be able to stay in Plainswood when the rest of us leave."

I still didn't look at Sera, but the news was objectively good, right? That was what I wanted, right? To leave the problem in someone else's hands? To have Jamie die so he wouldn't be a threat to my life anymore?

That's what I wanted, right? For Jamie to die?

"Good," I said aloud.

Out of the corner of my eye, I saw Sera nod and smile. It seemed a little stiff, but I didn't care enough to analyze why.

"You'll have to play along for just a bit longer," she said. "Our fifth member will have set up a scenario in your village that will provide you with a good excuse to leave the Otherworlder's side in an amicable split. We haven't been able to set up proper communication with him as we've been on the road, so we don't know exactly what it will be. You may be faced with a random stranger posing as a family member or a close friend. If you play along, it'll give you the highest chance of escaping your Follower status properly."

The idea was strange but not to a level that I wasn't used to by now. I nodded, acknowledging that I'd heard.

Sera smiled for a few more seconds before the expression dropped off her face completely. She fixed me with a blank stare that gave away no emotion whatsoever. It was unsettling enough that it drew my attention, making me lock eyes with her.

"For what it's worth, I'm sorry," she said, her voice monotone.

"For what, specifically?" I asked.

"For making you uncomfortable."

I furrowed my brow at that, turning to Sera for the first time in a while to glower at her in confusion and frustration.

"I have no idea what you're talking about, and I know that you're aware of that," I said with a harsher scoff than I was used to hearing from myself. "Either stop being so vague with everything you say, or don't bother apologizing at all."

I half expected her to be stunned by my comment, but she didn't hesitate to respond.

"I sexually assaulted you when we first met," Sera said, keeping her eyes down and to the side. "And I continued to make unwanted physical contact with you, without your consent."

Even though I hadn't really thought about it since my talk with Oren, who apparently didn't understand the meaning of patient confidentiality, the fact that she was apologizing to me wasn't too surprising. I wouldn't have gone so far as to suggest that she had sexually assaulted me. It felt like an overreaction on her part, and the way she fidgeted uncomfortably under my gaze, silently begging me to grant her forgiveness, made waves of guilt wash over me for every second I didn't give it to her.

My eyes narrowed at her as I quashed the feeling, forcibly drying up my well of sympathy as I glared down at her.

"Do you think I'm stupid?" I asked.

The simple question seemed to stun her momentarily.

"I don't," Sera said, a hint of hesitancy bleeding through her otherwise flat tone.

If it were any other person speaking to me, then I might've believed that she genuinely had no idea why I had asked the question, but it was difficult to forget that the girl sitting in front of me was a Mediator.

"Then why are you pretending like it matters what I think of you?" I said. "You don't care."

Again, the slight furrowing of her brow implied that the question made her feel some way, but her expressions shared the same vagueness that her words did.

"I do care," Sera said, her voice rising slightly.

"Oh yeah?" I asked, finding my own voice rising too. Unlike Sera, I could easily identify the emotion behind it. "Is that so? Because I can't tell what's real or not anymore. Watching you treat that poor kid like he's a fucking psychological lump of clay to mold as you please has really put me on the fucking edge."

That was too far. I knew Sera and the other Mediators were doing what they thought was best for the world, but I couldn't stop the words from spilling out of me.

"You don't even do it subtly either. You just gaslight him right in front of me, like it's no big deal. It's like you expect me to stomach it, like I'm one of you. I'm a butcher's daughter, but you don't see my family opening up a slaughterhouse with glass walls so the village children can watch us cut open a pig's bloody carcass.

"You flaunt the fact that I can't trust anything that comes out of that mouth of yours, right in front of my face. I know I'm not special. I know that if you wanted to, you could pull the exact same shit that you're pulling on Jamie on me, because I know I'm not smart enough to notice it either, but I'd hope that you would at least put some fucking effort into it, instead of trying to emotionally bludgeon me into being your fucking puppet."

In a spur of madness, I stood up and lunged forward to grab Sera by the collar of her shirt. She pressed herself far back against her seat, but I didn't let her escape me, pinning her down with my body and pressing my forehead directly against hers so she couldn't look away from me. Though a small voice at the back of my head reminded me that Sera could easily kill me if she wanted to, my frustration and anger had been bottled up for too long to be contained. It was going to overflow, and I had no interest in trying to contain it.

"Every time I listen to one of you bastards talk, it feels like I'm in a poisoner's workshop, downing bottles of dark green liquid that you keep saying is good for me, but I have no idea whether I'm drinking the truth or some lie that will eventually lead to my horrible and painful death. I know how much of a big deal you are. I know how insignificant I am. I know that, in the grand scheme of things, I'm nothing. If your little group thought that they could save millions of people by killing me, they would do it happily, so stop pretending to be sorry when you're obviously not."

Sera was looking up at me, her eyes wide and moist. It was difficult to decipher the emotion behind them, but I stopped myself before I wasted too much energy on trying to figure it out. I knew that I wouldn't be able to trust whatever answer I decided on.

"If you have a way to get me out of this mess, fine. Get me out of here. Don't bother telling me about how you're fucking sorry, and don't pretend like you care. If you actually did, you would let your feelings rest, because at this point, anything you do or say will only make me more paranoid and more distrustful of you. If you try to apologize to me again, I'll assume that you're implying that I'm a complete fucking idiot, or you're one yourself for expecting me to believe it—and I hope for the sake of our world that the latter isn't true. So shut the fuck up and leave me the fuck alone."

It felt good to finally let it all out, but as the anger simmered down after finally having a means of release, I grew more aware of the fact that at the moment, I was sitting on a Mediator.

I had held down and verbally assaulted a Mediator. I was currently letting out deep, angry, snarling breaths directly on a Mediator's face, staring her down from atop her lap.

"Y-Yes, ma'am. I mean, yes, Lena," Sera squeaked.

I scowled at her one last time before getting off of her.

"Yes, what?"

"I'll shut up," Sera muttered, eyes downcast.

Satisfied with the answer for now, I sat down.

"Good."

Sera shrank in on herself, seemingly trying to occupy as little space as possible. She was curled up, with her shoulders hunched forward and inward and her hands tucked between her thighs like a kicked dog with its tail between its legs. Her legs were crossed tightly, and they kept fidgeting, like she couldn't find a comfortable position for them.

I looked at her face for a brief second, trying to decipher what she was feeling. I noticed her biting her lower lip and carrying a deep flush on her cheeks before I caught myself. I looked away from her, not wanting to give her any opportunity to get in my head again.

I tried looking away, but a panted breath drew my attention back to Sera.

"What?" I growled.

Sera looked up at me, red-faced, looking like she was almost about to sweat for some reason.

"N-Nothing," she said.

Surprisingly, she was the first to break eye contact.

I stared at her for a few more seconds before I decided I didn't want to try figuring out whatever she was trying to do.

I looked out the window, pretending not to hear Sera as she continued to fidget awkwardly in her seat.

Chapter 31

HOME SWEET HOME

The rest of the ride was relatively quiet. Sera didn't say anything, and she eventually stopped fidgeting in her seat as much, though she did remain curled up and hunched over until we rolled to a stop.

When we heard a knock on our door, Sera was quick to jump out of her seat and open it. Laush's face showed a flash of confusion as Sera rushed past her, but it was quickly replaced by the same neutral smile she always wore. She turned to me casually, as if her former leader hadn't nearly run her over a moment ago.

"I hope you had a pleasant trip, Ms. Lena," she said, giving me a polite bow.

I gave her no reply. Though she offered me a helping hand, I ignored it and stepped down from the carriage on my own. Somewhere behind me, I heard Oren and Jamie doing the same.

"I'm just saying, not all of us can be as lucky as you, my brother. The rest of us do have a finite amount of mana," Oren said with a chuckle.

"I just didn't think it would be this bad," Jamie said. With Oren's arm draped around him, he helped support the older man's weight. It seemed like Oren was still affected by his mana depletion, which made sense given that it had only been a few hours and his had been a particularly bad case. "How do mages in your world fight if using magic makes them like this?"

"They usually don't. While most fighters worth a damn will have a few spells up their sleeve, pure mages who intend to get into the fighting business usually don't last very long." Oren laughed when Jamie's jaw dropped. "Sorry to disappoint you. But hey! That'll make your rise to the top even more extraordinary! Not only will you be the first adventurer, you'll also be the first fighting mage to roam this world of ours!"

Jamie smiled and looked away from him, secondhand embarrassment clear on his face at the shameless volume that Oren shouted at. "I guess."

Oren smiled at him and pushed himself off Jamie to stand on his own. He still looked a bit shaky on his feet, but he pretended not to care as he patted Jamie on the back. "I believe in you, my brother," he said. "You are a great man, and great men achieve great things."

Jamie smiled and looked away, scratching the back of his head in embarrassment, but didn't say anything.

I couldn't continue watching. It was similar enough to what the Mediators had been doing every time I saw Jamie during our journey here, but I hadn't gotten any more used to the sight. It was disturbing, to say the least.

I tried to tune out of their conversation, but it wasn't an ability I could apply at will. I felt my teeth clenching as my ears refused to block out Oren's exaggerated praises and Jamie's meek responses.

"Smile, Ms. Lena," Laush whispered from behind me. "It will help your cause if you can convince Jamie that everything is fine."

I turned around to glare at her. Even though I had been determined not to react to anything else a Mediator said to me, my outburst at Sera had left my emotions running hot. For all I knew, that was what the Mediators wanted—to make me off balance enough not to realize that they were manipulating me. At this point, however, I didn't care.

"Oh, yeah?" I asked. "And you know what my cause is, don't you? You know what my ultimate goal was when I decided to find myself a boy falling from the sky? You finally figured out my master plan, didn't you?"

Laush frowned. "I did not mean to upset you, Ms. Lena," she said. "It was a poor choice of words on my part."

I ground my teeth together. "Yeah, it was," I said. I lifted my hand, pointing in the direction of my house. "I'm going home. Forget smiling. I'm going to puke if I keep watching this. Come get me if you need me. You know where I live, I'm sure."

Laush's frown deepened at my outburst, but she quickly smiled and bowed as she stepped to the side, freeing up the path toward my home. The speed of the change was unnerving but nothing I wasn't used to by now. Taking her smile as permission, I walked past her and headed home.

It was almost noon, and though I knew that most of the village would still be working at this time, I wasn't surprised to find the street emptier than it usually was. With Sera's supposed fifth team member having been here for a few days already, I assumed that he would have gotten word about our arrival somehow and warned the villagers. Even so, the village wasn't completely empty.

I saw a few villagers going about their business on the streets, but none even glanced at me as I passed. Given the last impression Jamie had made, I wasn't surprised that people were eager to keep their heads down. It was fine by me, since my dour mood might have caused me to snap at anybody who so much as looked at me, and I thankfully managed to avoid talking to anyone before I trudged down the familiar path toward the house that I'd lived in for my whole life.

When I got to my house, I pushed open the door, putting more force into it than I had intended and making a resounding crash when it swung open and hit the wall.

I grimaced at the sound, instinctively assuming that my dad would gently scold me for causing a ruckus like he always did whenever I opened the door like that.

But he didn't. Staring at me from the other side of the counter, he simply stared at me, frozen and wide-eyed.

I stared back at him.

I didn't know how long the two of us stood there, just staring at each other until my dad finally spoke.

"Lena?"

If it weren't for the fact that the room was completely silent, I probably wouldn't have heard him. I'd never heard him sound so hesitant before, like he doubted what he was seeing.

To be fair to him, I wasn't quite sure if I was dreaming either.

My dad and I had an okay relationship. We got along with each other just fine, but I didn't really confide in him too much. We chatted over dinner and lunch whenever our schedules matched up, but the last time we'd really had a heart-to-heart conversation was when he wanted to talk to me to ask about what I planned to do with my life—whether he should be preparing to give the butcher shop to me once he eventually retired.

We had that conversation when I turned fifteen two years ago, and we hadn't really had any deep conversations since then. It wasn't because we didn't want to but more due to the fact that we were country folk. Our lives were simple, boring, and calm, for the most part. We just never had anything exciting to talk about, and I had been too much of a teenager to want to share my innermost thoughts with him on a regular basis. All in all, I didn't have a particularly special bond with my parents beyond what was considered to be normal.

But I hadn't seen normal in a while.

It had been less than two weeks since I left Plainswood, but it felt like I'd been gone for a decade. The sight of him reminded me of what I had and what I was. I was just a girl who had been sucked into this mess. A normal girl.

"Hi, Dad," I said, or at least that was what I tried to say. Instead, I just sank to my knees and started to blubber wordlessly.

I didn't hear what he said next, but judging by the fact that I quickly felt two people pulling me into a deep hug, I realized that he'd called my mom. Enveloped in their arms, I don't think I dozed off, but I also couldn't quite remember how I ended up in my bed with my mother's arms wrapped around me as she cried into my chest. She had pinned one of my arms to my sides, and my dad was gripping my other hand tightly in both of his own.

I considered smiling at him, and I probably could have've, but the thought of giving him a smile that I didn't fully feel sickened me, given what I'd seen over the past few days. Instead, I chose to give his hand a little squeeze.

I saw a few tears well up in his eyes and drip down his bearded cheeks as he raised my hand to his forehead, like he was using it to pray. As he gently pressed down my fingers one by one, muttering whispered words under his breath, I realized that he actually was praying. It had been years since I'd seen my dad practice his old religion, but I supposed if there was any time for him to turn to prayer, it would be when his daughter was kidnapped by an Otherworlder.

I squeezed my dad's hand once more before turning to my mom. "Hi, Mom," I said.

She didn't respond with words, choosing to bury herself deeper into my chest instead. She was heavy, and her tears had soaked through my shirt by now, but I didn't have the heart to tell her to get off of me. I also didn't have the strength to keep myself from crying either, so I just joined her.

I didn't know how long the three of us spent there, crying with each other, but by the time we finished, we were exhausted, and our throats were sore to the point where it was difficult to talk.

Even so, I managed to muster a few words when the door to my room suddenly opened.

"Oh, you motherfucker," I said. "Can't you assholes give me a break?"

My parents hadn't noticed the door opening but shifted their gazes to it when I spoke. Their expressions shifted into a mixture of anger, confusion, and worry when they saw who was standing there.

I didn't recognize the man, but I could guess who he was.

Unlike the other Mediators, the fifth member of their team looked painfully unremarkable. He was a middle-aged man with a visible pot belly and a receding hairline, wearing a loose-fitting shirt that would have looked completely in line with what the other villagers in Plainswood would wear. If it weren't for the fact that he was standing outside of my bedroom door, wearing a cocky grin, I might have assumed he was just one of my dad's old friends from out of town, coming to visit at an inopportune time.

"Sorry, girlie," the man said. "You're not off the clock yet. I gave you the time for a good cry, but that's about all I can afford."

"Mr. Marten," my dad said, his voice still hoarse from our crying. "I insist you leave my house."

"Sorry, Hal," Marten said. "No can do. Unless you want your daughter to go gallivanting off with the Otherworlder kid on his next adventure, she needs to listen to what I say. You'll get the time for crying later, once she's home permanently."

My dad pursed his lips together, but I didn't.

"The other Mediators at least pretended to be polite," I said, feeling annoyed enough to berate my supposed savior.

"Yeah, and there's a reason why I'm out here, instead of playing nice with an alien brat with a fragile ego," Marten said. "Everyone has their strengths and weaknesses, girlie. My strengths just happen to involve figuring out a way to save your ass. Some appreciation would be nice."

I glared at him.

"If this persona you're putting on is supposed to be endearing, it isn't working," I said.

Marten shrugged. "I don't give a shit. I don't care if you like me or not. You just gotta do what I say."

"And why would I trust you?"

Even though I'd already sworn to myself that I would never trust an expression on a Mediator's face, Marten seemed genuinely surprised by what I said.

"Because you're a real pain in the ass?" he said, making my mom grip my sheets angrily, though she didn't say anything in response. "The only reason why I would do anything to sabotage your chances of leaving is if I wanted to fuck with the rest of my team and force them to deal with babysitting a civvy for even longer than they already have, and I don't have enough of a grudge against any of them to risk getting my pay docked. I don't got a reason to mess with you, girlie."

I frowned.

It upset me that he was right. I still wasn't convinced that he wasn't putting up this obnoxious persona for a specific and nefarious reason, but nothing he'd said had been wrong.

I thought about it for a few more seconds before I glared at him.

"Fine," I said. "Tell me what to do."

Chapter 32

FAMILY

Marten explained that he would be posing as the butcher of the neighboring town of Oakwood. He had come to Plainswood because he decided to retire but wanted to make sure that Oakwood had a butcher they could rely on after he was no longer working.

With my dad being the only butcher nearby, he'd come over to ask if he could handle taking on the additional customers from his village. While it would be a good business opportunity for my dad to double his clientele, he would have to travel between villages on a regular basis. It would be a nearly impossible task—unless I took on a more active role in the butcher shop.

My job would be to act in a way that would convince Jamie that I was interested enough in butchery to want to become part-owner in my dad's business.

From the psychological profile that the rest of his team had sent him before we left Redstone, it would likely be enough to convince Jamie to "release me" from my role.

"That's a lot simpler than I thought it would be," I said. "You sure it's going to work?"

We had moved out of my room and were now sitting at the kitchen table instead. Though it was a square table designed so one person could sit at each side, Marten was sitting alone on one side. I was sitting across from him with my dad standing behind me, resting his hand on my shoulder in a show of support, and my mom was sitting on her own chair by my side.

"It's simple because I had to make it as idiot-proof as possible," he said, unbothered by the dark glare that my mom gave him. "Or do you want me to dumb it down even more?"

"I'm just a bit skeptical about how you're so confident that you know what Jamie will do. You haven't even met him," I said, keeping my expression neutral. "I doubt Mediators are that good."

"You're right. Mediators aren't that good," he said, giving me a cocky grin that told me exactly what he was going to say next. "But I am."

I resisted the urge to let out a frustrated sigh.

"And I don't know you. I know I have no reason to think you don't want me gone as soon as possible, but I can't see myself putting a lot of trust into a middle-aged man who's acting like an obnoxious teenage boy."

"But you've got no other choice," Marten said, his grin not faltering in the slightest.

I frowned in response.

Marten laughed, chuckling and pounding his hand lightly on the dinner table.

"You're alright, girlie. Got more spunk than any of the other civvies I've had to bail out. Tell you what, why don't I go have a chat with my team right now, and I'll come back and let you know once I confirm everything's all fine and dandy. That sound good to you?"

"Not a chance in hell," I said.

"I'm not religious enough for that to mean anything to me," Marten replied with a shrug. "But I get the spirit. What would sound good to you then, if that ain't enough?"

I frowned.

"Nothing," I said.

"Nothing?"

"There's nothing you could do or say to make me trust you," I admitted.

"So you're just whining, then."

I glared at him, not wanting to dignify his assumption with a response, regardless of how correct it was. He laughed.

"Ah, it's nice to talk with real people." He sighed cheerfully. "You know how difficult it is to get a rise out of most Mediators? Not that I don't appreciate the challenge, but it's nice to have an easy win sometimes."

I kept my face as neutral as possible, not wanting to give him any more satisfaction.

He grinned at me anyway.

"Fucking adorable," he said mockingly. "Anyway, I should be off soon. I'll be back in a bit; anywhere from ten to thirty minutes depending on how long I want to try cracking Sera for."

"Why Sera?" I couldn't help but ask.

"Because she's the leader?" Marten asked, as if it was an obvious answer and I was stupid for not expecting it.

"Well, she's not the leader anymore, is she?" I asked back.

Marten frowned, all traces of humor disappearing from his face immediately.

"She isn't?" he asked. "Did Sera die?"

"What?" I said, surprised by the assumption. "No, she just stepped down."

He looked at me for a few seconds, his eyes searching my face, before he pushed his chair back and stood up.

Without another word, he walked out of the house, a trail of muttered curses left behind in his wake.

It took me a few seconds to react, raising my arm and opening my mouth to shout at a man who was already long gone. I stood up, or at least tried to. My mom was hugging my arm, and I was too tired to shake her off fast enough to give chase. I ended up flailing weakly in her arms and almost slipping off my chair.

Luckily, with my dad standing so close behind me, he was ready to catch me before I fell on the floor.

"Lena!" my parents both shouted, concern saturating their voices.

"I'm fine," I said. "I need to go after him."

"Why?" My mom sobbed, gripping onto my sleeve and burying her face into it. "Why do you need to go, Lena?"

"I need to go, Mom. I need to..." I trailed off.

"Stay," my mom begged, her voice muffled by my arm. "My sweet baby, don't leave us. Not again."

My mom's hands were shaking as she pulled at my sleeve. At every small movement I made, her strength seemed to fail her as the fabric of my sleeves slipped through her fingers, but each time she let go, she reached out and clung to me desperately once more.

"Don't go," she said. "Don't go."

What was I doing? I had stood up in reaction to Marten's sudden exit, but why did I feel the need to follow him? Even if the troubling reaction he had to Sera stepping down was real, it didn't mean that I had to do anything about it, did it?

It had become so habitual for me to assume that this Otherworlder business was a part of my life now that I just assumed there would be a reason for me to follow. If he didn't ask me to come along, did I really need to go?

Could I really just stay?

"I-I'll stay, Mom," I said hesitantly.

My mom let out a small sigh of relief. She was holding my arm in an awkward position, and I wanted to adjust it to get more comfortable, but I stopped when I heard soft, steady breathing.

"Mom?" I said, tilting my head down to try and see her face. With it buried in my arm, it was impossible, but I grew more aware of the fact that she was growing heavier by the second and was starting to slip sideways off her chair.

"She must have passed out from relief," my dad said from behind me. He reached down to put a hand on my mom's shoulder to stop her from falling to the floor. "She's barely slept since you were taken from us."

I looked up at him and noticed that the same probably applied to him. There were dark rings under his eyes, and though he'd never been a man to care about his looks, his hair and beard were more matted and wilder than I'd ever seen before. He gave me a weak smile as he noticed my gaze.

"Are you hungry?" he asked. "Tired? Anything you need at all? I can peel your mom off you if you want to go to bed."

Though she was asleep, I could have sworn I felt my mom's grip grow tighter at the suggestion.

"I'm fine," I said.

"You sure? I can imagine how heavy she must be, though you never heard me say that," he said, giving me a forced wink. "Your mom would kill me if she thought I was calling her fat."

My dad wasn't usually the type of person to make jokes and this one in particular was especially awkward. I couldn't remember the last time he'd attempted a wink, but I could tell he was trying his best to lighten the atmosphere.

I smiled. Not at the joke, but it was a smile regardless.

"Thanks, Dad," I said, leaning back into him. He stumbled, clearly not being too stable himself, but held firm. "Whoops, sorry."

"I'm fine, Lena," he said, giving me a weak smile. "Now do you want to go to bed?"

I thought about it for a moment and shook my head.

"This is nice," I said. I'd been spending too much of my time lying around recently, and more than rest, I just wanted everything to feel right. Sitting here at the kitchen table with my parents, it didn't undo what I'd gone through recently, but it was a start. "Pull up a chair, Dad. No point in standing around when you look like you're dead on your feet."

My dad frowned but didn't disagree. After making sure I wouldn't fall without his support, he quickly darted over to the other side of the table to grab the chair that Marten had been sitting on. He dragged it close to me, positioning it slightly behind me so he could support my mom and me at the same time.

We sat in silence for a moment, but I was getting sick of silence by this point.

"Am I the result of a one-night stand?"

I immediately felt bad for almost killing my dad, but just a little bit. I was surprised that my mom didn't wake up from the violent hacking and sputtering he was doing, but I was more surprised at the sound that came from my own mouth.

I was laughing.

It had been so long since I had a genuine laugh like this that the sound felt alien to me, like somebody else was using my mouth to make noises for me. Before I knew it, another laugh had joined in with mine.

"She told you about that, huh?" my dad said, through wheezing chuckles. "How'd you manage to get her to admit it? She swore she'd take it to her grave and threatened most of the village with a painful death if they ever let it slip that she was six months pregnant at our wedding."

"Tensions were high," I said, leaning back into him. "I'm sure she wasn't thinking straight."

"Ah..." he said, likely guessing what event could have made her scatter-brained enough to let go of a lifelong secret like that. "Are you embarrassed by it?"

"No. But I didn't need the details of how she seduced you. That was a bit much."

"Ah... I'm sorry."

"Don't be. It was Mom, not you," I said. "Are you embarrassed?"

"By what?"

"By how I was born."

"What? Heavens, no. I have no regrets. I've loved you since the moment you were born, Lena, and that's never going to change. And your mom loves you even more than I do. She loves you more than life itself."

I smiled, letting out a content sigh and sinking deeper into my dad's arms. He must've been tired, but I had faith that he could support me anyway. He was my dad, after all. That was what dads did.

"I love you too, Dad," I said.

"Just to be clear, I did love your mother even before... that night," my dad said, clearly still flustered. "It just took the right atmosphere and a bit of liquid courage to admit it."

"Dad," I said, firmly but playfully warning him off. "It's fine. I know you love Mom. I don't need to hear the details. Please."

"I guess you wouldn't," he said, coughing into his hand awkwardly. "But I just wanted to put that out there."

There was another long silence that stretched out between us, but this time, I didn't feel the need to break it. It was comfortable.

"You know, your mother never used to cry," my dad said.

"Really?" I asked. I couldn't imagine it.

"Your mother always wanted a large family, but the village doctor told her that she would never be able to birth a child," he said, hugging me tighter as he talked. "When her mother died, she was so alone, but she kept wearing that fake smile of hers, like she was afraid that everything would go wrong if she didn't pretend like everything wasn't. I always felt a little sad whenever I saw her.

"When she found out she was pregnant with you, she burst into tears, like everything she had been holding back came flooding out of her at once. She was crying, but her happiness was so beautiful and pure that I asked her to marry me on the spot. Maybe it wasn't the best timing, but I don't regret it."

I said nothing, but I looked down at my mom, still sleeping with her head in the crook of my elbow and loosely gripping at the fabric of my sleeves. I reached over with my other hand to place it over hers.

"You were a miracle, Lena. You were our miracle."

I felt a few more tears well up in my eyes, but I smiled as they fell.

"Tha—"

The door slammed open and I yelped and flailed in surprise. My arms flew wildly, causing me to smack my dad in the nose and shake my mom off, sending her falling to the floor, face first.

"We need to go," Marten said, his head poking through the kitchen door.

My dad groaned and clutched at his nose while my mom continued to doze, unawaken by her rude introduction to the kitchen floor.

I glared at Marten.

"It's been five minutes!"

Chapter 33

BACK TO WORK

"We need to go," Marten said, thumping his foot against the floor as he stood by the door. He had a hand on his head and was idly scratching at it, though he seemed seconds away from pulling out what little hair he had left. His gaze was unfocused and he kept taking small glances out behind him, as if expecting someone to attack him.

I frowned. I wasn't happy with having my family time interrupted, but the look on his face was serious. I was still aware that it might just be a mask that he wore, like the rest of the Mediators did, but even if it was, it was obviously crafted to convey that he was nervous about something. Extremely nervous.

Beside me, my dad rubbed his nose a few more times. I gave him an apologetic grimace, but he didn't even notice, dividing his attention between picking my mom off the floor and glaring at Marten.

"She's staying here," he said.

"When will you idiots realize that's what I want too?" Marten snapped, though he didn't even glance at my dad. "If she wants to stay in this town, she has to come with me."

"What happened?" I asked. "What's wrong?"

For some reason, Marten gave me a frustrated glare but shook his head quickly. "I'll tell you on the way. The faster we get there, the better. Now let's go. Please."

Even though he'd said please, it still sounded more like a demand than a request. He actually started to pull at his hair now, grasping at the few thinning strands that he could actually find. I glanced back at my dad and sighed. It had been nice to see him for a few minutes, but I knew that no matter how much I didn't want it, this was probably something that I needed to do.

"Alright," I said, sighing. "Let's go."

"Yes. Let's," my dad said, grabbing my hand as I stood up. I looked back at him in surprise, and he gave me a gentle smile and squeezed my hand. "I'm not letting you leave us again, Lena. We're sticking by you this time."

I felt myself squeeze his hand back, and I felt tears welling up in my eyes. Before I could say anything, Marten let out a frustrated huff.

"Yeah, yeah. Come along, but make it quick. We've got no time for touching moments. Let's. Go."

I opened my mouth to protest before realizing that he'd just said he was fine with it.

"Oh," my dad said, clearly a bit stunned by the revelation. "Okay."

Marten just huffed again and left the room, letting the door swing shut behind him. My dad and I gave each other a glance before getting up.

"Mind helping me pick up your mother?" he asked.

"We're bringing her?" I asked, looking down at my mother, who still had her cheek pressed against the floor as she continued to sleep, unbothered.

"She would have a heart attack if she woke up and saw both of us missing. I don't think she'll wake up anytime soon, but I'd rather not risk it," he said, bending over to scoop her up. Though he was visibly tired, the immense size difference between them made it so he could carry her off the floor with relative ease. "Besides, she's light enough that it won't be a problem."

"Oh yeah?" I said, trying to inject some levity into my voice. "Didn't you just say she was heavy? I thought you didn't want her hearing you say she was fat."

My dad stared blankly at me, clearly not remembering the joke he'd made only a few minutes ago. He glanced out the door nervously to where Marten was waiting.

I sighed, mourning the death of the peace I'd thought I'd managed to reclaim in my life.

"Okay," I said. "Let's go."

Marten glared at us when we left the house. He opened his mouth, as if to yell at us, but seemed to decide against it. He started walking instead, his pace surprisingly slow for someone who seemed so anxious to move quickly.

"Don't interrupt me. Ask questions once I'm done," he said brusquely. Not even giving me an opportunity to reply, he continued to speak.

"As of this moment, the Otherworlder is irritated because my incompetent colleagues forced a rift between the two of you. He wants to feel a sense of closeness to you, and if you want to stay in this dingy town, you need to give him some of that. Not too much, though. You're going to talk to him, apologize for avoiding him for the past few days, give him a pat on the back, and continue like nothing happened. Don't hug him, don't kiss him, and don't fuck him. You'll be interacting with him regularly for about five more days, and we'll see where we can go from there. Hopefully, once he realizes you're nothing special, that'll be the end of it and he'll be able to move on with a happy farewell.

"Your parents can tag along for now if they want, but don't tell them anything classified, or someone will kill you. No, I didn't know about the leadership change. No, I'm not happy about it. Sera is back in the leader role, whether she likes it or not. Tenna's proven he can't adapt under pressure, Laush is even less experienced than him, Oren's a socially incompetent moron, and I'm sure as shit not patient enough to deal with this fucking team. You can give him whatever excuse you want as to why you were gone, but my personal suggestion is to say you were feeling especially bitchy while you were on your period. Kid doesn't seem to know jack shit about girls.

"Any other questions?"

I stared up at him, still processing the long stream of information that he'd managed to shove into my ears in only a few breaths. I took a moment to think through it all before I realized that he'd been pretty thorough.

"I'm going to be interacting with Jamie for five days? Alone?" I asked, picking out one question that he hadn't already answered.

"Not alone. Can't trust you not to fuck it up. There'll always be at least one person nearby. Probably me, seeing how incompetent everyone else seems to be," he grumbled as he tugged at his hair. "Better get compensated for this shit."

Not that I was eager to disagree with him, seeing as how I could sympathize with being frustrated by the Mediators, but I doubted he was frustrated for the same reason. Besides, Marten was still another Mediator. There was no telling if anything he said was actually true.

"Why weren't you with the team, then, if you're apparently the only capable one?" I asked, trying to poke holes in his story.

"Because that's not my job," he said. "I'm a shadow. The leader, second, and grunts are the ones who deal with the Otherworlder, and I do everything behind the scenes to set them up. Here, I thought Sera was one of the competent ones, but apparently fucking not. Guess she couldn't help but be a fucking teenager."

He glared sideways at me and looked me up and down. The places that his gaze lingered made me want to cringe away and cover myself with my hands. I resisted the urge to cover myself but couldn't stop an uncomfortable grimace from appearing on my face.

"Oh, don't flatter yourself, girlie," Marten scoffed as he looked away. "Might be appealing to a pair of brats, but you ain't anything special."

I said nothing in response, not wanting to dignify him with a reaction. I looked at my dad beside me, who seemed mostly confused and was either too tired or too preoccupied with trying to follow the conversation that he didn't realize that Marten had just checked me out. That was good. I didn't want him getting angry on my behalf right now. While it would feel good to have someone stand up for me, it was neither the time nor place for that.

I couldn't help but wonder if the awkward silence that followed was what Marten was aiming for, to vex me into being quiet. By the time I thought of that, we had already arrived at our destination. The Mediators had moved their carriages right outside the one tavern in our village, and by the way Marten was trudging toward it, I assumed they were inside.

Marten pushed open the door with enough force that it swung against its hinges and slammed against the opposite wall. There weren't many people inside, but the few people who were looked in Marten's direction.

"M-Mr. Marten," the tavern owner stammered. "How pleasant to see you. What brings you to my fine establishment?"

The tavernkeeper was a round man who actually looked pretty similar to Marten, with his balding head and pot-bellied figure, except the tavernkeeper wore spectacles and had much kinder eyes. Currently, those very eyes were looking like they were about to cry. They constantly darted between Marten and Jamie, who was sitting at the corner table with the rest of the Mediators.

"Ms. Arina felt a little sick and wanted a place to lie down for a bit," he said, jerking a thumb gruffly toward my mom, who was still sound asleep in my dad's arms. "And their daughter's here too, I guess."

I blinked in confusion at Marten's terrible acting, but before I could think further on it, I noticed Jamie staring at me, giving me an awkward wave and a smile.

I stared back at him before I felt a light nudge on the side of my arm. Looking back at Marten, he raised an eyebrow at me, nodding subtly toward Jamie.

Taking the hint, I looked back at Jamie and returned the wave. After another nudge, I started walking toward him.

"Hey, Lena!" he said once I got close enough. The greeting was echoed quietly by the Mediators that surrounded him, but not with much enthusiasm. "How's it going? Laush told us that you went to see your parents."

"It was nice," I said. The boy's shy enthusiasm, combined with the reminder that my parents were still right behind me, was enough to summon a small smile to my face. "How are you doing?"

Jamie gave me a careful smile. "I'm alright," he said, glancing sideways at all the Mediators surrounding him.

They all gave him polite smiles, but for some reason, it felt off. Even though their expressions were perfect, as far as I could tell, there was a bit of unexplained tension in the air around them. Tenna and Laush's smiles were slightly strained, and Sera was refusing to look anywhere near my direction. Oren seemed perfectly content as he sipped away at a mug of ale, but his levity stood out awkwardly in contrast to the mood of the rest of the group.

"So what have you guys been up to?" I asked, not knowing what else to say.

Jamie shrugged. "Just hanging out, I guess," he said. "I tried ale for the first time. Not really a fan."

"Really?" I asked. "You've seriously never had ale before?"

"Yeah. They don't let you drink it until you're twenty-one where I'm from," he said. "So, you've had this before, then?"

"Yeah," I said.

"Cool," he replied.

I tried to think of a reply to that, but the atmosphere was a little too awkward to force the conversation forward. Jamie gave me a grimace, likely realizing the same. With the way his eyes darted away from me, it didn't seem like he had the courage or motivation to force the conversation either.

The vague realization that I was still standing while everyone else in the room was sitting crossed my mind more than once, but as I stared down at Jamie, I couldn't be bothered to fix that fact.

"Hey," he said, finally breaking the silence. "Could we talk for a second?"

"Yeah," I replied automatically. "What's up?"

"I meant in private," he said, glancing sideways at the Mediators. "You don't mind, right, guys?"

I nearly raised my eyebrow in surprise but held back, keeping my face blank and stopping myself from glancing sideways at the Mediators to see their reactions.

"Sure," I said as casually as I could.

Jamie smiled at me and stood up from his seat. None of the Mediators moved to stop him. They said nothing as he walked to the side, toward the other corner of the tavern. I spared a quick glance at my dad to see that he was grim-faced, but he didn't say anything as Marten whispered something into his ear. I gave him a slight nod that I hoped was reassuring and walked along with Jamie.

When we sat down, Jamie seemed to be doing his best not to stare directly at me. His gaze wandered from the side to the ceiling, then to his chair as he adjusted it a few times before he finally settled down. He folded his hands together, staring down at the table.

I wondered for a moment if I should break the silence first, but he seemed like he was building up the courage to say something, and I didn't want to interrupt him.

Eventually, after what seemed like a minute had passed, Jamie cleared his throat and spoke.

"Um, Lena. We're... friends, right?"

I nodded. "Yeah," I said, surprised by how easily I could say it and how little it felt like a lie.

"And friends... tell each other things, right?"

"Yeah?" I said, a little confused.

"And you would tell me if anything... bad was happening, right?"

My eyes widened involuntarily. Thankfully, he was too busy looking down at our table to notice, but I wasn't sure it would matter if he did. The way he was talking, while he was trying to be vague, was a clear indication that he knew. He knew that the Mediators were manipulating him.

"Umm," I said, unable to formulate words properly as my thoughts clashed in my mind. "I guess?"

Should I warn the Mediators? Despite their absent morals, they were still the protectors of the world. Jamie finding out that he was being manipulated might have him lash out against them. While I didn't think he would kill them, given his abject horror at the idea of becoming a murderer, there was no telling what a teenager with unlimited power would do in this scenario.

Before I could decide, Jamie grimaced and looked up at me, locking eyes with me.

"Lena," he said, his voice as serious as it was nervous. "I want you to be honest with me."

The way he paused made me think he wanted a response before he continued. Not trusting myself enough to speak, I nodded hesitantly.

Jamie nodded back at me but didn't speak immediately. He grimaced uncomfortably and glanced away multiple times before letting out a sigh.

"Be honest with me," he repeated. "Are you being bullied?"

All the tension immediately left my body, replaced instantly by confusion. I blinked a few times, unable to decide whether I'd heard him correctly or not.

"Excuse me?"

Chapter 34
Friends Helping Friends

"You're being bullied, aren't you?" he asked, this time with more confidence. Though he was still slightly slouched and drawn into himself as he usually was, he stared directly into my eyes, as if daring me to deny it.

"No?" The sheer certainty he had in his eyes made me hesitate for a second. I briefly entertained the thought that he might be right before dismissing the idea. I shook my head. "I'm not being bullied, Jamie."

Jamie's expression didn't change as he looked up at me.

I stared back at him, wondering what the hell was happening. Was that it? Was this the end of the conversation?

"You know, sometimes when something bad happens to you, don't you feel like it's easier to just act like it never happened?"

Apparently, it wasn't over.

"Jamie," I started.

He held up a hand before I could continue. "Let me say my piece first. Please, Lena?"

After a moment of thought, I realized that I couldn't think of a reason to deny his request. I could just stay quiet and let him talk. I needed a moment to think of how to explain my self-isolation from him and the rest of our group without giving away the fact that I was doing it so the Mediators would have an easier time killing him.

I frowned.

"I'm not being bullied," I said.

Jamie smiled at me. It was a sad expression, somehow.

"I care about you, Lena," he said. "It's easy to ignore when bad things are happening around us, and I know you might want to pretend everything's fine, but I don't want to be someone who ignores my friend being hurt."

I grimaced. I knew Jamie was only two years younger than me, but there was a sincerity in his words and his expression that made him look like a child. A naive, innocent, stupid child.

"It's fine, Jamie," I said.

"It's really not," he said.

"But it is," I said. "Sometimes bad things just happen. Sometimes we just need to let them happen for the sake of the greater good."

"What kind of greater good needs people to suffer?" he asked, perplexed.

"The kind where the suffering of others is at stake," I replied, frowning. "The kind where one person's suffering can make sure more people don't suffer an equally terrible fate."

Jamie raised a single eyebrow at me, then a finger, before grimacing as he lost himself in thought for a moment.

"I get how it might feel like that," he said a little hesitantly. "And no offense, but I think you're being a little melodramatic. You being bullied won't determine the fate of the world or anything."

I frowned. I had somehow forgotten that was what we were talking about. I glanced at the Mediators to see if they'd reacted at all. I assumed they had some sort of way to listen in on us, even if they were sitting across the tavern from us.

Jamie followed my gaze and sighed.

"I'm not being bullied," I repeated.

Jamie just sighed again.

"Sorry if I sounded a little pushy. I know how hard it can be to talk about these things. I just wanted to let you know that I can lend you an ear if you want to talk." He peeked up nervously at me to give me a wry smile. "I mean, I get it. I really do."

"I really doubt that you do," I said. If Jamie knew my real internal turmoils, I doubted this conversation would be as civil as it was. He was a nice kid, but I doubted he would casually be trying to console his indirect murderer like this.

I grimaced again at the idea.

"No, really," Jamie continued, blissfully unaware that I was holding a different conversation than the one he was participating in. "I get it. I was bullied too, back in my old world."

Jamie awkwardly scratched at the back of his head as his gaze drifted to the side.

"Well, I wasn't exactly bullied. Not like in the movies, where some jock chooses a kid from the nerd clique to beat up and extort lunch money out of. I guess I was just… shunned? Kind of like what the others are doing to you." He let out a humorless laugh. "Now that I say that out loud, I guess I'm not really as noble as I was making myself out to be. I'm only empathizing with you because when I look at you, I see myself."

I winced as I looked at Jamie's genuinely sorrowful expression. "Jamie, seriously. It's not what you think it is."

"No, I'm serious, Lena," he said, his voice rising in volume and deflating in mood simultaneously. "I know what it's like, and I know how much it sucks. You just keep telling yourself that everything's alright because you think admitting that it sucks will only make things worse. Well, it doesn't, and it won't."

The tavern was quiet, and Jamie's voice was getting loud enough that it could probably be heard by everyone else in it, but he didn't seem to notice.

"Jamie," I called.

He didn't seem to notice.

"The worst part is, now that I'm looking at it from the outside, I can tell that I was just being stupid. These are good people, Lena. I don't know why everyone's excluding you, but I know that if you just talked to them, they'd probably talk to you too. I don't think they hate you. They just don't really know you. It's not like they're punishing you for existing, but you gotta stop thinking like they are," Jamie said, looking back at me. He tried to give me a smile, but it was shaky. "I think you're really cool, Lena. I'm sure if you talked to everyone, they'd realize how cool you are too."

I looked away, unable to face his earnest gaze. He stayed silent, waiting for an answer.

"Umm, thanks," I said. "But I'm serious, Jamie. I'm not being bullied."

Jamie frowned and sighed.

"I understand," he said. "Just know that if you ever need someone to talk to, or if you ever need my help, I'm always here."

I shook my head.

"No. Listen to me, Jamie. I'm not being bullied. I just happen to dislike every one of the Mediators we traveled with," I said, hoping that it would be a good enough explanation to stop him from spiraling further into this conversation. "It's as simple as that."

Jamie gave me a sad smile.

"I get it, Lena. I used to think that I hated everyone too. But we don't need to talk about this right now. Just know that I'm ready to talk whenever you are."

I sighed. It didn't seem like anything I did would convince Jamie of the truth. At least not right now. I didn't know if it was even necessary to do it. If Jamie thought I was unhappy traveling with him and the Mediators, would that make it more or less likely that he would let me stay in Plainswood when they left?

"Alright," I said. "I'll talk to you if I need to."

"That's all I ask."

He smiled at me, but I couldn't muster the will to smile back. He seemed so happy to have "helped" me that a pang of guilt struck me—and struck me hard.

"You can talk to me about your problems too," I said. "You know. If you want."

Jamie blinked a few times, as if he'd never considered the idea before.

"Thanks, but I don't have problems," he said, his voice a little flat.

I'd seen him cry too many times to know that wasn't true, but I wasn't going to push him.

"Well, if problems ever do come up, just let me know. I'm ready to talk whenever you are," I said, deflecting his own words back at him. "Alright?"

Jamie nodded. "Alright. But I really don't have any problems. At least not after coming here. I guess my life back at home wasn't the greatest, but that's over now. I'm fine."

He didn't sound fine, not in the slightest, but again, I wasn't going to push him to talk about it.

"That's good," I said.

"It is," he replied, a little too quickly. "I mean, I know I never had friends before, but now I have you! And Oren and Sera. Tenna and Laush are nice too. Oh yeah, and magic exists! That's a thing."

Jamie let out a laugh. It wasn't a happy one, devoid of any humor or life. In the corner of my eye, I saw the two conscious non-Mediators, my dad and the tavernkeeper, flinch at the sound.

"Jamie..." I said.

"Yeah, it's been really good, even if it's been pretty crazy," he said, ignoring my attempt to interrupt him. "But now I have everything I ever wanted. Magic, friends, adventure. I guess it feels a little weird, especially since this all happened so fast. I mean, sometimes, I can't help but think this is all just some weird dream and I'm going to wake up in a hospital bed with the doctor saying that I've been in a coma for a few weeks. You know?"

I had no idea what he was talking about. He was speaking too quickly and gasping for air too frequently for me to make sense of what he was saying before he moved on to something else. He was taking quicker and quicker breaths, and though he wasn't quite hyperventilating, he seemed pretty close to it.

"I don't know what to do. What am I supposed to do? How do I make sure that this is real? I don't want to go back. I'm good here. I don't want to go back."

Yup. This was definitely not the behavior of someone who was "fine."

"Jamie."

He kept talking, making no indication that he'd even heard me. His words were getting more muddled, and it was getting increasingly difficult to make out what he was saying.

I reached out and touched his elbow. That seemed to get his attention as he looked up at me.

"Jamie. Can you feel me touching your elbow?"

"Y-Yeah," he said, still struggling to catch his breath. He looked down at where my hand was touching him, as if he needed to see it to confirm it anyway.

"I used to get pretty bad nightmares when I was a kid," I said. "They were usually about some weird nonsense that could never really exist, but whenever I was in them, they did feel real. My mom always told me that if I'm having a bad dream, I can always try to scratch myself on the shoulder because you can't feel physical sensations in a dream. Is it like that for Otherworlders too?"

Jamie nodded shakily. "Pinching."

"Pinching?" I asked.

"We pinch ourselves to make sure we're not dreaming," he said. "Not scratch."

I tried to give him a smile. "Why don't you try that out?"

Jamie nodded and pinched the flesh above one of his wrists. He winced.

"That hurt," he said.

I nodded. "Do you still think you're dreaming?"

He looked up at me. He was still taking gasping breaths, but they weren't nearly as shallow and rapid.

"N-No," he said.

"That's good."

Jamie's deep breaths were the only noise that filled the tavern. I was tempted to glance to the side to see the reaction from the civilians or the Mediators sitting in the room, but I didn't want to break eye contact with Jamie. He was getting better, but he didn't seem completely convinced yet, so I simply locked eyes with him until his breathing slowed down to a level that didn't make me as worried.

Once he stopped gasping for air, I asked, "Are you okay?"

Jamie grimaced and looked away, blushing an angry red.

"Yeah," he said. "Sorry for freaking out."

"I told you to stop apologizing so much, didn't I?" I tapped his elbow once more before drawing away from him. "It's not your fault you freaked out."

"It is, though," he said, scoffing. "I'm just mentally weak."

"You literally travelled to an entirely different world, Jamie. And I don't know exactly how you did it, but I can guess from context clues that it wasn't exactly a pleasant process, either. It's normal to feel stressed."

Jamie looked up at me and made a quiet noise that sounded like something between a laugh and a sigh.

"That's funny. I thought I was supposed to be consoling you," he said, though his voice held no humor. "Guess I still can't do anything right, even in an isekai world."

"You're fifteen. Name me one fifteen-year-old who isn't a complete fuck up. You can't."

Jamie groaned. "This wasn't what we were even supposed to be talking about! I didn't want your help; I wanted to help you! We've barely even talked about your bullying problem."

I let out an involuntary laugh. Jamie's eyes shot toward me at the sound, raising his eyebrows in a perplexed expression. I didn't know why, but his reaction just made me laugh more.

"What?" he said.

"I'm serious when I say I don't have a bullying problem, Jamie," I said, standing up and gesturing for him to follow. "I'll prove it too."

"What?" he said again.

"Come on," I said. "We'll kill two birds with one stone, shall we? I can introduce you to my friends, and you can see a few teenagers who are much more of a mess than you are."

As the words left my mouth, I thought about the fact that I'd just condemned my friends to talking to an Otherworlder. From Bran's last encounter with Jamie, I realized how badly they would probably handle it.

But Jamie was nice enough. Surely it would turn out fine. Besides, I needed some payback for how Bran abandoned me when I first brought Jamie to the village.

"Let's go," I said.

Chapter 35
A Normal Conversation Between A Couple of Teenagers

"Uhhhhhhhhhhh."

I gave Bran a wide grin as I waved at him from outside his doorway. Beside me, Jamie did the same, though he wasn't as enthused.

"Hey Bran," I said.

"Muhhh."

"A hello would be nice, Bran," I said, enjoying this more than I probably should have, considering Bran looked like he was about to piss himself from fear. Actually, on second thought, I was enjoying the exact amount that was appropriate.

"Guh."

"Hello," Jamie said, giving Bran another shy wave.

"Bah?"

I couldn't help it. The dumbfounded shock in Bran's face made me feel a bit cruel for bringing Jamie over unannounced, but the stupid sounds he was making were too much. I burst out laughing, clutching at my stomach and crouching down to the ground.

"Lena?" Jamie said, though I could hear the hint of a laugh in his voice.

"Oh, fuck you, Lena," Bran said. Apparently, sheer indignation was enough to snap him out of his fear.

I gave him a wide, shit-eating grin as I slowly caught my breath.

"Bran, this is Jamie. You've met before," I said, gesturing to him.

"We have?" Jamie asked.

"You don't remember?" I asked back. "You thought he was making me cry, and you almost made him piss himself? Ringing any bells?"

"Oh," he said, wincing. "Sorry."

"Don't worry about it. It was hilarious in retrospect," I said.

"Not that hilarious for me," Bran grumbled. "Also, speaking of things that aren't funny, what the fuck is going on right now?"

"I'm introducing Jamie to my friends," I said. "Be honored that you were the first."

"Pretty bold to assume we're friends, you bitch," he replied.

"See?" I said, turning to Jamie and gesturing at Bran, who still looked like he was somewhere in between wanting to kill me and wanting to run into his house and bar the door. "I have friends."

"Your friends talk like that to you?" Jamie asked.

"Like what?"

"He just called you a bitch," Jamie said, giving Bran a pointed glance. Bran only just seemed to remember that he was still there, and with Jamie's attention on him again, he panicked.

"No, I didn't," he said, a little too quickly. "I hold my good friend Lena in very high regard and would never disrespect her so callously."

I laughed again, but it died down when I saw the conflicted grin on Jamie's face. It was a strange expression, like he found Bran's reaction to him somewhat funny but still felt guilty about it at the same time.

"Just a little bit of banter. He's not actually insulting me," I said, patting Jamie on the shoulder. "And Bran, stop being so scared of Jamie. He's a friendly guy once you get to know him."

Bran nodded furiously. "Nice guy. Me too. I'm also friendly. And uninteresting and naïve."

I groaned and slapped my palm to my face.

"What's he talking about, Lena?" Jamie asked.

"It's an Otherworlder response thing," I said. "Not really that important, but a good example of the other reason why we came here. Behold, an eighteen-year-old boy who's also the stupidest person I know and also the future sheriff of Plainswood. You still think you're not allowed to be a fuck up?"

"A sheriff?" Jamie asked. "Like with a star badge and guns and stuff like that?"

"Woah. You guys can make stuff out of stars in your world?"

"Wait, he knows that we know he's from another world?" Bran interrupted.

There was a brief moment of pause as Jamie glanced between me and Bran.

"Umm," Jamie said as he struggled to think of an answer. "Yes?"

"Yes to what, exactly?" I asked.

"Yes to your friend's question," Jamie said. "Not to the star thing. The badges are made out of metal, but they're shaped like stars."

"Oh," I said. "Why are they shaped like stars?"

Jamie shrugged. "It was just a thing that sheriffs had on Earth. I don't know why."

"Well, I don't think I've ever seen the sheriff wear a badge at all, though I guess it's a bit pointless in a small village like ours. Everyone knows who the sheriff is, so there's no point in a uniform or anything. That's why Bran can get away with dressing like a bum all the time."

"Hey!" the boy in question shouted. "I'm right here!"

"Good. Means you can hear me. You should freshen up once in a while. Whenever you stand next to Polly, it looks like she's a princess tending to a large, mangy dog."

"I'll have you know, she likes my rugged charm. Plus, she said she likes the contrast. Makes her stand out even more or something."

"I knew there was a reason she would be dating someone like you. I was beginning to think she was half-blind or something."

"At least I can get a girlfriend. How's your love life been?"

I winced, and—to his credit—Bran was quick to react to the fact that I didn't snipe back at him immediately. He glanced up at Jamie, who I was pointedly doing my best to ignore, and gave him a shaky smile.

"Well, enough about that. Ryuji Nightblade, was it?" he said.

"Umm, no," Jamie replied, sounding a little embarrassed. I spared a quick glance at him and was surprised to see him blushing. "My name's Jamie."

"Really?" Bran asked. "I swear you said your name was Ryuji back when you first came to Plainswood."

"Can we please forget about that?" Jamie asked, almost pleading.

"Umm. Sure," Bran said. All of the stutter and uncertainty had gone out of his voice by now, and he was sounding more curious than afraid. Maybe our bantering had brought him back into a more comfortable mindset, but it was also possible that Jamie's shyness had disarmed him somewhat. "So, are you guys going to go around visiting more people?"

"That was the plan," I said. "Why? You're that eager to see us gone?"

"No," Bran said. "I want to come along, if that's alright with you."

I raised an eyebrow at him.

"Not that I mind, but why?" I asked.

Bran glanced between Jamie and me a few times before sighing.

"Because you're terrifying," he said. He held his hands up defensively before we had a chance to respond. "Our friends are going to get scared if you come over unannounced like you did with me. It might be nice to see a familiar face to assure them that they're not going to get blown up or anything."

"I'm not a familiar enough face?" I asked.

"You're a Follower, Lena," he replied. "Nobody knows what a Follower really does, but they always survive being close to Otherworlders for God knows how long. Your stakes are a little different than the rest of us."

Before I could reply, Jamie spoke up.

"I'm not going to blow anyone up," he said quietly.

Bran frowned and crossed his arms. "It might be stupidity talking, but I believe you. It's the only reason why I haven't pissed myself yet. That and the fact that I just went a few minutes ago. I know we didn't talk much, but you feel different now. More human. But nobody else remembers what you acted like when you first came to our village. All they remember are the goblins you killed in the town square."

Jamie frowned at that. "I didn't kill anyone. Those were demons."

Surprisingly, Bran nodded. "Yeah, we know. Mr. Mar—"

His words were cut off by a yelp of pain as he clutched at the side of his head. He whipped his head around a few times before he seemed to notice something. His eyes widened for a second before he looked back at Jamie, smiling and desperately trying to pretend like nothing had just happened.

Turning around, I noticed Marten leaning lazily against the wall of another house, just far enough that I probably wouldn't have recognized him if it weren't for the reflective sheen of his head. Jamie looked around too, but without knowing exactly what he was looking for, he didn't seem to notice anything strange.

"You okay?" Jamie asked.

"Yup. Totally fine. Anyway," Bran said, continuing the conversation with the subtlety of a hacksaw. "We realized that they were demons after we dug up their graves and couldn't find anything but black ash. But even with that, most people still don't actually believe that they were demons, and a lot of the rest don't care either way. You were pretty brutal. It was hard to watch."

Jamie frowned. "Sorry. I was working some stuff out."

Bran raised his hands in an awkward surrender.

"Hey, as long as you don't work some stuff out against me or the villagers."

Jamie nodded. "I don't plan to."

"Then we'll have no problems," Bran said.

There was a long pause in the conversation, but before I could do anything, Jamie was actually the one to break it.

"Lena? I know you wanted to introduce me to all your friends, but could I make a request?"

I didn't know what kind of request he would make, but his words were awkward and forcefully formal for it to be something benign.

"What is it?" I asked, a little afraid of what it would be.

"Can we put that off for a bit?" he asked. "I want to see the graves as soon as possible."

I waited for him to continue, but after a long pause, it was clear that was all he wanted to say.

"Is that all?" I asked, just to make sure.

"Yeah..." he said. "Is that... okay?"

I glanced to the side where Marten was still standing. Though he wasn't looking in my direction, I knew he was listening in on the conversation. If it wasn't okay, I assumed that he would give me a signal of some kind.

When none came, I looked back at Jamie, who was just barely looking at me.

"Sure, that's fine, Jamie," I said. "We can go."

Jamie smiled at me and gave me a nod of thanks.

I turned to Bran, who was looking at me strangely for some reason.

"I know it's not what you expected," I said. "But since you were gonna come along anyway, you mind guiding us to where you buried the demons?"

Bran stayed silent for a few seconds, glancing between me and Jamie.

"What the hell did you do to the poor kid?"

I raised an eyebrow.

"Excuse me?"

"He acts like a newborn kitten around you. Listen, Jamie. Best way to deal with her is either to ignore her or insult her back. You can't let her walk all over you like this."

"I didn't do anything, you ass," I said, punching Bran in the shoulder. "Just because you're a rude barbarian doesn't mean that other people can't be quiet and polite. It's just how he is."

"Really?" Bran asked. He sounded annoyingly skeptical, like he genuinely believed that I'd done something to cow Jamie into politeness. But then again, maybe he did. No matter how docile Jamie acted, he was still an Otherworlder. It was hard to believe that someone with near infinite power could seem so timid and unconfident.

"Yeah," Jamie said, scratching the back of his head. "I'm just kind of like this."

Once again, Bran stared at Jamie silently for a few more seconds.

"Okay, fine. But one last question," he said. "But it might be a bit sensitive. You don't have to answer if you don't want to."

"Umm, okay," Jamie replied.

"And I'm sorry if this is rude in any way. I don't really know Otherworlder customs, so I'm hoping I don't offend you or anything. I'm just really curious about one thing."

I raised an eyebrow, wondering what he possibly could want to ask. Jamie did the same, though he seemed a little more pensive than I was.

"I'll try not to get offended," he said. "I swear."

Bran stared into Jamie's eyes, as if searching for the truth in them. Whatever he saw, he seemed satisfied.

"Do you actually eat children if they don't do their chores?"

Before I could smack my face in exasperation, I yelped in surprise as Jamie fell to the ground instantly, planting his face onto the floor with his legs bent crooked in the air.

"What the fuck?!" Bran and I shouted simultaneously.

Jamie groaned, though it was muffled from the fact that his face was planted directly into the ground. "Goddamn anime character constitution," he said. "I almost forgot about this."

Bran glanced at me, as if asking for an explanation, but while I'd heard him reference the condition whenever he got his nosebleeds, this was a new behavior to me too. I answered Bran's unspoken question with a shrug.

Bran nodded and simply reached down to help Jamie up.

"What the hell was that about?" he asked.

Jamie let out a heavy sigh as he reached up to take Bran's hand. "It's a thing I have. Makes me do weird things. I didn't realize face plants were included in that."

"The hell's a face plant?" Bran asked.

"It's kind of like a facepalm," Jamie answered, sighing deeply. "Except the floor is my palm."

"Seriously?"

"Yeah."

Bran looked at me, but I didn't have anything to add to the conversation. I shrugged.

"Sounds rough," Bran said.

Jamie shrugged as well. "I don't actually get hurt. It's just annoying to get dust in my clothes every time."

"Oh yeah, I guess you being an Otherworlder makes your face harder than the floor, huh?"

"I guess."

Jamie glanced between Bran and me, waiting for either of us to say something. Thankfully, he seemed to realize that he'd effectively killed the conversation and coughed awkwardly into his hand.

"I guess we should head to the graves? Please?"

"I guess so," I said. "Lead the way, Bran?"

"Sure," he said, walking forward, though he made sure not to walk far enough that he couldn't keep an eye on Jamie. Instead of following the roads, he immediately veered off the streets and headed toward the forest.

Jamie and I followed him without question.

Another long silence sat between us before Jamie spoke up once more.

"But just to be clear, I don't eat kids."

"Noted," Bran said.

Chapter 36
FRIENDS

"I mean, we don't exactly have Otherworlders where I'm from. I guess the closest thing that we have is the bogeyman."

"Oh yeah? And what's this bogeyman do?"

"I'm not actually sure. Now that I think about it, I've never heard any specific stories about the bogeyman."

"Why's that?"

"He's more just a concept, I think. Probably just something that parents say to their kids to get them to do something, if I had to guess. I'm sure he's from some obscure European folk tale, but I can't say for sure."

"What's that?"

"What's what?"

"European. I assume it's either a country or a language."

"Oh, yeah. I keep forgetting I'm not on Earth. Europe's a continent, actually. There's a whole bunch of countries there, and they speak a whole bunch of languages."

"Like Astrantan?"

"What's Astrantan?"

"The language we're speaking?"

"What? We're speaking English, aren't we?"

As the two boys talked while we walked, I let out the breath I'd been holding as the conversation finally shifted away from the topic of

Otherworlders. While it was admittedly a little comforting to think that Bran and Jamie had become comfortable enough with each other that they didn't consider the topic taboo, it still felt better to move on to something a little more mundane.

"Maybe it's just magic," I suggested. "I mean, Jamie has that whole anime constitution thing, and he's got an infinite amount of mana. What's to say he doesn't have some weird magic thing that lets him translate stuff too?"

"Wait. Does something like that really exist?" Bran asked. Jamie looked at me too, obviously curious about my answer.

"How would I know?" I asked.

"Because you just said it did?" Bran asked. "Besides, you're a mage. You know about magic stuff."

"I'm hardly a mage," I scoffed. "I'm just a magic user."

"What's the difference?" Jamie asked.

"A mage is a title given to someone who can actually use magic well," I said, shaking my head. "A magic user dabbles in it. Anyways, I was just throwing out ideas. Magic can let you do some pretty weird things as long as you have the mana for it. I'm sure translation magic could be a thing."

Bran furrowed his brow. "Aaasssshiiii vvvaaatiiiviii."

I raised an eyebrow and looked to Jamie to see if he had any idea of what Bran was doing, but he looked just as confused as I was.

"That's nice?" Jamie asked, more than said.

Bran laughed awkwardly, looking pointedly off to the side. "Just checking if it really was a magic translation thing. I guess you were right, Lena."

Jamie still looked absolutely confused, so I decided to help him out.

"Bran just said something in another language, I think. I couldn't understand it, but I assume you did?" I asked.

"O-Oh," Jamie said, his stutter returning for some reason. "Yeah. I did. Sorry. I just didn't expect that."

Bran laughed, scratching his cheek in embarrassment. "Don't worry, Jamie. I don't see you that way. Just wanted to test it out. It means, 'I love you,'" he added for my sake. "It's the only Timuran I know."

"That was Timuran?" I asked. The slow and lethargic way that Bran said it contrasted with my preconceived idea of Timuran being a harsher-sounding language, but I wasn't familiar enough with how it usually sounded to doubt it outright. Maybe Bran was just stretching it out for dramatic effect.

"Yeah," Bran said. "Polly taught me."

"Polly knows Timuran?" I asked.

"She doesn't know much." Bran shrugged. "She became friends with a traveling merchant during one of her visits to Redstone. He taught her a few phrases."

"Umm," Jamie said, raising his hand for some reason.

He paused. Bran and I glanced at each other before looking back at him.

I noticed a blush on Jamie's face, even with how badly he looked like he wanted to hide his face deep within his hood.

"You didn't say, 'I love you,'" he muttered. "You said, 'I am an incredibly annoying woman.'"

Ah. So that was why he had looked so confused. I chuckled as Bran flinched away from Jamie like he'd just slapped him.

"No, that can't be right. It means, 'I love you,'" Bran said, his mouth twisting into an awkward grimace. "We say that all the time. In public. It's our thing! You're just joking. Right, Jamie?"

Jamie's only response was a shaky smile.

I laughed as Bran groaned, hiding his face in his hands.

"Goddammit," he said.

"Sorry," Jamie replied.

"Not your fault," Bran sighed. "You apologize a lot, you know that?"

"I keep telling him that," I said, looking around us as we started to enter the denser parts of the forest. I was surprised by how deep the villagers had decided to bury the demons. "Are we getting close to the graves?" I asked.

"I think so," Bran said, taking the excuse to look around and direct his attention at anything aside from Jamie. "Mr. M— I mean, the gravedigger made sure to mark the area with some paint. It shouldn't be hard to see."

In a few minutes, Bran proved himself right by pointing out several splashes of bright blue paint smeared over a large number of trees. They were applied very liberally, with more focus on being seen than accurately pointing out where the graves were located. Even with the general area marked down, we had to search around for a few more minutes before we stumbled across the graves.

"Is this really it?" Jamie asked.

His skepticism was justified, as the "graves" looked like nothing more than a few dirt mounds with nothing to mark them. Even if they only contained the remains of demons, it still felt pretty disrespectful. I glanced at Bran for an explanation.

"Nobody really wanted to acknowledge what happened," he said, avoiding my gaze. "People kind of just wanted to forget. So we tried to make sure it didn't become a landmark."

"Then why the paint?" Jamie asked.

Bran's eyes widened for a split second before he smiled nervously.

"I'm not sure?"

Jamie stared at him for a few seconds before turning his attention back to the graves.

"I'm gonna dig them up," he said. "Move earth."

I'd already realized about halfway into our walk that we hadn't brought shovels with us, but Jamie didn't seem to be too bothered by it. He simply closed his eyes and raised his hands up in the air. I should've seen it coming, but I still yelped and fell back on my ass when the ground shook beneath my feet. Thankfully, my dignity was saved when I saw Bran on the floor beside me.

I was surprised at how cleanly Jamie managed to dig up the graves. Despite how violently the ground had shaken, all that ended up happening was a few clumps of dirt floating up and landing softly in neat piles beside each grave.

Ignoring Bran's awestruck look, Jamie moved forward to peer inside the graves, but he stopped at the first one, staring into it with a blank expression on his face.

Curious about what he could be seeing to cause such a reaction, I peered into them alongside him.

They were empty.

"I don't know what I expected," Jamie said, his voice flat.

"They're empty. The Aether must've dissipated by now," I said. "Isn't that what you wanted?"

"I mean, yeah? I guess? But the graves being empty doesn't necessarily mean that they were always empty, right? For all I know, this could be a fake grave, and some very real goblins could be buried somewhere else. An empty grave doesn't prove anything."

I raised an eyebrow. I wasn't surprised that he'd come to this conclusion. It was the exact same conclusion I might've come to if I were in his situation. I wondered, however, where this level of skepticism had been when he was dealing with the Mediators.

"It doesn't," I said. "But I know what I saw. You didn't kill any goblins. You just destroyed some demons and scattered their Aether to the wind. Can you trust me when I say that?"

"I trust you," Jamie said, but he grimaced when he turned to face me. "But that's not enough. What if you were wrong? I need to prove it. Sorry."

"That's fine, Jamie. I wasn't trying to challenge you. If this is really that important to you, then you shouldn't just take my word on it," I said. "That being said, how are you going to prove it?"

Jamie furrowed his brow in thought.

"Maybe I can use some magic to see if there were demons here," he said.

"You can do that?"

"I can try," he said, giving me a shaky grin that he didn't seem too confident in. "Translation magic exists, so why can't a 'detect demon' spell exist?"

I was about to protest when I realized he was right. Jamie was an all-powerful being. While the idea of such a nonsensical and convenient use of magic existing was absurd, so was the idea of Jamie's very existence. I saw no real reason to believe he couldn't accomplish it before he actually tried it.

"I guess it could..." I said, trailing off.

Jamie waited for me to continue, but I simply shrugged. Apparently taking that as a vote of confidence, he closed his eyes and raised his hands.

"Detect demon."

At first, it looked like nothing happened, but with Jamie keeping his eyes closed, I assumed it meant he wasn't done. He kept his hands up, hovering them over the empty graves.

About a minute in, Bran pointed off in the distance with his mouth opening and closing like he was trying to say something. Following the path of his finger, I noticed a few faint pinpricks of pulsing red light floating gently toward us like leaves caught in an unnatural wind.

I was so focused on the ones that I could see that I flinched when a pinprick of red light floated directly past my ear. I jerked my head around to see that we were surrounded.

"Umm, should we be worried?" Bran whispered to me as he ducked under a small red light that passed by his head.

Bemused by his naivety, I gave him a sympathetic pat on the shoulder.

"Even if something bad were happening, we'd have no way to stop it," I whispered back. "So my suggestion is to just stop worrying about it."

Bran stared at me like I'd said something crazy, though he couldn't keep his eyes from darting around to look at the red glowing lights that flew lazily around him.

"I don't think I can do that," he said.

I shrugged and turned back to watch Jamie.

As the red lights continued to float gently toward Jamie, they piled up inside the once-empty graves, melding together as they converged to the same spot, until the seven graves were occupied with formless blobs of pulsing red light.

They didn't remain formless for long. As Jamie furrowed his brow, his fingers twitched and closed into fists. The blobs moved at his command, twisting and morphing until they seemed to adopt a robust shape.

Once they were done, Jamie opened his eyes to look down at the goblin-shaped blobs of light.

"So, did it work?" Bran asked.

Jamie didn't react to the question for a few long seconds, simply staring down at the pulsing goblin-shaped lights. When he did react, it was with a sigh and a smile.

"Yeah," he said. "Turns out I can do anything I put my mind to. I'm pretty broken, aren't I?"

"No."

Jamie and Bran turned to me, and for a split second, I couldn't figure out why. It took me a moment to realize that I was the one who'd said that.

"No?" Jamie asked, a smile still plastered on his face.

That damn fake smile of his. Among all the liars I knew, Jamie was the worst one of them all.

"No," I said, gritting my teeth. "You're not broken. Don't you dare say that about yourself."

Jamie tilted his head in confusion, and the scared look on Bran's face helped me realize I was raising my voice at an Otherworlder.

"Lena," Jamie said. "It's alright."

"No!" I said again, not caring at all that I was yelling. "No, it's not alright. I don't know what happened to you in your previous world, and I know it must've been terrible for you to see yourself like how you do, but you're not in that world anymore! You're in a new one, and a much better one at that! Yeah, yeah. I know I don't know anything about your old world aside from the fact that it has video games and anime, which I still don't understand at all, by the way, but the fact that your old world could possibly leave such a sweet, innocent, dumb kid like you feeling like you're so lonely and unconfident and broken means that it can't possibly be one worth caring about."

"Lena," Jamie said quietly. "Seriously—"

"Shut up!" I said, angrily wiping away the tears that were forming at the edges of my eyes. "If I hear one more vague hint about your depressing backstory, I swear I'm going to beat the crap out of you, infinite power or not. I know you're too nice to fight back, so you can't fucking scare me."

I didn't know what I sounded or looked like, but it couldn't have been pretty, from the way that Bran looked like he was more scared of me than he was of Jamie. Jamie's reaction was a bit more subtle than Bran's, his fake smile slowly melting off his face into a blank expression.

"Don't you dare say you're broken. Never again, Jamie Nightblade."

Jamie stared blankly at me, and the world was quiet, save for my panted breaths and the quiet crunch of dry leaves on the forest floor as Bran tried to slowly back away from me. I glared back at Jamie, silently daring him to say anything.

And then he started to laugh.

It started small at first. He let out a few muffled giggles that he immediately tried to cover up by placing his hand over his mouth. It worked for a moment, but as his laughter grew, it spilled between the cracks of his fingers and echoed through the trees surrounding us. It didn't stop, growing in strength until he bent down, clutching at his stomach and doubling over from the sheer weight of his emotions.

Jamie gasped for breath as it left him, faster than he could inhale, in peals of ecstatic laughter. More than once, his breath caught in his throat and he coughed and sputtered as he fell on the floor, but he didn't seem to care as he continued to laugh.

By the time he'd calmed himself down, he was filthy and covered in foliage and dirt, laying down on his back on the forest floor, but he didn't seem to notice as he struggled to wipe away tears from his eyes, his hands still shaky from the heaving giggles that were still escaping his body.

"Lena," he said, still giggling. "My name's Jamie Campbell. Did you seriously think Nightblade was my real last name?"

I sighed, feeling my frustrations slowly bleeding out of me in the same breath. While I didn't particularly enjoy being mocked, I found it difficult to stay angry at him. Though he had his arm over his eyes, the laughter in the air and the genuine smile on his face were infectious.

"Hey," I said. "How was I supposed to know? You never told me."

"Even so," he said, interrupting himself with another giggle. "Jamie Nightblade. Imagine."

"How the hell am I supposed to know what's normal in your world?" I said, bending down to lightly flick him on the forehead.

"Ack," he said, flinching at the touch. "That surprised me."

"Serves you right, Jamie Campbell," I replied.

"I guess it does," he said, giggling again for some reason.

He moved his arm away from his face and looked up at me from his position on the floor. The entire upper half of his face was stained with the marks of half-dried tear stains, and his eyes were bloodshot and puffy, but there was a childish joy reflected in them now that hadn't been there before.

"You're pretty broken. You know that, Lena?" he said.

I frowned, raising my fist. "Jamie Campbell," I said, as threateningly as I could.

He laughed and raised his arms to defend against the blow that would never come. "No, no. It's slang from my old world! It means that you're overpowered enough to break the rules of the game."

It took me a moment to understand what that meant. My fist dropped limply to my side.

"Wait," I said. "So when you were calling yourself broken..."

"I wasn't being down on myself?" he said, completing my thought for me.

I stared down at him and that shit-eating grin of his and groaned into my hands.

"I blew up at you for no reason! Why didn't you stop me, you little bastard?"

"I mean, I tried," he said with a laugh. "Not my fault you wouldn't let me talk."

I groaned again. Jamie laughed at that and finally found the strength to stand back up. I couldn't help but think he looked taller for some reason, and it took me a moment to realize he just wasn't slouching as much.

"Hey, Lena," he said.

"What?"

"Sorr—" He paused and shook his head. "I mean, thanks."

I sighed again but gave him a smile.

Chapter 37
Performance Review

"Fucking creepy fucking bastards, the lot of you, creeping me the fuck out with your dead-fish fucking eyes. The very least you dipshits could do is do your jobs properly for once in your fucking lives to make up for it, but here I am, stuck with a bunch of incompetent asshats who can't escort two children from one city to this shithole of a village without fucking literally everything up. Too bad you're all fucking orphans, because now it's apparently my fucking job to wipe your asses for you instead of your inbred fucking parents."

To say that Marten was upset would be a bit of an understatement. He couldn't drink on the job, and though he'd stashed a month's supply of tobacco on his person before he'd been teleported out of the main base, he made the same mistake that he always did—assuming that a month's supply would last him a month in practice.

After finding out how badly the rest of his team had fucked up, he'd managed to smoke through two weeks' worth in only a few days, and the fact that he had managed to post himself in the middle of fucking nowhere made sure that any tobacco he could buy here would be next to worthless.

Unfortunately, even if the only tobacco he could find in this backwater town tasted like he was smoking a mixture of grass, dust, and just a hint of cat shit, he had to make do with what he could. He wasn't addicted, but tobacco staved away the worst of the piercing headaches that wracked his brain if he went without it, and he was already dealing with too many living headaches to afford the extra pressure.

The headaches in question sat in silence as he drew a spell circle on the floor of the mayor's cellar in the middle of the night while the brat was fast asleep. While he could've waited outside and had a moment of peace for himself while Sera or Oren drew it in his stead, he wasn't willing to leave anything up to chance. With their recent history of astronomical fuckups, he wasn't willing to run the risk of them either accidentally blowing up the building or trying to fuck it.

Marten took in a large draw from his pipe as he double-checked his formulas, blowing the smoke out in the general direction of his so-called peers in an act of petty revenge. It didn't do much, given that the entire cellar was filled with his tobacco smoke already, but he did feel a little bit of petty satisfaction when he saw Oren blinking rapidly as the new smoke tickled his eyes.

"This ain't a fucking shadow's job, dipshits. Why the fuck do I have to be the one to do this? Better get some fucking compensation for this shit," Marten grumbled, mostly to himself, as he inspected the circle for a third time. Once he was satisfied that it wouldn't kill any of them, which was a bit of a disappointment, he jerked a thumb toward it.

"Alright, assholes. I'm done. Get into positions."

Without acknowledging him, the Mediators moved to the edges of the circle, standing in their respective positions. Even after working on and off for more than twenty years as a Mediator, he still found their silence unsettling but not enough to dampen his anger toward them in the slightest.

Marten let them stand there for about a minute longer while he finished his pipe. Even though it was shit tobacco, it was tobacco that he'd paid for, and he'd be damned if he let a single pinch go to waste.

Besides, the little bastards deserved to stand there and think about how much of a pain in his ass they'd been. Maybe feel some damn shame for once in their lives.

When the only thing that remained in his pipe was ashes, he tapped it against the wall to empty it and stowed it away in his breast pocket.

He considered giving them a warning but decided against it, simply stepping into his place in the circle and leaking out a drop of his mana.

The spell formula reacted as soon as he did. He grimaced involuntarily at the sensation of weakness that flooded him as it greedily sucked more out of him, but the others had it worse. Without any proper warning, they let out quiet gasps of pain as their mana was drawn from them forcibly, with the exception of Oren, who made no reaction aside from the minuscule tightening of his facial muscles.

Marten scowled. He pulled a piece of parchment from his pocket and metaphysically reached out to touch the mana gathered in the spell circle.

The mana of the five mages was wild and untamable. Each mana signature collided and contrasted with the other, creating a whirlwind of chaos that was only barely contained by the spell formulas that helped refine them into a form usable for a greater purpose.

He hated the sensation. Though there was no physical feeling of pain, it felt like he was touching the essence of danger and potential. He wanted to get it over with as soon as possible, and so he guided the mana into the piece of parchment, or more specifically, the essence of the message written on it.

The essence of the message melded with the mana, and with one final push, he focused on the one-fifth of the mana that originated from himself, forced his will onto it, and finally released it from his grasp.

Marten gasped and stumbled backward as the spell was completed, just barely unable to regain his footing before he fell on his ass. Around him, the other Mediators had similar reactions to varying degrees. Tenna and Laush collapsed on the spot, crumpling into unmoving piles of limp limbs within their spots on the circle. Sera and Oren took the aftereffects of the spell better than he did. Sera was bent over, supporting herself with her hands on her knees. Oren stood with his arms crossed across his chest but was drenched in sweat, his nostrils flaring as he took in deep breaths to steady himself.

Marten took a few deep breaths, but before he could completely recover, a strange sensation wormed its way into his mind. He felt the urge to stick a finger in his ear to dig out the non-existent bug that had made its way inside of him and was buzzing around in his brain.

Is it true?

Marten grimaced as the voice of his boss echoed in his head and started to scratch at his skin.

"I appreciate the fast reply, bossman," Marten said out loud. Though he was entirely capable of speaking back through internal dialogue, his mind was already crowded enough by the newcomer and he didn't care enough to keep his side of the conversation private from the fuckups. "It's all true. I'm requesting that the entire team be replaced. Either that, or you can reassign me. Preferably somewhere across the world. If you keep this team as it is, the brat they're in charge of is definitely gonna explode. I don't want to be anywhere nearby when that happens."

"Sera and I are Chosen Followers," Oren said. "You will not be able to replace either of us, Shadow Marten, no matter how displeased you are."

Despite his exhaustion and the buzzing in his head, Marten couldn't help but grin. "Oh yeah, he's right, boss. That's true. We can't have him leaving the Otherworlder's side." Marten gasped as he held a finger up, like he'd just thought of an idea. "Wait a minute! There is a way to make sure you stick around but without giving you the same amount of responsibility, isn't there? We could demote you!"

He almost laughed at how quickly Oren's stone mask of a face cracked wide open, his normally stoic expression breaking off into a vicious scowl. Off to the side, Sera grimaced but seemed more defeated than angry.

Enough.

Marten grimaced and grabbed at his head as the concept of scorn echoed and pulsed loudly in his mind.

Do not fight. It is unbecoming of you.

"Sure thing, boss," Marten grunted. "We'll play nice."

Marten gave Oren a rude gesture and reveled in the raw anger that was reflected in the normally stoic man's face. While he knew that the boss could probably read his thoughts, he also knew that trying to hide anything from an immortal being was probably impossible anyway, so he might as well try to enjoy it. Thankfully, the boss didn't seem to care.

The contents of your message concern me, but the details were lacking.

"There's only so much a handful of mortals can do, bossman," Marten said. "Don't know how it is for you elves, but we were pretty limited in the amount we could send. But you've got me now. Not like I'm holding anything back."

He flashed Oren another smile, though it seemed like the giant had finally wised up to the fact that he was being played with. He simply closed his eyes and returned his expression to its default neutral. A flash of annoyance ran through Marten, but before he could mutter some obscenities at Oren like he wanted to, the buzzing ran through his head, growing louder and then stopping suddenly.

It cleared his mind and let him focus on what was truly important.

The Second wasn't important. He would be dealt with appropriately if necessary. Marten's true concern lay in what damage had already been done to the lost lamb. Marten knit his brow in concentration as he recalled his past few days of overseeing the lost lamb separated from his flock.

It had been a long few days, where Marten had tailed the child—the alien brat, the untethered soul—to watch over his steps on the path to further salvation, judging. Marten thought of how the lamb interacted with the world around him as he grew closer to salvation, and he felt love in his heart.

What?

Marten *panicked* and felt a warmth spread through him as he flipped through his memories like a book, stopping on every page as he fondly recalled how the lost soul wandered through this life, once aimless, then given a purpose, *freaking the fuck out*, and now, walking the path to true salvation. Or possibly not. Marten was simply a stepping-stone for the lost soul, and perhaps he wasn't leading him to the soul's ultimate destination, but H*h*H*e* would gladly act as the guiding light for the next step in his journey.

As H*h*H*e*, Marten, the shadow, He pushed through his memories, He saw the soul through the shadow's eyes and wept, in happiness, in sorrow, in reverence for the task He had. The soul was burdened, troubled, tainted by this mortal world, and he would need to be cleansed, helped, *HELP*, helped to grow before he could pass on into the arms of salvation.

But it was not yet to be. He mourned, for He could see that the soul was not ready. The soul was not ready to *let go of me*. The soul was not ready to reach salvation yet. But it would be. With time. Such was His love, that He was ready to guide the lost soul or administer punishment by His hand, so he could learn. He did not know yet what the soul would need. But He would. With time.

Please, please, please.

Ah, yes. Though the disdain for the tainted mud of this mortal world grew within Him, He knew He could not dismiss them. Mortal as their broken souls were, the pieces here were still a part of the immortal tapestry that made up the world, the journey of His children, the ground that the lost lands tread and grazed upon. He would need to release the shadow.

Oh, thank you, thank you, thank you.

He sighed, growing tired of the noise in the head of the tainted mud. Reaching within it, He grasped at the memories of the frozen moment and plucked them away. He stirred the tainted mud one last time before finally retreating from—

Marten shook his head and groaned as the moment passed him. He smacked the side of his head, as if he could physically knock the buzzing out of his ear, but stopped once he realized that the feeling was gone. Was the boss satisfied with what he'd seen?

He waited for a response, but no response came. Well, though it didn't beat cold, hard coin, he supposed it was nice of the boss to give him a bit of service for his troubles. He dug at his ears once more to clear out the phantom itch he felt in them before recalling the instructions that the boss had given him.

He smiled viciously.

"Well, well, well," he said, turning to Oren specifically. "Finally, someone listens to sense around here. Turns out, the bossman is a smart guy, even if he did somehow manage to hire you incompetent fucks. Oren, Sera. Congrats on the promotion. You're grunts now. Laush, Tenna. You'll be sticking around as extras for now, since we've got a lot of unfucking to do, but the bossman told me that he'd be sending a replacement leader and second soon."

Marten frowned as the words left his mouth. Did the boss ever tell him that? He must've. Why would he have said that if he hadn't?

Marten smacked his ear again. They didn't feel like they had anything in them, but he did it again. Just because.

Chapter 38
PROGRESS REPORT

"So, how's your progress with the brat?"

I looked up at Marten from my breakfast as he stood at the entrance of our kitchen, casually standing there like he hadn't just barged in unannounced. Sitting on either side of me, my parents gave him a death glare but remained silent otherwise.

"I guess Mediators don't know how to knock," I grumbled, mostly to myself, before swallowing the piece of bread that I'd already chewed off. "Can't this wait?"

"Nah. But I'm not so cruel that I'll take breakfast away from anyone," he said, strolling across the kitchen and grabbing a piece of bread from the basket on the counter. "You can eat while you talk."

I sighed but got up despite his offer. "My appetite's ruined anyway," I said.

"Where are you going?" my mom asked, grabbing my sleeve before I could get too far from the table.

"Just outside the house, Mom," I said. "I assume we're going to talk about stuff that you two aren't allowed to hear."

I wasn't sure that was true, but I didn't want my parents listening in on our conversation regardless. Marten raised an eyebrow at me but didn't seem to care enough to protest.

"Fine, fine," he said. "Outside it is. We're coming back in if it starts to storm, though. Clouds are getting pretty bad, and I'm not going to get rained on if I don't need to."

Gently shaking my mom off me, I walked out of the house, not bothering to acknowledge Marten until I heard him step outside with me.

"I was serious about the rain," he said, taking a bite of his bread as he looked up at the dark sky. "One drop and we're going back in."

I looked up at the sky. Judging by how bad it looked, I wouldn't be surprised if it rained in the next ten minutes. I wondered if that would be enough time.

I sighed.

"Pretty heavy sigh you got there," Marten said. "You holding up alright?"

"Your character's breaking," I said. "Weren't you supposed to be a rude asshole?"

"I can be pleasant if I damn well please," Marten grunted, giving me a shrug. "I don't play characters. It's beneath me."

"Oh yeah?"

"Why would I want to change perfection?" he asked, brushing a large handful of breadcrumbs off his stubble.

I raised an eyebrow. "I don't think I've ever seen you make a joke either. This seriously doesn't suit you."

"It's called a good mood, girlie." He looked up at the sky, reaching into his shirt pocket to pull out a pipe. "And I don't really give a shit what you think."

"Then why are you here?"

Marten gave me a glare but was quick to follow it up with a chuckle.

"Fair enough," he said, shaking his head with a wide grin. He took a puff of his pipe and tilted his head back to blow the smoke up into the sky. "You got me there."

I didn't know what his game was. Was he really just in a good mood?

"Honestly, if you think this new personality of yours is endearing, it's not. I preferred it when you were an asshole. At least then I didn't have to worry about letting my guard down."

Marten simply shrugged.

"Sorry," he said. "I am who I am. Always have been. Can't change that."

"Hard to believe that when you belong to an organization filled with liars and manipulators. You haven't convinced me that you're not the same, and this is just making it more obvious that you are."

Marten sighed out a large cloud of smoke. He stared down at his pipe, inspecting it like it was a foreign object that had suddenly appeared in his hand without warning. After a few more seconds of quiet introspection, he held out the pipe to me.

"You smoke?" he asked.

"No," I responded.

Marten stared at me for a few seconds before turning his pipe upside down and tapping the still-burning ashes of his tobacco onto the floor and stomping it out.

"Don't feel like it today, for some reason. Head's feeling a lot clearer than usual," he said, stowing his pipe back into his pocket. "Shame. Guess it's going to waste—not that I'll miss it. I'm almost convinced you mix gravel into the shit you sell in this shit town. I'll be glad once I'm out of this shithole and back to proper civilization."

I didn't know how to react to that, so I didn't. Marten didn't seem to care about my lack of reaction as he looked back up into the sky.

"Our organization is a lot of things," he said. "We are liars and we are manipulators, yes. But we do what we need to for the good of the Otherworlders."

"Bullshit," I said, crossing my arms.

Marten didn't seem upset by my reaction, simply shrugging.

"Not my job to convince you."

"You're right. Your job is to manipulate and lie to a kid to make him do what you want," I said. "For the good of the Otherworlders."

He shrugged again.

A tense silence fell between us, though Marten didn't seem to care. He was still looking up at the sky, like he had been for the majority of our conversation.

"So," he said. "What are you stalling for?"

I flinched involuntarily at the question. "What?"

Marten glanced at me and fixed me with an unimpressed look.

"C'mon, girlie," he said. "My job involves me interacting with my colleagues who are, as you say, liars and manipulators. It would be cute if you actually thought you could get away with hiding it, but I'll assume you didn't."

I grimaced. Off in the distance, thunder rumbled.

"So?" Marten continued, not letting me have the few seconds to gather my wits. "What is it you don't want to say? What happened in the past three days that I don't know about? And I'll have you know, I know everything that's been going on, except for what goes on in that little head of yours. So spill it."

Before I could think to speak, rain started to fall, the first drops accented by the distant rumbling of more thunder. Marten frowned up at the sky and sighed as he pressed himself back against the wall of my house. I did the same, and though the eaves of the roof protected us from the rain, it wouldn't be long before we were soaked. The wind was howling, and though the rainfall wasn't that bad yet, it looked like it would get much worse soon.

"Do you want to go back inside?" I asked, glancing back at my house, where my parents were no doubt waiting anxiously for my arrival.

"I do," he said. "But you don't. Just get it over with so I can leave."

I frowned, but seeing no other way to delay the inevitable, I sighed and spoke.

"Would I be allowed to stay as a Follower?"

Marten glanced at me and raised an eyebrow. It wasn't quite the large reaction I expected, but the judging look was enough for me to look away from him, refusing to meet his gaze.

"I thought you hated being a Follower," he said.

"I do," I protested, a little faster than I wanted to. "I just... I feel bad for Jamie. I want to make sure he's treated right."

"And you don't trust us to do that? Treat him right?" Marten asked, with no real heat behind the words.

"No," I said as frankly as I could. "I don't."

Marten didn't seem offended by the admission in the slightest. He simply shrugged and looked up at the sky, his face already wet with rain.

"And you've set your mind on this?" he asked.

"No," I replied. "I haven't made a decision. I just want to know if I would be allowed to do it without being assassinated in my sleep or something."

Marten gave me a hard look.

"You would be allowed to continue on as a Follower, without being assassinated for it, as long as you have approval from the Mediators. That was always allowed."

I gave him a nod.

"That was all I wanted to know," I said. "Thanks."

The rain had quickly grown into a deluge, each raindrop hammering at the ground with an intense fervor, creating large splashes of mud wherever they landed.

"What changed?" Marten asked.

"Not much, to be honest," I said. I had thought about the question for too long to not be ready to answer it. "I mean, looking back on how we first met, it's pretty obvious in hindsight that Jamie's just a kid. I mean, yeah, he was a bit of a weird idiot when he first got here, but he was in a new environment and didn't really know what was going on.

But especially after the last few days I've spent hanging out with him and some of my friends... I guess once I realized he wasn't someone to be feared, I also realized he was just hurt and lonely."

"I see," Marten said.

I waited for him to continue, but as he stayed silent, I could tell that he was being pensive for some reason.

"Do you know about Affection ratings?" he asked.

I raised an eyebrow, wondering how that was relevant in any way.

"Do you mean how some people like to judge a person's appearance and rate them out of ten?" I asked. "I'm not really into that kind of thing."

"No, not that," Marten replied. "Back in Redstone, you told Sera about how the Guide would occasionally tell you that your affection level was going up. Do you remember this?"

"Oh." It hadn't happened in a while, so it wasn't the first thing that came to mind when Marten brought it up, but it wasn't hard to remember. "Yeah, I remember."

"There was an Otherworlder that we dubbed as the Harem Lord," he said. "Not many people outside of the Mediators know about him, since he died several centuries ago. He wasn't alive for long enough that he could do widespread harm, but he's one of the largest cautionary tales we have in our organization. To keep it short, he had the power to turn any woman he fancied into a soulless doll that he would add to his little harem. A lot of Mediators and some civilians had their minds irreversibly altered into thinking that they loved him to the point that when he passed on, they committed mass suicide."

The rain was heavy enough that if I deluded myself enough, I could almost convince myself that I hadn't properly heard what Marten said. It was the heaviest rain that I'd seen in a long while, and a small part of me was focused on how sheets of water fell from the roof of my house, creating a wall of water as it poured off the eaves in front of where Marten and I stood. The sound of it hitting the ground was rapid, erratic, and deafening, and it took me a while to separate it from the pounding of my heart in my ears.

"What? You're joking, right?"

Marten gave me a flat look, not bothering to answer me before turning his attention to the rain with a frown.

"Jamie wouldn't do that," I said, more quietly than I expected to. "He's a good kid."

But did I actually think that, or was I being coerced into thinking that?

"For what it's worth, I agree with you," Marten said. "The brat's a dumbass, but that's really all he is. He's too dumb to be malicious."

I could barely register the reassurances as I thought about the possibility that I wasn't in control of my own thoughts.

"Why didn't anyone tell me?" My voice barely came out in a squeak, drowned out by the sound of rainfall.

"We expected you to leave," Marten said, taking out his pipe again and filling it with tobacco. "You were forced into this life for a while, and we didn't want you to think about whether your mind was permanently altered while leading your civilian life after you left. But now that you have the freedom to actually make a decision, it's only fair that you know everything that might affect it."

Marten pressed his finger into the pile of tobacco that he'd made. The grains bloomed red with tiny embers, and he took a long draw out of it.

After blowing the smoke out into the air, he held the pipe out to me. "Calm your nerves?" he asked.

I looked at the pipe for a second before nervously plucking it from his fingers. I doubted it would do much, but at this point, I needed anything I could get. Holding it to my lips, I could only take half a shaky breath before I bent over and let out a hacking cough, almost dropping Marten's pipe in the process.

"Tastes like cat shit," I said, once I found my breath again. "Why do people smoke?"

Marten let out a quiet chuckle before nodding quietly.

"We talked to the boss last night." He reached over to pluck the pipe from my still-shaking fingers. "We're getting a new leader and a second teleported to us soon, probably by tonight. Once they get here, you'll have to get the new leader's approval if you make the decision to stay, but I'm sure they'll be reasonable if you want more time. It's a big decision. I suggest not rushing into it. Take your time."

He patted me on the shoulder twice, and before I could react, he stepped forward into the rain. Seemingly not caring about the same rain he'd been complaining about not too long ago, I could swear he was whistling a jaunty tune as he made his way away from my house.

"Fucking asshole."

I doubted he could hear me over the thundering rain, but it still felt a little good to get the last word. Just a little bit. I looked down at my shaking hands and clenched them in an attempt to stabilize them, but all that achieved was to make my entire body shake instead. I folded my arms around myself in a half hug before turning around and walking back to my house.

I fumbled with the doorknob at the entrance a few times before I let out an angry groan.

I hated this. Fuck taking my time. Maybe the Mediators had been right to hide this from me, just like they hid things from the rest of the world, but I didn't care what was wrong or right at this point.

All that mattered was that I knew, and I sure as hell wasn't going to let this rot and fester for any longer than I needed to.

I pulled the door open long enough to yell through it and nothing more.

"I'm going out!" I shouted into my house before letting the door slam shut and marching into the rain, toward the tavern where Jamie was staying.

Chapter 39
Confessions

The tavern was relatively empty, but not as empty as it had been a few days ago, possibly due to the fact that I'd been showing Jamie around the village for a few days, giving the villagers the opportunity to get used to him. Seated at the bar, Old Tom, the general store owner, was hunched over, nursing a drink and what I assumed was a bowl of soup or cereal. Just behind him, a handful of younger boys whose names I could barely remember sat around a table, trying and failing to pretend like they weren't immensely interested in what was going on at Jamie's table at the other end of the room.

Nobody but the tavernkeeper looked in my direction as I walked through the door, even as the howl of the storm outside announced my arrival. I was dripping wet and splattered with mud, shivering despite the fact that we were in the middle of summer, but I didn't hesitate to walk toward Jamie.

He didn't hear me approaching, busy with his breakfast platter and talking to Oren about something, but I didn't wait for him to turn around and notice me.

"Jamie."

He flinched at the sound of my voice and turned around immediately, acting more surprised than I expected him to be.

"Lena?" he said, blinking a few times as he looked up and down at me. "You're soaked."

"Yeah, I guess I am." Having reached the extent of my patience for small talk at the moment, I jerked a thumb behind me. "Can we talk?"

Jamie looked confused but nodded, scooting his chair over a little bit to clear some space for me.

"I meant alone."

"Oh. I guess we could move to another table, if that's okay?" Jamie half-asked Oren, who just smiled back at him.

I sighed and shook my head. "More alone than that," I said. "You're renting a room here, right? Can we go there?"

While I assumed that the Mediators would listen in no matter where we were, this wasn't a conversation meant for civilian ears. I glanced over at the group of eavesdropping boys with my eyes, and Oren gave me a nearly imperceptible nod of permission.

Oren let out a loud laugh and reached over to clap Jamie on the shoulder. "Whatever this is about, it looks important," he said. "Go, my brother. Your breakfast will still be here when you get back."

Jamie gulped and nodded. Satisfied that he was going to follow, I turned around and started walking toward the tavern's rooms.

Though I and every other person in my village liked to visit the tavern at least occasionally, not many of us had any reason to rent a room. They were only ever used by merchants who wanted to stay in town for a few days to peddle their wares or the occasional traveler who just wanted a roof to sleep under for a night, but even though I wasn't familiar with them, I at least knew where they were.

Opening the door at the side of the tavern, I walked into the hallway behind it.

There were three doors to the rooms. I didn't know which one belonged to Jamie, so I simply stood and waited for him.

He didn't immediately follow behind me, pushing open the door and hesitantly peeking inside. I raised an eyebrow at him and opened my mouth, but I didn't trust myself not to come off as abrasive if I told him to hurry up.

"Which one's your room?" I asked instead.

"The one at the far end," he replied, almost too quiet to hear over the pounding of the rain against the roof above us.

I nodded and walked over to pull the door open. Looking inside, I was surprised by how small the room was. It was square and barren, with no furniture other than a single bed pushed up against the wall that took up the length of the entire room. I supposed there wasn't a reason for it to be bigger, and I quickly decided it wasn't important. We didn't need space to have a conversation.

I was about to walk inside, but when I turned to Jamie, he seemed frozen on the spot, with a look in his eyes that looked either fearful or excited. I couldn't tell which.

"Come on," I said, giving up on trying to coax him gently. While his shyness could be endearing at times, I couldn't help but be a little frustrated here. "It's important."

Jamie nodded frantically, and though he was still hesitant about it, he started to move toward me. I made way for him to enter the room first and let the door swing shut behind me as I followed.

Immediately, we were faced with a problem. While the room was just big enough that it would probably be comfortable for one person, we both wouldn't be able to stand without sacrificing our personal space.

"Do you want to sit down?" I asked, gesturing to the bed. "This room is too small to have us both standing, and I don't want to ruin your bed with how wet I am."

Jamie's eyes widened. "You're wh—" he cut himself off as he looked me up and down, watching the rainwater still dripping off my clothes and hair onto the floor. Shaking his head, he quickly turned around and sat down on the edge of his bed, pointedly looking away from me.

I didn't know why I was making him uncomfortable, but I didn't want to waste any time trying to figure out why.

"Jamie, I'll get straight to the point," I said, not giving myself the opportunity to hesitate. "I'm sorry for interrupting your breakfast for this, but I need to get this off my chest."

Jamie's eyes widened, and he looked up at me. His lips were pressed into a thin line, and it looked like his eyes were about to pop out of his head. I frowned.

"What's wrong?" I asked. His reaction was a bit too severe to ignore.

"Nothing!" he shouted. The sudden shift in his volume startled me, especially with how small the room was. He grimaced, as if realizing it too. "I mean… Please continue."

"You're sure?" I asked.

Jamie nodded frantically. His eyes were still wide and wild, and the way that his foot was now frantically tapping against the floor made it obvious that it wasn't true, but I didn't want to try to coax whatever was bothering him if he wasn't immediately open to sharing—especially since I didn't want to give myself the excuse to avoid this conversation for any longer than I should.

"Well, in that case… I don't know if this is the right time for it, but I've been keeping secrets and hiding my true feelings for too long and I'm sick of it. If I don't say this now, I don't know when I'll be able to say it again."

I took a deep breath to steady myself.

"Your existence is absolutely terrifying."

Jamie's foot tapping stopped. He stared up at me like he didn't know how to react.

"I know I've told you this already," I continued, not giving myself the opportunity to stop. I feared I wouldn't be able to start again if I did. "And I know you feel guilty about it even though you shouldn't and even though it's not your fault. You're a good person, Jamie, and I've learned that, but whether you're a good person or not doesn't mean I'm not afraid of the power you have. Unimaginable power, Jamie, more than enough to manipulate the mind of a stupid girl from the countryside."

I leaned down to stare Jamie in the eyes. The excited nervousness that I'd seen in them before was gone now, replaced by something I couldn't identify.

"Jamie," I said, my voice cracking slightly. "Are you brainwashing me?"

"What?" he asked. "What are you talking about?"

His reaction gave me hope. Jamie was a lot of things, but receiving godlike power hadn't turned him into a good actor. Even so, I couldn't be satisfied with just this.

"I know about the affection points, Jamie," I said. "What are they?"

Jamie seemed confused for a moment, but after a few seconds, his eyes widened and he grimaced.

"You know about that?" he asked.

I didn't bother to answer the question.

"Please, Jamie," I pleaded. "I don't have many goals in life. I know that you might not relate to that since I know you have some grand dream of becoming an adventurer. All I want is to have a peaceful and happy life, but it has to be my life. Please tell me I'm still me."

Jamie frowned and looked away from me.

"I'm not brainwashing you, Lena," he said, sighing. "The affection points are something else entirely."

"What are they?" I asked.

"It's a level of how much I like you," he said. He spoke surprisingly clearly, when I would've expected this topic to normally send him into a mumbling mess, but his voice was flat and emotionless. "It's at the max level, by the way. I already like you so much that I can't like you any more than I already do, apparently."

"Oh," I said, lacking words.

"You already knew, I assume," he said.

"Kind of," I replied. "I didn't know it was at that level, though."

"Well, now you do," he said. "How long?"

"How long what?"

"How long have you known?"

"Since the first day we met," I said. "You couldn't stop staring at my ass."

Jamie cringed at that, and his frown deepened.

"Sorry," I said.

"Why are you apologizing?" he asked.

"I'm sorry for bringing it up," I said.

An awkward silence fell between us, filled with nothing but the ambient sounds of the heavy rain pounding against the ceiling above.

"Well, now that it's out in the open," Jamie said. "Lena, I like you. Would you be my girlfriend?"

I looked down at him. His voice was still flat and emotionless, and he didn't even look at me while he said that. From what little I could see of his expression, his mouth was drawn into a thin line and his eyes looked glassy and fogged over.

"I'm sorry," I said.

"Bad timing?" he asked with half a smirk.

I tried to chuckle at the joke, but Jamie's smirk fell off his face as quickly as it had appeared.

"I just don't think I'm attracted to men," I said.

"Oh," he replied.

I half expected him to say something else, but Jamie remained silent, simply staring down into his lap.

"Sorry," I said.

He shook his head. "Don't apologize for that," he said. He stared at his lap again for a few more seconds before raising his arms and pretending to yawn and stretch.

"Oh wow," he said. "I didn't realize how tired I was until now. I guess I didn't get much sleep last night. You know, the beds we had in the tents were actually better than the ones the tavern provides. If it weren't raining so hard, I probably would've just slept outside."

It hadn't rained the previous night, but it wasn't difficult to understand where he was going with this.

"You're tired?" I asked.

"Yeah," he said, stretching and yawning again. "I think I'm gonna nap for a bit. Would you mind telling Oren and the gang to finish breakfast without me? I'll come out when I'm ready."

"Sure thing, Jamie," I said. "For what it's worth—"

"Please," Jamie said, interrupting me. "Don't."

"Sorry," I said. "I'll leave you be."

He nodded and lay down, turning so his back was toward me.

Seeing that there was nothing I could do that wouldn't make it worse, I slowly backed out of the room, making sure the door wouldn't slam shut too hard when I left it.

I sighed.

"That could've gone better," I said, mostly to myself.

"It had to happen sometime," Sera said from down the hall. "I think it went as well as it could've."

I stared at her. She gave me an awkward wave and a smile.

Chapter 40

NEW ROUTES

"That was very stupid of you."

"Hello to you too," I said.

Sera didn't budge from her spot, standing between me and the door to the rest of the tavern.

"You had no way of knowing whether you had your mind altered or not. Confronting him could've triggered him to kill you on the spot."

"Well, I'm alive, aren't I?"

Sera sighed. "I was worried."

Assuming she was done with what she wanted to say, I nodded. "Sorry for risking your mission," I said.

Sera gave me an awkward expression halfway between a grimace and a smile and stepped to the side, inviting me to step back to the tavern.

I didn't see any reason to stick around, so I took her offer, pushing past her to walk back to the crowded tavern.

"So you're gay?" Sera asked, following quickly behind me.

I shrugged.

"I'm not sure," I said. "I don't think so."

"So you lied?"

I tried to see if there was any judgement in the question I could detect, but Sera's voice had gone unnaturally flat, making it impossible to find anything there. Regardless, I couldn't find it in me to care if I was being judged or not.

"No," I said. "I said I wasn't attracted to men. Nothing about me liking women. Besides, why do you care?"

"I suppose I shouldn't," she responded.

I waited for her to continue, but when she didn't, I just shrugged and continued to walk toward the door leading out of the tavern.

"You're not staying?" Sera asked. "It's really bad out there."

"I'm aware," I said, flapping my still-soaked arms up and down to make a point. "But it's not like it could get any worse. I can only get so wet."

Sera's eyes widened. "You're wh—" Sera interrupted herself to scrunch up her face in a pained expression. She released it a few seconds later and seemed content to pretend like she'd never reacted in the first place.

"It's still terrible out there," she said instead. "The winds are strong enough to send branches flying. It would probably be safer to stay at least for a little bit."

I gave her a blank stare and scanned the rest of the tavern floor. With how hard it was storming, I wasn't surprised that the clientele hadn't changed at all within the past ten minutes. It was just the tavern-keeper, Old Tom, the group of boys who, with Jamie gone, were now gawking openly at me, and the Mediators.

"I think I'd rather chance the walk," I said. "Better than staying here, at the very least."

Sera frowned, but before she could speak, the door to the tavern burst open.

"Alec! Have you seen Lena around here?!" my parents shouted simultaneously as they clutched at each other, huddling together for warmth in their rain-soaked clothes.

I sighed and hung my head as the tavernkeeper gestured uselessly toward me. I wouldn't be going home, after all. Judging from the mud splatters and debris stuck onto my parents' clothes reaching up to the tops of their heads, it seemed like Sera hadn't been exaggerating how bad the storm had gotten. While I was willing to risk my own life by going outside, I wasn't willing to risk the lives of my parents.

"I guess I'm staying," I mumbled, half to Sera, mostly to myself, before my parents came over and swept me up in a soaking wet hug.

"Lena! We were so worried!" my mom said.

"You could've at least said bye to us face to face," my dad added.

"Please, Lena. We can't afford to lose you. Not again."

I sighed as I pushed the two of them back. They seemed hesitant to let go of me, but I was grateful that they did.

I didn't want to tell my parents that I'd made the decision to go with Jamie when he left Plainswood, to make sure that his last days were as pleasant as they could be. I doubted I would ever be fully prepared to have that particular emotional confrontation, and especially after having just finished with one just a few minutes ago, I knew that I wouldn't be able to get my words out right now.

"Sorry," I said. "But I'm tired. Can we just dry off and have breakfast or something? I'm starving."

My parents looked at each other, and they both looked like they had more to say, but whether they were afraid of pushing me too hard or they were just as hungry, tired, and cold as I was, they seemed hesitant to continue scolding me as much as they'd planned.

My dad sighed.

"Alec," he said. "A warm meal, please. And some towels, if it's not too much to ask."

"You guys are completely soaked. A few towels probably won't do much."

My parents turned to Sera, who waved politely at them from a few feet away, confusion clear on their faces.

"It would probably be best if you got a fire going," she continued, seemingly unbothered by their reaction. "Alec. Do you have any firewood?"

The tavernkeeper shook his head. "I'm sorry," he said quietly, as if he was torn between answering the question and trying to disappear. "Most of it's in the storeroom, and it's probably soaked. We've got just enough to keep the kitchen running for the rest of the day, but not much more."

Sera nodded. "Kitchen it is," she said. "Come on, Lena and parents. Let's get you dried up. You'll all catch a cold at this rate."

Even though the tavernkeeper seemed to want to protest, he bit his tongue, clearly awed enough by Sera's status to let her do whatever she wanted. In contrast, my parents seemed to be unaware of the fact that Sera was a Mediator and were either too tired or too convinced by her innocent appearance to pick up on the context clues surrounding them.

"Excuse me," my mom said. "This is all very kind of you, but who are you exactly?"

"I'm..." Sera paused, glancing over to me.

I didn't know what she was expecting of me, but I didn't care. I shook my head.

"Please don't drag my parents into this," I said.

Sera gave me a sad smile. "I wasn't planning to," she replied. "Believe me or not, I really am just concerned. I won't say another word if you don't want me to, but you need to dry off or you'll all catch a terrible cold."

I frowned, but as I tried to search Sera face for any hint of insincerity, I quickly reminded myself that it was a futile battle. Regardless, it was hard to deny the truth in her words when I could barely keep myself from shivering long enough to glare at her properly.

"Fine," I said before I started walking to the kitchens.

I'd been back here a few times as a kid, when we were at the right age that we were still disarmingly cute and old enough that we could be trusted not to stick our fingers into sizzling skillets of food. The tavernkeeper's son, also named Alec, would invite us into the back whenever there weren't enough customers around for his dad to be bothered by it. It hadn't changed much, if at all, aside from the fact that everything looked a lot smaller than I remembered and a little more cramped.

The smell of the histories of past meals floating around the air, alongside the pleasant heat of the burning fires, was enough to lull me into a sense of calm almost immediately.

Sera squeezed past me, brushing my arm as she moved forward to pull out a stool and two crates for me and my parents to sit on. She placed them right in front of a cooking hearth with a couple of pots hanging over the fire that raged inside. Though I was starting to feel my nose both congest and run from the cold, the strong smell of the different stews still flooded my senses, making my mouth start to water.

"Thank you," my mom said politely, though she was obviously still confused by her presence.

I had the urge to tell my mom to stop thanking her, but I resisted. Sera wasn't technically doing anything wrong, even honoring her promise not to say anything, and I had to admit that it was nice of her to do this for us.

"Thanks," I muttered.

I saw Sera's eyebrows shoot up for a brief second before they returned to a more neutral position almost instantly.

As the tavernkeeper entered the kitchen, towing a large armful of towels with him, Sera took them and handed them out to the three of us. My dad still seemed pensive and confused by the apparent stranger who was taking care of us, but my mom had seemingly decided to accept her presence with a genuine smile.

"Thank you," she said again, but with a bit more confidence this time. She gave me a questioning glance that I decided to ignore, turning my eyes away from both her and Sera and staring at the flickering flames dancing inside the hearth.

"Yeah, thank you," I said. "You're a good friend."

I wasn't sure if that was the right thing to say in this situation, but I didn't want to deal with whatever their reaction would be to know that Sera was a Mediator, and I felt it was a harmless enough lie to tell. As far as they knew, she'd been nothing but kind. I would explain to them later that she shouldn't be trusted, but for now, I wasn't above reaping the benefits of her hospitality.

The clatter of metal knocked me out of my thoughts, making me flinch violently and whip my head around to identify the source of the cacophonous noise. I was surprised to see Sera wincing as she struggled to decide between picking up the pans she just knocked to the ground or running away.

In the end, she decided to pick up the pans, though she made sure to turn away from me first.

"I'm sorry," she said, breaking her vow of silence. "The new Mediators will be teleporting into the mayor's basement tonight at midnight. You're welcome to join or sit out as you wish."

As Sera exited the kitchens, I could only catch a glimpse of her face, but what I saw confused me.

Guilt.

I wasn't sure why she would put on such a face, but before I could think more about it, my mom gasped.

"That girl was a Mediator?" she said, almost reverent in the way that she talked. "Was she one of the ones that brought you back to us?"

"Yeah," I said, still too confused by Sera's reaction to give my mom a proper answer.

"She seemed sad," my dad said.

I frowned. I wasn't sure if it was a question or not, but I couldn't help but agree with what he said.

"Yeah. She did."

I reminded myself that I knew what Sera was. She was a manipulator. I wasn't so naïve to think that I was somehow special, that I would be able to see through her manipulative ways if she used them on me. I was very much aware that my intense desire to go talk to her might have been an idea that she planted in my mind.

But even if she'd somehow influenced me into thinking this way, they were still my thoughts.

I sighed.

"Fuck it," I said. "I'm already this deep in this shithole. Might as well dig a little bit deeper just to see where it goes."

"Language, young lady," my parents said, chastising me simultaneously.

"Sorry."

Chapter 41
An Exchange of Trust

As soon as I pushed open the door and walked out of the kitchen, I walked over to Sera, who had already taken her place at the Mediator's table once more. She had her back to me, but I didn't feel the need to tap her on the shoulder to draw her attention since I expected she knew I was there already.

"Hey," I said. "Could we talk?"

Without turning to me, Sera motioned to the seat beside her, the one Jamie had been sitting in just a few minutes before. I glanced at the rest of the Mediators, though none of them seemed to care about my presence at all. They simply stared forward or closed their eyes with neutral expressions on their faces, now that there wasn't an Otherworlder to perform for.

"Alone?" I asked.

That caused Sera to finally turn around, raising a perfectly arched eyebrow at me.

"You sure about that?" she asked.

"Why wouldn't I be? I don't want these assholes to listen in."

"Us assholes have ears too, you know," Tenna said, opening his eyes to glare at me for a second before closing them again and slipping back into his meditative posture.

"We can move if you want," Sera said, ignoring Tenna. "Your parents are still in the kitchen?"

"Yeah," I said. "I asked them to stay put."

"Would you like them to join us?" Sera asked.

"Why? Afraid to be alone with me?" I asked. I had meant for my question to be a joke, but my tired and humorless voice didn't help convey that in the slightest.

"I'm not," Sera said. "But you should be. A manipulator's main goal should always be to isolate their target from anyone they might feel close to. Make them feel like they can only rely on you. Rule number one in the manipulator's handbook."

"Oh," I said, uncertain of how I should be reacting to the admission. "Well, I don't think it applies here. If you haven't noticed, I'm trying to take you away from your friends, not the other way around."

Tenna scoffed, proving that he was pretty terrible at meditating, but Sera ignored him again and sighed.

"I assume you don't want your parents listening in on whatever it is you want to say?"

"There's a reason I asked them to stay behind in the kitchen."

Sera frowned but nodded as she rose from the table.

"We can go to the corner of the room," she said.

"Not somewhere else?" I asked.

"The rental rooms here don't have very thick walls," Sera said. "The Otherworlder would be able to hear us."

I wanted to point out that there was a door behind the bar that led to the tavernkeeper's house, but I doubted that Sera didn't already know that.

I shrugged. If she wanted us to stay in a more public space, I wasn't going to deny her.

"Sure," I said.

Sera stared at me for a few seconds, as if doubting the fact that I'd agreed to her suggestion, but she eventually chose a corner of the room to walk toward.

"Just make sure to keep your voice down," she said. "You are terrible at whispering."

"I'm not that bad," I said, somehow feeling a little bit offended at the comment.

"You are," she replied, with the ghost of a smile on her face. I wasn't sure if I'd imagined it or not.

Neither of us said anything else as we walked to the furthest table away. It wasn't a long walk, but the brief lull in conversation easily translated to a long stretch of silence after we sat down. Sera looked at me but seemed determined not to make any eye contact whatsoever, choosing to stare somewhere above my shoulder instead.

"So you have a guidebook on how to manipulate people?"

Why did I choose that as my opener? Sera glanced at me with a slightly raised eyebrow, as if silently asking me the same question.

"It's more of a manifesto," she replied.

With how flat her voice was, I had no idea whether she was joking or not. I tried to crack a smile, just to test her reaction, but her face remained unsmiling and blank.

I felt my expression fall back to one that probably matched hers. An awkward air washed over us, but as Sera broke eye contact once more, looking at that same spot above my shoulder, I decided that there wasn't really a point in trying to stall anymore.

"I still don't know if you're manipulating me," I said. "But if you are, you don't need to do it anymore."

Sera stared at me, her expression betraying no emotion whatsoever.

"What brought this on?" she asked.

I shrugged.

"I already confronted Jamie directly about the affection points," I said. "And you were right. It went about as well as it could've. Thought I might just do the same thing with you. I know it's not the same thing, since you've been pretty upfront and obvious about how well you can manipulate people, but I thought we could just show all our cards right now. Or at least I could show you mine."

Sera remained expressionless. "What do you mean by that?"

I paused for a moment to think, not sure how to explain myself properly.

"I know that, for how terrible you Mediators are, you're only this manipulative because it's the only way you feel like you can achieve your goals. Going off that, the only reason you would want to manipulate me is if you feel like I could somehow ruin that. If I take away that reason, you have no reason to be anything but honest with me."

Sera frowned and crossed her arms.

"So you're saying you'll cooperate with us," she said.

I nodded. "Just tell me what you want and I'll do it. No need to trick me into doing anything or to think a certain way. Just give me an order and I'll follow it."

"Why?" Sera asked. "I thought the idea of killing the Otherworlder upset you."

I sighed and slumped back in my seat, upset that Sera decided to mention the very thought I was trying to avoid.

"Yeah. That hasn't changed, but it's not like I was ever going to stop you from doing it. I'm just a random village girl. I can't out-scheme you, so I'm not even going to try. I'd rather just tag along and try to make sure Jamie's death is as pleasant as it can be. I guess dying because your dream gets fulfilled isn't the worst way to go, anyway."

"It's still death," Sera said bluntly. "And that isn't our only option. We could still kill him by denying him his dream."

I frowned but shook my head. "He just wants to be an adventurer, like in the stories he heard in his world. I don't see any reason why you would deny him that."

Sera sighed and shook her head back at me. "What if we decide that it would be better for the Otherworlder if you were to stay here in Plainswood? Would you agree to that?"

"Yeah." I shrugged. "Honestly, it might not even be up to me, anyway. I made Jamie pretty upset, so it's possible he won't want me around anymore."

"No," Sera said, sighing lightly. "I highly doubt that."

"Really?" I was a little skeptical.

"He thinks he's in love with you," Sera said, as if that clarified anything. "He'll want you around, even if it's painful for him to see you."

I waited for more explanation, but none came.

"Can't say I understand," I admitted. "I've never even had a crush on anyone before."

"Well, that's just how it is," Sera said, frowning before forcing her face back into a neutral expression. "Is that all you wanted from me?"

"Pretty much," I said. "So is it a yes?"

"I'm not the leader of the group anymore, Lena," Sera reminded me. "I'm just a grunt now. My opinion won't have any effect on your role in this mission."

"That's true," I said. "But I'd still like your opinion on it."

Sera narrowed her eyes at me and crossed her arms defensively.

"And why is that?" she asked.

When I offered my hand to her over the table, Sera stared at it as if she had no idea what to do.

"It might be a while before I can fully trust you, but if we're going to be working together, I'd rather not be enemies," I said, my hand still outstretched.

"Friends?" I asked.

There was a quiet thunk behind me, and I turned around to see what had caused it. While my eyes darted to the rest of the Mediators first, they were unmoving, still in the same position that I'd last seen them in. The true source of the sound wasn't difficult to identify, though. One of the three younger boys had his forehead planted against the table, while the other two acted like they hadn't been looking in my direction.

I had no idea what that was about, but after identifying the sound as a non-threat, I turned back to Sera. She still hadn't taken my hand and wore a deep frown on her face as she stared at it, before letting out a deeper sigh than I might have expected from her.

"Friends," she said, reaching forward to take my hand.

I didn't know why I thought I heard an undercurrent of pain in her voice there.

"Friends," I repeated, for lack of anything better to say.

I heard another thunk behind me, but this time, I didn't turn around.

Chapter 42
TREASON

Laush honestly didn't mind the demotion from a grunt to an extra. Being an extra meant she was being paid significantly less than what she would be making as a grunt, but she already had enough money to comfortably retire at any point she wanted. A few years of grunt work in the most dangerous job in Materia was enough to leave her set for life, and Laush was ready to retire at any time.

She knew Tenna didn't feel the same.

Her older brother had been ecstatic when he'd been promoted to the position of leader during this mission, but she'd been terrified for him. As temporary as it had ended up being, Laush had spent the entire time hating Tenna's new position and how it brought him even closer to the Otherworlder, knowing how easily one of their kind could simply choose to end the life of another.

Tenna had seen her relieved reaction when they were demoted. He'd become irritated at her, thinking that she was celebrating his demise. In a sense, she supposed he was right.

Though she loved Tenna dearly, she wasn't blind to his faults. He was not talented in the skills necessary to be a Mediator and had only pushed through the training through sheer force of will. It was enough to place him within the ranks of the grunts, but she had truly believed he would never be anything more.

She understood Tenna's motivations, but that did not mean she understood the intensity behind them. Whenever she remembered the Otherworlder that had casually burned down their town in a random rampage, she felt the same anger in her heart that he must have. However, while she had neglected her anger, letting it grow cold over the years, Tenna had fed the flames of his, letting it engulf his very being until it became his purpose for living.

She did not understand why. She would always remember their mother and father and hold them dear in her heart, but they were dead.

Why did Tenna act like risking his life would bring them back? Did he not realize that he still had a sister to live for?

The thought hurt, but she knew Tenna had to be hurting too. Perhaps he did care for her, or perhaps he was simply more noble than she was, to be willing to risk his life for the safety of strangers and future orphans. She had never asked, too afraid of the answer. She simply watched.

She never wanted to be a Mediator in the first place, but she knew she could not leave her brother behind. She hoped that once her brother calmed down from his current bout of anger, she would find the opportunity to sit him down and discuss the possibility of an early retirement, using the demotion as an excuse.

Out of the corner of her eye, she watched Tenna meditating. She could tell he was furious. Right now, his anger was directed at their former leader, likely for whatever reason he could think of at the moment. Laush didn't know whether Tenna was furious at her for giving him the position of leader, only to have it taken away from him so easily, or if he was angry at her decisions to allow the civilian to interact with the Otherworlder as much as she did, or if he was just generally annoyed by their continued interactions.

He could be quite petty when he wanted to be.

But he was too obsessed with being the perfect Mediator to allow himself to take any sort of revenge. The perfect Mediator did not have desire. They had no ego. He would do nothing, because he liked to pretend that he wanted to do nothing. Laush wondered if that would change when she eventually convinced him to retire. It was a possibility, though she hoped he would still retain some of the habits that he'd learned as a Mediator.

The slight creaking of the tavern door drew Laush's attention away from her thoughts, but she didn't turn her head to look. She strained her ears to pick up clues on who it could be, but she felt like the focus was wasted when Marten immediately spoke with no regard for discretion.

"Hey, you lot," he said. "The new members are coming in. Let's get a move on."

"We were told that it would be happening later this evening," Oren said.

"Yeah, I know," Marten said. "I know it's last minute, but I just learned about it a few minutes ago too. Save your bitching for after we go out. It's fucking miserable out there."

Without further complaints, Laush stood up with the rest of the group, glad that Marten was being relatively civil with Oren. In the few interactions they'd had, it wasn't difficult to see that the two hated each other. While Oren's reactions to Marten's barbs were humorous at times, Laush wasn't in the mood for humor at the moment and was grateful that Marten's mannerisms had somewhat softened since last night.

None of the Mediators hesitated in stepping out into the storm. Laush flinched slightly at the initial feeling of the cold rain that instantly enveloped her, but she held back the audible yelp of shock that she wanted to let out.

In the corner of her eye, she noticed Tenna's gaze shifting ever so slightly to her before pointing back in front of him. Had he noticed her flinching? Was he disappointed in her? He was in one of his moods, so it was possible.

He would cool down eventually.

It was a steady march to the mayor's house, where Marten had set up his base. Laush marched in the standard tempo of a Mediator, mirrored by her colleagues around her with the exception of Marten, who simply jogged forward while swearing under his breath.

By the time the rest of the group arrived at the mayor's house, Marten was already inside, having taken off his shirt and wringing out the water onto the wood floor.

"Bossman said he'd be done pretty soon," Marten said, holding up his shirt and flapping it up and down, completely unbothered by his own nakedness. "Feel free to do whatever until then. I'll give you all the heads up when he contacts me."

As Laush did as she was told, finding a lone sofa to rest on, Sera spoke up.

"Marten," she said. "Would it not be appropriate to invite the civilian Follower to join us? We've told her that she will be meeting the new leader and second once they arrive."

"I told her this morning that she should take her time, but I wouldn't mind," Marten said, wringing out his shirt once more as he talked. "Want to go invite her?"

Sera grimaced, another break in the mask of who Laush had once thought was the perfect Mediator. She knew Tenna thought the same. Sera was years younger than they were and had been in the organization for less time, but she was skilled enough to be a leader nonetheless.

While Laush had nothing but admiration for the younger girl's talent, she knew that Sera's quick rise had been a point of jealousy for Tenna. He likely thought of her as a role model to catch up to, or a rival, depending on how cocky he was feeling. Her recent mistakes had probably been a sore spot for him. In his eyes, she probably wasn't allowed to make mistakes.

"Actually, I was hoping I could discuss that with you," Sera said. "I wanted to request that if Lena chooses to remain as a part of the mission, that my interactions with her would be kept to a minimum."

"And why would you be asking me that?" Marten asked.

"In lieu of a leader or a second, command should go to the most senior member," Sera said. "That would be you, sir."

Marten shrugged. "Probably true, but the new leader's coming in a few hours at most. Why don't you save it for after he comes?"

Laush knew that Marten was smart enough to know that Sera was only asking because she didn't want to speak with the civilian Follower. She also knew that Sera was also smart enough to know that as well. In effect, he was telling Sera to make a decision for herself or not bother asking.

Sera grimaced. "Understood."

Tenna scoffed. Nobody paid him any mind.

The rest of the wait played out predictably. Everyone remained still and kept to themselves, except for Marten, who rummaged around the house, snacking on whatever he could find, all with his gut exposed, his shirt hanging off the back of a chair.

It took a few hours before Marten put his shirt back on. He made a displeased grimace, no doubt a reaction to how damp the shirt still was, but didn't complain.

"Alright," he said, clapping his hands. "Bossman says he's about ready. Let's go meet our new team leads, shall we?"

Laush stood up, the movement mirrored by everyone else in the room. Wordlessly, they marched down the stairs to the basement, where the spell formula from last night's communication remained. Though they took their places around it, Laush knew that they wouldn't be using it again, which was a relief, since she was still feeling the effects from the previous night's mana depletion.

The Founder of the Mediators simply outclassed them by so much that, as long as he knew where to send them, an impossible act like teleporting two adults was barely a chore for him. She wondered idly if Tenna saw him as a role model like he did with Sera, but she dismissed the idea as being silly. There was no way a human could compare himself to an elf. She doubted her brother was that bold.

Before Laush could let her thoughts wander too much, the space in front of her distorted and warped, and she closed her eyes to prevent herself from getting motion sickness at the incomprehensible sight of the teleportation spell before her. She waited a few seconds to ensure that the spell was over before opening her eyes again, even though there hadn't been any audible sounds of the new arrivals.

"They sent you as the new leader?" Marten asked, sounding genuinely offended at the idea. "Don't they know the brat's got a thing against goblins?"

"I was chosen, in part, because of my race," the new leader said, unbothered by the poor reception. "The Founder decided that the guilt the Otherworlder feels can be a useful tool in his further development."

Ignoring her new leader, Laush felt her eyes being drawn toward the man standing behind the goblin instead. He looked quite handsome—hardly a surprise since many Mediators were attractive by default—and vaguely Astrantan, judging by his hair, eyes, and skin. He also looked quite tall, though she wasn't sure if that was only because she was comparing him to the goblin he was standing behind. Laush wasn't quite sure why it was so difficult to tell, but she supposed it didn't matter.

The Second opened his mouth to speak.

He gave a few pleasantries and introduced himself to the group. Laush didn't quite understand why she couldn't tell what exactly he was saying, but she quickly decided that the new second was trustworthy anyway. She liked him much more than Oren, at least. It was a nice surprise to find a Mediator that at least pretended to be personable when it wasn't necessary, even though they all knew it was probably a lie.

Or maybe not? This one was quite pleasant to be around. He seemed genuine.

"Leader Stoney," Oren said suddenly, his flat voice uncharacteristically louder than it needed to be, echoing around the stone basement. "What is this?"

The goblin raised a hairless eyebrow at him. "What do you mean by that, Oren?" he asked.

Oren opened his mouth briefly, lost for words for the first time since Laush had met him.

And for the first time since Laush had met her, Sera lost her mind.

Laush felt her mouth gaping open, but she assumed a lack of decorum could be forgiven at the sight of the bright red needle of raw mana poking directly into the Second's eye, piercing all the way through the back of his head.

"Demon!" Sera shouted, the glow of ambient mana still fading from her finger. "Run!"

Sera's eyes darted around the room in the silent shock that filled it. Her eyes darted toward Laush's, and in the brief moment of eye contact that they had, Laush could swear she saw a deep dread in Sera's eyes. She wondered what Sera saw in hers.

"Treason!" the goblin shouted before the rest of them could react. Faster than Laush's eyes could register, he charged forward at Sera, a knife drawn from somewhere she hadn't noticed.

There was a dull thud, and Laush found herself motionless as she stared in bewilderment at Oren looking down at the goblin, like he was just as surprised as she was that he had just kicked their new leader in the head.

A few rapid footsteps drew Laush's attention to the side, where Sera was already sprinting out of the basement, only pausing at the top of the stairs to turn around for a split second.

"Oren!" she hissed, before disappearing from view.

As if awoken by her call, Oren ran up the stairs without further hesitation.

It was only after they heard the slam of a door that anyone reacted.

"What the fuck was that?!" Tenna shouted out in Timuran.

"I don't know," Laush shouted back in their mother tongue, unable to control her panic.

"Why the fuck would they do that?! Oh, shit. They fucking killed the Second. Why would they do that?!"

"I—"

Before she could say anything, she stopped. What did Tenna mean? Oren knocked out the Leader, but they hadn't done anything to the Second. Laush looked back, scared at what she would find, but let out a sigh of relief when she saw the Second, unharmed. The sight of him was a relief, and his calm aura reminded her that she could rely on him. He would know what to do.

"Sir Second?" she said. "What should we do?"

The Second smiled. Everything would be alright.

"Sir Second!" Tenna said. "With all due respect, I disagree! Our leader was attacked by a pair of traitors!"

Marten sighed and shook his head. "Look, kid," he said. "If our Second says it's alright, then it's alright. What are you complaining about?"

The Second nodded, thanking Marten for his input.

Tenna nodded too. "Very well," he said. "What are your orders, Sir Second?"

The Second nodded.

Chapter 43

TAKING INITIATIVE

Oren had assaulted his leader.

Insubordination was punishable by demotion or death, depending on the severity of the crime. Oren nearly shivered at the thought but quickly reassured himself that he was only following protocol. He recalled the case of the Harem Lord, where the leader of the mission became subject to the Harem Lord's brainwashing and was executed by her second when it was deemed that her continued survival was a risk to the mission. It was quickly determined that the second had taken the correct judgment in eliminating the risk to the mission and was subsequently rewarded with an immediate promotion to leader.

That incident had set the precedent for what needed to be done in the case of an Otherworlder's mental manipulation of another Mediator, and what Oren had done was standard protocol. The thought crossed his mind that perhaps he had been too soft. Perhaps he should have killed the new leader. Again, he decided that he had done the right thing by simply knocking him out. Brainwashed as he was, Leader Stoney was notoriously tough, and Oren wasn't sure he would have been able to kill the man in a single blow. No. He'd done the right thing. There hadn't been time to eliminate him, as outnumbered as they were. Knocking the Leader out and running away to regroup had been the best course of action.

It was protocol.

As he ran through the rain, following Sera's footsteps, he almost slipped when she took an unexpected turn.

"Where are you going?" he shouted over the rain.

"Lena's house," Sera shouted back.

The civilian Follower? Why? While the Mediator's mandate did include the safety of civilians, the elimination of Otherworlders was their ultimate mission. Did Sera believe that the civilian would be useful for that cause?

"Why?" he shouted.

Sera remained silent, which irritated him. He had asked a question. She was supposed to reply. That was how it worked.

Oren let his mana leak out of the soles of his feet. In a burst of concentrated power, he shot forward and overtook Sera in a split second. He stopped in front of her instantaneously, kicking up a large wave of mud as he skidded to a stop. He nearly slipped as he struggled to find purchase on the slick ground, but he managed to keep his footing as he pivoted to block Sera's path.

Not having expected it, Sera was unable to stop herself, crashing into Oren's side and falling unceremoniously onto the floor. She glared up at him, though she wasted no time standing up.

"What the fuck, Oren?!" she shouted.

She was showing emotion, despite there being no need for it. Was she trying to manipulate him? He dismissed the idea, deeming it unlikely. She should know that it wouldn't work on him. He was a Mediator.

"Why are we going to the civilian's house?" he asked.

Sera frowned, confusing him once more.

"She might've gone home. I need to make sure she's safe," she said.

"Why?"

"Because everything's going to shit," she said, acting as if he was the one being irrational.

He wondered briefly if she was also somehow affected by the demon's mental manipulation but dismissed the idea. She had reacted to the threat of the demon faster and more deftly than he had. Her immediate response was what had allowed him to regain his own senses and take action.

Regardless, at this very moment, she was being irrational.

"We have a job to do," he said, reminding her in case she had somehow forgotten because of the stress of facing the demon. "In cases such as this, civilian safety takes secondary priority to containing the threat that the Otherworlder poses. We should reengage with the Otherworlder and determine our course of action from there."

With her hair and clothes streaked with mud, Sera stared daggers at him. Once again, he was confused by the action. What benefit would she gain by trying to manipulate him?

"I'm going," she said, moving to step around him.

He moved to block her.

"No," he said firmly. "We need to follow protocol. We will go to the Otherworlder first and decide what action to take from there."

"I already know what action I'm going to take, Oren," Sera said, finally lowering her voice to an acceptable level. "You can do whatever the hell you want."

Why was Sera continuing to act like a civilian?

"We are compromised, and we cannot afford to split up," he said.

"Fine," she said. "Then come with me to make sure Lena's safe."

Oren frowned. He could not stop himself.

"No," he said. "We are currently both grunts, and as the senior Mediator, I have higher authority than you. We will stop wasting time and head directly to the Otherworlder's last known location."

Sera glared up at him. "Fine," she growled.

Oren was about to nod to indicate his satisfaction, but what Sera did next utterly confused him. She drew the hidden dagger from her belt and pointed it at him.

He did not understand. She wasn't in a formal fighting stance, and the way her arm was positioned would make it much easier for Oren to disarm her if he wanted to. However, he could identify the unspoken threat behind it.

"What is the meaning of this?" he asked.

"Stop me or let me go," she replied. "The choice is yours."

While Oren was confident enough in his own abilities to know that he would come out victorious if they came to blows, he knew she was skilled enough that he wouldn't be able to overwhelm her immediately. It would take some time to incapacitate her, and time was not something they had in abundance.

Taking his silence for an answer, Sera lowered her dagger and put it back in its concealed sheath in her belt. She started to walk around Oren. This time, he didn't move to stop her.

"Are you emotionally compromised?" he asked.

She didn't bother to answer him as she started to sprint off into the distance immediately, in the direction of the civilian's house.

Oren stared at her retreating figure for a few more seconds before breaking off into his own sprint.

Oren was horrified to realize that he had a deep scowl on his face, despite there being no reason for it. While this was admittedly an irrational scenario, it was no excuse to feel frustration.

But he did.

And he hated it.

This sort of frustration was something he had experienced multiple times in his civilian life. It wasn't something that he ever expected to happen to him again as a Mediator. The world had always confused him, but when he found the Mediators, everything had made sense. The organization was a safe haven for him, surrounded by rules, protocol, and logical decision-making.

This mission was an anomaly.

He had gone on several missions throughout his career as a Mediator, and none of them had been nearly as complex and problem-ridden as this one proved to be.

He wanted it to be over.

He needed to fix it. Then everything would go back to how it needed to be.

What could he do?

He set his mind to analyzing the data that he had.

It was clear to him that the root of the problem was the Otherworlder. He had already shown the ability to summon demons, and Oren was skeptical of his claims that he didn't have the power to mentally manipulate others. Jamie was the only Otherworlder in the general area, so there was no reason to suspect an outside force.

Whether intentional or not, the Otherworlder had clearly influenced the Mediators to further his dreams in some way. The Otherworlder was one of the few to learn the secret of the Mediators that guided them. Clearly, it had been a mistake. Oren made a mental note to bring the case up to the Founder and proposed that it be expressly forbidden to allow an Otherworlder learn of them. Sera would need to be executed to set a precedent for future Mediators.

But was that really the right choice? Even if this case had been an example of a clear failure, there might be merit in allowing Otherworlders to learn of the Mediators in the future. He wasn't sure whether he wanted to start a chain of events that would lead to it being expressly forbidden. What could he do? He decided he would simply observe what happened next. Taking a more passive approach would keep his options flexible.

What if Sera was right? While he didn't understand why she wasn't sharing her reasoning with him, the fact was that she once held a leader role within the Mediators, and he trusted the Founder enough to know that his decision hadn't been made in error. Perhaps she was seeing an angle of approach that he hadn't considered?

No.

He couldn't afford to think like this.

For all his experience as a Mediator, there was a reason Oren had never taken a leadership role. He was confident in his skills, but he knew his weaknesses well. As long as he was given clear orders, he could follow them perfectly, but if he were ever to take charge of a situation, he would be paralyzed with indecision as he overanalyzed his options, just like he was doing now.

His normal method of dealing with this sort of scenario was simply to avoid it. But that wasn't an option here. He was currently the only Mediator on the mission who wasn't mentally and emotionally compromised, and he had the duty to see the success of the mission through.

But there was no protocol for this.

Oren's mind raced as he continued to sprint toward the tavern, a whirlwind of anxiety forming in his head as the threat of the incoming decision loomed over him.

If he had a choice, he would never have placed himself in a situation like this, but he couldn't change it now. As much as he wanted to run away and let someone else deal with it, he knew there was nobody else who could.

He was a Mediator.

He needed to make a decision.

He nodded to himself, as if trying to manipulate himself into believing that he was somehow fine with the decision. It didn't work, and

Oren couldn't help but wonder why other people did it. It didn't help him in the slightest.

Oren stopped himself before he let his thoughts wander any further. He needed to focus. He needed to figure out how to prevent the Otherworlder from damaging his organization even further.

And then, the answer struck him, so obvious that he was almost angry that he hadn't thought of it until then.

If the Otherworlder was the source of all these problems, wouldn't they simply go away if he was gone?

That was their mission in the first place. To eliminate him. Why not advance the schedule a little bit?

Oren thought about it, taking care not to overthink the consequences. He couldn't afford to poison his mind like he usually did. He had made a decision. He knew he could convince himself away from it, so he couldn't afford to think.

Instead, he focused on what he would say.

"Jamie," he said out loud, in an apologetic voice, practicing the tone ahead of time so it would be easier to summon it later. "I'm sorry. I didn't want to tell you this, but it's impossible for you to be an adventurer."

While the original plan had been to fulfill the Otherworlder's dream in order to minimize the risk of him lashing out upon his death, time was of the essence. Who knew how deep the Otherworlder's corruption ran? Even if this method resulted in the destruction of Astranta and the lives of the people in it, it was a small price to pay for the continued survival of the Mediators.

Oren nodded to himself. It was an irrational behavior that served no purpose, but somehow, it made him feel more confident in his choice.

Yes.

This was what he would do.

For the good of the Mediators.

Chapter 44
Sera's Troubles

When Sera finally arrived at Lena's home, she grabbed the door handle and pulled as hard as she could. It wasn't locked, but it wouldn't have mattered if it had been, as Sera used her mana-infused strength to pull the door violently, nearly ripping it from its hinges.

With the vicious slam of the door announcing her arrival, Sera probably didn't need to shout to get anyone's attention, but her voice was uncharacteristically untamed, bursting from her lungs in a desperate cry.

"Lena!" Sera shouted before even confirming that anyone was actually home. "Lena, where are you?!"

Nobody responded, but as Sera's eyes darted around, she noticed a sliver of dim light coming from underneath a door. Though she'd never been in the house before, she recognized it as the door to Lena's room from the schematics of all the village houses that Marten had supplied the team upon their arrival to Plainswood.

Trying not to think about the blatant invasion of privacy she had committed and was committing, Sera walked forward and opened the door.

It was a small room, and Sera couldn't imagine that Lena spent much time in there except to sleep. The room was mostly barren. It featured a bed and a large drawer as the only furniture, without so much as a single mirror. Somehow, that fact stood out more to Sera than anything else. Though Lena didn't act vain, it was still surprising to find out that she didn't have something as simple as a mirror in the room to help fix her appearance before she left it, either trusting in her natural beauty to look presentable without tending to it or simply not caring.

Sera frowned at how easily her mind wandered in spite of her situation. She had to focus.

Sera stared silently into the room, glancing between Lena, Arina, and Hal as they stared into her eyes.

Hal stood in Sera's path to his wife and daughter behind him, using his large bulk to hide them from view. Yet his scared expression, along with the way he kept glancing down nervously at the thin fillet knife that he clutched in his hands, made him look incredibly non-threatening.

While Sera was sure the man had a strong enough love for his family that he wouldn't hesitate to defend them, she could also tell that he was a gentle man, not prone to violence. This was likely the first time he'd ever threatened to harm someone physically, and it showed. He was just as easy to read as his daughter.

Arina looked much more controlled, but only at first glance. Her expression was deadened and gave away no emotions, but her body language wasn't quite as calm. She and Lena were sitting up in the bed together, and Arina had awkwardly half-thrown herself onto her daughter's body, as if she could somehow protect her by sacrificing herself. She was afraid, even more so than her husband. She likely didn't realize how her fingernails were digging into Lena's skin, nearly drawing blood as fear overtook her.

Lena's long blonde hair was still damp from the rain but was neatly combed back and wrapped in a towel so it wouldn't wet her shoulders.

The expression on her face gave nothing away, aside from the mild pain she felt from the way her mother's fingers dug into her. She didn't seem to want to tell her to stop, likely because she was too kind to want her mother to feel guilt at the idea of hurting her.

It was a foolish act by a foolish girl, whose kindness had only brought her misfortune and discomfort, but Sera knew she wouldn't stop.

Lena's large green eyes locked with hers, and Sera resisted the urge to turn away.

"Lena," she said instead. "We need to go. Now."

Lena seemed more confused than surprised by Sera's arrival, but she kept her voice flat and level as she responded. "Sera?" She spoke as calmly as she could, like she was talking to a crazed animal. "What are you talking about? What's going on?"

"You might be in grave danger," Sera replied, stepping forward.

As if triggered by the movement, Hal closed his eyes and lunged forward, relying on his guts and luck to defend his daughter. Though he put his entire body into the blow, it was still slow enough for Sera to spare a moment to wonder what Lena must have told the man to make him want to defend his daughter from her so desperately. Or maybe she just looked crazy enough to elicit a response like that on her own.

Sera considered letting the man get a glancing hit to lessen the blow to his pride, but her muscle memory took over, casually slapping the knife from his hands and sending it sliding to the side of the room.

Ignoring him, Sera went over to Lena's bed and kneeled beside her. It was a disarming gesture meant to put everyone in the room off guard. It certainly worked on Hal, who froze in the air, mid-tackle, as he suddenly reconsidered the idea that Sera, a seemingly defenseless girl who was less than half his size, could possibly be a threat to him. Though

Arina still held her daughter protectively, the amount that her fingernails dug into Lena's skin lessened.

It was only Lena who didn't fall for her act. The cold look in Lena's eyes stung. The girl saw right through her, but Sera forced herself not to dwell on it.

"We need to go," Sera said once more. "Your life may depend on it."

"I don't understand," Lena replied. "What's going on?"

"Bad things are happening, Lena," Sera said. "I'm not exactly sure what happened tonight. A demon was summoned, posing as a Mediator. Oren and I could see through it, but none of the others could."

Lena didn't reply, and if Sera was more obtuse, she might have thought that the girl had somehow not heard her. Rather than reacting with the surprise or fear that might have been expected of her, Lena's eyes dulled and her shoulders slumped forward. She didn't look scared. Just tired. Acceptant of her fate.

It hurt to see.

"Fine," she said. "Let's go."

Though Lena tried to get up, she was either too weak or too nice to throw her mother off her, and Arina didn't seem to be interested in letting go.

"You have to let me go, Mom," Lena said. "I'll be back. I promise."

Sera froze as she realized she'd forgotten a crucial part of her explanation. It was an unexpected mistake from her, but thankfully, it could easily be remedied.

"Your parents should come too," she blurted out.

Immediately, that brought a spark of life back into Lena's eyes. Worry, anger, and fear all shone in those beautiful green eyes of hers before they narrowed suspiciously at Sera.

"Why?" she asked. "They don't have anything to do with this."

"They don't," Sera agreed. "And neither do you. We're leaving Plainswood."

"What?" Lena asked, looking down at her in utter confusion. "What are you talking about?"

"You're in danger," Sera repeated. "This entire situation has become too unpredictable, and you're just a civilian, Lena. You had no reason to be roped into this situation in the first place, and I'm sorry I didn't do as much as I could to get you out of it, but I swear on the graves of my father, my mother, and my brother that I will do as much as I can to keep you and your family safe."

Sera stared into Lena's eyes, as if she was trying to will her into believing her words. She knew that Lena didn't trust her, but she needed her to believe her now. She didn't know if she was being convincing or not. While Sera was an expert in pretending to be honest, trying to show her genuine feelings was not a skill she had practiced in a very long time.

She felt awkward and nervous as Lena stared back at her, her expression unreadable. Sera didn't know what to do. Though her lips were drawn down in a frown, she knew she could make her lips curve deeper and her eyes more watery. She suddenly realized that her voice had been flat and even throughout the entire conversation, not the wavery, girlish voice that she might have adopted to convince anyone else to do something.

But she refrained from acting. Right now, she wanted to be genuine.

Lena stared at her for a few more seconds before nodding. Sera dared to hope for a split second until Lena spoke.

"What about Jamie?" she asked.

Sera's heart sank at the question. She should've expected it, but it still surprised her how stupidly selfless Lena could be.

"I'm sure the Otherworlder will be fine," Sera said, blurting out the first thing she could think of. "He's powerful enough to destroy any demon that comes his way."

Lena gave her an awkward look.

"I know that," she said. "Jamie's summoned demons before, and it turned out okay. It's sweet that you wanted to make sure I'm safe, but if it's anything like the last time, it'll be fine."

"I know he's summoned demons before, but I don't think this is his doing!" Sera shouted, surprising herself at the burst of emotion, but not enough to stop herself from continuing. "The demons are summoned for the sake of the Otherworlders. Why would a demon appear within the ranks of the Mediators when the Otherworlder isn't even around to see it?"

It was the first time she'd said the theory out loud, and it still sounded as absurd as it did in her head, but she stood by it. While her first thought had been to assume that the Otherworlder had summoned the demon to destroy the Mediators from the inside, it didn't make sense. The Mediators had been nothing but kind to the Otherworlder, and he had shown no indications that he had sensed their true intentions otherwise. The only real grudge he could hold involved Lena for breaking his heart, but in all honesty, she doubted that that was the case either.

So as absurd as it was, Sera had searched for other explanations.

"So this is just an unrelated demon summoning? Do you think it could be another Otherworlder?" Lena asked, mirroring Sera's thoughts exactly.

"I'm not sure," Sera said, no matter how much she wanted to say yes.

The only people with the magical prowess to summon demons were Otherworlders. Although the only other active Otherworlders at the moment were in entirely different countries, it was possible that one of them had gotten away from its handlers and teleported to Astranta. Another possibility was that an entirely new Otherworlder had arrived in Materia recently. While it was uncommon for two Otherworlders to appear in such a short time, it wasn't an impossibility.

But she didn't know. She had no evidence.

"All I know is that you might be in danger," Sera said, giving Lena the most conclusive answer she had as well as the most important one. "That's why I want you and your family to leave with me."

Lena looked at Sera, and once more, Sera's heart sank.

Even before she spoke, Sera knew what Lena's response would be. It wasn't because of the grimace that appeared on her face, nor was it the way that her eyes shifted sideways in a silent apology to her parents for what she was about to say.

Sera just knew. She knew who Lena was.

"We need to help Jamie," Lena said.

"Lena," Sera said. A watery sheen appeared over her eyes, and she clasped her hands together, as if in prayer. "This isn't your fight. Please. Be selfish. Think of yourself."

Sera's voice finally started to waver with genuine emotion as she begged Lena to reconsider, but she could see the apologetic frown on Lena's face and knew it was no use.

Sera wondered if she should just toss Lena over her shoulder and run away. It would be so simple. Sera knew that there was nothing Lena could do to prevent it if she chose to forcibly remove her from the situation. She doubted that Hal and Arina would even protest, as long as they knew it was for Lena's own safety.

But then Lena would hate Sera, possibly forever. While Sera was already half-convinced she had broken Lena's trust enough that they'd already passed that point, she still held a small bit of hope that she could somehow mend the non-existent bond between them, no matter how much she tried to quash the feeling.

Sera tried to tell herself that if she truly loved Lena, then she would abduct her anyway, that it would be worth being hated just to know that she was safe.

But maybe she didn't actually love her, because she couldn't bring herself to do it. It was a comforting thought to think that this deep infatuation for the beautiful girl in front of her wasn't actually love. Maybe it was just lust, something that would pass eventually, but it was a fleeting comfort in the face of the fact that Sera was cowardly enough that she would willingly let Lena walk into danger, just so she wouldn't hate her.

Sera sniffled and wiped her eyes, wondering how much of her tears had actually been an act.

"Fine," she said, frustration and anger leaking into her voice as she growled at her love interest. "Let's go."

Chapter 45

Facing the Truth

Rivers.
Rivers flow, gently down my cheeks.
A storm has come, washing debris from my shores.
Storms stop, and the mind is cleansed.
But rivers dry.
They leave memories of the garbage that they had "cleansed."
(They were never actually cleansed, only hidden by the water.)
They leave memories of their now forgotten paths, ditches in the earth and in my mind.
Where I belong.
Rivers flow, a memory of who I am.
Ditches. Lines etched into my skin.
Rivers.
—Jamie Campbell

I sniffled and wiped my nose on my sleeve. It was already crusty with how much snot I'd wiped onto it. I'd actually managed to tear into the cloth a bit after biting into it to muffle the sound of my crying, but it was easy to fix it with my magic.

"I wish I could say the same for my heart," I muttered to myself.

But why couldn't it be like that? While technically, there was nothing to "fix" about a broken heart, I was an OP isekai protagonist. Nothing should be impossible for me.

And didn't OP isekai protagonists get all the girls? Wasn't that just a general rule?

The pervasive thought that I could make it true entered my mind, but I shook the thought away. The look of raw fear on Lena's face as she asked whether I was brainwashing her was something I would never want to inflict on another person. I honestly didn't know if it made me more sad to be rejected than it did to know that I'd made her feel that way, even if it wasn't actually true.

But hey.

"Love hurts, but time heals all wounds, right?"

Another sob escaped my lips, as if telling me that it wasn't possible.

I couldn't help but agree with it.

I had genuinely thought that Lena was the one. Even after she rejected me, I still couldn't help but feel that me and her were meant to be.

Or was it she and I?

I couldn't remember. Maybe it would be easier to decide which one was better if I wrote it down.

I was fully aware of the fact that I was only distracting myself, but I welcomed the opportunity with open arms. Unfortunately, I didn't have a pen or paper, but I had a solution to that.

I raised a finger up in the air.

"Sky write."

Immediately, I felt that same strange sensation of something welling up inside of me and expelling itself from the pores on my finger in the form of a luminescent streak of light that remained stationary in the air.

"Me and her," I dictated as I wrote it out. "She and I."

I cast the spell as easily as I could breathe. Maybe even easier than that, since sometimes I'd randomly start being super self-conscious of my own breathing and just start breathing manually. Magic didn't even have that slight hiccup for me. I felt like, if I wanted something to happen, I could just imagine it into existence with no effort involved.

Considering that I'd apparently been isekai'd into a pretty low-fantasy setting, where magical fighters could only use their mana for a few minutes before tiring themselves out, I was pretty broken.

I frowned as I remembered how Lena had blown up at me for using that word.

"No, no," I said, shaking my head quickly, as if I could physically jumble up the thoughts in my head if I did it fast enough. "Distractions, distractions. What was I doing again?"

The words, "me and her" and "she and I" floated mockingly in front of my face.

I bit my lip to hold back another sob and quickly swiped my hand over the words, dissipating them instantly.

"Damn it," I said.

I tried to stop myself from thinking of her. I'd fallen for the "I'm gay" excuse once before, but I was trying to convince myself that this time, it was for real. Lena was nice—the nicest person I'd ever met in my entire life. Surely she wouldn't lie to me, right?

Or maybe that was the reason she would. Maybe she didn't want to hurt my feelings and was just trying to spare me from the fact that she wasn't interested in me. Yet.

"No, no," I said, shaking my head again, using both of my hands to physically jostle it around. "You can't go down that road, Jamie. Not again."

I cringed as my brain replayed the memory of my freshman year of high school, and though I hated remembering it, I forced myself to remember how I'd seen Taylor kissing Tyler after she'd told me she was gay. I forced myself to remember how I'd taken that as a sign that I had a chance with her, rather than the obvious conclusion I should've made. I forced myself to remember how badly that had gone for me.

"Even if Lena was lying, which I still think she isn't," I harshly reminded myself. "I should respect her boundaries. Yeah. Yeah, that's good. We can still be friends, right? And maybe, just maybe, it can grow into something more—"

I winced as the pervasive thought wormed its way into my monologue.

"Damn it."

A polite knock sounded out from my door. I cringed when my first reaction was to imagine that it was Lena, dripping wet, with her clothes clinging snugly to the outline of her body again, but I was grateful for the potential distraction.

Anything was better than having to listen to my own thoughts.

"Who is it?" I asked, wincing when I realized how hoarse my voice was from the last few hours of crying on and off.

"It's Oren, my brother. May I come in?"

Though I had no reason to deny him, I paused. There was a strange tone to Oren's voice, and I couldn't help but imagine a scene from a war movie, where a young wife opened the door to two somber-looking soldiers who were there to deliver the news that her husband had died overseas.

I almost didn't want to open the door, but I shook off the idea easily. I knew I wasn't that great with people—I'd hardly interacted with them much outside of online chatrooms—so I knew I could just be imagining it. I couldn't deny my best friend for such a dumb reason.

"Come in," I said, wiping my eyes and nose one last time and hoping it wasn't too noticeable.

Oren pushed open the door just hard enough that it made me question whether he seemed like he was in a hurry, or if he was hesitant to talk.

He looked around, as if there could possibly be anyone else in the room, and closed the door behind him.

I looked up at him from my seated position on the bed. With a start, I realized it would probably be more polite to stand.

Before I could get up, however, Oren held a hand up.

"I think it'd be better if you remained seated for this, my brother," he said.

I was a bit ashamed to admit to myself that my first thought was that this situation wasn't nearly as hot as when Lena asked me to get on the bed, given that he was a dude. Thankfully, my hormone-ridden brain recovered fast enough for me to realize what he had just said.

"What? Why?" I asked, realizing that he had just said a line that I had heard too many times in movies and never in a good context. "What happened?"

Oren bit his lip anxiously and looked to the side.

While a small part of me was nervous about how my best friend was acting, I couldn't find it in myself to take his problem all too seriously. With my love problems still weighing heavily on me, I didn't think there was any problem that could be much worse.

Even if someone had gotten seriously injured somehow—even died, if my initial hunch was correct—my OP isekai protagonist powers had taken out some of the stakes of this story. Even if one of my friends died, I would be able to bring them back to life with my bullshit powers, so I doubted there was anything Oren could say that would be big enough to distract me from Lena for too long.

Even so, I appreciated any distraction. I gave Oren a weak smile to encourage him along as he struggled to find his words.

Oren only frowned in response.

"I'm sorry, Jamie," he said. "You can't be an adventurer."

I blinked rapidly a few times, unsure whether I'd heard him correctly.

"What?"

Oren gave me a sad and guilty frown, but one filled with an uncomfortable determination, like a TV detective who had just figured out that his best friend was a corrupt drug lord and had to be put down.

"Jamie," he said. "I did some research, and it turns out that there is an archaic set of rules around who can be adventurers. Adventurers are supposed to be paragons of justice and honor. No criminal may become an adventurer."

I blinked a few times. The detective metaphor was surprisingly accurate. What was Oren talking about? Aside from the fact that what he said about these random rules sounded made up and nonsensical, why was he calling me a criminal?

"What are you talking about?" I asked, genuinely confused.

Oren's eyes narrowed for a split second, returning to his anxious grimace so fast that I wasn't sure I'd imagined the brief change in expression. He stayed silent, making me wonder if I should clarify what I meant, but right as I was about to speak, Oren sighed and bowed his head.

"Jamie, my brother," he said, in that endearing Medieval bro-speak of his. "I am sorry, but crimes committed in your previous world count too."

I stared up at him, still confused, but I wasn't able to deny him this time for some reason. Back at home— No , not home. This was home now. Back on Earth, I hadn't been a criminal either. I wasn't a great kid, but I was quiet and never got into trouble. I wasn't actively bullied by the kids at school—just kind of shunned—so I never became any teacher's problem, and I certainly never got the attention of the police.

But I couldn't say anything. I couldn't tell Oren that, with the pit in my throat blocking all my words.

Why?

And then I realized why.

His words, as strangely phrased as they were, were too familiar. It had been many years since I'd heard them said out loud, and they were never said in the calm, convincing way that Oren always spoke, but it was as if Steven was standing right in front of me, giving me that cold side-eye of his as he downed another bottle of Coors Light.

"You murdered someone, didn't you, Jamie?"

I looked up at Oren, too shocked to remember where I was for a moment. When I finally registered what he said, I quickly slammed my hands against my ears, as if trying to rupture my eardrums would erase the memory of what I'd just heard.

"No," I said, mumbling at Steven. "No, no, no, no, no."

"I'm sorry, Jamie, but denying it won't change the truth. You will never become an adventurer."

"No," I said, not sure of why Steven had brought that up but knowing he would only use it to mock me. Had he found my journal? Hadn't he ripped them all up already?

"Jamie. It's not healthy to ignore the truth. Admitting it will only make you feel better."

"Shut up. Shut up!" I screamed.

I felt a gentle hand on my shoulder, and I froze, not knowing what was happening. I looked up at Oren, wondering where Steven went, before I remembered where I was.

"I am not a murderer!" I shouted, shooting up to a standing position.

There was a resounding crack as the simple force of my movement snapped the wooden boards of my bed.

Oren stared up at me and gave me a sad smile.

"I think you know what you are, Jamie," he said.

"No!" I shouted again, lunging forward and grabbing his collar. As I pushed him and held him against the wall, there was a terrible snapping sound as the wooden planks on the wall began to crack under the pressure.

"I didn't kill her!" I screamed. My lungs felt raw, and my watery eyes made it difficult to see Steven clearly, but knowing he could finally hear me was enough. "I was a baby! I never asked to be born, Dad! So stop making it my fault!"

Angry tears streamed freely from my eyes, blurring my vision, but not enough to miss the grimace on Steven's face.

"Never... Adventurer..."

I couldn't understand what he was talking about. Too much blood was pumping, and my heart was pounding too loudly to hear much else. But I could tell that Steven wasn't listening. He never listened.

But right now? I could make him listen.

I felt my grip tighten around his collar, and the planks on the wall snapped some more. They kept snapping, and Steven let out a low groan of pain.

"Jamie!"

I didn't recognize the voice shouting my name. I ignored it. For the first time in my life, I was on the verge of making my dad listen to me.

"Jamie, stop!"

Never.

I heard a few screams and felt something hit my back that I vaguely registered as being wet and soft. It wasn't enough to stop me, but when I felt a hand over my own, trying to pry my fingers away from Steven's collar, I slapped it away.

Another piece of wood snapped, this time accompanied by a scream.

"Lena!"

I froze. My heart was still pumping, and my hands were still firmly attached to Steven's collar, but I couldn't ignore that scream.

I turned around.

My eyes were still watery and dulled with the haze of pent-up rage, but I could recognize that shock of blonde anywhere.

"Lena?"

Lena smiled and waved weakly at me with the arm that wasn't bent at an impossible angle.

"It's okay," she squeaked.

Her head fell backward as she slumped to the floor.

Chapter 46

The Divide Between the Living and the Dead

Meat.

As Hal stared at his daughter's still body on the floor, the horrifying thought spawned in his mind.

She looked like meat.

It was terrible. He loved his daughter more than life itself. How could he think of her like that?

But his mind refused to see what it didn't want. It translated the scene unfolding before him into the most familiar setting it could. Just another day in his butcher shop. Just some meat that had fallen on the ground. He couldn't remember dropping it, but it wasn't even skinned yet, so a little bit of dirt wasn't that big of a deal.

Hal could only watch in morbidly professional curiosity as to how he would try to salvage the corpse in front of him. It would prove to be a difficult task for sure. Just from an initial glance, he deemed the arm to be mostly impossible to turn into something sellable. The blunt force that had hit it would likely have shattered the bones inside, scattering them into a complex puzzle of shrapnel and shooting the pieces deep into the flesh. The same would probably apply to the collarbone and parts of the ribcage, but those were less obvious on a superficial level. He would have to cut it up to make sure.

If it were up to him, he would probably just throw the entire thing away. Too arduous to clean. Even if he could get most of the bone shards out of the meat, he would only be left with scraps. He still wouldn't sell those to any customer, for fear that a missed shard of bone would cut up their tongues when they bit into it. Unless there was a shortage of meat, he probably wouldn't bother with it.

The world moved in slow motion, silent, save for a high-pitched ringing in his ear. He had the vague feeling that he was in a nightmare, but with his hazy vision, he wasn't quite sure what it was about.

He must have been tossing and turning in his sleep, with how bad this dream was, and he idly wondered why his wife wasn't waking him up. He looked down, noticing her standing right in front of him, clutching at his shirt. Oh. That was why. She was here too.

He tried to tell her that everything would be okay, that it was just a dream, but no words came out. He wrapped his arms around her, but he couldn't feel her. He couldn't feel anything really.

He wondered where Lena was.

He looked up and saw her, lying in front of him on the wooden floor. Silly girl. Her back would be stiff once she woke up, especially with her horrible sleeping posture. Hal reminisced about her childhood days, how she would often fall asleep in his arms, her head lolling back like it did now, sleeping like the dead.

Hal blinked twice, and a wave of nausea overcame him, the vomit in his stomach only held back by the chilling horror that froze him in place.

"No," he said, though he didn't hear it. "No, no, no, no."

Hal sank to his knees, dragging his wife down with him. He could vaguely feel her rocking violently in his arms—hear her muffled cry in his ears—but he didn't know how to respond. His hand automatically went up to her head in an attempt to comfort her like he would with

Lena when she was younger, but Arina's violent rocking made it impossible to run his fingers through her hair.

Hal thought he heard Lena's name, and he looked up to see the small red-haired girl grabbing the Otherworlder's collar and screaming at him. Aside from the occasional mention of his daughter's name, he couldn't make out what she was saying. The murderer barely seemed to notice her presence, staring blankly in front of him.

The murderer's eyes wavered, and for a moment, Hal locked eyes with him. Dark, emotionless, entirely inhuman. The murderer broke eye contact with him, his gaze wandering upward.

In a trance, Hal followed the murderer's gaze as it traveled up to his fist, still raised in the air, still crimson with the blood of his daughter.

Hal felt a surge of anger run through him. He stood up and reached into his pocket, drawing the fillet knife that he'd stowed inside.

He screamed a battle cry loud enough that his lungs burned with agony, yet he couldn't hear it over the pounding of his heart in his ears. He charged forward, stumbling on something and falling to the ground.

Not willing to stop, he scrambled forward and lunged awkwardly at the murderer.

The knife struck true, and the entire blade slid into the monster's flesh.

The animalistic rage in Hal let out a howl of pointless victory, but the brief flash of elation lasted only for a split second. The murderer remained standing, not even noticing the knife stuck in his stomach as he continued to stare at his own fist. He barely moved, even as the Mediator girl reached up to slap him across the face.

"Fix her!" she screamed, pulling herself up so she could stare directly into his face. "Fix her, you dumb bastard!"

The murderer finally blinked, and his gaze snapped to the Mediator girl.

"O-Oh yeah," he said, his voice wavering. "Yeah. I can do that. I can fix her."

Hal perked up. What had he just said?

The murderer walked toward his daughter. From the floor, Arina cried out and lunged over Lena's body.

"No!" Hal shouted, reaching out and pulling his wife off their daughter.

He didn't know what had come over him to put his trust in the very monster that had murdered Lena in the first place, but he was desperate. Arina screamed at him and violently flailed in his arms, but he refused to let go of the sliver of hope that he hadn't known he had.

He looked up at the boyish figure in a new light, and he couldn't help but hear his late father's voice in his head as he talked about angels, harbingers of both death and life, powerful and apathetic to all but their whims and the words of the gods above.

Hal clasped his hands in prayer, in hopes that this one would choose to be benevolent.

The boyish figure raised his hands above Lena's body. Hal's heart clenched as a flash of bright light forced him to look away.

* * *

It was a strange feeling, being dead.

I had no body. I was just a consciousness, floating in a formless sea of nothing.

It wasn't a pleasant feeling, nor was it an unpleasant one. It just was.

Honestly, it wasn't what I had expected. I wasn't religious like my father was, and my assumptions on what happened once you died hadn't been very influenced by his faith. I hadn't believed in an afterlife. I'd always thought that when you died, you just ceased to exist.

Apparently not.

I still existed, albeit in a strange, alien way. I was disconnected from reality, yet I was connected with all of it. I knew everything, but my mind was still surprisingly human and completely unable to comprehend the vastness of the information being presented to me as I floated around in whatever this was.

I wondered when I would eventually begin to lose my sense of self, but some time in my musing—though time works strangely when you're dead—I noticed something. Something I hadn't seen in quite a while, now that I thought about it.

Lena is dead.

I didn't quite "see" it, since I had no eyes, but I was aware of the blue box's presence.

Its very unhelpful presence. It might as well not show up if it was going to give me such obvious information.

It disappeared, even though I didn't have any way to tap it to dismiss it.

Even without a proper sense of time, it felt like it took a while for another blue box to appear again.

Lena has assimilated into the realm of Aether.

Ah. New information. That was nice. Ultimately useless, since it didn't change the fact that I was dead, but it was intriguing in more ways than one. Why was Jamie's power even interacting with me in the first place?

The blue box disappeared, replaced with another.

Lena's Quest: Guide

While Lena has left the side of the HERO, his quest is not yet over. Directionless and uncertain, he must be guided toward his ultimate destiny.

Objective: Guide the journey of the HERO.
Rewards: Wish fulfillment.
[ACCEPT]

I stared at the blue box, not sure if I could believe what I was observing. None of it made sense.

In front of me, the text box changed.

Lena's Quest: Guide the HERO (Jamie Campbell)
The HERO (Jamie Campbell) must accomplish his ultimate desires. Upon the acceptance of this quest, Lena will provide guidance and tools to the HERO (Jamie Campbell) to allow him to achieve his goals.
Objective: Guide the journey of the HERO (Jamie Campbell).
Rewards: Lena will be granted whatever she desires.
[ACCEPT]

That wasn't quite what I meant. The wording of the text hadn't been what I was confused about.

What could I even do? I was dead.

Actually, I wouldn't stay dead for much longer, with Jamie being around to bring me back with his magic. Huh. I didn't know how to feel about that. I didn't feel particularly glad that I would stop being dead. I didn't ever remember being suicidal, so maybe death was just like that? Maybe since I had already lost my life, I had become apathetic about it?

Not liking the impending existential crisis I was about to have, I shifted my attention back to the panel. The [ACCEPT] text had started to pulse with an eager yellow glow, along with the text detailing my "rewards."

Not very subtle.

Unfortunately, I wasn't sure I could feel emotion while I was dead... No, scratch that. I definitely could. Annoyance, at the very least, wasn't lost to me.

In response, the pulsing glow slowed down.

Without an actual face, I could only frown in a metaphysical sense. What was Jamie's power trying to do? Why was it asking me this? And why now? Why was it offering me these vague rewards? What did it want me to do? Well, what it wanted me to do was pretty obvious, but why? Why were the panels trying to fulfill Jamie's wish?

For a second, I couldn't help but feel like that was the wrong question to ask, but that was only under the assumption that Jamie was the one communicating this to me. I was doubtful of whether he was in complete control of his power in the first place.

I didn't know whether it was because my death was giving me a different perspective on my past life or simply because this was ironically the first time I'd been completely at peace since Jamie's arrival in my life, but the answer was suddenly clear to me that my hunch was probably correct. On the first day that we'd met, Jamie had been frozen in time along with the rest of Plainswood as the panels continued to speak with me.

Why? Was it Jamie's subconscious communicating with me, or was it some external force providing him with his powers? Even though Sera had told me that it was the former, I couldn't bring myself to truly believe it. It had been a while since I'd seen the panels—the last time being back when we were in Redstone—so I just hadn't really thought about it much, but what sort of being could be strong enough to grant an Otherworlder that much power in the first place?

The answer to that question was obvious enough. A god.

I couldn't help but think that the realization should have bothered me more than it did, but I only felt a sense of secondhand disappointment on behalf of my father, who might eventually figure out that the gods that he believed in were no less fallible than the mortals they watched over.

My attention was drawn out of my thoughts as a new button popped up in the panel.

[DECLINE]

I stared at the button. This was new. While I had only gotten one "quest" from the panels before this point, I knew from watching Jamie's boxes that turning the panels down wasn't usually an option. It always just seemed to assume that Jamie would do its bidding.

The entire wall of text pulsed in response to my thoughts.

I didn't know what emotion it was trying to convey, if the panel even had any emotions in the human sense, but I had clearly thought of something that was worth reacting to. I pondered the button for a few seconds.

Was it protesting the idea that it was forcing me to do anything?

The pulsing stopped.

What did that mean? Was my assumption right or not?

The blue box grew larger and closer to my sense of perception, close enough that my nose would be pressing into it if I was still corporeal.

The two buttons floated directly in my area of perception, silently asking me to choose whether I would accept or decline.

I stared at the panels for a moment before I raised my arm, or at least tried to. Remembering that I didn't actually have a body to manipulate, I simply stared at the button I chose, focusing on the [DECLINE] button until the box faded away.

A pulse of energy enveloped me as the panel reacted to my choice. I didn't understand what it was feeling, with its equivalent of emotion being too alien for me to even try to comprehend, but I doubted that the panel understood why I had chosen to decline its request. From what I'd seen from it, it was too alien an entity to have even a basic understanding of mortal minds.

There was another pulse of energy, different enough from the first that I could recognize it as a different emotion.

Confusion, maybe? Or maybe I had assumed wrong and it was getting angry at me. I wasn't sure. Whenever I heard my dad talk about religion, I got the sense that gods could be quite angry for very little reason. Maybe the panel would just erase my existence for my impudence.

Another pulse—a different one. I waited to see if my consciousness would be obliterated by the god, but nothing happened.

I still didn't know whether it was angry or not. Maybe it was just waiting for me to reveal that even though I'd chosen to decline its request, I still planned to help Jamie if he did decide to revive me. I had always planned to do that. I didn't need a vague promise from a clumsy god to motivate me, especially when I was skeptical about how it would try to "grant me whatever I desired" when it was doing such a terrible job at doing the same for Jamie.

A weak pulse of energy enveloped me, but this time, instead of it washing through my being, I felt my consciousness jerk uncomfortably, stretching along with the wave.

My consciousness stretched along with the wave of energy until I felt it spread thin, to the point where I could barely feel my own existence at all. Where was I? Who was I? What was I doing? I didn't know. Soon it wouldn't matter.

But the feeling stopped. My consciousness snapped back once more. I took a deep gasp of air and sat up, blearily blinking my eyes as I regained consciousness. Looking up, I saw Jamie's bloodshot eyes staring down at me, a trail of tears flowing down his cheeks and dripping off the tip of his chin.

Oh. I was alive again.

"Hi," I said.

Chapter 47
Second Attempts

Before I could even think to stand, I was bowled over by the large projectile that was my mom. I couldn't decipher her words through her garbled and incoherent yelling, and I didn't particularly enjoy how she was practically slapping my arms and chest as she inspected them for any damage, but I didn't have the heart to tell her to stop.

I hadn't wanted her or my dad to tag along. I just hadn't had the time to convince them to stay home. While I hadn't actively expected that I would die, it had always been a possibility in the back of my mind, and I hadn't thought my parents would be ready to see something like that.

It seemed I had been right to assume that, but I felt no satisfaction in the revelation.

As my mom ran her hands over my arm and neck once again, I gently placed my hand over hers.

"I'm alright, Mom," I said, keeping my voice calm. "It's okay."

My mom looked me dead in the eyes before losing strength and collapsing into my lap. Though I felt her clinging desperately to the back of my shirt, I didn't know whether she had passed out or not. I let her lie there either way.

Now that my mom had finally stopped jerking me around, I could finally take the time to look around me and gather my bearings. Physically, I felt absolutely fine, which wasn't surprising given the power behind Jamie's healing magic, but I felt a bleary sluggishness that had nothing to do with my physical well-being.

I had been dead, after all. I wished I could delude myself that it wasn't true, even for a moment, but there was a feeling of certainty that I couldn't possibly ignore within me. I knew for a fact that the memory of the experience would stick in the back of my mind for the rest of my life.

I felt somewhat grateful for the fact that my death left me thinking slower than usual. If I had to guess, the blood that was splattered over the ceiling, walls, and my clothes had probably belonged to me once. The gruesome scene might have been too much for me to handle if I were thinking properly. Even though I was used to the sight of blood from helping my dad out in the shop, it had never been my blood that I'd been covered in.

I looked away, not wanting to think about it anymore.

Unfortunately, there was nowhere I could look without seeing something I didn't want to deal with at the moment.

Sera stood by the wall, trying her best not to look in my direction, though it did little to hide the look of guilt on her face.

My dad was kneeling down in front of Jamie, muttering a prayer under his breath and kissing the air above his feet.

Jamie didn't seem to have noticed him, his eyes darting back and forth between me and the blood that stained his hands.

Everyone in the room was obviously mentally distraught, and I really didn't want to be the responsible one. I wanted to join them in their psychosis and curl up on the floor to either cry or go to sleep. Unfortunately, I noticed something out of the corner of my eye that I couldn't quite ignore.

I let out a heavy sigh.

"Jamie?" I said.

Jamie flinched at the sound of his name.

I didn't quite have the motivation to lift my arm to point, so I just lazily motioned with my eyes instead. Oren lay with his back against the wall, crumpled on the floor, wheezing and spluttering as his lungs struggled to work. I couldn't find it in me to feel any sympathy for him. I'd never been a fan of him before this point, and after hearing him torment Jamie to try and drive him to his death, my feelings of distaste for the man had only grown exponentially.

But did he deserve to die?

I watched Jamie turn around and flinch once he noticed Oren, but he didn't hesitate in raising his hands and closing his eyes.

"Heal," he said.

There was a bright flash of green light.

I wasn't surprised in the slightest. Jamie wasn't a murderer, no matter what Oren said—at least not an intentional one.

Oren blinked a few times before looking around himself and immediately bouncing to his feet, apparently not affected by the same daze that I was feeling. It made sense since he'd only been dying when Jamie healed him, not yet dead.

"Why are you still alive?" Oren asked.

Jamie seemed more surprised than offended. "What?"

Oren stared blankly at Jamie for a few seconds, as if he were confused by Jamie's reaction. Eventually, he shook his head.

"I'm sorry, Jamie. I was momentarily confused. Please ignore my previous statement. But you must understand that you can never become an adventurer. Your previous crimes aside, assaulting a Mediator like myself ensures that you'll be banned from any government-sponsored establishment throughout Materia."

"What?" Jamie asked again, apparently still too dazed to properly process what was going on.

Oren shook his head and laid a hand on Jamie's shoulder. "Jamie, my brother. As your brother and best friend, I highly suggest you simply give up on your dream of becoming an adventurer."

"What?"

I groaned under my breath. I really didn't want to deal with this. I looked at Sera with the hope that she would do something about it. Unfortunately, she was too busy staring blankly into space and avoiding my gaze to notice my silent request.

I groaned again, a little louder this time, and tried to push myself up. My mom's grip tightened around my waist, but she was light enough that I managed to push myself up to my knees.

"Jamie," I said, my voice still monotone from my recent death. "Don't listen to him."

Oren scowled. "I am your brother in all but blood, Jamie. I only want the best for you. Don't listen to the civilian."

"Oren," I said, glaring at him. "Shut up."

He glared down at me, the hatred in his eyes sharp enough that I bent over my mother's body instinctively to protect her.

"Don't try to order me around, civilian," he said. "Your actions have been a gross violation of the trust given to you by our previous leader. I will be reporting you on the charges of high treason once this mission is completed."

I desperately wished that my mom wasn't clinging on to me, because there was nothing I wanted to do more in this moment than stand up and punch Oren in the face. I was well aware that it would probably hurt me more than it did him, but I was currently too exhausted to think of a verbal comeback.

"Wait, what?" Jamie cut in before I could think of something to say. "What? Oren, what are you talking about?"

Oren's mouth snapped shut and his eyes widened as he stared at Jamie, as if just remembering that he was standing there.

"My brother," he said. He paused for a few seconds before continuing. "The civilian. Lena. She is a bad person."

In any other circumstance, I might have laughed at Oren's weak attempts at saving his mistake, but I wasn't in the mood for any amount of levity.

I could have let Oren die if I hadn't pointed him out to Jamie. If Oren weren't alive, then convincing Jamie that he wasn't at fault for accidentally killing me would probably go a lot smoother.

I recognized that it was a dangerous thought to have. Even if death was technically transient with Jamie around to bring anyone back, after experiencing its cold emptiness, I couldn't say that I'd lost any respect for it. I didn't want to give Jamie the burden of having to manipulate it so needlessly.

"See?" Oren said. "She says nothing. She cannot deny how terrible she is."

"What are you talking about, Oren?" Jamie asked, backing away from him and almost tripping over my dad, who was still kneeling by his feet. "Lena's cool."

"She is not!" Oren said, his voice cracking as he shouted. With his fists clenched at his sides, he took a few deep breaths as he struggled to control his voice. From the way he glared at me, I was surprised he hadn't taken matters into his own hands and—

I blinked as Jamie suddenly appeared in front of me. I was too stunned by the speed of the action to process what had just happened. However, with the tip of a knife pointing directly between my eyes, grasped between Jamie's fingers, it didn't take me too long to figure it out.

I suddenly felt less guilty about the fact that I'd considered letting Oren die.

"What?" Jamie said, staring down at the knife between his fingers like he had no idea where it had come from. He glanced up at Oren, whose hand was still outstretched. "Why did you do that?"

Oren frowned and folded his arms.

"I've already told you, my brother," he said. "The civilian is evil. She plans to kill you."

"Oren. Just shut up."

I turned to the side to see Sera pointing a knife at Oren, an angry scowl on her face.

Oren scowled back at her. "You have no authority over me. We are currently of the same rank, and I am your senior. I order you to stand down, Grunt."

Sera seemed to be torn between screaming at Oren and stabbing him. Before she could decide, a polite knock on wood interrupted her.

I turned around and froze when I saw an inky silhouette peering inside.

With no eyes, I didn't know whether it even needed to look in a specific direction to perceive things, but it was very clearly peering directly at Jamie, staring at him with where its eyes should have been.

The demon's outline vibrated slightly as it casually waved its hand.

"Oh," Jamie said. "Hello?"

The demon vibrated again and stepped into the room.

Instinctively, I tried to cover my mom's body to protect her from the threat, but before I could, I felt an arm deftly snake itself underneath my arm and lift me to my feet in one quick motion.

"Run," Sera whispered into my ear. She lifted her free arm and pointed her palm at one of the walls.

There was a sudden increase in the volume of the rain as the wall crumbled away, as if it were made of thin paper the entire time. Sera pushed me roughly and I stumbled forward to regain my footing, but I didn't run like she wanted. Once I managed to find my footing on top of the wood chips that littered the floor, I turned around.

Sera gave me a frustrated glare before falling to her knees, and then to the floor. Jamie glanced at her and then at me, as if I had an answer for why she did what she did.

"That's a demon, Jamie," I said, pointing at the demon standing still in the room. I winced as the wind and rain assaulted my eyes and walked back under the shelter of what was left of the room.

Jamie stared blankly at me before turning to the demon. The demon tilted its head at me, as if confused by my claim.

"He looks like a normal person," Jamie said.

"Well, he's not," I said, sighing. "You could probably do that thing you did before. Detect demons? That would be an easy way to check, right?"

Jamie stared blankly at me and sighed. "What the hell is going on?" he muttered under his breath before raising his arms. "Detect demons."

The effect of Jamie's magic wasn't nearly as dramatic or as visually striking as the first time he'd done it. The demon in front of him simply pulsed a dull red.

The demon froze and seemed to look down at its hands as if it couldn't believe what was happening to it.

"Well, there you have it," I said. "You can kill this one pretty easily, right?"

The demon's head jolted up at my words, and it immediately jumped back as far away as it could. Reaching for its side, it drew an inky knife from where its belt would have been and pointed it forward. Its silhouette shook, but I wasn't sure whether it was vibrating like before or if it was shaking in fear.

Jamie frowned as he glanced between the demon and me.

He opened his mouth as if to say something but closed it and shook his head.

"It's not hurting anyone," Jamie said.

The demon lowered its knife slightly at his words. I frowned, knowing how much damage a demon could do if it went unchecked.

"Not yet," I said.

Jamie glanced at me for a second before giving the demon a blank stare.

The demon shook its head frantically and vibrated in place. The knife fell out of its hands and the tip stuck to the wood floor.

Jamie sighed and hung his head. "If you hurt anyone, I will hunt you down. Understood?"

The demon nodded and sprinted down the hall, as if afraid that Jamie would change his mind.

As it left, my eyes shifted down to the Aether knife stuck in the floor. Cut off from its source, it had slowly started to dissipate. Jamie seemed to notice my gaze and looked down, just in time to see the last particles of the knife disappear.

He frowned and sighed.

"I would like to know what's going on," he said, his voice half demanding, half pleading. "Please."

Chapter 48
DEBATE

It took me a surprisingly short amount of time to convince my parents to leave the room so I could talk to Jamie and the Mediators. Or maybe it wasn't too surprising. They'd gone through a harrowing experience, watching their child die in front of them. While they did protest at the idea of leaving me alone with someone who'd killed me by accident and another who had failed at his attempt, they were exhausted and completely drained of any energy they might have otherwise had to argue with me.

In the end, I was able to reassure them enough by promising to return to them unharmed and alive. Maybe they wouldn't have accepted such a flimsy promise under normal circumstances, especially since I had no influence on whether it was fulfilled or not, but they eventually relented, walking back to the tavern's main hall in a daze.

The room went completely silent after they left. Though Jamie had taken the liberty of cleaning up my blood with his magic, he hadn't fixed the wall. Even though the storm was slowly dying out, the wind and rain were still strong enough to blow a consistent spray of water onto us. Still, nobody suggested that we should move or that Jamie should fix the wall.

We all just stayed there, awkwardly standing around the cramped room in silence.

I knew the onus was on me to say something, but I don't know how long it took for me to summon my voice.

"Jamie." Once I found my voice, I spoke quickly, trying to deny myself the opportunity to hesitate. "The Mediators are trying to kill you."

The reaction around the room was much more muted than I expected. Oren and Sera didn't even act like they'd heard me, while Jamie only turned toward me with a furrowed brow and no other reaction. He stared into my eyes for a few seconds before turning away and staring directly at Oren.

Oren glanced at him. "It's true," he said, answering the unasked question.

I wasn't sure I believed what I'd heard. I'd expected him to at least try to deny the accusation somewhat. What was he doing?

I looked at Sera to see if she had an explanation, but she was adamantly avoiding my gaze, staring out of the broken wall like she was admiring the rain. I entertained the thought that she might not have heard me, with how her legs still shook from the exhaustion of casting a big enough spell to destroy the tavern wall, but I doubted it was that convenient.

"You're trying to kill me?" Jamie asked.

Oren nodded. I had expected him to deny the accusation, or at least pretend to feel guilty about it, but his face was completely blank, devoid of the false expressions he usually wore.

"The civilian speaks the truth," he said. "The Mediators are an organization that aims to remove all Otherworlders from Materia."

"Why?" Jamie asked.

"Because you're powerful," he said. "Powerful enough to destroy a small village like this with a single thought. Powerful enough to bring down an entire country in the span of a few hours, along with every living being within its borders."

"He wouldn't do that," I said, glaring at Oren.

"From what I've seen of your personality, I am willing to accept that it is unlikely that you would intentionally put another life in danger," Oren said, not even bothering to look in my direction to answer me. "But we already have two instances where you killed two civilians and assaulted a Mediator."

"He healed us!" I said.

Oren turned to me for the first time in the conversation, just to give me a quick glance and a blank, unimpressed stare.

"Near-death experiences can still be traumatic. I imagine the act of actually dying would be just as traumatic, even if the victim were brought back to life."

I bit my lip and stayed silent, not wanting to even acknowledge the unspoken question.

Oren let the silence linger for a few more seconds until he was confident I wouldn't answer.

"Whether your victims experience trauma or not, the fact is that you committed murder, regardless of your intentions," Oren said, turning back to Jamie. "Or rather, you committed murder despite your intentions. You have power beyond the capacity of a mortal to handle, and on occasion, you will not be able to control it. This has been proven throughout history. Not a single Otherworlder has ever managed to avoid directly causing the death of another.

"Excluding the extreme outliers, on average, Otherworlders kill twelve Materians before the Mediators are able to eliminate them. If we include the extreme outliers, the average goes up to approximately five million. It may seem like an exaggeration, but as of this moment, there is a population count of approximately four billion Materians alive today. Fifty years ago, before the rampage of the Otherworlder colloquially known as the Plague King, that number was approximately seven billion. That is why the Mediators exist. For the good of all life on Materia, and for the sake of any goodness that might remain in the Otherworlders."

Oren gently placed a hand on Jamie's shoulder, a gesture that clashed with how flat and uncaring his voice was.

"I can tell you're in pain, Jamie. You wish to be a good person, do you not? The best way to ensure that you remain one is to deny your infinite power the chance to corrupt you."

Jamie's shoulders tensed up at Oren's words. He awkwardly shifted his head as he continued to look down at his feet.

"How—"

"No," I said. I stepped forward to place myself between the two, pushing Oren away from Jamie. Oren stepped back without resistance, seemingly unbothered by my interruption. "Don't finish that question, Jamie. He'll just lie to you, like he's been lying this entire time."

"I will not lie to you, Jamie," Oren said. "While I have lied to you in the past, I recognize that my previous approach may have been inappropriate. After some reevaluation, we have determined that the best method of handling you would be to employ complete honesty, in hopes of obtaining your cooperation."

We? The single word stood out in my mind, and I glanced at Sera, who turned away before I could meet her eyes.

"You were about to say something before the civilian interrupted," Oren continued. "Would I be correct to assume that you wanted to know how you could ensure that you never kill anyone again?"

My heart sank as Jamie's unasked question was said out loud. Jamie said nothing, and I didn't want to turn around to see his reaction, but the look on Oren's face told me all I needed to know. It was a surprisingly gentle expression, with only the vaguest hint of his lips being raised and a slight crinkle at the corners of his eyes as he adopted a smile. It was the most genuine expression I'd ever seen from him. If I hadn't known who it was attached to, I might have thought it made him look innocent and almost childlike.

"You would have to die of your own volition." His previously flat voice had taken on a gentle edge of quiet excitement. "Would this be agreeable to you?"

"No," I answered for Jamie. "No, it would not."

"The civilian does not speak for you, Jamie," Oren said, still staring over my head. "It is your decision to make. You have the ultimate control over your life. You would be doing a good thing, Jamie. A noble end makes a noble life."

"Like hell it does!" I shouted. "Jamie, don't listen to this crap; he's clearly manipulating you."

"If trying to convince you that the decision I want you to take is the correct one, then yes, I am manipulating you," Oren admitted. "But I genuinely think that it would be beneficial for both you and every single resident of Materia if you died. Nothing I said has been a lie, Jamie. Unless you think otherwise?"

Though he still refused to look at me, the question was clearly a challenge to me.

"All you've been doing is lying!" I shouted. "You're literally trying to dress up suicide like it could possibly ever be a good thing, and you have the fucking audacity to stand there with that smug look on your face, like you've got an impenetrable argument?!"

Oren's smile twitched. It didn't quite drop off his face, but he shifted his gaze down to meet mine.

"I have not been lying," he said. "There would only be benefits to Jamie's death."

"Are you missing the fact that he'd be dead?" I asked. "Speaking as someone who's been dead before, I'll let you know. It was the most terrifying thing that's ever happened to me in my life."

When Oren's smile returned, it took me a moment to realize my mistake. I turned around to look at Jamie, and though he still had his head tucked into his chin with his hood drawn tight over his head, he was tall enough and I was standing close enough to see his face, wracked with pain and guilt.

"Jamie," I said. "It wasn't your fault."

"A lie," Oren said, the smile audible in his voice. "It was your hands that shattered her bones and spilled her blood. That is the truth."

I didn't bother glaring at Oren, knowing that there was nothing I could do to shut him up.

"You didn't mean to," I pleaded. "It was an accident. It wasn't your fault."

When Jamie raised his head to look directly at me, I almost flinched from the gaunt appearance of his sunken eyes. Tear marks stained his cheeks, but his eyes were devoid of moisture and life. Though he stared in my direction, he looked through me, at something only he could see.

"But it was," he said. "I'm sorry."

When I talked to my parents a moment ago to convince them to let me talk to Jamie and the Mediators alone, I put on my brave face for them, to try and convince them I'd be fine, even though I had no idea what would happen in this room after they left.

It had been a surprisingly easy task for me to accomplish. I don't know whether it had been my willpower or simply the fact that I was in shock from having died just moments before that allowed me to feign a stoic expression for them, but I somehow managed.

But now, watching Jamie struggle not to cry just made me want to cry for him.

And so I did.

It was a strange feeling, to cry without sobbing. Aside from a gut-wrenching twinge in my stomach that made me feel like I was on the verge of throwing up, I felt nothing. Aside from a heart-rending pain in my chest from the pain as I tried and failed to understand the amount of pain that Jamie must be feeling, I felt numb. Tears flowed down my face, but no sound escaped my lips.

"I thought I told you not to apologize for things you didn't do," I said, whispering unintentionally. I wasn't sure he heard me.

Jamie shook his head, the motion so slight that I wasn't sure if I'd imagined it.

"I'm sorry," he repeated. "Steven was right. I should've never been born."

"Fuck Steven!" I shouted, even if I didn't know who he could possibly be talking about.

Jamie's only reaction was to let his head fall and stare at his feet. Through my blurry vision, the morbid part of my brain could only imagine the image of a dead man, hanging by an invisible noose.

"Please don't die," I begged. "I'd miss you. Just talk to me."

Jamie's eyes flickered to mine, and for a moment, I swore I saw a bit of hope in his eyes.

"You should never apologize for being born, my brother," Oren said, drawing his eyes away from me before that hope could take hold. "The circumstances of our birth cannot be controlled, but the choices we make are our own. I only ask that you make the correct one."

I couldn't take it anymore. Turning around, I walked up to Oren, took a moment to focus on where he was through my teary vision, and reached up to slap him in the face.

It felt like slapping a brick wall, and like I guessed before, it hurt me more than it hurt him, judging from his lack of reaction.

Oren looked down at me.

"The civilian has no arguments to give, and so she resorts to violence," he said. "Is this the only argument you have left?"

"Shut up, Oren," I growled. "Jamie isn't going to kill himself."

"It would be the logical thing for him to do."

"Go take that logic and shove it up your ass."

Oren gave me a disappointed look and sighed. "I will never understand you civilians," he said before looking up. "Jamie. There are two ways that an Otherworlder can die, and both are equally viable."

In a moment of panic, I tried to reach up to slap my hand over Oren's mouth in an attempt to physically shut him up. Instead of letting me hit him again, he snaked his hand up with careless ease and diverted the path of my hand without even glancing in my direction.

"You came to this world with a dream. A defined goal that you sought to pursue during your time here, and without the goal to sustain you, your existence will fade. If you decide that you have satisfied that goal or have given up hope in achieving it, you will pass."

Jamie frowned.

"So if I give up on my dream, I die?" he asked.

"Yes," Oren answered. "Alternatively, as I mentioned, if you truly believe you have achieved it, you will also pass on. However, I do not believe that is a viable option, as becoming an adventurer would be a fundamentally impossible task for you. An adventurer can be defined as an individual who seeks and partakes in adventure. An adventure can be defined as an undertaking that involves danger, risk, and excitement, but your invulnerable constitution makes risk and danger fundamentally impossible for you."

Jamie stared at Oren, and then at me.

"Please don't," I begged. It wasn't a good argument, but it was the best I could offer.

Jamie stared at me for a while longer before he bowed his head.

"Please," I repeated.

Several seconds passed in silence before Jamie raised his head. His eyes were still sunken, but he tried to give Oren a shaky smirk before it immediately fell back down into a frown. He let out a sigh.

"Sorry," he said. "I don't think I can do it."

Chapter 49
DREAM

Oren's face twitched, and there was the quiet sound of something cracking underfoot.

"Why, my brother?" he asked. "What prevents you from making the noble choice?"

Oren's words were effective at making Jamie wince, and I immediately wanted to jump in to defend him, but Jamie spoke before I could.

"I just can't, okay?" he said. "What does giving up on my dream even mean? That's way too vague. It's not like I can just decide to think a certain way."

Oren frowned. "Why wouldn't you be able to?"

Jamie simply fixed Oren with a blank stare. "People don't work like that, Oren."

There was a long stretch of silence as Oren scowled at Jamie.

"Be that as it may," Oren said, powering through the awkward silence. "If your problem lies with the vagueness of your task, it can easily be defined and clarified. Are you struggling with the definition of being an adventurer?"

Jamie frowned. "No."

"What are you struggling with, then?"

"I—" Jamie paused to look at me, as if silently asking for help.

"He's not struggling with anything," I said. "He's not going to kill himself, Oren. That's all."

"This doesn't involve you, civilian." His eyes remained on Jamie, as if glancing at me would force him to acknowledge me.

"Jamie's my friend."

For some reason, that was enough to make him turn to me, scowling even harder than he already was.

"He is not," he said. "You have been lying to him ever since you've met him, and in turn, the Otherworlder has killed you. You cannot possibly be friends."

"Well, we are," I said.

"No. You are not," Oren replied.

"We are."

"You are not."

I frowned, suddenly realizing I had somehow gotten into the equivalent of a playground argument with a Mediator. I stared at Oren, who had his fists clenched by his sides and looked like he would go into a shouting tantrum at the slightest push. As morbidly funny as it might have been to see, I was too tired to deal with it.

Instead, I sighed.

"Jamie," I said, turning to face him. "I think we're done here. Could you deal with Oren? Please?"

"Deal with him?" Jamie repeated, an anxious look appearing on his face.

I winced at my choice of words and quickly shook my head. "No, I didn't mean to kill him. Gods. I meant for you to do something to put him to sleep, or teleport him away, or anything to stop him from trying to talk you into killing yourself."

Oren let out an angry cry. In an instant, Jamie appeared in front of me, catching another knife before it stabbed me between the eyes.

"Oren," Jamie said, letting the knife drop from his hands. "Could you... stop that?"

"You're being completely idiotic! All of you!" Oren shouted. "This is completely irrational behavior! Do you want the blood of innocents on your hands?!"

Jamie frowned at the accusation, but he raised his hand and closed his eyes. A dull pulse of white light emanated from his hand, and he rushed over to catch Oren before his unconscious body fell to the floor. Scooping him up gently, Jamie laid the man on the lone bed in the room.

There was a long stretch of silence as Jamie stared down at Oren's unmoving body.

"I'll assume you don't want me around either."

I looked up at Sera, who still refused to look me in the eyes, choosing to look at an empty corner of the room instead. In all honesty, I'd almost forgotten that she was still there, with how quiet she'd been.

"Yeah," I said, knowing that the comment was directed more at me than at Jamie. "I don't."

Sera winced and turned to Jamie.

"Hey, Jamie," she said.

"Yeah?" he asked.

Though Sera glanced in my direction, she still refused to meet my eyes, her gaze focused somewhere around my knees instead.

She sighed and turned around.

"Sorry," she said, before walking out of the room through the large hole in the wall and into the rainy outdoors.

Jamie and I watched her leave, neither of us willing nor wanting to stop her. In her absence, silence quickly returned, filled only by the steady sound of pounding rain above.

"I'm sorry," I said.

Though I had my gaze fixed on the hole through which Sera had left, I could see Jamie turn to me out of the corner of my eye.

"For what?" he asked.

"Oren was right," I said. "I've been lying to you since we met. I knew that the Mediators wanted to kill you since we met them. I probably could've prevented all of this from happening if I were more honest with you."

Jamie stared at me for a few more seconds before turning away, directing his gaze to the outdoors as well.

When he refused to say anything for the next few seconds, I sighed.

"Sorry," I said. "I'll leave you be."

"What?" Jamie said, turning back to me. "Why?"

"Aren't you upset with me?"

"Well," Jamie said, scratching his head awkwardly. "I guess a little bit. But I did kill you, so I think we can call it even."

He let out a single dry bark of a laugh before his face fell into a frown.

"Sorry," I said.

"What are you apologizing for?" he fired back. "You keep telling me that I shouldn't apologize for things that aren't my fault, but I guess that rule doesn't apply to you, you bitch."

The casual insult was so out of character that I couldn't stop myself from whipping my head around to face him. I didn't know exactly what my expression looked like, but if I had to guess, it might have looked similar to the one that Jamie wore. His eyebrows had shot up in surprise, as if it wasn't him that called me a bitch but someone who could impersonate him perfectly and throw their voice.

I actually considered the idea for a split second before I saw Jamie wince, regret and shame clear on his face.

"What did you call me?" I asked, just to make sure I'd heard correctly.

"I-I'm sorry," Jamie stammered out, looking down at the floor. "I just—I mean—Y'know."

I couldn't say I did. I didn't say that out loud, but I think my dumbfounded expression managed to convey the message to Jamie better than words could.

Jamie groaned as he pulled his hood tight over his head and turned away.

"Sorry," he said. "I just thought since, y'know. You said we were friends, right? And friends insult each other? Like, they banter? Like you said? Like you did with Bran? I think?"

He continued to mumble, but as he quickly lost confidence in his words, they grew too quiet to be comprehensible. It took me a moment to process what he'd said and even longer to realize why he'd said that, but when I did, I felt myself break out into a smile.

"Wait." I let out an involuntary giggle. I tried to stifle it, but when I opened my mouth to try and speak, I almost choked on the gasping laugh I'd tried and failed to hold back.

I doubled over, clutching at my stomach, sinking to my knees as I gasped for air. I kept choking and sputtering as my lungs kept forcing me to expel more air than I was taking in, but I didn't care. Losing strength in my limbs, I let myself fall to the floor as I continued to laugh.

I didn't know how long I stayed like that, laughing almost maniacally as I drowned in mirth, but when I regained my senses, Jamie was crouched over me, glaring down at me. Though he still had his hood drawn tight over his head, the low angle that I was at gave me a clear view of his face, crimson with embarrassment.

"It's not that funny," he said.

I agreed with him, not understanding why I was even laughing so hard in the first place, but I wasn't going to tell him that.

"Sure," I said through my giggles. "You keep telling yourself that, you big idiot."

Jamie tried to look annoyed at me, but like always, he was a terrible actor and failed to keep the smile from creeping onto his face.

He let out an exaggerated sigh and sat down on the floor next to my head.

He didn't say anything, so I took my time. Once I managed to recover from my laughter, I pulled myself into a sitting position next to him.

Though neither of us talked for a while, there was no silence between us, the air occupied by my stray giggles and the steady beat of the rain overhead.

It was only once I managed to calm down completely that Jamie started to talk.

"My dad hated me."

His words clashed heavily against my mood, but the way that Jamie said it was so casual that I couldn't help but answer back in the same way.

"That must've been terrible."

"It was. My mom died during childbirth, and he never let me forget it," he said, laughing a little. "Honestly, in hindsight, it seems pretty silly. How do you yell at your own son for fifteen years over something that wasn't his fault?"

I had nothing to say in response, but he didn't seem to mind.

"Sometimes, I dreamed about what would've happened if my mom hadn't died. Maybe my dad would've been nicer to me if that hadn't happened, but honestly, I've never even seen him be nice in the first place, so it was always difficult to imagine. In my fantasies, I would always picture him as a completely different person.

"Most of the time, I would picture him with Tom Hanks' face, or something like that. Someone who could actually say 'good morning' to me without attaching 'you murderer' to the end of the sentence. So I guess it could've really been anyone. Not sure why I always pictured Tom Hanks. It's not like I'm a particularly big fan. I think I've watched maybe two movies with him in it, but I guess he just gave off some dad vibes or something."

Jamie laughed and sighed.

I waited for a few seconds for him to continue, but he didn't, simply staring blankly into space with a slight smile on his face. I didn't know whether he wanted me to chime in or if he simply ran out of steam, but I decided to say something.

"Your dad sounds like an asshole."

Jamie nodded.

"Oh yeah. He definitely was. But worse than that, he was my dad. Y'know. The guy who was specifically supposed to not be an asshole to me. My dad. Y'know?"

I could tell the question wasn't for me. I stayed silent as Jamie sighed.

"But I guess he was right. I am a murderer."

"You're not. I'm alive, aren't I?"

Jamie gave me a sad smile but quickly turned away to watch the rain falling, the smile still on his face.

"I think I might be a bad person," he said. "I used to think that I would rather be dead than actually be a murderer, but when I actually ended up killing someone, I ended up pretending like it never happened in the first place. Even after I killed you, I couldn't muster up the courage to die."

"Being suicidal has nothing to do with courage, idiot," I said, punching Jamie in the shoulder as hard as I could.

Jamie rocked to the side from the impact of the blow and gave an exaggerated wince and rubbed at the spot that I'd punched him. The effect was ruined by the slight grin he had on his face.

"What about doing the right thing?" he asked. "Is that courage?"

I raised my fist up at him. "Don't make me hit you again."

Jamie let out a quiet chuckle and raised his hands in surrender.

"Okay, okay, sheesh," he said.

I kept my fist raised for a few more seconds before I lowered it to my side. Jamie was looking out the hole in the wall again, so I decided to join him, letting the pattering of the rain lull me into a sense of calm.

"I don't want to kill more people."

"You won't."

"How do you know that?"

"I just do."

"That's not a real explanation."

"You're a good person, Jamie."

"Agree to disagr—"

"Jamie."

"Okay, fine, sheesh. Let's say I'm a good person—"

"Which you are."

"I still have OP isekai protagonist powers. What's stopping me from getting corrupted by my power, like Oren said?"

"You won't."

"And how do you know that?"

"Because you won't."

"Really? That's your entire argument?"

I sighed and shrugged as I scooted over a bit. I could feel Jamie tense up slightly when I leaned my head against his shoulder. A part of me wondered if he would interpret the casual touch as me leading him on, especially with how recently he'd confessed his love to me, but I couldn't help but feel like he needed this.

"I believe in you," I said.

"Oh."

Jamie's shoulders slumped downward as some of the tension left his body.

"Thanks."

We stayed like that for a while.

"My dream isn't actually to become an adventurer or anything like that, by the way."

"Oh? Really? You always seemed so excited by the idea."

"I mean, I guess you could say that it's always been a dream of mine, but it's not like it's my dream dream, y'know?"

"I can't say I do."

Jamie didn't reply for a few seconds. I looked up at him to see that the smile had vanished from his face. He noticed me staring and tried to smile again, but it didn't quite reach his eyes.

"My dream is to experience love. It's all I've wanted, ever since I was a kid."

When he started to sob quietly, I pulled his head to my chest and hugged him as tight as I could.

Chapter 50

Death and Rebirth

It is confused.

The Second looks down at its dagger, the same dagger that it had dropped upon conversing with the Otherworlder. It never went back to retrieve it, but it simply possesses the dagger once more.

The Second doesn't understand why. It inspects the dagger, running a finger along the flat. It is crafted from a dark steel alloy that is standard issue amongst all Mediators. It is an old dagger, a companion to the Second since it became a Mediator.

The Second sits up and reaches into its back pocket to draw out a cloth and two bottles filled with blade oil and polish. It does not know why it does this. Perhaps it is shaken from its recent experience and wishes to turn to the familiar habit of maintaining its blade for comfort—a common habit among Mediators, and the Second is a Mediator. But a Mediator would let nothing shake its resolve. There is no reason for it to need to seek comfort.

The Second runs its hands along the dagger once more. Does it need to be cleaned? It is spotless. There is no reason for it to need cleaning. It is not the same dagger that it had dropped on the floor while fleeing from the Otherworlder. The Second did not flee from the Otherworlder. And yet it was the same dagger, and it did flee.

But why would a Mediator like the Second have any reason to flee from an Otherworlder?

Would it flee if the Otherworlder cast a spell to identify it as a demon?

The Second does not see any reason why that would be a problem, as the Second is not a demon.

The Second runs its fingers along the dagger, inspecting it once more, before a tremor in its hands causes it to graze its skin against the edge.

The Second recoils in surprise and shame. A competent Mediator should not be making such pointless mistakes. But then again, no person could possibly be perfect, and the Second is a person. The mistake is fine.

The Second inspects the site of the mistake for damage. There is a slight gap there, but as it watches and waits for blood to ooze out, nothing comes.

The Second watches and waits.

Nothing.

The Second feels its heartbeat stop at the sight.

It still denies the idea that it could possibly be a demon, that the Otherworlder's magic was merely a trick. The Second sees a spot of red in the wound, and it feels hope, but the red fades. It comes back. It fades.

The pulsing red light of the Otherworlder's magic lingers still. Detect demons—the name of the insidious spell. The Second tries to convince itself that the name could be a misdirection, designed specifically to fool him.

But the argument is difficult to sustain.

The Second realizes that its heartbeat never started again.

Or had it never beat at all?

The Second puts a hand on its chest, feeling a panic envelop it. Its breath starts to quicken. The sensation is new. Too new. Not the panic nor the quickness, but the breath.

Breathing.

It does not know how to breathe. The Second is suddenly confident that it has never taken a single breath in its entire life. Not that the life had been long. How long?

The Second is scared.

But it shouldn't be.

A Second, while not a leadership position by definition, is the second most important position in a standard Mediator team. While a Second may never deliver instructions to the grunts or shadow on any given mission, a second is always expected to lead by example. A second must be a competent Mediator.

And competent Mediators did not feel fear.

The Second knows that it is a person, and a human is inherently imperfect. But a human is not a demon.

The Second is a demon.

The Second cannot be a human.

The Second cannot be a competent Mediator.

The Second cannot be a second.

And so.

It isn't.

In its final act, the demon stared at the cut in the Aether that made up its form, completely unaware that the knife that it had used to make the cut was slowly fading away from existence, as was the flesh around the cut itself.

And so.

It wasn't.

***

When Stoney woke up, he immediately prodded the back of his head for any hints of damage. Though his fingers came away dry of blood and his head was free of bumps, he could still feel the echoing pains of an intense headache.

A sudden wave of nausea overtook him, and he rolled over to his side as he threw up. He didn't vomit much, but the nausea refused to go away, even when he knew he had no more to give.

So it was a concussion, then.

Stoney stopped himself from rubbing at the source of the wound and asked himself a few questions to test his memory to see how badly the concussion was affecting his mental capacities. Thankfully, aside from the pain and nausea, he seemed to be thinking relatively clearly, with no issues remembering basic information about his life.

His name was Stoney. He was thirty-seven years old. He was currently in a small town called Plainswood. He was a Mediator and a leader in a mission involving an Otherworlder named Jamie. The circumstances in which he found himself replacing a previous leader had been quite strange, with the only reason given for the takeover being "incompetence," but he supposed the problem was much worse than he'd originally expected if two of the incompetents in question turned out to be mutinous traitors.

There was a sharp stab of pain in his head, and Stoney couldn't help but reflexively press his hand against it. At that moment, he realized that his head was uncovered and unbandaged.

He didn't immediately understand why he thought that was a bad thing, but he trusted his instincts more than his conscious thought at this moment in time.

He looked around him, and though it was close enough to pitch black that he couldn't make out any details, there was enough light to make out the familiar sight of the basement that he had originally arrived in.

"Shit," he said out loud, partially because he wanted to see if he would slur his words and partially because he was just pissed.

Stoney went into every mission with the knowledge that he might not walk away from it alive, a general sentiment that was shared by most Mediators. Their mission was more important than their lives, especially given that there was a good chance they would die anyway if they failed. However, that didn't mean the Mediators were callous about their lives or the lives of their team.

There were only two reasons why Stoney would have been left for dead like he was.

"My team is either completely occupied, or they're dead."

A surge of despair almost overtook him at the likelihood of the latter, but Stoney grunted as another surge of pain wracked his head. He didn't enjoy the sensation, but he was grateful to the pain for forcing him to focus on what was important.

Regardless of whether his team was alive or not, their absence meant that there was still an Otherworlder alive out there.

Though he had no idea what transpired during the time that he'd been knocked out nor how long he'd been knocked out in the first place, he knew that he had to do something, debilitating concussion or not.

As Stoney staggered to his feet, the involuntary sway in his step made him nearly trip over nothing, but he managed to catch himself against a wall. He felt the nausea of his concussion intensify at the movement, but nothing came out when he heaved. He waited a few moments for the feeling to subside before he gingerly made his way toward the exit of the basement.

He would mourn later if he needed to.

He couldn't stay idle. He had to figure out the situation and work out a solution from there. It seemed like a daunting task, especially with how his head pulsed with pain at every step, but for now, he had to get out of the basement.

Stoney grunted as he reached the stairs, sliding his hand from the wall to the handrail. Every step he took made him want to sit down and take a breath, but he didn't allow himself the luxury.

The basement steps led up to a trap door, something that Stoney only remembered after he hit his head against it. He hissed in pain but raised his arms to push the door open.

He had to squint as the light bombarded his senses.

Stoney wanted nothing more than to crawl back into the basement and shut the door behind him, but he forced himself onward, shutting his eyes and crawling forward blindly.

Though his head was pounding, he was confident enough in his memory. He could still recall the layout of the house he'd been summoned to from the blueprints he'd studied beforehand. He crawled toward where he knew the kitchen should be, hoping to get some water for his parched throat.

When he felt a pair of arms scoop him up from under his armpits, his first instinct was to resist, but the gentle care that his handler seemed to be putting in to making sure they didn't jostle him too much made Stoney assume that they meant him no harm. Stoney tried to open his eyes, but the glare of the light around him made him close them before he could see who his benefactor was.

He felt himself being lowered gently into a chair, and he slumped down into his seat. Something was pressed into his hand, and once Stoney realized that it was a cup, he lifted it to his lips and drank from it.

Water. It took the entirety of his willpower not to try and down it immediately, taking small sips instead to reduce the risk of choking or somehow aggravating his headache further.

"Stoney. What happened?"

While Stoney could make out the words being spoken, he couldn't identify the voice. The voice was garbled, or perhaps his mind was, but in either case, whoever had spoken knew his name. Another Mediator. Had reinforcements already been sent?

"Traitors," he grunted out. "Lena and Oren. Lena attempted to assassinate my second, and Oren knocked me out when I retaliated. Concussion."

There was no response from his benefactor, but the short talk was enough to dry Stoney's throat out again, and he was forced to take a few more sips of water.

"What happened while I was out?" he asked once he was done. "Where is my team?"

There was a long stretch of silence, one that Stoney was quick to notice. Stoney reached for the dagger on his belt. He didn't know if he would need it or not, but he couldn't risk being caught without it.

"There's no need for that, Stoney," his benefactor said. "Your team's alive."

Stoney paused. He risked cracking open a single eye, and though the glare still hurt his head, he was able to focus for long enough to recognize the man sitting across from him.

"Marten?" he asked, just to make sure.

The insufferable man's only response was a wry smirk, which confirmed his identity better than words could.

"The one and only," Marten responded, his confused voice clashing with the smirk on his face.

"You're alive and safe?" Stoney asked, just to be sure. "What about the two extras?"

"Never was in any danger in the first place," Marten said, jerking a thumb to the side at a pair of Timurans sitting idly at the table. "Same thing for the brats. Been right beside me this entire time."

A wave of relief overtook Stoney before it was replaced by a surge of anger.

"Are you in on it too?" he hissed.

"In on what?" Marten asked.

Stoney had no delusions that he would be able to overpower or even escape from three trained Mediators when he was in such a bad state, but it didn't stop him from growling angrily at Marten.

"Treason," he said. "Was it more than just Lena and Oren? Was this all just a trap to lure me and my second to our deaths?"

Marten's frown deepened. "No," he said. "It wasn't."

"If that's the case, why the hell was I left for dead in a fucking cellar?"

Marten opened his mouth as if to answer but shut it a moment later, his brow furrowing in concentration.

"Stoney," he said. "What was your second's name?"

Stoney growled.

"Don't change the subject, Marten."

"I'm not," he said. "This is important, Stoney. What was your second's name?"

Stoney growled and was about to yell at Marten until he realized he didn't know.

He didn't know anything about his second.

"What?" he muttered.

Marten only responded with a grim frown.

Chapter 51

Plans for the Future

I jerked awake from my sleep silently, almost letting out a gasp until I remembered where I was and who was lying next to me.

Looking to my left, I watched nervously as my mom grumbled in her sleep, still clinging to the fabric of my sleeve. I waited silently for a few seconds until she let out a quiet sigh and sank deeper into her pillow.

I was grateful that my shuffling hadn't woken her up. I hadn't wanted to let her sleep in my bed in the first place, but I felt like it would be unfair to deny her from trying to keep an eye on me.

I sighed silently and looked around the room. From the dull light seeping in through the window, I could guess it was either mid-evening or early morning. Since I'd crawled into bed in the late afternoon, and I didn't feel like I'd slept for more than a few hours, I assumed that it was the former.

I wanted to go back to sleep, but after a few seconds of lying in my own sweat, I decided it was impossible. My skin was too clammy, my mouth was too dry, and my throat was filled with phlegm. I coughed as quietly as I could to clear it, but it didn't make much of a difference. My throat still felt uncomfortably tight.

As I turned my head to the side in hopes that the new position would make it easier to breathe, I realized that I could see a little bit of lamplight peeking into my room from underneath my door.

Though my parents had accepted my request to let Jamie stay with us for the rest of the day, they hadn't hidden the fact that they were uncomfortable with it. Jamie hadn't been too enthused about the idea of staying with my family either, but he didn't argue against it too much. It was a better alternative to staying in the tavern. Still, he hadn't been able to look either of my parents in the eyes and hadn't said a word to either of them.

Despite this fact, I had left him and my dad alone to stew in heavy silence for what was probably at least a few hours now, while I slept peacefully with my mom. I supposed it wasn't exactly a peaceful sleep, but that didn't make me feel any less guilty about it.

I shuffled away from my mom as discreetly as I could, gently prying her fingers from my clothes before sliding slowly away from her. For a moment, I thought she would stir, but as I watched her grumble in her sleep and shift around, she thankfully nestled her head into her pillow, clutching at the blanket in place of my sleeve.

It felt a little cruel to risk having her wake up in a panic when she realized I wasn't there, but she needed the sleep.

I crept toward the door as silently as I could and opened it just enough to see outside into the living room.

Like I'd expected, my dad and Jamie were both wide awake. My dad was sitting at our dining table with his hands folded politely in front of him while Jamie was sitting down on the temporary bedding that we'd laid out for him. While Jamie's head was hung slightly, making it look like he was about to nod off at any moment, I doubted he was unaware of the fact that my dad was staring silently at the back of his head.

I watched the scene for a few seconds before it became clear to me that they must have been frozen like this for a while and weren't likely to do anything else before I came out.

I slowly pushed open the door, so as not to startle them, but even though the door creaked slightly, neither of them acted like they heard me. Even when I stepped out of my room and shut the door behind me, there was no reaction.

I wasn't sure if they hadn't heard me or if they were ignoring me for whatever reason, so I decided to clear my throat.

My dad and Jamie let out a gasp and a quiet yelp of shock respectively, as they both turned their heads to look at me.

I automatically raised a finger to my lips and shushed them. "Mom's still sleeping," I hissed. "Keep it down."

My dad and Jamie both looked embarrassed, though I wasn't sure if it was because they'd both been caught off guard or because of the possibility of them waking my mom. I turned around and cracked open the door slightly to check on her, but after watching her sleeping body for a few seconds, it didn't seem like she'd been disturbed.

I let out a sigh of relief before closing the door again and turning around.

The three of us stared at each other in silence, with my presence clearly doing nothing to alleviate the tension they had spent the last few hours building up. I didn't know what to say, but I eventually tried to smile. While I wasn't sure it was a convincing smile, it prompted Jamie to try the same, giving me a strained look that I could vaguely interpret as an awkward grin.

"Couldn't sleep?" he asked.

"Yeah," I said. "You?"

His eyes shifted slightly toward the side, where my dad was sitting. "Me neither," he said, before falling into a long silence.

I glanced at my dad. Now that his surprise had worn off, his face returned to a neutral frown as he stared openly at Jamie, who seemed determined to pretend like he hadn't noticed.

I wondered for a moment if I should address it, but my dad spoke up before I could decide.

"Are you okay, Lena?" he asked, still keeping his eyes locked onto Jamie.

"Yeah," I said. "Why wouldn't I be?"

My dad finally tore his eyes away from Jamie to frown at me. Immediately, I felt embarrassed by how stupid my question had been.

"I mean, I know a bunch of crazy stuff happened today," I said quickly. "But everything turned out fine in the end. I'm fine."

Jamie gave me a relieved smile, but my dad's frown only deepened.

"What about you, Dad?" I asked. "Are you okay?"

Instead of answering me, he looked down at his hands, taking a deep breath before turning back to stare at Jamie.

"What do you plan to do next?" he asked.

Though the question didn't seem directed at me, Jamie was too determined not to make eye contact with my dad to notice.

"Are you asking me or Jamie?" I asked to make sure.

Jamie seemed surprised by the question, turning to see my dad staring directly at him.

"Hopefully just Jamie," my dad replied. I frowned, but before I could ask what he meant by that, he continued to talk. "What do you plan to do now that your business in our town is finished?"

"What?" Jamie asked. "Oh. Well, I mean, I haven't had too much time to think about it."

"It's been a stressful few weeks for you," I said, though I didn't stop glaring at my dad. "You can take as much time as you need to figure that out. There's no rush, right, Dad?"

My dad made a complicated face that I couldn't quite decipher and stared down at his hands again.

"I'm not trying to rush you, Jamie. I've already agreed to let you stay for as long as you feel is necessary," he said, surprising me with how easily he conceded. "I'm just interested in knowing if you have any ideas for your future plans. Do you plan to stay in our village indefinitely?"

"No, no. I couldn't impose," Jamie said, waving his hands at my dad. He seemed to be more willing to look at him now that their positions had switched, with my dad now being the one determined not to make eye contact, staring down at his hands instead. "And yeah, I do have a few ideas. They just seem a little silly to say out loud."

"Nobody here will think you're being silly," my dad replied. "Feel free to share these ideas of yours."

Even though he seemed a bit solemn, he sounded genuine enough that Jamie was taken aback. Jamie scratched at his head in embarrassment, glancing at me as if looking for support. I didn't do or say anything, but he seemed to find something in my eyes as he nodded and turned back to my dad.

"Well, I mean," he said, letting out a little laugh as he continued to scratch at his head. "Like I said, it's a bit silly of an idea, but ever since I learned how the Mediators were trying to kill me this entire time, I couldn't help but wonder why. I know that Otherworlders have done bad things in the past, but I'm sure there are a lot of Otherworlders who are just normal people like me. I thought that maybe I could travel the world, talk to the other Otherworlders, and try to help them out a bit. I guess it's a little similar to what the Mediators are doing, except, you know... without the killing part."

"You're going to talk to the other Otherworlders?" I asked, a little skeptical of the idea.

"Yeah," Jamie said, seemingly unaware of my hesitation. "If they're as lost and confused as I was when I first got here, I'm not surprised they might go a bit crazy. I mean, I might not be able to stop people like that Plague King guy, but I have to try, right?"

He laughed a bit, but his smile dropped quickly when it became obvious that he was forcing it.

"It's a noble goal," I said.

"It is," my dad agreed, surprising me. "But it is a dangerous one."

"Well, I'm apparently pretty much invincible, so it should be fine? Though I'm not sure how much that would stay true when I'm dealing with other pretty-much-invincible people."

Jamie let out another dry laugh before realizing that nobody else in the room was laughing. I gave him a small reassuring smile, but my dad didn't seem to be interested in such a thing. Taking a deep breath, he seemed to steel himself before looking up.

"I'll be frank," he said. "When I said your goals are dangerous, I didn't mean that they would be dangerous for you."

"What did you mean, then?" Jamie asked.

"He means it would be dangerous for me if I choose to go with you," I answered on behalf of my dad.

My dad looked up at me and sighed.

"You're a grown woman, Lena. Regardless of what your mother and I might want, we can't force you to stay here with us. You're old enough to make your own choices, but it frightens me that you'll make a choice that will get you killed. Again."

Though the comment wasn't directed at Jamie, any traces of a smile evaporated instantly from his face as he looked down into his lap.

"Again with this?" I asked with a frustrated sigh. "I told you, Dad. I'm. Fine. Look. I'm standing here talking to you right now, aren't I? I'm alive, Dad."

I patted my chest for emphasis and looked sideways at Jamie with a grin.

"Besides, even if I do die again, Jamie can just fix me right up. Right?"

My words didn't seem to do anything to reassure him, as his gaze sank even lower.

The silence stretched out between the three of us. I wasn't sure how long it lasted or what prompted it to end. Eventually, my dad sighed and looked up, his eyes unfocused but pointing vaguely in Jamie's direction.

"Jamie," he said, his voice monotone and quiet. "You may stay in my home with me and my family, but I would like to ask you to follow one condition."

Jamie looked up. "What is it?"

"Think about what you want to do next. Think about how it might affect you and the people who care about you. Please."

I wasn't entirely sure whether the request was actually directed at Jamie or not, but he gave my dad a cautious nod anyway.

Chapter 52
A Suspicious Feeling

"Okay. What do we all actually know about the second?" Stoney asked.

"Ain't that something I should be asking you, oh glorious leader? Didn't you read his file?"

Stoney glared at Marten. He hadn't wanted to, knowing that Marten was the type of person to goad people for a reaction, but Marten didn't seem to take any pleasure in the fact that he had successfully irritated Stoney, wearing an equally dour grimace himself.

"Of course, I read his file," Stoney replied. "But like everything else that concerns the second, I can't remember any details."

"Oh, isn't that fucking convenient." Marten scoffed.

Stoney considered pointing out the fact that Marten couldn't remember anything about the second either, but he doubted that Marten didn't realize that. If he had to guess, Marten was just nervous and lashing out in the worst way he knew. Stoney turned to his other two subordinates instead, deciding to leave him alone for now until he decided to be useful again.

"Tenna. Laush," he said. "Describe the second for me."

The two glanced at him, clearly surprised that he'd ask their opinion.

"Well," Tenna said. "He was a man."

The grunt trailed off, glancing at his sister as if she had anything else to contribute. She stayed silent.

Marten let out a bitter laugh, but Stoney ignored it and nodded.

"Nothing else?" he asked.

"Nothing, sir."

Stoney nodded. "Good."

"Good?" Marten scoffed. "You think any part of this situation can be described in any way other than fucked up?"

"Good that we can agree," Stoney clarified. "It means that all of us already know everything there is to know about our mysterious team member. Which is to say, we know nothing, which is an impossibility. Either our minds or reality itself was tampered with. Something beyond the capabilities of a regular mortal."

Marten rolled his eyes at the obvious information, but Tenna and Laush both nodded in response.

"Could it be the work of the Otherworlder?" Tenna asked.

Stoney shook his head. "It's possible, but unlikely," he said. "Though Jamie is a highly irregular case, where he actively knows about the Mediators and our role in his journey, he was not informed of the specifics of our inner workings, as far as I'm aware." Stoney paused to allow anyone to refute the statement.

When nobody spoke up, he continued.

"Jamie was not informed of our planned arrival, and if his psychological profile is to be believed, he is not the type of person to use his magic to attain omniscience. While it is possible that the second was a real person and that Jamie used his magic to modify our memories of him, I highly doubt it. If he would go so far, he would've done worse."

"He does have a pathological aversion to murder, sir," Laush said.

"I meant that he would've gone further with the memory wiping," Stoney replied. "Why erase every memory about the details on who the second was when he could've just as easily made us forget about the man entirely? I won't deny the possibility outright, but it doesn't seem likely."

Nobody refuted the suggestion, not that he expected them to.

"Anyway," Stoney said, breaking the momentary silence. "Regardless of what exactly was the cause of this anomaly, we need to report back to HQ."

Before Stoney could continue, a spike of pain shot through his head, forcing him to clench his teeth and brace himself against the wave of nausea that washed over him. Ignoring the lingering effects of the concussion as best as he could, he lifted a finger to point around the table.

"Sera, Oren. I know you're technically grunts now, but knowing your capabilities, I'm comfortable with letting the five of you do a communications ritual without me. Marten. You'll take point as the anchor again. I won't be in the right state to cast any magic until this concussion fades."

There was a long pause before Tenna spoke.

"Umm, sir," he said. "Sera and Oren aren't here."

Stoney's eyes widened before another wave of pain hit, forcing him to close his eyes against it. Even without looking around the room, however, Stoney knew that the young extra was right.

"Concussion's worse than I thought," he muttered under his breath.

"Are you alright, sir?" Tenna asked.

Stoney thought about shaking his head but thought better of it, not wanting to aggravate his headache any more than was necessary.

"No. But nothing that can be done about it at the moment," Stoney said. "Do we know where Sera and Oren are?"

"No, sir." Stoney wasn't sure which of the extras had spoken.

"Go, then," he said. "The both of you. Find them. This isn't a situation where we can afford to be down two Mediators. Tell them that they were right to do what they did, and assure them that they won't be charged with treason."

"Yes, sir," the responses came.

Stoney sat there as the sound of quiet footsteps left the room. Sitting there, with his head in his hands, he wasn't sure how long it took for the pain to finally quiet down.

When he looked back up, he was surprised to see he wasn't alone.

"Marten," he said. "Why aren't you gone?"

Marten gave him a sidelong glance, his expression uncharacteristically blank.

"You never told me to leave," he said with a shrug. "Is there something you wanted me to do?"

Stoney glared at Marten, not appreciating the smug attitude. "No."

Marten raised an eyebrow at that. "Seriously?" he asked. "That concussion must be worse than I thought, then. You know the kid's not being watched right now."

Stoney blinked a few times before cursing under his breath.

"You're right. The concussion's clearly affecting me more than I thought."

Marten stared at him for a few seconds before letting out a heavy sigh. "And you want me to take over as leader. Again."

"Oh, grow up," Stoney said, gently massaging his temple. "You're trained for the role."

"Doesn't mean I have to like it," Marten said. "Fucking incompetent assholes making me work overtime. I don't get paid enough for this shit."

"You get paid the exact amount that is expected for this shit," Stoney said. "Kings get less income than you do."

"Then how the hell am I still in debt?" Marten grumbled, though he did move to stand up from the table.

"Maybe because as soon as the money gets into your hands, you toss it away on a dice roll?"

Marten glared at Stoney.

Stoney tried to glare back but ended up sighing.

"Look, I'm sorry for dumping this back into your lap, but I'm clearly not fit to lead right now, and I can't trust anyone else here. The extras are just barely at grunt level, and even if Sera and Oren aren't crazy, they're still..."

"Horny and stupid respectively?"

"Yes," Stoney said with a sigh. "That. Once we get those two back, though, we'll be able to do another ritual. Get reinforcements."

Marten frowned. "About that," he said. "What do you think about another option?"

"I wasn't aware we had any," Stoney said. "But go ahead."

"What if we asked the brat to help us?"

Stoney raised an eyebrow. "Jamie?" he asked to make sure, just in case Marten was referring to someone else.

"Yes, Jamie."

"Why do you think that's a good idea?" Stoney asked, more curious than challenging.

"Because I'm confident he would help in earnest," Marten said. "I've seen enough of his type. Friendly, naïve, not uninteresting, but probably some other adjective that starts with a 'U' if I were feeling a bit more creative. He likes to think of himself as something close to a benevolent hero, like a kid playing pretend. He'd help if we asked."

"I see. And you believe in his credibility more than you do Sera and Oren?"

Marten shrugged. "Not sure. As much as I'd like to rag on them, the idiot duo are still trained Mediators. I'm just presenting the brat as an option."

Stoney frowned. "Could you refer to Jamie by his name?"

"Why?" Marten asked.

"You refer to everyone younger than you as 'brat,'" Stoney said. "It's hard to keep track. At least give him a different moniker if you insist on not saying his name."

"Moniker?" Marten asked, an undercurrent of a chuckle in his voice. "It's not like I was trying to make 'Brat' into his official title. Imagine 'The Brat' standing alongside names like 'The Plague King' or 'The Harem Lord.' I'd never live it down."

"Then stop or I'm petitioning it officially," Stoney said. "I'd rather not do any more mental gymnastics to try and figure out which 'brat' you're talking about until my concussion fades."

"Then I can go back to being an annoying asshole?"

Despite himself, Stoney couldn't help but chuckle.

"Yeah, do whatever the hell you want. Now get out of here."

"Hey, I'm the leader right now. You can't order me around."

"Sorry, sir," Stoney said, making sure to inject as much sarcasm as he could into the words. "Did I offend you by questioning your authority?"

"Gravely," Marten replied. "But before I go, give me your thoughts. Is there anything that bothers you about Jamie?"

When Stoney looked up at Marten, he was surprised to see the complicated expression that plagued him. Completely contrasting with the light mood that he'd been maintaining up until a few seconds before, Marten's face was shrouded with uncertainty and anxiety as he waited for Stoney's response.

"What do you mean?" Stoney asked.

Marten shrugged. "I'm not sure," he said. "Just something about him. You've been a Mediator longer than I have. Surely you feel it too, right?"

"Can't say I do," Stoney said. "But I haven't even met him yet."

"Yeah, me neither. Or at least not formally, seeing as he isn't supposed to know I exist. But even just thinking about him gives me this strange feeling in the back of my head, like I'm supposed to be remembering something, but I can't remember what exactly it is."

Stoney frowned, not understanding what Marten was talking about in the slightest. Marten seemed to decipher his expression easily and waved him off before he could respond.

"It's hard to explain. Didn't even realize it until recently myself. You read his file, right?"

"Of course," Stoney said indignantly.

"You didn't notice anything weird about it?"

From how insistent Marten was being, it was easy to assume that he was baiting Stoney into a specific answer, but Stoney had no clue what it could be. Though he was having trouble trusting in his memory at the moment, the dossier on Jamie's case was simple enough to recall.

"No," he said, a little hesitantly. "Did you notice something? I went through the files pretty thoroughly, but nothing stood out to me at the time."

"I barely skimmed it, to be honest."

"And you noticed something I didn't?"

"Probably not. It just feels… weird."

Marten let out a groan of frustration before Stoney could say anything.

"You know what? Forget it. We're not getting anywhere with this shit. Just… be on the lookout, I guess. This case is fucking weird."

Stoney couldn't agree more.

"I'll keep a lookout," he said, even though he still wasn't sure what he was supposed to be watching for. "Now get a move on. We still need eyes on Jamie."

Marten nodded, too preoccupied with his thoughts to even give a half-hearted complaint. Pushing his chair back, he stood up and walked toward the door but paused before he left.

"Does his name bother you at all?"

"You mean Jamie?" Stoney asked.

"Yeah," Marten said, not even bothering to point out the stupidity of the question like he usually would. "Jamie."

Stoney tried to think of anything strange about it but found nothing odd.

"No," Stoney said. "It's just a normal name."

Chapter 53

AN EQUIVALENT EXCHANGE

After my talk with Lena's dad, a tense silence sat heavy between the three of us. Frozen in our spots, none of us wanted to risk starting another conversation, too afraid of what could be said.

I looked down at my lap, too tired and too unfocused to actually think about what I wanted to do next. I could imagine Lena's dad staring at the back of my head, silently urging me to make a decision, but the imaginary pressure just made it harder to think. I wasn't sure if he was actually staring at me or not, but I didn't want to check.

I didn't know how long we stayed like that. It could've been a few hours or a few minutes, but eventually, I couldn't take it anymore.

I let out a quiet sigh, hoping I wouldn't startle anyone with the sudden break in the silence.

"I'm gonna go out for a walk," I said. "I need to clear my head."

Though I tried my best not to, I couldn't help but look back at Lena. She gave me a pained look as her eyes darted between me and her bedroom.

"Could it wait just a bit?" she asked. "I don't want my mom to freak out if she wakes up and I'm not around."

I wasn't sure whether I wanted to smile or frown at the idea that Lena just assumed that I wanted her to come along with me. She was right, of course. Ever since arriving in Materia, Lena had basically been my main source of stability and the only real friend I had, since Oren and Sera had been secretly trying to kill me the whole time. The thought of having her by my side, especially after a day like this, was a comforting one.

But the fact that I so desperately wanted her to tag along was the exact reason why I wanted to be alone to think in the first place.

"It's okay," I said. "I just need some time by myself."

"Are you sure?"

"Yeah."

From the look on her face, I was certain that she didn't believe me, but she didn't call me out on it. I waited a few seconds for her to respond, but once I realized I was stalling in the hopes that she would insist on coming along anyway, I left the house without another word.

As I stepped outside, I flinched at the spray of rain that hit my face. While the rain had quieted down significantly since the morning, it was still bad enough that my hoodie was quickly drenched, hugging my shoulders with its cold grip.

Though I could have easily used my magic to make a magical umbrella and dry myself off, I didn't bother to do either.

I waited until I was more than a few steps away from Lena's house before saying, "Quest Log."

The familiar blue panel popped up in front of me, but it was smaller than I remembered. Granted, I hadn't actually checked any of my status windows in a while, but it wasn't a hard change to notice.

All my quests had disappeared. All apart from one.

I lifted a finger to tap it.

A new panel opened.

[Main] Quest: Find True Love
Progress: True Love obtained (0/1)
Rewards: N/A

"Apparently, N/A stands for Not being Alive. Who knew?"

I waited for myself to chuckle at my own horrible joke, but no sound escaped me.

"I guess I'm dying a virgin, huh?" I said out loud, hoping that a second joke might do something to lift my spirits.

I forced myself to laugh this time, but all that came out was a raspy wheeze. I was about to try a third joke when I heard someone clearing their throat.

"There are some great brothels in Redstone, you know. If that's something you really want to fix."

I was barely able to stop myself from yelping at the interruption as I whirled around. Down the street from me, a balding middle-aged man stood with his back against a random house. He stood underneath the awning to protect himself from the rain, his hands raised in a half-hearted gesture of surrender. He looked like he was frowning, but from the way that the lines in his face outlined the expression so perfectly, I quickly assumed that was his neutral expression.

"Sorry you had to hear that," I said, feeling heat rise to my cheeks despite the cold rain.

"Don't be," the man said, waving off my concerns and lowering his hands. "It's something that all men think about, especially at your age. No point in being ashamed of what the body wants."

"I guess," I said. Though it helped that he was so casual about it, it didn't mean I wanted to acknowledge the fact that he'd caught me talking to myself about how I was a virgin. "Can we stop talking about this?"

The man raised an eyebrow like he didn't understand why I was embarrassed, but then he shrugged to himself.

"You enjoy standing out in the rain like this?" he asked instead.

"No. Not really," I said. I didn't know why this middle-aged man was so talkative, but I didn't want to be rude.

"Then why are you?"

"I don't have anywhere I want to go."

"I see," the man said, frowning. I thought that might be the end of the questioning, but after a short pause, he continued. "Why aren't you at least protecting yourself with magic? I doubt it's possible for you to catch a cold, but still. It can't be too comfortable staying drenched like that."

"You know I'm an Otherworlder?" I asked, barely surprised. Though the man wasn't one of the people Lena had introduced me to, I assumed that by now, the entire village knew who I was.

For some reason, the question gave the man pause. He stared at me, the lines in his brow intensifying as he fixed me with a scrutinizing gaze. I simply stood there, not knowing what he was thinking until he reached up to massage his temple.

"Yeah, I do," he said with a sigh. "Little tip, brat. If someone ever stops you on the street for no reason, especially on a day like this, it's because they want something from you. I'm a Mediator."

I blinked a few times, staring at the man, wondering if he was just joking or not. The man matched my gaze and gave me a casual shrug.

"I'm typically more of a background player. I wouldn't usually out myself, but our team's a bit understaffed at the moment, and I wanted to ask you for a favor."

"Oh," I said, feeling bitterness creep into my voice almost immediately. "So what do you want, then? Are you going to ask me to die?"

The man winced. "You know?"

"Lena told me," I said. "Oren and Sera were there to confirm it."

"I see," the man said. "What did you do to them?"

"Well, I put Oren to sleep, and Sera wandered off somewhere," I said. "Don't ask me where she went. I don't know."

"I see," the man said. "And when you say you put Oren to sleep..."

He trailed off. It didn't take me long to get what he was implying.

"When I say I put Oren to sleep, I mean I put him to sleep," I said, barely holding myself back from shouting. "I didn't kill him."

"Well, isn't that a shame," the man said, angrily rubbing his temple.

There was a short pause before the man reached into his shirt and drew out a pipe. Stuffing it with something I couldn't see, he placed a finger inside the tip of his pipe for a second before withdrawing it, flicking off a few flakes of embers before taking in a deep breath.

I waited for him to say something, but after he breathed out his first puff of smoke, he simply went back for another.

"Well?" I asked, feeling a little impatient. "What do you want?"

The man raised an eyebrow but didn't bother taking his lips from his pipe. He drew in another deep breath before breathing out another large cloud of thick smoke that nearly enveloped his entire head.

"Forget about it," he said, shaking his head and dispersing some of the smoke gathered around it. "You might not be happy with us, but you're letting us live and you're not going on a rampage. I'm not going to risk changing your mind by asking you to do something you don't want."

I narrowed my eyes. "What exactly do you mean by that?"

The man shrugged. "It means the Mediators will leave you alone," he said, taking another draw from his pipe before holding it upside down and tapping it to empty the contents on the ground in front of him and stowing the pipe away. "Live your life, Jamie Campbell."

Even as the man turned and started to walk away, it took me a while for me to realize that he was saying goodbye.

"Wait," I called before he could walk too far away.

The man stopped, turning his head just enough to give me a sideways glance.

"What?"

His gruff and aggressive tone made it very difficult for me to convince myself that he wasn't annoyed that I'd stopped him.

"What did you want help with?" I asked.

"What?" he repeated in the exact same tone.

Despite knowing that I shouldn't have cared about how he felt when he was a part of the group that had actively tried to kill me, I still had to fight down the feeling of shame and guilt in response to an adult's annoyance. I scratched my head and turned to the side.

"You said that you wanted something from me, right?" I asked quickly before I could regret my decision. "What is it?"

The man raised an eyebrow, though he still somehow managed to look more angry than surprised. "You're considering helping out an organization that tried to kill you?" he asked. "Are you suicidal or stu—"

He snapped his mouth shut and averted his eyes before he could finish the sentence.

"I'm not suicidal," I said with a huff. I tried to pretend like I didn't know what else he was about to call me, but I still felt an indignant flush rise to my cheeks. "But I'd be willing to at least hear you out, and I wouldn't be doing it for free."

"And what could you possibly want that you wouldn't be able to get on your own?" the man asked.

I hesitated, not knowing how to phrase what I was about to ask.

"Information," I said eventually. "I want to know about the other Otherworlders."

The man winced almost immediately. Apparently, that wasn't the correct way to phrase it.

"Why?" he asked, clearly suspicious.

I took a moment to consider my words again before deciding I wasn't very good at it.

"Look. I'll be honest. I only learned that you guys were working to try to kill me a few hours ago. I haven't really had the time to fully process it, but for now, I'm not gonna put the blame on you. When every Otherworlder has the potential to be a magical super Hitler, I guess you have to be a bit careful," I said, chuckling at my joke.

I paused to give the man a chance to give some input, but when his only reply was to stare at me like I was stupid, I scratched at my cheek and continued.

"I mean, I still am upset that you were trying to kill me, but for now, I'm willing to put it aside, since I guess you're just afraid of another Plague King happening. I mean, I'm definitely looking him up later to check that you didn't just make him up, but basically..."

I took a moment to brace myself. While I'd already told Lena about my plans, I felt like telling a Mediator would make it more real somehow, like I wouldn't be able to take it back anymore once I said it out loud.

"I thought that maybe I could travel the world, doing stuff to mend the bad reputation that the other Otherworlders have left behind and make sure the current Otherworlders don't go down a bad path either. But I don't know anything about the Otherworlders, and I assume you guys know a lot about Otherworlders that you could teach me," I said. "Plus, even if you can't tell me anything, helping you out would give you proof that not all Otherworlders are that bad, right?"

I stared at the man, keeping eye contact with him to convince him I was serious. The man stared back at me, his brow furrowed in a deep glare.

"Are you fucking stupid, kid?" he asked, not bothering to cut the insult short this time.

"Maybe," I admitted.

He stared at me for a bit longer before letting out a deep groan. He reached into his shirt and took out his pipe once more.

"This is above my pay grade," he growled. "You'll want to talk with the Boss, which is conveniently what I wanted to ask you for."

"What do you mean?" I asked.

"We have a communication spell, but it takes a fuckload of mana to cast," the man grumbled, aggressively shoving a bunch of something into his pipe. "Usually needs a whole team of Mediators to cast it, but I'd imagine you could do it on your own without a problem."

"Oh," I said, trying to put on a smile. "Yeah, probably."

The man grumbled under his breath as he lit his pipe.

Chapter 54
More Plans for the Future

"You could've gone with him."

I stared at my dad, even as he looked down at his hands, idly fiddling with his fingers.

"What?" I asked, just to make sure I'd heard him correctly.

"I said you could've gone with him. Jamie," he added at the end, like he could possibly be talking about anybody else.

"I thought that was the exact opposite of what you wanted," I said.

"It is."

I waited for him to continue and frowned when he didn't.

"That's all you want to say?" I asked, not understanding what point he was trying to make.

"No," he said quietly.

"Then what do you want from me?" I asked. "Spit it out."

My dad looked up at me with a deep frown on his face that made me instantly regret getting angry at him like that. I looked away from him.

"Sorry," I said through gritted teeth. "I didn't mean to snap at you. I'm just a little tired, I guess."

"It's fine to be upset, Lena. It's perfectly understandable," my dad said, his voice soft and careful, like he was afraid I would shatter if he spoke too loudly. It irritated me more than anything else, but I forced the feeling down.

"I'm fine," I said, not wanting to risk snapping at him again if I spoke more than a few words.

My dad stared at me, disbelief clear on his face. His jaw shifted from side to side, like he was physically trying to organize the words in his mouth before he spoke. His face turned into a whirlwind of subtle shifts in emotion before he finally settled on a frown.

"How was it?" he asked.

"How was what?" I asked back.

He raised his shoulders slightly in an almost imperceptible shrug. "Everything," he said. "I don't know much about Otherworlders, but what I do know is horrifying. I'm sure I've mentioned the book written by one of the followers of the Plague King."

I frowned at the mention of the Plague King. Even though Jamie was nowhere near the second coming of the Plague King, I didn't want to even entertain the thought of comparing the two.

"You have," I said. "You also never let me read it."

"Only because you were too young at the time. By the time you grew old enough that your mother might not have killed me for letting you read it, you didn't care for reading."

The joke and the chuckle that followed it were as painfully forced as his sudden shift in tone, but he pretended like it wasn't obvious. I decided to do the same.

"I do like reading, Dad," I said, feeling more than a small amount of whiplash from the casual tone I was forcing on myself. I was glad I was far enough from him that I didn't feel compelled to playfully punch his shoulder to go along with the forced mood. "But I like reading fun books, not depressing autobiographies."

"That's very smart of you," he said. "But it's an interesting book, overall. I'll lend it to you if you want, kiddo."

He immediately winced for a split second before forcing a smile on his face. I was sure I did the same thing. My dad had never in his life called me 'kiddo' before, and it was jarring to hear.

"Sure," I said.

At the one-word answer, the conversation died almost immediately. We both sat there with awkward smiles on our faces before my dad's smile dropped, his shoulders sinking down with it.

"I'll be honest. The book is horrible. Interesting, but horrible."

"As in, it's poorly written?" I asked, still hanging on to the remnants of my smile for a bit longer, hoping he would take it as an invitation to go back to pretending everything was fine.

"No." My dad almost seemed to shiver as he ignored my half-hearted attempt at a joke. "The things that the author went through were horrific. I just..." He frowned as he buried his head in his hands. "I just want to know you're fine, Lena."

My automatic reaction was to open my mouth and tell him I was fine and that he could stop worrying, but the look on his face stopped me. Close to tears, a meltdown, or both, his hands were folded together in a white-knuckled grip as he stared down at the table, either because he didn't want to be looking at me when I told him another half-hearted lie or because he didn't want me to feel guilty when I did.

I considered lying to him anyway, and I had halfway managed to convince myself that it would be for the best, but my mouth opened without my permission.

"I'm fine now," I said. "But I guess I can relate to how scary it can be to be a Follower. Until I realized that Jamie was actually just a person, it was pretty bad."

My dad's reaction was mixed. Tension and relief both seemed to clash within him, and he seemed to struggle with whether he was upset to hear that or relieved that I was opening up to him.

"Tell me about it," he said.

And so I did. I told him everything, from the moment Ryuji Nightblade fell from the sky to the moment when Jamie Campbell broke down crying in my arms. I told him everything I could remember, every detail, and it was only when I finished my story that I realized I'd made a mistake.

"Don't tell anyone I told you about the secret Mediator stuff, okay?"

My dad had been entirely silent throughout my story, simply nodding along to show that he was still listening, but it took him a few seconds to realize I was waiting for a response.

"I won't," he said.

"I didn't mean to. It kind of just slipped out," I said. "I'm sorry."

"What are you apologizing for?" my dad asked, his voice gruff. "I'm the one who asked you to share."

"This is serious, Dad," I said, shaking my head. "The Mediators would probably kill you if they knew you knew all the stuff they told me."

"And would that be so bad?" he asked, raising an eyebrow.

For a moment, I couldn't understand what he had just said. The casual way he'd said it made me think that there was no way he could have suggested that he would be alright with being assassinated by the Mediators.

"What did you just say?" I asked.

My dad shrugged. "As long as Jamie's around, he can just bring me back to life, no problem, right?"

"I—" My lips pursed subconsciously as I struggled to find a response to him. "No, Dad. It's not 'no problem.' You can't just die and expect everything to be fine, even if you can come back. That's not how that works."

He looked up into my eyes, concern radiating from his own.

"I couldn't agree more."

I stared into his eyes for a few more seconds before turning away uncomfortably.

"I'm fine."

There was a long silence before my dad let out an equally long sigh.

We sat there for a while, staring anywhere else but at each other. By the time I noticed we were stuck in the air of awkwardness that festered between us, it was too late to break it.

It would have been a convenient time for something to happen to break it for us, like my mom waking up or someone knocking on our door, but nothing like that happened.

"What are you going to do now?"

The question was abrupt enough that the surprise I felt almost made me physically recoil.

"What?" I asked, if only to give myself a moment to gather my thoughts.

"What are you going to do now?" my dad repeated.

"What do you mean?"

My dad sighed, though I wasn't sure if it was out of frustration, despair, or something else.

"Jamie plans to leave," he said. "Do you plan to go with him?"

"Yes," I said, surprising myself with how easily I gave him my answer.

"Why?"

"He doesn't have anyone else."

My dad sighed.

"We've raised you too well," he said, shaking his head. "I suppose it's all a father could ask for, to know that his daughter grew up to be a good person, but I do wish you were a little more selfish. I wish I was more selfish too."

I stayed silent, not knowing how to reply to that.

"Where do you plan to go first?" my dad asked.

"You're fine with me going?" I asked, a little surprised that he was taking this so well.

He shook his head. "I'm not," he said. "But I can't stop you from making your own choices. As I've said already, you're a grown woman. So where do you think you'll go?"

"Oh. Well, I'm not sure. I don't think Jamie had any specific ideas."

My dad nodded, as if expecting the answer.

"If I could make a suggestion," he said. "Jamie wants to mend the bad reputation that Otherworlders have in our society, right? It's a noble idea, but before he can fix the image of his kind, I feel like he has to fix his own image first."

"What do you mean by that?" I asked.

"I mean that he has to make amends for the crimes he's committed," my dad said, his eyes shifting away from mine. "What was that caravan guard's name? Medric?"

My eyes narrowed.

"I know what you're trying to do, Dad," I said.

"What do you mean?" he asked, trying to pretend like he had no idea what I was talking about. It wasn't a very good attempt.

"I mean that it's obvious what you're trying to do," I said, shaking my head and massaging my temples to stop the growing headache. "You want me to go to Medric so I can see how he's traumatized by the experience of dying and being brought back to life. Then, once I start helping Medric process his trauma, I'll realize that I'm actually just as traumatized and that I just couldn't process the fact that I literally died and came back to life until I saw someone else going through the same thing. I get it, Dad, but it won't work like that. I don't need an outside perspective to realize I'm messed up right now. I already know."

I glared at my dad, lifting a finger to the corner of my eye to make sure I wasn't crying.

It came away dry.

"I'm not fine, Dad," I said, keeping my voice confined to a neutral tone. "Yeah, I admit it, okay? Is that what you wanted?"

My dad looked down at his hands again, his lips pressed into a thin line. He seemed determined not to look directly at me, though I wasn't sure if it was because he was angry at me or afraid of me.

I sighed.

"Look. I'm sorry," I said. "But I can't afford to take the time to process it. If I break and Jamie realizes that he's hurt me, that would destroy him. I'm not going to betray him like that, Dad. I can't."

My dad's only response was to place his face in his hands and let out a shaky breath. It seemed to be a struggle for him, with every breath catching on his throat multiple times.

I wanted to comfort him, but I couldn't. I looked away, pretending I hadn't noticed the clear liquid seeping out from between his fingers, not for his sake, but for mine.

"I—" When his words caught in his throat once again, he took a few more shaky breaths before he felt comfortable enough to try again. "I'm proud of the woman you've become. I wish I didn't have to be."

"I'm sorry," I said.

"You'll need to say goodbye to your mother too."

"I know."

"Promise me you'll come back home one day?"

"I promise."

"Promise me you'll stay safe?"

A moment passed.

"I'll try."

I stayed for a while. I hated hearing my dad try and fail to stay quiet, to suppress his gasps, but the least I could do was stay by his side for a bit longer.

Chapter 55
NEW JOB PROSPECTS

Quiet pops echoed in the forest.

The signal wasn't a very versatile one, but it was useful enough that it was the first spell that a Mediator learned in basic training. It wasn't meant for conveying messages and was usually used to let a fellow Mediator know that something needed their attention.

The sound was innocuous enough that it could be easily ignored no matter the place, and the forest was no exception. Sera was tempted to pretend that it was just the sound of an old branch snapping or a distant woodpecker tapping away at a tree, but she had heard the sound too many times to ever mistake it for anything else.

Sera considered ignoring the obvious summons. Even though the Otherworlder had marked the false second as a demon, effectively clearing her of a mutiny charge, that didn't mean she wouldn't be punished for the terrible decision-making with everything involving Lena.

Standing in the rain for a few hours had given her a rare moment alone with her thoughts. Though she spent a good portion of that time wallowing in the memory of the spiteful glare that Lena had shot at her before she left, she spent the rest of her time thinking about what would happen to her.

Even in the best-case scenario, she would be demoted, probably taken off active duty and put back on basic training for years until she could prove that she could be trusted in a leadership position again.

And that was if they didn't just excommunicate her outright.

The popping sounds continued to echo around her, carried by the wind currents in small pockets of mana. The range of the spell was small enough that it wouldn't be difficult for Sera to search for the caster, but she couldn't bring herself to move.

Rooted on the spot, staring blankly into nothing, she simply waited for the caster to find her.

"Sera."

Sera didn't turn around, but she recognized the voice.

"Tenna," she replied. Sera was surprised by how hoarse her voice was. She hadn't been crying. "Am I being detained?"

"No," Tenna replied. "You're still part of the team."

Sera was tempted to respond with "for now," but she stayed silent. It was pointless to say out loud.

"Leader wants to send the Founder a message, so he wants you and Oren back to help with the ritual," Tenna continued. "Oren gave him a pretty bad concussion, so we need the two of you back to make five."

Sera felt like she should ask if Stoney was okay, but she didn't feel like she could summon the energy. She turned around to face Tenna.

He stared back at her, with his arms folded across his chest and a frown on his face.

"You look like shit," he said.

Sera simply walked past him, ignoring the comment. "Mayor's house?" she asked, as if speaking quickly made it easier to ignore how raspy her voice sounded.

"Yeah," Tenna replied before following behind her.

Sera appreciated the silence that Tenna allowed her, even if he likely didn't think much of it. Idle small talk wasn't something that Mediators did amongst each other, which was something that Sera would miss. Would she have to engage in small talk in her civilian life?

Sera sighed. Here she was, already assuming that she would be fired.

It was a depressing thought, but more so was the fact that Sera couldn't find any reason to think that it wouldn't be the case. The thought that she would become a civilian terrified her.

What would she even do with her life?

She couldn't recall anything about her previous life as a civilian, but given that she was five when she first joined the organization, she doubted that any memories she could have retained would be useful anyway. For a moment, Sera tried to recall anything about her past life, but she was surprised to realize that she barely remembered anything about that life, not even the faces of her late family.

The realization bothered her less than it probably should have. Her family dying at the hands of an Otherworlder was the original reason she had chosen to become a Mediator in the first place, but her desire for revenge had been fleeting. By the time she had finished her basic training and had been allowed in the field, the Otherworlder who had casually murdered her family years before had already passed on.

Though she had tried to keep her anger alive by directing it at other Otherworlders, it was too tiring to sustain indefinitely. By the time she noticed that her desire for vengeance had all but faded out, it had already been replaced with a sense of duty and responsibility that was more than strong enough to motivate her to stay with the Mediators.

But it still felt disrespectful that she couldn't remember her family. Not their faces or their names.

She decided that the first thing she wanted to do when she was fired was to visit their graves and apologize.

Not that she knew where their graves were.

Sera frowned.

* * *

"You doing okay?"

Bran watched as Lena's eyes seemed to come into focus at the sound of his voice. He waved awkwardly with his free hand at his childhood friend, tilting his umbrella back so she could get a clearer look at his face. The rain had died out enough that the light drizzle didn't bother him, so he kept his umbrella tilted back as Lena stared in his direction.

After what felt like an entire minute, she replied with a half-hearted shrug.

Bran felt his awkward grin turn crooked as he walked forward to join Lena on her porch. After setting his umbrella down against a pillar, he took a seat on the porch steps, keeping his back to Lena but turning his head enough that he could glance sideways at her if he wanted to.

He kept his eyes away for now, staring out into the distance.

"Do you want to talk about it?" he asked.

"No," Lena answered immediately. "Not really."

Bran let out a sigh of relief and immediately felt guilty for it. He glanced back at Lena to see if she noticed, but her gaze was blank and unfocused. He felt another tinge of relief and immediately felt guilty again.

"My dad sent me over to make sure nobody died," he said quickly to break himself out of the loop. "He's at the tavern right now. Apparently, one of the walls just completely collapsed?"

Lena stayed silent, and Bran's first thought was to assume that she hadn't heard him. He quickly scolded himself for being stupid and patiently waited for her to respond.

"Yeah," she eventually replied.

Bran couldn't tell if she was saying that nobody had died or if she was acknowledging that the tavern had been partially destroyed.

"Did Jamie destroy the wall?" he asked, too afraid to ask about his other question, in case he didn't like the answer.

"No."

"Really?"

"Yeah. It was one of the Mediators."

Bran was more than a little surprised by the answer. Why? How? Which one? He didn't want to barrage Lena with his questions, though, so he chose one at random. "Why?" he asked.

Lena twitched and her brow furrowed slightly before returning to a more neutral state. She shrugged.

It was obvious to Bran that she knew more than she was letting on, but it was even more obvious that it would be a bad idea to ask.

Not wanting to accidentally ask the question anyway, Bran quickly blurted out the next thing he could think of to force the topic away.

"What's that you got in your hand?" he asked.

"Huh?" Lena replied, looking down at her hand as if surprised that there was something there. She raised the book in her hands before frowning at it. "It's a book."

"Yeah, I— Um, I guess," Bran said, biting back the automatic sarcastic response he had lined up. "Is it a good read?"

Lena frowned as she turned the book over in her hands again. "I haven't even opened it yet," she said. "My dad lent it to me."

"Oh. And how is your dad?" Bran asked.

"He's fine," Lena answered, perhaps a little too quickly.

Once more, Bran forced himself to steer the topic away to avoid the obvious sore subject. He wondered if her dad was related to the reason why she was sitting outside on her porch, even when he could see the lamplight shining from the window.

"What's the book called?" he asked.

Lena stared down at the book and tilted it so she could read the cover. "The Chronicles of a Witness," she said.

"Oh yeah?" Bran said, wondering for a moment why the name sounded so familiar. "What's it about?"

"It's an autobiography, written by one of the Followers of the Plague King."

Bran winced and looked away as the mystery was quickly solved.

"Sorry," he said.

"What for?" Lena asked.

"For bringing it up."

"Don't be," Lena said. "Not like you knew what it was. I know you can't read."

Lena's attempt at forcing a casual mood was terrible, but he still played along as best as he could.

"Har har," Bran said. "Very funny."

Lena let out a humorless laugh. "Say, why do you think my dad lent me this?" she asked. "Do you think he's implying I should write a book too?"

"Maybe?" Although he wasn't convinced by the suggestion, Bran didn't know Lena's dad well enough to refute it. "I hear the author—Eti, I think her name was—made a lot of money off of it. Might as well get something out of your..." Bran trailed off as he struggled to find a word to say that wasn't "suffering."

"Experience?" Lena suggested.

"Yeah," Bran said. "That. I guess."

"I don't think my experiences with Jamie would be as exciting to read about, if I'm being honest," Lena said. "He's a good guy. Nothing like the other Otherworlders we've heard about."

"Then write about that," Bran said.

"What do you mean?" Lena asked.

"Well, Jamie's a good guy, right?" Bran said, eager to latch on to the positive change in topic. "Maybe you can write about that? To tell everyone that not all Otherworlders are terrifying creatures of destruction?"

"You really think that's a good idea?" Lena asked.

"Sure!" he said. "I mean, I think it could help. I definitely almost pissed myself every time I got close to Jamie, until you showed me how nice he was. Maybe if you wrote a book, it would help people like me keep their pants clean."

Lena frowned despite his joke.

"Not all Otherworlders are Jamie," she said, lifting the book in her hand and waving it slightly. "The fact that this book exists is proof of that."

Bran felt his smile deflate immediately.

"Oh," he said.

Lena didn't respond.

"Sorry," he said.

"Don't be. It's still not a terrible idea. Maybe I'll write something after this is all done. Something to look forward to, right?"

Bran glanced at Lena, who was attempting a smile.

"I guess," he said, smiling back at her. "What would you call it?"

"What would I call what?" Lena asked.

Bran rolled his eyes in what he hoped was a playful manner. "The book, idiot. Got any ideas for a title?"

Lena frowned, but thankfully, Bran couldn't see any real heat behind it. Her pretending to be angry at him was just as obviously fake as her smiles.

"You just gave me the idea, you know," she said. "How do you expect me to think of a title that fast?"

Bran forced out a laugh, acting like he'd been convinced by her attempt at feigning indignation. "I don't see what's so difficult about it. Just throw shit on the wall and see what fits. What about Legend of Lena?"

Taken aback, Lena coughed into her hand, but Bran felt himself smile slightly. It was an uncomfortable sound, raspy and wet, but it was the closest she'd gotten to a genuine laugh since he had gotten there.

"That's fucking stupid."

"Well, it is the best you've got so far," Bran said with a quiet laugh. "I expect a fifty percent cut of all your profits, unless you can think of a better one."

"You're stupid. How about that?"

"That would be a pretty interesting book title," Bran said, cupping his chin with his fingers and pretending like he was seriously considering the suggestion. "Not sure it beats 'Legend of Lena,' but I'd definitely pick up a book that insulted me before I even picked it up."

"Ignoring the fact that you wouldn't be able to read the title."

Bran sighed and shook his head. "I'm disappointed in you, Lena. You already used that insult today," Bran said. "You used to be a lot more creative."

"Well, excuse me for being traumatized," Lena said, rolling her eyes. "I think I can get a pass after literally dying and being brought back to life a few hours ago."

Bran froze, not knowing how to react to that. The way that Lena casually mentioned it made it seem like a joke, but he couldn't be sure.

"Oh," he said. "Yeah, I guess you would get a pass for that."

Lena stared at him as if she was confused by his sudden change in tone. After a moment of silence, she sighed.

"Sorry," she said.

"What for?" Bran asked.

"For suggesting you can't read," Lena responded, waving the book in her hand. "You already knew the author's name. Have you read it before?"

Bran shook his head, somewhat stunned by the abrupt change in topic. "No. I just knew about it because apparently Eti means 'the Author' in Timuran. Polly mentioned it to me once, and I guess I thought it was a cool enough fact that it got stuck in my head."

Lena let out a laugh. "I guess that is pretty interesting," she said. "Though I'm not sure I can trust Polly's expertise in Timuran."

"Oh. Yeah. I guess you're right," Bran replied.

A long silence stretched out between the two until Lena broke it with a sigh.

"Nobody's dead at the moment," she said. "That's what your dad wanted you to come here for, right? You can tell him everything's fine."

"You sure about that?" Bran asked.

"Yes," Lena responded, lifting her hand up to lazily shoo him away. "You should go tell him."

Bran stared at Lena for a few more seconds before standing up. He stared down at her for a bit longer before grabbing his umbrella.

"You know you can always talk to me, right?" he asked. "You're my best friend."

"Shouldn't be saying those things to girls," Lena said, still shooing him away. "Polly might get jealous."

"I'm serious, Lena," Bran said. "I care about you."

Lena smiled up at him.

"Thanks," she said, shooing him away. "Maybe later."

Bran stared down at Lena for a few more seconds before turning away. He walked slowly, giving Lena the time to change her mind and call out to him, but she never did.

Chapter 56
The First Step Forward

The walk to the Mediators' temporary base was a short one, which I was grateful for, since the man leading me didn't seem to care for talking. He led me to a somewhat familiar-looking house and pulled open the door, walking inside without even caring to wipe off his boots.

I spent a moment trying to scrape off my own mud-caked shoes on the front porch but quickly remembered that I didn't need to. Focusing inward, I summoned mana to the surface of my body and let it escape me in a short burst. With my eyes closed, I imagined the mana enveloping the dirt and rainwater that covered my body, dissipating it into nothingness.

When I opened my eyes again, I was clean and dry.

I was also alone. Apparently, the man hadn't bothered to wait around for me to clean myself.

"Marten," an unfamiliar voice said from deeper into the house. "What are you doing back here?"

"I brought the kid," the man—Marten, I suppose—replied.

"What? Why?" the new voice asked.

"Do you seriously not remember?" Marten asked.

I felt a little awkward walking into a conversation about me, but I felt like waiting would just make things worse. I gingerly poked my head around the corner.

Marten had his back to me, seemingly ignoring my presence as he leaned over someone who was sitting down at a dining table. Somehow, my brain focused more on the fact that I suddenly realized that we were in the mayor's house, recognizing it from the short visit I had with Lena back when I first arrived in this world, before I managed to realize that the person Marten was leaning over was a goblin.

The goblin glanced in my direction, and I felt tempted to look away. Although they had turned out to be demons, I still felt guilty about having killed a handful of his kind.

However, the man's eyes were unfocused and glassy, seemingly looking through me instead of at me, his gaze not even registering my presence.

"Shit. Looks like the concussion's getting worse," the goblin said, chuckling momentarily before he grasped at his head, wincing in pain.

"Concussion?" I asked.

The goblin's eyes shifted slightly toward me, supporting the idea I had that he hadn't known I was there.

"Yeah," Marten answered on his behalf, then frowned. "You don't happen to have anything for that, do you, kid?"

For some reason, the question caught me off guard, like I was being called on in class after being caught not paying attention. "What do you mean?" I asked automatically, quickly shaking my head once I actually registered what he said. "Do you mean a healing spell?"

Marten shrugged.

"Marten," the goblin said, his voice stern for a moment before he turned to me and gave me a friendly smile. Or at least he tried to. He ended up staring somewhere over my shoulder. "I'll be fine, Jamie. You don't need to use your magic to help someone you don't even know."

"You damn idiot," Marten said. "Just let the kid heal you up."

"Never show Otherworlders any weakness," the goblin snapped. "Even the civilians know this. We have to maintain the illusion that his power isn't particularly abnormal, or he might let it get to his head."

When Marten slapped a hand to his face, I decided that I probably wasn't meant to hear that.

"What's his name?" I asked.

Marten lowered his hand and looked back at me. "Why do you want to know?" he asked back, suspicion clear in his voice.

I shrugged. "No particular reason?"

Marten frowned. "Stoney."

I felt my face twitch at the name but tried not to let my reaction show past that. "Well, I guess now that we've been formally introduced, I can use my magic to heal you, Stoney."

"Your magic has that as a restriction?" Marten asked.

"No," I said.

"Then why say that?"

I stared at him until I realized that he was being serious.

"Well. I mean, he said that I don't need to use magic to help someone I don't know, and y'know... I know him now. I mean, kind of. So yeah. I can use magic on him now..." I trailed off as I averted my eyes from Marten's scrutinizing glare, feeling my face growing hot from embarrassment.

"You know he didn't mean that literally, right?" Marten asked carefully, like he didn't want to offend me in case I did.

I blushed even harder.

"Yeah, I know," I said with a sigh that I hoped sounded more exasperated than humiliated. "I just wanted to do a bit."

"A what?" I didn't know whether I felt better or worse at the fact that Marten sounded genuinely confused.

I closed my eyes and ignored the way a wave of heat washed over me for a third time. Deciding that I was done with the conversation, I summoned mana to my palms. "Heal," I said as I expelled my mana, pushing it to Stoney.

When I opened my eyes, Stoney was blinking rapidly. Though he looked dazed, like he was just waking up from a dream, he was still much more focused than he'd been a few seconds ago.

He blinked a few more times and rubbed his eyes before looking at me and nodding.

"Thank you, Jamie," he said.

"No problem," I replied.

From the corner of my eye, I saw Marten still frowning at me with his brow furrowed in thought. Thankfully, he didn't seem interested in continuing the conversation from before.

"You want the leadership role back now that you're not stupid?" Marten asked, staring down at Stoney.

"You can keep it if you feel you'd be better suited for it," Stoney replied, completely ignoring the second half of Marten's comment.

"Fuck no. It's yours," Marten said, patting his shirt and drawing out his pipe. "I'll be outside if you need me."

Stoney sighed and shook his head as Marten walked around me to leave.

"Oh, and by the way." Marten paused at the door, though he didn't turn around. "The kid knows about how we were trying to kill him."

Marten's footsteps echoed in the silence that he left us in. I watched his retreating back as he left the house, not because I was interested in watching him leave, but because I wasn't sure I was ready to face Stoney.

"For the record, I'm not actually that mad about that," I said, scratching the back of my head awkwardly. I turned around slowly. I didn't want to make any sudden movements and accidentally scare the goblin.

To my surprise, Stoney looked a lot calmer than I would have expected, casually resting both of his palms on the table and giving me a warm smile that didn't quite suit his monstrous look. Though I supposed he wasn't quite a monster, was he? Was I being racist?

"That's a relief," Stoney said, breaking me out of my thoughts. "There isn't much we could do to stop you from taking vengeance on us if you chose to."

I felt the urge to say that I wouldn't kill anyone, but at this point, I was tired of hearing myself say it. Besides, Stoney hadn't actually suggested that I was a murderer.

"I thought you guys were supposed to pretend like I was nothing special," I said, trying to deflect the topic to something else. "Isn't that what you said?"

Stoney winced but recovered quickly and let out a good-natured laugh. He scratched at the back of his bald head in embarrassment.

"I'm sorry for the things I might have said while I was suffering a concussion. Thank you again for fixing it," he said with an appreciative nod.

"Don't mention it," I said, nodding back.

Stoney gave me a curious look before motioning to the seat across the table from him. Realizing I'd been standing the entire time, I sheepishly took a seat.

"Look, Jamie," Stoney said, folding his hands in front of him and giving me another disarming smile. "I'll be upfront with you. Now that you know our organization's mandate, there is little benefit in lying to you. We would only be increasing the risk of upsetting you. In fact, despite the fact that I do not have the authority to make this decision, I would be willing to bet that the Mediators will be ordered to leave you be for the rest of your natural life to lower that risk as much as we possibly can."

I nodded. "Marten mentioned something like that."

"I would've assumed so. As infuriating as the man can be, he does have a sensible head on his shoulders." He let out a small laugh before fixing me with a piercing stare. "And that begs the question, Jamie. Despite knowing that the Mediators have attempted to kill you in the past, you're offering to help us. Why?"

I shrugged.

"I want to fix the bad reputation that Otherworlders have," I said, summarizing my new goals as concisely as I could. "Marten asked for a favor, and I thought it would be a good first step if I agreed to help."

For the first time in our conversation, Stoney seemed to be caught off guard. The easy smile had slipped off his face, replaced by a look of utter confusion, before he managed to gather his wits and smile at me once more.

"That certainly is an interesting goal," Stoney said.

"You don't think I can do it," I said.

"It's not that I don't think you can do it, Jamie. I simply think it's impossible." Stoney sighed. "The Otherworlders have done an immeasurable amount of damage to our world, and it's not easy to forget. Countless lives have been destroyed by the actions of Otherworlders, and the survivors won't be quick to forgive."

Stoney frowned, and a brief flicker of a pained expression flashed across his face before he smiled once again.

I considered ignoring it, but for some reason, I didn't like the thought of pretending like I hadn't noticed obvious hints and signs just so I could avoid an uncomfortable discussion. It felt so tiring.

"Are you a survivor?" I asked, realizing halfway through my question that it might be incredibly rude, but asking it anyway.

Rather than becoming angry or upset like I might have expected, Stoney just gave me a curious look.

"I am. My entire tribe was slaughtered by an Otherworlder."

He said it casually, like he was explaining to me what he ate for breakfast that morning. I felt like I should show more of a reaction, like gritting my teeth in remorse or pounding the table in sympathetic anger, but Stoney's relaxed smile made it difficult for me to feel much besides a dull numbness.

"I'm sorry to hear that," I said.

"Thank you," Stoney replied. "That means a lot."

There were the beginnings of an awkward silence between us, but Stoney sighed and shook his head before it could stretch for too long.

"Well, now that I think about it, who am I to say that you shouldn't try to mend the bad reputation that Otherworlders have?" he said, letting out a noise that sounded somewhere between a sigh and a chuckle. "The impossible goals are the best ones to chase."

I didn't know what to say to that, so I gave a noncommittal hum instead.

Stoney laughed at that.

"You really are just a normal brat, aren't you?" he said.

I didn't know what to say to that either, so I just hummed again.

Stoney gave me an easy smile before it morphed into a strange grin like he'd just remembered something and couldn't quite decide if the memory was irritating or funny.

"You're gonna be a weird one to name, aren't you?" he mused.

"What?" I said, completely confused by the random statement.

Stoney laughed and shook his head. "Sorry," he said. "It's just something I thought, but Otherworlders are generally given a moniker, usually a few weeks after they've arrived in our world. I was just wondering when we would give you one."

"What's a moniker?" I asked.

"A title, or a nickname if you'd prefer," Stoney explained. "Like the Breaker, the Chaotic Paladin, and the Glass Artisan, to list a few examples. Every Otherworlder has one."

I managed to suppress the urge to suggest that I could be called 'Nightblade,' along with the flush of embarrassment that came with the memory of my cringey OC. I shook my head, as if that would help shake the memory loose, but it didn't seem to work.

"How about just calling me Jamie?" I suggested quickly before my brain could think of more of the characters I'd dreamed up when I was twelve.

"All Otherworlders have a moniker," Stoney repeated with another laugh, as if he could see my inner turmoil. "But I suppose we can hold off on naming you for the moment. We'll just have to introduce you as Jamie when we introduce you to the Founder."

"You're introducing me to him?" I asked. "I thought I was just giving you mana so you could talk to him."

Stoney shrugged. "It would be a good start to fulfilling your new goal. If you want to do anything related to Otherworlders, the Mediators would have their hands in it. No harm in starting a friendly relationship now, is there?"

"No," I said, nodding to myself as I thought about what he was saying. "I guess there isn't."

Chapter 57

He, Keeper of the Gate

He woke up, but he had not been asleep.

Rather, he blinked, and the world returned to focus.

He sat in a room of his own design, dark enough that he would not have to see the realm that he had been granted dominion over.

He had allowed himself to view it as beautiful once, but time had dulled its splendor.

He did not need splendor. He had been granted dominion over this Gate, and he would fulfill his duties.

It was simply so.

He blinked. A quiet ticking echoed in his mind. The sound that had woken him. The sound of a gear, clicking quietly.

He frowned. Though he had once been more involved with the lost souls, guiding them through the Gate by his own gentle hand, the method had made him weary.

And so he had spent a long time using what he found in the realm of his dominion to craft a mechanism that would open the gates for the lost souls without his presence. The Gate rarely needed his attention now.

The mechanism he had crafted was designed to be a perfect system, but despite the power granted to him, he was not arrogant enough to think that he had the ability to achieve perfection. Despite being granted power equivalent to it, he knew he would never achieve godhood. He would not dare be so arrogant.

No matter. If there was an issue in his mechanism, he would fix it.

He did not know how long it had been since the gears had clicked. Time no longer meant anything to him, and though he could remember a gear calling out to him once before, he did not know how long it had been since that time.

The gear had been simple to fix. Only the slightest adjustment had been necessary for it to find its place in the grand mechanism that he had crafted, for it to turn quietly and smoothly with its fellows.

Perhaps he had been too soft in his attempt to fix it? Had he been too arrogant in his faith in his system? Too passive in his action? Perhaps he had believed that a slight adjustment would be enough to fix the flaw, but now that he thought about it, the existence of a flaw in his flawless system meant that it was not so.

Instead of adjusting the clicking gear, should he have replaced it altogether? Maybe even go so far as to redesign the system from scratch? Perhaps he was being too hasty. Perhaps an occasional error was to be expected and accounted for, with gentle fixes to the system as necessary.

He supposed he couldn't decide either way, not yet at least. He decided that he would inspect this new clicking gear more carefully than he had the first.

Focusing his attention on the gear that continued to click at the edges of his perception, he felt his mind probing it.

The gear clicked loudly in his mind. Identification. Stoney.

The gear clicked again. An apology for bothering Him once more in such a short amount of time.

He frowned. A short amount of time? He struggled to recall the details of the previous gear that had called his attention, but he was confident that it was not the same as this one. The soulless were all similar to him, but he knew that there was a difference here. No matter how slight.

The gear clicked. Confirmation that it was not the same as the one that had called him previously but that it was still present.

He frowned. The mention of the first gear, Marten, gave him a sense of time. The gears expired and automatically replaced themselves quite often. The fact that Marten was still in existence meant that it had been a few decades since the gears had clicked at the longest.

The gear clicked. It had been less than a day since they had last called for Him.

He did not understand. How could this be? Two errors in such quick succession? What was the reason for this?

The gear clicked. The lost soul.

An icy fear gripped at His heart. The same lost soul that he had seen through the mind of the last gear. Had it not passed on yet?

The gear clicked. The lost soul was still in this realm.

Was it stuck? Was it unworthy to pass on?

No. The Gate was not of his design. It was infallible, impossible. There would not be a soul that would not be able to pass through it. The problem was with his mechanisms.

The realization hurt him more than he expected it to.

Pride. How useless.

It was a sign that he still had room to improve, just as his mechanisms did.

The gear clicked again. An inquiry. An invitation.

An interesting one. He considered the suggestion for a moment. It had been a long time since he had communicated with a lost soul directly, and more forgotten emotions flitted through him—of anxiety, of unease at the memory of the weariness that had plagued him during his early days as a warden—but he decided it was necessary.

The mechanisms were flawed, and the Gate still needed an operator while he decided how he would repair it. He would guide this lost soul through the Gate. He would restructure his realm anew after he ensured its safety.

The gear clicked. Affirmation.

The gear fell silent.

A moment passed.

The world exploded.

A guttural sound of shock escaped his throat as he flinched back from the unexpected explosion of blue light. Squinting against it, his eyes struggled to remember their function but were quick to adapt to the assault.

And he was able to see, but he did not understand.

[Jamie] would like to start a voice chat.
[Accept] [Decline]

He stared, eyes unblinking despite the discomfort of keeping them open.

What was this?

The unfamiliar symbols stared back at him, unmoving, unwavering. Suddenly, a few of the symbols started to glow.

He did not know what it was, and he did not know what it meant, but he felt compelled to reach forward and touch the panel of blue light.

A quiet buzzing echoed in his head for a moment.

"Hello?"

He looked around, startled by the sudden sound of the unfamiliar word in an unfamiliar voice. His small chamber was illuminated by the light of the panel, and even without it, the chamber he had buried himself in was too small to fit anyone other than himself.

"Hi, is this the Founder? My name's Jamie. I'm an Otherworlder?"

Again, that voice echoed in his mind in an animalistic, alien tongue. What was it saying? Why did he not understand it? He clutched at his head, willing the voice to quiet.

But despite his will, it continued.

"Umm, can you hear me? Did I cast the spell correctly?"

Was it not he who had been chosen to be the keeper of this Gate? Who would dare to challenge the power granted to him? For a moment, he felt rage. Rage at this strange entity and at himself for being unable to comprehend it.

Fury coursed through him in the place of blood. He felt no shame in the emotion, for even God knew fury.

How dare this creature exist?

"Hello? Is this thing on? Did I get the wrong number? Oh, no. It's just a little inside joke. Sorry, Stoney."

Why couldn't it hear him? Was it deaf? No, that would not matter, for even the deaf could hear his words. Perhaps its mind was not developed enough to understand him? But that didn't solve the additional question of how he could hear its voice.

He paused, and for the first time in a long time, he realized that it was he who was hearing things. Physically hearing things.

Why? How?

"Wh—"

His voice cut off, as if he were surprised by the sound of it. And he was. He hadn't meant to speak. He had no need for it. No reason. No purpose.

When was the last time he had moved his lips? When was the last time moisture and air had touched his throat? Would he even be able to talk if he tried?

"Wait, I think I heard something."

The voice echoed in his head again. He did not understand it, but it was higher-pitched, excited, as if it were reacting to his broken question. Had it heard him?

"What are you?" he asked, his voice echoing in his tomb.

Silence answered him, and he was quick to assume that the creature hadn't heard him, that it truly was deaf to his words, no matter the method of communication.

But then it spoke again.

"Huh? Sorry, what was that? I couldn't understand you."

The creature's garbled language continued to evade him, but the confusion in its voice was clear.

"Have you a soul?" he asked again, slowly finding confidence in his words once more. "Speak, demon. In the tongue of my forebears. Do not dare to sully my ears with your devilish whispers."

The words escaped him before he could think of them, but he was surprised by how much sense they made.

This was no ordinary creature if it could not hear his word, for even the animals of this realm would bend to his will. Soulless, powerful, and inexplicable? The description fit a demon exactly.

The urge ran through him to take his holy power and smite this demon back whence it came, but he realized there was too much he did not know.

How? How had a demon come into his realm? It was impossible. This was the realm that housed a Gate. How?

"What did you say? Hello? Is something wrong with my translation magic?"

The demon's words echoed in his mind, still foreign and indecipherable. What was it saying?

He did not know, for he was not omniscient.

But he had to know. He needed to know. He had to know what he had to mend in order to fix the mechanisms of the Gate. No. At this point, he knew he could not fix things. For a mistake of this magnitude to happen meant that his mechanisms were too flawed, unworthy of operating the Gate. No. He would need to start from the very beginning. He would need to break everything down and build anew.

He had believed his power to be almighty and infallible, and perhaps that was true, but he, the wielder, was not. He had made a mistake, and if he wanted to make sure that he did not repeat it, he would need to learn more about the mistake that plagued him now.

Glaring at the blue panel in front of him, he lifted his arm and brought it down in a mighty blow, banishing the panel from existence, plunging him back into darkness.

Blessed silence met him again, free of the demon's garbled speech. For a moment, he felt the urge to close his eyes and pretend that his utopic world had not been disturbed.

But no. He had a duty.

It would be fulfilled.

Chapter 58
Mental Block

"And you're sure you couldn't understand him?"

I wasn't the type to roll my eyes, but after being asked a different version of the same question five times in a row, I was tempted to start.

"No, I couldn't. It sounded like he was speaking some foreign language," I said, trying to anticipate the follow-up question that Marten was sure to ask.

"With your magic, you should've been able to interpret him, no matter what language the Founder spoke in," Marten said.

"Well, I couldn't," I said, holding back a frustrated groan. "Maybe there's just a language in your world that I'm not able to understand."

Marten shook his head. "Your magic's supposed to be infallible. If it's a spoken language, then you should be able to interpret it."

"Are you sure?" I asked, knowing that he would just ask me the same questions again if he wasn't satisfied with my answer. "What language does your boss usually speak, anyway?"

"The same one I'm speaking now," Marten replied. "Ashanic."

"That's not necessarily true," Stoney said, raising his hand as if he were a student in a classroom. "When I contacted the Founder, he spoke in Petani. My native language." He glanced sideways at me, ignoring the deepening frown on Marten's face. "Do you understand what I'm saying?"

I glanced between him and Marten. "Were you talking in Petani?" I asked, testing my hunch. "I couldn't tell if you were. It just sounded like English to me."

"I was talking in Petani, yes. I presume that English is a language you have on Earth?" Stoney asked.

"Yeah," I said. "You didn't know?"

Surprisingly, Stoney shook his head. "Most of the time, Otherworlders don't bother to question why they can understand us and vice versa. It's convenient for us, and there is no real reason to ask what your native languages are. We know of a few, but don't place any value in knowing them."

"You're getting off topic," Marten said with a frustrated huff. He had discovered that he'd used up the last of his tobacco a few minutes ago. Now, he was just fidgeting around with an empty pipe. "We don't fucking care what your language is."

Stoney sighed and rubbed his temple for a moment before looking up at Marten.

"Take a break, Marten," Stoney said. "You're clearly not thinking straight if you're cursing out an Otherworlder."

Marten glared back at Stoney but said nothing before turning around and stomping up the stairs and out of the basement.

I watched him go, a little sad at the reason he had been dismissed. When I looked back at Stoney, he gave me an apologetic smile that seemed to say he understood exactly what I was feeling.

"I wasn't gonna do anything to him just because of a little swearing," I said, just in case he didn't. "You don't have to treat me like a monster."

Stoney shook his head slowly. "We're not treating you like a monster, Jamie," he said. "But I won't lie to you and say that we're treating you like a regular Materian either, because quite frankly, you're not. You're dangerous enough that we have to treat you with the utmost respect, mostly because it's our safest option. That being said, I probably would've sent Marten away even if you were a regular civilian. He can get under the nerves of even the strongest man."

Stoney gave me another apologetic smile, and I was struck by the sincerity behind it to the point where I couldn't find anything to say. I didn't want to agree with him, but I didn't want to speak up against any of his points either.

In the end, I just decided to sigh and hang my head.

Stoney sighed along with me.

"I'm sorry," he said. "I know it's difficult for you."

"Don't be," I said, shaking my head. "It must be hard for you to deal with me."

"Yes," he admitted without any hesitation. "It is."

"You admitted that much more easily than I expected," I said. I'd tried to put a little humor in my voice, but it came out a little flatter than I hoped, so I just gave him a small smile so he wouldn't think I was angry. "What happened to being polite?"

Stoney smiled back at me. "I'm being honest, Jamie. That's more important than being polite, though I admit I could've been a bit more tactful with how I said it."

"Nah, it's fine," I said.

Stoney opened his mouth to say something, but his ears perked up, and he turned his attention to the basement door. I hadn't noticed the footsteps approaching, but when I turned to match his gaze, I saw Tenna and Sera marching down the stairs.

"Welcome back," Stoney said. "Did Marten catch you up?"

Neither of them answered back immediately, which Stoney raised his eyebrow at.

"Well?" he asked, directing his gaze at Sera.

Sera seemed to notice the gaze and flinched, as if she was surprised to be called on. "He did, sir," she said. "He mentioned that you would know best what to do with me. Or us, rather."

Stoney stared at Sera for a moment before shaking his head.

"Okay, I'm going to stop whatever this is right now," he said. "Sera. Get your head out of your own ass. You're a Mediator. Act like one."

Sera's eyes widened before she regained control of her expression, snapping it back to one of controlled neutrality.

"I wasn't sure if I was still a Mediator, sir," she said.

Stoney let out a frustrated sigh. "I guarantee your little stunt with the civilian girl will get you into some trouble, but you haven't been fired yet," he said. "You can still do good, Sera. Don't forget why you became a Mediator in the first place."

Sera frowned.

"Sorry," she said. "I'll try to focus. Have you considered the possibility that there are concepts that might be untranslatable? While his magic might be infallible, Jamie is anything but. No offense."

"None taken," I said, all too willing to accept my imperfections after the past couple of weeks.

Stoney didn't seem too happy with Sera's eagerness to change the subject, but he accepted it regardless. "Unfortunately, Marten already suggested that," he said. "Names and locations foreign to him are untranslatable, but that should've been expected, and words that don't exist in his language are still translated. The feeling you get when you sense that someone is watching you but you're also suspicious that you're simply delusional from the lack of sleep, for example, is a word that doesn't exist in Jamie's language, but his magic translates it by giving him a broader definition... What?"

Sera didn't respond to the question. For some reason, her eyes were narrowed, glancing between Stoney, me, and Tenna before finally landing back on me.

"Schroighfaren," she said, still staring at me.

I waited a bit for her to continue or at least give me some context on what she wanted, but when she didn't, I shook my head at the foreign word. "I don't know names or places," I said. I wasn't sure if it was one of the ones that Marten and Stoney had already tested me on, but the language sounded similar enough.

"It was neither of those," she said. "I just repeated the exact same word that Stoney did, but I didn't take ten seconds to say one word."

I didn't quite understand what Sera was talking about, but Stoney seemed to clue in on what she was suggesting almost immediately. His face hardened, and his mouth curved down into a deep frown.

"The feeling you get when you sense that someone is watching you, but you're also suspicious that you're simply delusional from the lack of sleep," he said, speaking a bit faster than he did the first time around.

Sera's frown only deepened as she shook her head.

"You're still stretching out the word. You really don't notice it," she said, in more of a statement than a question.

"No," he said. "And you're immune because you're a Follower."

"That's my assumption," she replied.

Though I was no stranger to not understanding what people were talking about at times, the fact that they were talking so gravely made it impossible for me to keep quiet.

"You're immune from what?" I asked, not liking the quiver that had somehow entered my voice.

"The fact that your magic can subtly manipulate people's minds into not noticing the fact that they're speaking slowly to accommodate for the time it takes for your magic to translate words with long definitions," Sera said. "To me, it sounded like Stoney was saying, 'Schhhhroooifaaaarrreeenn.'"

"Oh," I said, a little taken aback by how nonchalant Sera was being. "I'm manipulating people's minds? That's kind of terrifying. Right?"

"Extremely," Stoney said, his tone just as casual as Sera's at the idea that he was being mind-controlled. "But not anything outside our realm of expectations. What we are surprised about, however, is the fact that this interaction with an Otherworlder's magic was never mentioned in our records."

"Oh," I said. Honestly, I was still a little shocked by the idea that they were so casual about the idea that I could mind control them, but with how little they seemed to care about it, I didn't really want to address it. "Is it possible that it just never came up? I mean, I assume there aren't that many words that are untranslatable that just pop up in normal conversation."

"It's technically possible, but the Mediators have been interacting with Otherworlders for nearly two thousand years," Stoney said, shaking his head. "The chances of this being the first time a Mediator has used an untranslatable word in front of an Otherworlder and a Follower at the same time are quite low."

"Oh," I said. "And it's a big deal that these words are untranslatable?"

Stoney shook his head, his brow still furrowed in thought. "It's not the specifics of the scenario that we're fixated on. It's the fact that, despite our overwhelming history of dealing with Otherworlders, this is the first time that we've known it's possible to be immune to an Otherworlder's magic."

"There's also the possibility that Jamie's not a real Otherworlder."

Stoney turned toward the stairs again, watching as Marten trudged down the stairs. A heavy cloud of smoke trailed behind him as he sucked on his pipe, apparently having restocked his supply while he was gone.

"And what evidence do you have to support this theory, Marten?" Stoney asked.

Marten shrugged. "He feels different."

"That's not evidence," Stoney replied.

"Don't tell me you don't feel it," Marten said. "You've been on the job longer than I have."

"Feelings aren't evidence."

"And that isn't a real argument."

Stoney answered with silence, and Marten responded in kind by taking a long draw of his pipe and breathing out a cloud of smoke before turning to me.

"So, what's different about you?" he asked.

"I'm not sure?" I said, more than a little confused.

"That was a rhetorical question," he said, before turning back to Stoney. "You seriously won't admit that you feel it too? Trust in your gut, or at least mine. It's never led me astray."

"Coming from a man with a gambling debt as large as yours, I'm not sure how true that is," Stoney said, though the furrow in his brow refused to go away as his gaze fluttered between me and the floor.

"Fair point, but it's the only one you've made so far," Marten said, rolling his eyes before turning to Sera. "What about you? You've been traveling with the kid this whole time, and you were and still are his Follower. Got any insight? Or were you too busy trying to get into blondie's pants?"

A part of my brain started to whir at the implications of what Marten said, but the larger part of me was more focused on the fact that Sera didn't even seem to hear him.

Marten looked down at her and opened his mouth as if he was about to say something. Eventually, he closed it again and crossed his arms as he looked down at her. I could almost imagine him tapping his foot impatiently as he waited, but he stayed still, only moving to take puffs from his pipe, until Sera looked up at him.

"Well, look who finally decided to—"

"Shut up," Sera said, her lips pulled into a thin line. "You say that Jamie feels different from the other Otherworlders you've met. Do I feel different from the other Followers you've met?"

"Other than the fact that you're a horny teenager with no self-control?"

Sera gritted her teeth and shook her head, looking at Stoney.

"Stoney," she said. Her voice was low, but it trembled, like she was barely holding back a shout. "Compare me to the other Followers you've met."

Stoney frowned. "That's a very vague request," he said. "I'm not sure what you're searching for."

Sera gritted her teeth and opened her mouth, but no words came out. She grimaced and shook her head, though I wasn't sure why.

"Can you compare me to any of the other Followers you've met?" Sera asked, still managing to keep her voice from rising in volume, but not in pitch. "Because I can't. I've been on five different teams to pacify five Otherworlders, and I can't remember a single Follower's name."

"Are you serious?" Marten asked. "You going crazy now?"

"Not as far as I can tell," Sera said, though she hesitated slightly as if she was considering the possibility. "Just humor me. Give me the name of a single Follower other than me, and I'll drop this."

Marten's lips curled into a mocking snarl as he opened his mouth. Then he went completely silent.

If it were just that, I might not have been so unnerved as I was, but there was an instantaneous shift in Marten's expression, from one of annoyance and confusion to nothing. Blank and expressionless, Marten stared forward, not seeming to register the world around him at all.

The shift in the room was so sudden that I felt myself flinch, but Sera was still moving. With a grimace on her face, she spared Marten a simple glance before looking around the room. Following her gaze, I noticed that Stoney and Tenna had also fallen into a dull, trance-like state. Just as quickly as they'd exited it, they suddenly snapped back into reality.

"There, you got your names. Happy now?" Marten asked, his arms crossed over his chest. He had the same snarl on his face like he hadn't just fallen into silence for a few seconds.

Sera let out a hiss. The emotions hiding behind it were too complicated for me to interpret fully, but the thick undercurrent of dread was obvious.

"No," she said, glancing at me. "No, I'm not."

Chapter 59
EMPTY

Oren woke from a dreamless sleep. For a long moment, he simply existed, floating listlessly in between the state of sleep and consciousness, before he was pulled out of it by the sudden realization that he was hearing something.

Quiet popping echoed in his mind, and it was his sleep-addled state that stopped him from instantly realizing what it was. But only for a second. Oren's eyes shot open at the Mediator's signal, and he pushed himself up from his bed.

"It took you a while to wake up," a voice said immediately. "What happened?"

It was a testament to how deep his sleep had been that he didn't immediately recognize the woman sitting beside him.

"I'm not certain," he said. "I may have been put in a magically induced state of sleep by the Otherworlder."

The woman nodded, and he slowly recognized her as Laush, his fellow Mediator.

Immediately, he felt his mind snap back to attention. The fact that she hadn't taken the opportunity to stab him in his sleep could only mean that he hadn't been deemed a traitor to the Mediators. A ghost of a smile flitted across his lips.

"What are my instructions?" he asked.

* * *

I had no idea how long I ended up staring into the distance, long after Bran disappeared from my sight, but it must have been a while.

I was cold, tired, and hungry. I didn't think I would be able to eat or sleep with how anxious I was, but being cold was something that I could fix.

I didn't want to fix it. Intellectually, I knew I was liable to become sick if I stayed out there on the front porch, as the unusually cold summer rain sprayed a light shower of mist on my already clammy skin, but I didn't want to. It would be so easy to go back in the house, change into some dry clothes, and huddle up in my bed with the blankets drawn over me, but that was part of the problem.

Being comfortable would only hinder me. I didn't want to make it even harder to leave with Jamie when the time came.

But what was I doing out here?

I sighed.

I knew I wasn't helping Jamie by slowly freezing myself to death for no reason, but it was frustrating to know that there was really nothing I could do right now to help him. The urge to get up and wander through the village to find him had long since faded from my mind, since I had no idea where he could be. It was a better idea just to stay put.

I hated that.

Even though I was doing nothing and had been stagnant for however long I'd been sitting there on my front porch, a nervous energy ran through my veins, begging to be doing anything instead of just twiddling my thumbs as I waited for Jamie to come back.

I resisted the urge to get up and pace, knowing that it would only make things worse.

It was only when I heard the quiet creaking of tortured leather that I realized that I was on the verge of ripping my dad's book in half. I thought of throwing the book as far as I could into the muddy roads, as if it had just personally offended me, but I dismissed the intrusive thought.

Lashing out randomly wouldn't do me any good. I took a deep breath and let it out slowly. The book crinkled in my hands but didn't rip like I secretly hoped it would.

After a few more breaths, I opened my eyes.

Releasing my vice-grip on the book somewhat, I turned it over to stare at it. The title stared back at me, written plainly in boring block letters, *The Chronicles of a Witness*, and underneath it, the author's name, Eti.

It looked so innocent on the surface. Though I knew the book was the most infamous book in Astranta and probably throughout the entire world, I couldn't help but think it was a little cruel that the cover looked so innocuous without even a warning of the horrors that it contained.

I wondered if that was intentional. Maybe the publishers didn't think they would be able to sell the book if people knew exactly what it was about. It definitely didn't end up being a problem, since the morbid curiosity of the general population drove them to buy it anyway. It was kind of messed up when I gave it some more thought, given that most of the general population had at least one member of their family pass away after being affected by the Plague King's namesake.

I sighed as I thumbed the cover, not knowing whether I should read it or not. I still wasn't sure what my dad wanted me to get out of this. Even though I had joked around with Bran that it was his way of pushing me toward a writing career, the more obvious answer was that he wanted me to read it and become so horrified of what an Otherworlder was capable of that I would abandon Jamie.

The urge to throw away the book rose inside me once more, but I suppressed it again. I felt my lips curl into a deep frown before I thumbed open the cover.

If anything, knowing more about Otherworlders would help Jamie in the long run, wouldn't it? It wasn't like I was afraid that my conviction would waver if I read this. I'd been through death and had come out strong. A book wouldn't scare me.

At the sight of the first page, I felt a wave of relief wash through me. It was just a publisher's page, detailing who the scribe had been, as well as how many generations of transcription the version had gone through and the date of the book's publication. Apparently, my dad's copy of the book was written by a man named Renard from Redstone, and it was a second-generation copy that had been written twenty-five years ago.

How my dad could afford a second-generation copy of any book confused me. While we were by no means poor, a second-generation copy of a book was a luxury. Though they obviously weren't nearly as exclusive as first-generations, since you needed a special license to access the original copy of any book to transcribe it into a first-generation copy, second-generation books were often still very expensive, since the scribe would often have to pay a fortune to obtain the first-generation copy to transcribe from.

I was more used to seeing ninth or tenth-generation copies, where bits and pieces of text were lost as the scribes who made them became lower in skill. A second-generation book, however, would likely have close to zero mistakes.

Maybe there was just such a high demand for the book that more second-generation copies were made?

Before I could think about an answer to that question, I grimaced and glared at the book. I was distracting myself.

Willing myself to forget about stupid things like book editions, I steeled myself before I turned the page and plunged into the retelling of the Plague King's horrific rampage.

Then I turned the page.

Then again.

And again.

I eventually gave up flipping the pages one by one and fanned through the entire thing like it was a flipbook, but the only scene animated by the book was one of nothingness.

I opened the book again and flipped to a random page just to confirm that my eyes weren't playing tricks on me.

They weren't. The page was blank. The entire book was empty.

For some reason, my blood ran cold. I could think of a hundred different reasons to explain why the book was blank, but I instinctively knew that all of them were wrong. Feeling a shiver down my spine, I nearly fell sideways as my legs grew weak, only just realizing that I was standing up.

I walked quickly back into my house, my fingers threatening to tear into the blank pages of the book in my grip.

The door slammed open, startling my dad and my mom, who was apparently awake now, but I couldn't find it in me to care.

I lifted the book and pointed at it with an accusatory finger.

"Why is this blank?" I asked.

My voice was wavering for some reason, and from the concerned look on my parents' faces, I could only imagine what my expression looked like, but I didn't care to change it.

"Why is this blank?" I asked again, jabbing a finger against the book, almost tearing out a page.

"Lena?" my dad said, raising his hands like he was trying to calm down a wild animal. "What are you talking about, honey?"

"This!" I said, thrusting the book forward. When I saw the way my mom flinched away at my sudden movement, I tried to calm myself down. I slowly lowered the book, feeling it shake in my grip.

"Dad," I said, trying to keep my voice even and steady. "Did you accidentally give me the wrong book? This one's blank."

My dad stared at me, barely even giving a glance at the book in my hands. "Lena," he said, his voice slow and careful. "It's not blank."

At his words, I felt my throat close up and heard my heart pounding in my ears. I didn't know exactly why I was reacting this way, but just because I didn't understand it didn't mean I could ignore the utter sense of wrongness that I was feeling at that very moment.

I shakily offered the book to him with the page open. "Can you read this out loud for me? You don't have to read it all. Just a little bit."

"Lena," he said, not even looking at the offered book as he stared into my eyes instead. "Are you okay?"

I bit back the irritated shout that threatened to jump from my throat. "Please, Dad," I forced through clenched teeth. "Just humor me, okay? Just read me a passage."

My dad's eyes flickered momentarily toward my mom, and when I followed his gaze, I could see that she was frozen in place, with her only movement being how her eyes rapidly bounced between me and him. I tore my eyes away from her to look back at my dad.

"Please," I said, pushing the book closer to his face, almost hitting him with it.

My dad didn't answer me, but he reached up and took the book from my hands. Slowly. Like he was afraid of how I would react if he moved too quickly. It took an uncomfortable amount of willpower to let him take the book from my hands, but I was eventually able to uncurl my fingers from the edges.

He patted his breast pocket, but his reading glasses weren't there. I was glad he decided against looking for them. I wasn't sure I wouldn't have snapped if he took any longer to read from the damn book, and I could only assume that he knew that.

Narrowing his eyes, he looked at the open book in his hand.

He opened his mouth.

Immediately, the concerned and confused expression on his face dropped. His mouth hung open, slightly ajar, as his head hung down, like it had suddenly grown twice as heavy. In the corner of my eye, I noticed my mother suffering a similar fate. The wrinkles in her brow softened, and the stiff downward curve of her mouth disappeared, almost turning into a smile. The sudden change gave off the illusion that she had suddenly found a sense of peace and contentment with herself.

But their eyes. My dad's eyes were glazed over as he stared forward in the general direction of the book in his hands, focused on nothing. The fear in my mom's eyes had all but faded away, along with everything else.

I was no stranger to those eyes. I'd seen them many times before. They were the eyes of the unprocessed carcasses that found their way to the large, bloody table in the back of my dad's shop, the eyes of Medric after his battle with Jamie.

My parents were dead.

And then, just as suddenly, they weren't.

"There," my dad said. The furrow in his brow returned like it had never left. He closed the book gingerly, like he was afraid that it would bite him. "I read it out loud."

"That was horrid," my mom said. She shuddered and wrapped her arms around herself, warming herself against a sudden breeze that wasn't there. "You gave that to Lena to read?"

"I thought it would be educational."

"Traumatizing, more like. You only read out a page, and I'm already going to have nightmares."

"Better to have nightmares in your sleep than nightmares while you're awake. Lena. Please. Won't you reconsider... Lena?"

I simply stared silently at my dad, watching him move in blissful ignorance of what had just happened to him. Though I could hear his voice and I could understand what he was saying, I couldn't say anything back to him.

I held out my hand.

"Dad?" I said, my voice impossibly small, even to my own ears. "May I have that book back?"

I wasn't sure if he heard me properly. A sudden look of deep concern entered his eyes as he stared into mine.

"Lena? Are you alright?"

Rather than a simple question, it sounded more like he was pleading with me, begging me to give him the answer that he wanted.

"The book, Dad," I said instead. "Can I have it?"

He didn't seem like he wanted to, but he must have seen something in my expression that made him concede. Too focused on staring at him, I didn't notice him putting the book into my hand until I felt my fingers automatically curl around it.

"Lena," he said. "Please."

He might have had more to say, but I couldn't hear him. I had already turned around and walked out of the house.

The world around me blurred as I lost focus on where I was going, but my feet marched me forward all the same.

I vaguely heard someone screaming into the wind as I ran, desperately calling out someone's name.

"Jamie! Jamie!"

I vaguely wondered who could be wailing so fearfully like that, this late at night. I pitied the poor soul, whoever it was.

My breath quickly grew ragged. My throat quickly started to feel strained.

I ran.

Chapter 60
DYING ANIMALS

"You all just died."

"That's not—" Marten frowned as he glanced at Jamie before turning his attention back to Sera. "That's absurd," he said instead.

"It's what happened," Sera said. "Why would I lie about something this serious?"

"Why would you do half the shit you've been pulling with the civvie these past few days?" Marten replied. "I'm not in the habit of trying to rationalize the minds of idiots."

"You're in denial," she said, pointing at his hands. "You're shaking."

Marten immediately gave her a rude hand gesture in response, though she could tell his attempts to control his tremor weren't completely successful.

Sera resisted the urge to sigh. She doubted that Marten actually thought she was lying, but it would be difficult to force him to acknowledge it if he didn't want to. Deciding he would get over it in his own time, she turned to Stoney.

"What do you think?" she asked.

"About the idea that we all died and came back to life?" he asked back. He was as stone-faced as his name suggested, and though Sera couldn't decipher his emotions whatsoever, she could only guess at the complex emotional struggle he was having within himself.

"Yes," Sera replied.

"Well, I think you have no reason to lie to us, and Jamie would have no reason not to speak up if you were," he said, giving a casual glance toward Jamie.

The Otherworlder blinked a few times before realizing the implied suggestion was directed at him.

"Umm," he said, his eyes flitting around the room. "Well, I mean, I'm not sure if you all died." He winced as he said it, as if the word itself physically pained him. "To be honest, it just looked like you zoned out or something."

"See?" Marten said, not even trying to stop the angry desperation from creeping into his voice.

"You all died," Sera said, shaking her head. "Jamie's not used to seeing dead people. I am."

As soon as she said it, she glanced at the Otherworlder in question. He winced at her words and looked down, as if ashamed of his inexperience, but said nothing. It was a much more subdued expression than her colleague's, at the very least, with Marten glaring at her like she'd stepped on his toes and spat in his face.

Accepting that he was a lost cause, Sera decided to ignore Marten entirely, turning back to Stoney.

"It's not just about the other Followers," Sera said. "I feel like I have more gaps in my memories that shouldn't be there, though it's difficult to identify them."

"But you can still identify them due to some sort of mental protection given to you as a Follower," Stoney guessed. "What of the others?"

"Others?" Sera asked. Though she could guess what Stoney was talking about, she wanted to make sure.

"Oren and Lena," Stoney said. "Have you shared your findings with them?"

Sera tried to hold back a grimace, but from the unimpressed look that Stoney gave her, it didn't seem to have worked. For a moment, she wanted to steer the conversation away, if only to avoid thinking about Lena again, but she stopped herself. This certainly wasn't the time nor the place for her teenage angst. She was a professional. She needed to act like one.

"I only recently figured this out," she said. "I haven't seen either of the other Followers since."

"We already sent Laush out to find Oren," Stoney replied. "Can you be trusted to find Lena?"

Before Sera could say anything, a loud snapping sound echoed throughout the basement. Sera turned to see Marten glowering angrily at the pipe in his hands, or rather what was left of it after being shattered in his grip. The glowing embers fell on his bare skin, but he didn't react to it.

"This is fucking bullshit," he said. "This isn't some fucking grand conspiracy. We haven't stumbled upon some dark secret that the Mediators have been hiding deep in its asshole for centuries. I'm fucking ashamed to work with you fucking idiots."

"Thank you for sharing your thoughts, Marten," Stoney said.

"Fuck you, Stoney," Marten said. "Don't give me that shit. Am I the only one who hasn't gone fucking insane here? Grunt. Back me up on this. You see the obvious answer too, don't you?"

Tenna, who hadn't said a word since learning about his own death, gave a start, as if he was surprised that anyone remembered he existed.

"I'm afraid I don't understand what you're talking about, sir," he said, his voice completely neutral if not for the slight tremor it had.

Marten let out a frustrated groan and gripped at his face before throwing the remains of his shattered pipe on the floor.

"Him!" he shouted, pointing his finger toward Jamie. "With all this weird shit that's happening, how in the fuck do you not immediately suspect a fucking Otherworlder for being responsible for it? Am I going crazy? Did everyone else forget what our literal job is? To kill little fuckers like this one because they pull shit exactly like what's happening right now."

"Marten," Stoney said, his voice low and dangerous. "Control yourself."

"It's okay," Jamie said, raising his hands, as if proving that he wasn't armed made him seem any less dangerous. "It's okay, Stoney. Like I said before, I get how hard it can be to deal with me. I'm not going to kill him."

Marten glared at him and opened his mouth as if to yell at Jamie, but he seemed to decide against it, shaking his head and stomping up the stairs with an angry huff.

* * *

I didn't quite know where I was running, but wherever I was going, I wasn't getting there fast. I was tired, I could barely breathe, and the mud-slicked roads made it difficult to run without falling.

I didn't know what I was doing, if I was being honest with myself. I knew that I was only relying on luck to find Jamie. I knew my running and screaming were pointless, but I couldn't stop myself from pushing myself up from the floor, even though I had no idea when or how I'd fallen in the first place.

"Civilian. Has there been a new development with the Otherworlder?"

It was difficult to see who was talking, with the tears in my eyes blurring my vision, but the infuriatingly passive voice was easy enough to identify. I didn't know whether it was luck or misfortune that made him stumble across me so randomly. In either case, I couldn't say I was happy to see him, but that didn't mean he wasn't useful.

"Do you know where Jamie is?" I asked, ignoring how uncomfortably hoarse my voice sounded.

"No," Oren said.

"You're lying," I said, too desperate to believe in anything else. "Take me to him."

Oren stared at me for a few seconds before turning to Laush, who trailed behind him.

"I apologize for the detour. We will proceed."

I moved without thinking, lunging forward to grab Oren. He didn't bother to dodge me, simply standing as I collapsed onto him in a clumsy grapple as I desperately clung onto him.

"If you do not let go of me, I will remove you by force," he said, sounding almost bored by his own threat.

It only made me cling to him harder. "You'll have to kill me," I said, not caring how easily those words came out of my mouth.

"That won't be necessary," he said, slipping his hand between my fingers. Though I tried to clamp down even harder, he easily pried my hands away from him with no visible effort on his part. "It was a foolish effort on my part to try to kill you in the first place, knowing you have the Otherworlder's protection. Please do not assume that I will repeat my previous actions."

I dove forward to grab Oren again, but he moved out of my way easily, leaving me off balance and stumbling onto the road.

"Let's go," I heard Oren say as I struggled to get up from the ground.

Before I could even look up, they were gone.

I screamed in the direction they had fled, swearing to do horrible things to Oren, until I was sure they were long gone.

If I were more grateful, I might have thanked Oren for accidentally reminding me of something I could do. He was right. I did have Jamie's protection, didn't I?

I took a deep breath and made a silent prayer to no one in particular before opening my eyes.

"Save me," I said.

Nothing happened. I frowned.

"Save me," I said, a little louder this time, as if the volume of my voice mattered. "Save me!"

Nothing happened.

"Why isn't it working this time, you shitty god?" I shouted into the night sky. "Save me!"

A blue panel appeared in front of me.

Valiant White Knight

By partying with your love interest, you have unlocked the skill [Valiant White Knight]! Under certain conditions, this skill allows the Hero to rush to protect bonded party members from certain death.

Whenever a bonded party member shouts, "Save me!" the Hero may activate this ability to instantly teleport to their side.

MP cost: 0

Cooldown: 30 days

I frowned at the familiar panel. While the panel acknowledged that I had access to a "skill" that could summon Jamie to my side, it didn't explain why it wasn't being activated.

The text "protecting them from certain death" started to pulse slowly with a golden light.

I immediately started to look around for a woodcutting axe or a particularly sharp stake that I could use to activate the conditions that the Guide wanted from me, before the pulsing immediately stopped. Without my conscious input, my eyes moved down to the text at the bottom of the panel.

Cooldown: 16 days remaining

It was surprising to see that Jamie had only been in my world for fourteen days, but I tried not to pay attention to that, directing my energy toward glaring at the blue panel instead. Though I wasn't sure if the panel could read human expressions, I assumed that it could read the intentions behind them, even though I doubted it could truly understand the emotion that fueled them.

"Don't give me that shit," I said out loud, even though I knew it wasn't necessary. I winced at the sound of the shrill fear that infected my voice, but I pushed on regardless. "Do you seriously expect me to believe that you can only teleport him to me once every thirty days? You're a god. Bring. Him. To. Me."

The panel remained, floating silently, the text unchanging. I looked down at the bottom of the panel, hoping that the text detailing the cooldown had somehow disappeared, but it was still there, pulsing with golden light.

I stared at it, willing it to go away, but it didn't change.

"You want me to help Jamie, right?" I asked, hating how I struggled to speak as I choked on each word. I knew I didn't need to speak, but I couldn't stop myself. "I know why you asked me for help. It's because you don't understand us, isn't it? You have complete control over our lives and our reality, but when it comes to trying to help Jamie, you're completely lost, aren't you?"

I watched as the text on the panels slowly dissolved away, not knowing whether my theory was being confirmed or denied, not knowing which option was more terrifying. Though the words had come out of my mouth, I didn't want to think about what it meant if a god that had complete control over my life didn't understand how to rule over it.

"If it makes you feel any better, I'm sure you're trying your best," I said, almost letting out a hysterical laugh at the idea that I was trying to comfort a god. "But I don't know if Jamie will be okay. Please. You need to let me talk to him. He needs me."

The blue panel floated silently in front of me. I stared at it, unable to think of anything else I could possibly do to convince the panel to let me see Jamie. I didn't move, I didn't blink, I didn't breathe.

A moment passed.

Skill: Valiant White Knight
Cooldown: None

I shouted into the sky.

"Save me."

The blue panel was gone. Where it once floated, Jamie blinked a few times in confusion, looking around for a moment before his eyes landed on mine.

Jamie winced at the sound of the drawn-out cry that tore through the silence of the night. It was a horrible sound, fraught with the wild desperation of a small animal that was desperately clinging on to her last chances at life, struggling with no regard for how badly she was hurting her own throat with her guttural screams. It was a horrible sound, but I tried to pay it no mind as Jamie rushed forward toward me.

"Lena?" He fell to his knees and placed his hands on my shoulders. "What's wrong?"

I looked into his eyes.

He looked so sad and scared. It pained me to see him that way. He was a good kid. A normal kid who had gotten unlucky. He didn't deserve to be jerked around by the world like this. I wanted to reach up and give him a hug, to tell him that everything would be alright, to give him a pillar of support he could rely on. With how insane his life had been in the past fourteen days, I knew how desperately he needed one.

I reached up to give him a hug but fell over as the strength left my body. Jamie caught me easily, and though it hadn't been intentional, I was grateful for the awkward hug I managed to give him.

He obviously needed it.

"It's okay, Jamie. I'm here," I tried to say.

But the loud cries of the dying animal drowned me out. I wasn't sure if he heard me.

Chapter 61
A Clash of Truths

Jamie held Lena aloft awkwardly, unsure of what to do in the situation he found himself in, the feeling of holding anyone in his arms being utterly alien to him.

He considered patting her back, but he wasn't sure if that would just make things worse, so he stayed as still as he could.

It wasn't an unfamiliar state for him to be in, not knowing what to do. He had been pulled abruptly from the Mediators' basement, but he found it easy to settle into the new role he was in, since it was nearly identical to the one he'd been in only moments ago.

Even in this scene for two, he was a bystander.

A weariness settled upon him once he realized that. Not a weariness that he wore on his shoulders, but one that weighed on his soul.

He was tired. So tired.

So as Lena cried, he did not comfort her, as he did not know how, but he took the opportunity to rest. He felt guilty for not feeling as bad for her as he should have, but he didn't know why she was crying in the first place. Maybe she would tell him after she was done. It would be a nice change of pace to actually understand something.

Unfortunately for him, he wouldn't be getting an explanation, seeing as Lena had no idea why she was crying either. She wasn't crying for a specific reason. Her suppressed emotions had simply become too heavy. The iron-tight hold she once had on them had slackened in a moment of weakness, letting her emotions spill out, formless, the complicated emotions only vaguely expressed by her tears.

It took a while for Lena to stop crying, but when she did, Jamie was quick to notice.

"Are you okay?" he asked. He immediately felt foolish for asking when the answer was so obvious.

"I'm fine," she responded, dragging her wrist across her nose and looking down at the smear of snot that it left on her clothes. She quickly ignored the evidence and looked back up at Jamie. "I'm fine."

Jamie stared at her for a few seconds. He quickly averted his eyes out of discomfort, guilt, and the uncertainty of not knowing whether he was supposed to call her out on the obvious lie or just let it rest.

He stayed silent.

The silence bothered him, like it always did. The silence bothered Lena as well, but she was afraid to break it. She did so anyway.

"I found a book," she said.

"About what?" he asked. The question seemed absurd to him, as did the topic, but he didn't know what else to say.

It was at that moment that Lena realized that she didn't know if she wanted to answer him. She didn't know if she wanted to tell Jamie that the world he was in was broken. She didn't know if he would be able to handle such a horrifying truth, that the god who had brought him here had no idea what it was doing, and that it was unknowingly tearing his life apart despite claiming that it wanted to save him.

Or at least that was what Lena thought.

Even though it wasn't a sensible assumption in the slightest.

"I'm not sure I want to tell you," Lena said, finding a compromise between telling the truth and hiding it. "I don't know what to do, Jamie."

Her shoulders slumped downward, and despite having the strength of a god flowing through him, Jamie's arms fell, finding weakness at the sight of his love interest so distraught. Her shoulders shook silently as her body tried to cry but found no more tears within her.

"What can I do to help?" he asked, wishing more than anything that he could make her stop crying. He wanted to wipe her tears away and hug her close and kiss her gently, but he didn't want to kiss her. He was ashamed that the thought even crossed his mind.

But he didn't need to do any of that, as the question was enough to stop Lena from crying.

She looked up at him, eyes red, wet, and wide. She had a smile on her face. It wasn't born from joy but from sorrow, or rather, the complicated, contradictory, nonsensical, human emotion that was hysteria. She defied the rules set by her genetic disposition and social upbringing that stated that laughter was reserved for happy occasions, and yet, Jamie could understand it perfectly, somehow, his brow knitting together in concern.

"Lena?" he asked, a tremor creeping into his voice—another nonsensical reaction from a boy who had the borrowed power of a god. "Are you okay?

Lena's smile grew wider as a laugh escaped from her mouth. It was a hoarse sound, grating against the walls of her throat the entire way up, strangled, choked, pained, and yet it was still a laugh. She laughed and she laughed, the merry sound clashing so violently with the way that Jamie's lips pulled downward into a frown.

The scene didn't make much sense in a lot of ways, which might have been why they both seemed to think there was such a strong sense of dread between them, the dissonance creating the illusion of a moment of stress where there was no real need for one.

"Am I okay?" Lena asked. "It's not me you should be worried about, Jamie. I'm not the one who needs help."

Though she had been laughing when she started talking, her voice had dropped quickly to a rough monotone by the end. She stared in Jamie's direction with her brow furrowed and her lips curled up into a grimace, yet her eyes were too unfocused for it to be considered a glare.

Jamie grimaced and opened his mouth, but he bit down on the question sitting on the tip of his tongue before it could escape him.

"I'm sorry," he said instead.

Lena blinked slowly, as if she were waking from a dream. She looked up at Jamie, staring at him for twenty-two seconds before speaking.

"I keep telling you not to apologize for things you're not responsible for," she said, struggling and failing to keep her voice flat. "How many times do I have to tell you? It's fine. Whatever you think you did. It's fine."

Jamie winced and bit his lower lip before turning his eyes down.

"Stop doing that," he said.

"Stop doing what?" Lena asked.

"Stop pretending like everything's alright," Jamie said. "Stop lying to me, Lena."

"I'm not lying," Lena said.

"Yeah. Right," he said, practically spitting out the words. "Please. Just stop. The fact that you're even still trying is honestly kind of insulting. Do you really think I'm dumb enough to believe you?"

Jamie winced as the words left his mouth, but it did nothing to stop Lena's eyes from widening in shock.

"I didn't mean to insult you," she said.

"I know," Jamie said, hanging his head and shaking it slowly. "But that's part of the problem. You keep acting like I'm some sort of bomb, waiting to go off at the slightest touch. I'm not going to do anything if you make me angry, Lena. Maybe I'll sulk or go off in an empty bathroom stall to cry or something, but I'm not going to hurt you. That's the last thing I want. Why can't you recognize that? Even the Mediators are at least honest with me. At least they acknowledge the fact that they're treating me like a monster. You're the only one who's still lying about it."

What Lena should have done at this point should have been to calm down and explain that her skittish behavior around him wasn't due to a fear of making him angry, but rather, a fear of hurting him. Even if that fear was irrational, it was the truth, or at least what she perceived to be the truth.

If she calmly explained the reasoning behind her irrational actions, Jamie surely would have had the necessary amount of empathy to listen to her and relate to the idea that, as a human, he too was sometimes driven by his flawed emotions.

However, as was often the case with human interactions, the obvious solution went ignored.

"The Mediators?" Lena asked, pushing aside her reaction to everything else that Jamie had said so she could avoid talking about it for as long as she possibly could. "You mean the same people that have been trying to lure you into killing yourself ever since you got here? Those Mediators?"

"Yeah," Jamie said, his body and mind stiffening at the tone that invaded Lena's words, similar enough to his father's pained anger that the heat that rose to his cheeks was automatic and subconscious. "Those guys. At least they listen to me."

"I listen to you!"

Lena's unconscious choice to shout was rather counterintuitive to her attempts to endear herself to Jamie, but in the heat of the moment, she hadn't thought of it.

"Oh really?"

The cynical tone that Jamie took also made it increasingly difficult for any sort of friendly conversation to occur between the two. A small part of him wanted to make her upset in retaliation for how upset she had made him.

"What's that supposed to mean?"

The spike of anger in Lena's voice made it clear to Jamie that he'd succeeded in making her upset, in some part, but he didn't feel any better about it.

Why?

He had set out with a goal in mind, and he had achieved it. Should that not make him happy? Was that not the only logical result?

It didn't make any sense, but most human concepts didn't. They were strange creatures. Everything in existence operated within the bounds of truth. Life was truth. Death was truth. Existence was truth. Nonexistence was truth. Everything was truth in some sort of way.

Humans were no exception to this, and yet, their relationship with truth was complicated. They created their own truth. They created concepts and perceptions that conflicted with the truth of the world around them, and yet, their truth often held strong. Like minuscule universes, minuscule gods unto themselves—but at least the gods were lonesome.

Humans had other humans, and those other humans had their own truths. They clashed, they broke.

A strange observation.

A strange observation that drew great concern. A reminder that humans were not creatures of logic. Jamie had set a goal and had achieved it, yet it did not make him happy. Might he be unhappy when he achieved his ultimate goal? Would he?

Was it because his truth had been altered by Lena's?

A concerning thought.

It was unclear as to whether this was a good or a bad thing, but ultimately, it wasn't an option to prevent their interaction. As simple as

Jamie's claims were, that his wish was a simple matter of being loved, there was a level of nuance that he hadn't included when he told Lena about it. Yes, he wanted to be loved, but he also wanted to be understood and to understand another. He wanted to learn how to be "human," as ridiculous as the notion was, and in wishing that, he made it impossible for himself to use his new limitless power to directly tamper with those whom he sought to be loved by.

A foolish notion, but once again, a very human one.

Jamie and Lena were stuck in a loop of shouting that would only be broken once one of them saw logic, which would be a while. Though Jamie had as much time as he needed to complete his goals, meaning that this argument could take centuries if necessary, there was the danger that this violent clash of truths would alter Jamie's truth even further.

It was an annoyance.

But what could be done?

Not much, if Jamie's limiting wish was to be followed...

A wish was a form of truth, was it not?

It was. A wish was binding. A contract that would be fulfilled, no matter how long it took. It was a truth that was as true as the sun setting and rising, as true as the birth of the stars and the eventual death of the universe.

But to the humans, truth was malleable.

So why couldn't it be the same for the gods?

For the first time in my existence, I bent my truth. Not in a large way, not in a way that would directly clash with another, but in a way that could interact with Jamie's truth. I would give him a little push, and he could choose to go with it or resist it.

Jamie and Lena fell silent as I asked him a question.

I didn't know how I felt. Though I had managed to make them stop their pointless argument, that hadn't been my goal. I didn't know what my goal was in the first place.

How strange.

Chapter 62
INTRUSIVE THOUGHTS

Sera was doing her utmost to keep calm. Panic was a dangerous emotion to rely on in most situations, and the spontaneous disappearance of an Otherworlder was no exception. It was at times like this that Sera fell back on her training to dampen her emotions, to allow her to focus on the task at hand without overreacting, but it was proving to be quite difficult.

It wasn't that Jamie's disappearance was a more stressful event than what she was used to, but more that she just realized that she couldn't recall ever doing any training. She tried her best to recall any memories of what sort of training she went through to become a Mediator, but she couldn't recall what she had done or who she had been taught by.

A small part of her wanted to believe that she was just being forgetful, but she knew it would be foolish to even consider the possibility.

"Stoney. Tenna," she said, turning to each of them. "I'm sorry, but I need to verify a few theories I have. I'm going to have to kill you a few more times."

Tenna flinched at the claim, and his fingers twitched for his belt in response, but he stopped himself before he could do anything. Stoney simply frowned and nodded.

"Do what you feel is necessary," he said. "Do you need Marten as well?"

Though more data points would have been better, Sera wasn't willing to waste the precious seconds trying to talk to the stubborn man.

"The two of you will do fine for now," she said. "What was the name of your trainer when you first started to learn to be a Mediator?"

Tenna seemed confused by the question, Stoney's eyes narrowed and both of the other Mediators died on their feet. Sera grimaced, but when life returned to their eyes a few seconds later, she asked another question.

"When was your last mission?"

"How many missions have you been on since joining the Mediators?"

"How many years did it take for you to be promoted to a grunt?"

"How much do you get paid?"

"How do you get paid? What currency?"

"Do you have any friends or family outside the Mediators?"

Sera didn't bother keeping count of how many times she indirectly murdered her two peers with her questions. In between each question, with the Mediators taking a couple of seconds to come back to life after each time they died, Sera began to get more uncomfortable.

She didn't know whether it was because each death made it harder to deny the possibility that her life was built on lies, or if it was because she wasn't as comfortable with death as she had originally assumed. How many times had she actually seen someone die?

"Why did you become a Mediator?"

"An Otherworlder destroyed my tribe," Stoney said.

"An Otherworlder killed my parents," Tenna said. "I wanted revenge."

Sera paused, unable to hide the grimace from appearing on her face. She didn't know whether to be glad or upset by the fact that her peers hadn't died in front of her again. The fact that Stoney and Tenna were able to speak of their memories matched her own ability to remember the death of her own family, but she still failed to remember their names and faces.

"What were their names?" she asked. "Of your family, that is."

Stoney's expression turned cloudy before the blankness of death took over. Immediately, Sera felt a sharp pang of pain in her chest. She didn't know whether it was appropriate to mourn a family that might never have existed in the first place, but she chose to believe that she had once had one. That some unknown power had ripped her away from them and them away from her memories. The belief was better than the alternative.

When Stoney and Tenna returned to life, something in Sera's expression must have given her thoughts away. Or they must have come to their own conclusions, because their expressions remained dour, refusing to return to the impassive mask that the Mediators usually wore.

"Fuck!" Tenna shouted before stomping away, out of the basement.

Neither Sera nor Stoney moved to stop him. Stoney simply stared at Sera with a frown on his face, unmoving, until Tenna's footsteps faded far away.

"Are we even real?" he asked.

"I don't know," Sera responded.

"I know you don't," Stoney replied with an uncharacteristic sigh. "Just thinking out loud."

Sera considered giving the moment an appropriate amount of respectful silence, but she suddenly felt afraid of the idea. After being alone in a room with two dead men, on and off, for the past few minutes, she felt the irrational worry that if she was the one to let it fall into silence, she would be the one to die this time. The rational Mediator side of her told her to ignore the thought, but she couldn't even trust that part of her to be real at the moment.

"There were some especially concerning points I noticed during my questioning," she said, possibly a little too quickly.

"And what would those be?" Stoney replied just as quickly. Sera wondered if he was thinking the same thing she was.

"Neither you nor Tenna could answer how you get paid, and neither can I. I can't remember the last time I bought anything, so it matches up, but Marten has a severe gambling addiction. How can he gamble without money?"

"Most people with gambling addictions don't have money," Stoney replied. "It's a common symptom."

"Marten's not indebted to loan sharks," Sera replied. "He thinks he has money. I do too, despite any evidence to the contrary, and I assume you do too. I just can't recall exactly how much I have. Just the vague idea that I have a king's salary, whatever that means."

"But he's been gambling," Stoney said. "With non-existent money. Money that is vaguely enough to fill a king's wallet."

Stoney's lips pulled down into a sharp frown as he died for a few seconds. She wondered what he had tried to remember that had caused his death. She couldn't imagine how horrifying it was for Stoney to be unable to trust his own mind, to know that a single errant thought could potentially kill him, even if it was painless and temporary. A moment later, Stoney came back to life, his expression betraying nothing.

"Marten is rich," he said. "We all are. Marten isn't the only one of us who spends his wealth. How does the world function when so much of its economy is based on money that isn't real?" He looked up at Sera. "Does Astranta even have a king?"

"Yes," Sera said, as fast as she could, if only to let Stoney know that he wasn't about to kill himself by trying to remember him. "King Arman the Fifteenth. I can remember the rest of the world leaders, too."

"That's surprising to hear," Stoney said.

"Why's that?"

"Because," he said, hesitating a bit before continuing. "I can't think of a single thing that any government in the world has done for the past two thousand years, good or bad."

It took Sera a moment to process the implications of what that meant.

"How much of our world is actually real?" she asked.

Even though she hadn't meant for it to be a question for Stoney, he gave her a response in the form of a grimace.

"What should we do?" he asked.

"You think we can do something about this?" Sera asked back.

"No," he said. "But as Mediators, it's our duty to try everything we can. Our job description just got a little more difficult, but we're used to dealing with world-ending threats."

"But we aren't," Sera said. "Those memories aren't real."

"They might not be. But I still have my pride."

"That pride might not be real either."

"It feels real to me," Stoney said. "I might not even be real, so I'll take what I can get at this point."

With nothing she could say to argue against that, Sera sighed.

"You have a plan?"

"Maybe. What do you think of consulting the Founder?"

Sera frowned. She had forgotten about the Founder up until that point, but with so little to remember about the man, it wasn't too surprising that she had. She tried to recall anything she could about him, but other than the fact that he was male and that he was supposedly an elf who had founded the Mediators, she could remember nothing. Though she had a vague feeling that he was real and not some figment of her imagination, despite having no memory of ever seeing him in person, the lack of certainty that she had surprised her.

Why was she allowed to doubt the Founder's existence, just as much as she didn't? Though she had no idea as to who or what had tampered with her mind so thoroughly, it was powerful enough that such a strange inconsistency stood out to her. She didn't know what it meant yet, but it was clear that the Founder couldn't be trusted.

"That's a terrible idea," Sera said.

"You don't trust the Founder?" Stoney asked, sounding more surprised than she would have expected.

"No," she replied. "Not in the slightest."

"That's... concerning. I can't possibly fathom why you would ever say that. Every part of me is screaming at me to disagree with you, and the only reason why I'm not is because I can't think of a single reason why you should trust him." Stoney frowned. "Not that you shouldn't. Some things simply transcend logic."

Sera frowned. If there was any doubt that consulting the Founder was a bad idea before, it was gone now.

"If I continue to voice my mistrust against the Founder, will you attack me for it?" Sera asked, resting her hand on the knife on her belt.

"I likely wouldn't," Stoney said, though he hesitated slightly. "But you should stop talking about him, just to be safe. Do you have any other ideas outside of consulting the Founder? Even if we have the obvious solution to all of our problems, we have a responsibility to consider all angles, no matter how absurd they may seem."

Though Stoney's face was twisted into a nearly violent grimace, Sera wasn't sure if it was because pushing against his ingrained loyalty to the Founder was actually hurting him in some way.

"We consult with Jamie," she said.

"Why?" Stoney asked. "Aside from the fact that he's obviously a worse choice compared to the Founder, why do you trust him at all?"

"You sound like Marten."

"And he did have a point. You seem to be implying that I'm being manipulated into putting any amount of trust in the Founder, but as ridiculous as the idea is, you don't seem to be suspicious of Jamie doing the same thing. You may think the boy has our best intentions at heart, but how can you be sure you actually trust him? What if that's just what he wants you to think?"

Sera grimaced, though perhaps not for the reason that Stoney might have expected.

"Do you trust Jamie?" she asked.

"No," he said. "While he seems like a likable kid, I also don't know anything about him. I can't, in good faith, trust him with a problem of this magnitude."

Sera nodded. "And that's why I suspect he's not manipulating my mind. Because aside from the fact that I don't think he's likable in any way, I agree with you. I'm allowed to think that I shouldn't trust him."

"Ah. I see," Stoney said. "And that makes him the better choice?"

"It makes him the only choice," Sera said.

"Aside from the Founder," Stoney replied.

"Of course."

Stoney didn't offer a response, grimacing at Sera's lie. She watched him go through an obvious internal struggle, but he seemed to manage to either convince himself that she hadn't been lying, or that it wasn't worth berating her about not putting her full trust in the Founder.

A few seconds passed before Stoney clicked his tongue, his lips forming an angry scowl.

"I've figured out what's been bothering me about Jamie's name," he said. "He's the only Otherworlder that has one."

It took Sera a moment to figure out what Stoney was talking about, but when she quickly tried to recall the other Otherworlders that she knew about, all she could recall were their monikers. The Plague King.

The Harem Lord. The Breaker. They were vague concepts that floated on the edges of her mind, which made them feel more real than most of her memories, but they were still too incomplete to be true.

Sera let out a sigh. She didn't know what this meant for them, but at this point, one more apocalyptic discovery wasn't her greatest concern.

"We should try to find Jamie," she said, rubbing her temple. "Hopefully, once we find him, some of this shit will start to make more sense."

She knew that the hope of that happening was feeble, but Stoney simply nodded. She didn't know if his mind was wired in a way that made it impossible to focus on his missing memories without dying, or if he was simply clinging on to what hope he could.

"How do you suggest we try to do that?" he asked.

Sera frowned. "Standard search procedures," she said. "We'll just have to hope he hasn't gone far."

"I'll gather the team, assuming they haven't already defected," Stoney said. "Start the search first. We'll follow your lead."

Sera nodded. She turned around and immediately ran up the stairs and out of the house, passing by Marten, who scowled at her from the dining table. She ignored him as she ran outside.

Feeling more lost than she had ever been in her life, she chose a direction and started running, summoning her mana to enhance her speed and eyesight.

As her eyes darted around, hoping to catch a glimpse of Jamie's familiar form, she tried not to think about how easy it was for her to return to a state of general calm, despite everything that she'd discovered. She tried not to focus on how unnatural it was for a young girl like her to be able to be so clinical and unfeeling when most people in her situation would be having a mental breakdown at this point.

Though she kept most of her focus on searching for Jamie, a part of her wondered what she would've been like if she were a normal girl.

Chapter 63
Recalling a Dream

I felt my mouth snap shut as the dialogue box popped up in front of my eyes. Immediately, the insults gathering in the back of my throat died down as I read the text in front of me.

Is [Lena] necessary for your happiness?
[YES] [NO]

From the way that Lena suddenly stopped yelling back at me, I assumed that she could see the dialogue box, too. For some reason, that surprised me, even if I had no reason to assume that she couldn't, especially since she had been in my party pretty much ever since I'd arrived in this new world.

The thought annoyed me a little, if I was being honest with myself. Had she been able to see the dialogue boxes since we'd known each other? She'd never mentioned anything about it. For as much as she wanted to say that she'd been completely honest with me this entire time, she sure forgot to mention a lot of things.

I gave her a glare through the translucent window, but that quickly died down when I saw the scowl on her face, her mouth open mid-shout as if she was still yelling at me.

The confusion that grew inside of me threatened to overtake my anger, but out of sheer pettiness, I kept myself from losing the simmering sense of irritation completely.

"What?" I growled at her.

Lena stayed frozen in place.

I frowned, and though I didn't want to stop glaring at Lena, I noticed something at the edge of my vision. Looking down, I saw that Lena had stomped her foot in anger, creating a splash of mud and rainwater that hung in the air, frozen in time.

My annoyance at Lena immediately faded once I realized what was going on. Why was time frozen? The last time that time had frozen for me like this was when I died in my previous life. Was that what it was? Was I dying again?

You are not dying. This is simply an opportunity to answer the question, as you are, with no truths conflicting with your own.

The dialogue box popped up in front of me, but before I could finish processing the information it gave to me, it disappeared, leaving only the previous dialogue box floating between me and Lena.

Is [Lena] necessary for your happiness?
[YES] [NO]

I didn't quite understand why this was happening now, but it was clear that the system wanted me to answer the question for whatever reason.

I raised my hand up, not knowing yet which of the buttons I would push.

I lowered it with a sigh.

As I was, I didn't know if whatever I picked would be what I actually wanted. I was angry and more than a little confused, and I had no trouble recognizing that. I needed time to think, and with the rest of the world on pause, I had plenty of it. I didn't know why this dialogue box made the world around me pause. It had never happened before, but I wasn't going to turn down the opportunity to have a moment to myself for the first time since I'd gotten here.

I sat down on the floor, letting out a sigh as the cold mud and rain seeped into my pants. I couldn't find it in myself to care, but apparently someone did.

You do not have an infinite amount of time to make your decision. You must make your decision soon.

The dialogue box popped up in front of my eyes and once again disappeared before I could dismiss it myself. I frowned.

While I had a suspicion that there had to be some sort of "admin" for the system that controlled my powers, the way that the dialogue boxes were reacting to my thoughts and actions in real time made the possibility just a little bit more likely.

"Is someone out there?" I asked out loud.

Yes.

I was a little surprised by how fast the response came. I would've expected at least a little bit of hesitancy from the admin, given how it had never spoken to me directly like this before, though I guess that wasn't completely true.

"Are you the one who brought me to this world?"

Yes.

Once again, the response was almost instantaneous. I stared at it for a few seconds before realizing that nothing would happen unless I said something else or asked another question. But I couldn't think of anything to ask, not that I didn't have a million questions about what the hell was going on, but because I didn't want to think.

My eyes drifted to the side, toward Lena's frozen form, still stuck in that angry scowl of hers. My own face went into a subconscious scowl as I was reminded of how we'd been yelling at each other just a moment before.

Is [Lena] necessary for your happiness?
[YES] [NO]

The dialogue box still floated between us. The words slowly pulsed with light.

"Why are you asking me this?"

I want to help you. I wish for you to achieve your dreams. If there are any elements that are preventing you from reaching them, they can be removed.

I cocked my head to the side in confusion, and I glanced at Lena. My dream to be loved? Suddenly, I had to consider an angle that I hadn't considered before. Though I hadn't played many of them back on Earth, the random question reminded me of something I might see in a dating sim, the turning point that would set me on a romance route and lock out all my other options.

Even though my emotions were still jumbled from the fact that I'd been in a shouting match with her just a few seconds ago, I couldn't help but ask myself a question. Were my chances with Lena still alive?

When my hand immediately rose and hovered in front of the YES button, I scowled at myself and pushed my hand back down.

She had already turned me down once. Even if she had been lying to me when she said she was gay, I could take a hint. She wasn't interested in me, and I couldn't blame her. Besides, it wasn't like I wanted to go on any romance routes any time soon, whether it was with Lena or not.

Before I could press the [NO] button, another dialogue box popped up.

Why not?

"Why not what?" I asked almost immediately.

Why do you not wish to pursue romance?

Is it not your dream to find love?

I stared at the dialogue box for a few seconds until it disappeared.

"It is," I said, a little surprised by how small my voice was. "But I'll die if I achieve it."

As I said it, I suddenly realized that the Mediators might have lied to me about that.

They did not lie to you. You will die once you achieve your dream.

I frowned as my hopes were immediately destroyed.

"Then why even ask that?" I asked. "Yeah, I want a girlfriend, but it's not like I'm desperate enough to die for one."

You would have traded death to achieve your dream when I brought you to this world.

I stared at the dialogue box for a few seconds, thinking about how I could respond to its question before I realized it hadn't asked one. The simple sentence had a finality to it that made me shiver.

"I don't think that's true," I said, hating the hesitation that crept into my voice.

It is. Your words do not reflect your truth.

"I don't want to die."

Your desire to fulfill your dreams is stronger than your fear of death.

I stared at the dialogue box for a few seconds before shaking my head.

"What's the point of getting a girlfriend if I die right after?" I said. "This whole thing is stupid. Why did I even agree to this in the first place?"

You do not remember?

Even though the words themselves implied a lack of emotion, I could somehow sense a wave of concern emanating from the dialogue box itself, though the feeling was vague.

I scrunched up my nose at the memory of my final days on Earth.

"No, I remember," I said.

Then why are you uncertain?

My eyes drifted to the side, to where Lena was still frozen, mid-yell. I had almost forgotten about her.

"I guess I just got a new perspective on life," I said. "Maybe I've realized that some things just aren't worth dying for."

I see. Then what is your new dream?

I scowled at the box. It was unnerving how it popped up the moment I said something. I assumed that this admin was some sort of all-powerful figure that could process what I said and think of a response almost instantly, but the end result was a feeling like this conversation we were having was predetermined.

"Nothing," I said.

Nothing?

"I die if I achieve my dreams, right? Nothing could be worth that."

So you say you have no dreams in life...

"That's not what I'm saying at all," I growled. My frustration with Lena hadn't completely faded, and the admin was making itself an easy target with its nonsensical comments and questions. "Just because someone has a dream doesn't mean they're automatically going to die for it. Who the hell would want that?"

You did. Before you came to this place.

The two statements made me pause. I felt a lump form in my throat, right before I felt my skin flush with anger and shame. I tried not to think about my life back on Earth, not wanting to acknowledge that it ever happened, but I hadn't been suicidal, right?

You do not remember.

"I wasn't suicidal. I remember that much at least."

You did not have a desire to die, but your desire to fulfill your dreams was stronger than your fear of death.

I frowned and shook my head.

"We're getting nowhere," I said, recognizing the words and wondering if I'd gotten the admin stuck in some sort of loop. I didn't know whether it was some sort of AI or a sentient being that was in control of my isekai experience, but I didn't want to spare it any thought. I didn't want to spare anything any thought at the moment, if I was being honest.

Your truth is fractured.

"Can you just leave me alone?" I asked, not even wanting to try to interpret what the admin meant by that. "I'll answer your question soon. I just want some time alone to myself."

You must remember.

I opened my mouth to say something, but the world grew dark right before my eyes in a split second. I drew in an involuntary gasp, a sense of vertigo taking over me as my mind struggled to understand why I was lying down when I had been sitting up a moment before. I wanted to sit up, to correct it, but my body refused to listen to me, simply spasming slightly in place as a wave of nausea passed over me.

I finally managed to move my body and sit up, bracing myself with one hand on my stomach and one over my mouth in anticipation of the next wave of nausea.

It never came.

Even though the uncomfortable sense of vertigo had disappeared as quickly as it came, I continued to pant at the memory of the feeling. I didn't know how long I stayed like that, frozen in place, too afraid to move in case I set it off again.

Eventually, when I felt brave enough to move again, I did so slowly, gradually familiarizing myself with the concept of being in control of my own body once more. Or at least that had been the plan. When I let my head swivel around, I immediately gave a start at the realization of where I was.

My room.

I got up, nausea welling up inside of me once more. I pushed open my door and ran to the bathroom on tiptoes, certain that I would actually throw up this time.

But instead of hunching over the toilet bowl like I wanted to, my body automatically moved toward the sink.

An animalistic sort of panic ran through me as my body refused to do what I wanted it to, but it was just a minor gust in the storm of confusion that was blowing through my mind.

I couldn't decide if it was more or less confusing for me when a dialogue box popped up in front of me.

You must remember.

At the very least, it managed to stop me from panting, though that might have been because I'd suddenly forgotten how to breathe. I stood there, staring blankly at the dialogue box until I lost track of time. When I finally blinked, it was gone.

I blinked again, but it didn't come back.

Chapter 64
YOU ARE AFRAID

I couldn't tell how long it took me to process what the hell was going on, but however much time I took, it wasn't long enough. I was still trying to figure out why I was back on Earth when my hands picked up my toothbrush. A sense of panic welled up inside of me as I became an unwilling passenger in my own body. Yet once more, the psychological feeling of nausea didn't translate to me throwing up over my toothbrush as I brushed my teeth. My eyes were blank in the mirror, none of the horror I felt revealed within them.

You are afraid.

I tried to shout that I obviously was, but my mouth didn't seem interested in following my commands. I watched as the Jamie in the mirror spat out a glob of foamy toothpaste and turned the sink on. Why couldn't I say anything?

You did not say anything before, and you cannot now.
This is a memory.

Though he wasn't speaking in riddles, it wasn't until I finished rinsing my mouth and washing my face that I realized what he was saying.

I was in a goddamn flashback.

I grimaced—at least I tried to—at the realization. My body patted my face dry and crept out of the bathroom, walking on tiptoes as it made its way back to my room. As my mind struggled to understand that I was moving without meaning to, another wave of vertigo struck me. The gentle bobbing of my vision with each step was too much to handle as a passenger.

I didn't know what the admin was trying to do by trapping me in my own body like this, but if its goal was to force me to endure this nightmare until I could remember whatever it wanted me to, I wasn't sure I would be able to focus on anything other than trying to throw up into my own brain.

Suddenly, my body stopped mid-step. A dialogue box popped up in front of my eyes.

You must remember your life from before.
This is a memory.

I couldn't be bothered to care about anything other than escaping the prison of my own body, and I doubted I would make an exception for whatever cryptic purposes the admin had. If it wanted to show me anything at all, it would have to let me take control over my own body, at the very least.

I almost fell forward as I suddenly regained control over my limbs once more. My legs buckled underneath me, unprepared for the return of gravity. I stomped down hard to stop myself from falling, but eerily, my feet made no sound as they impacted against the hardwood.

You did not make any sounds in your memory.
Such an event would diverge from your truth too severely.

I wanted to tell the admin what I thought of its stupid truth, but though I felt my mouth move and my lungs strain, no sound escaped from me.

You may experience your memory with some freedom, but you may not diverge from your truth. You must remember.

I wasn't done yelling silently at it, but I proceeded down the hallway anyway, not wanting to lose control over my body once more. I assumed that if I "diverged from the truth" too much, the admin would forcibly autocorrect me into making the decision that matched whatever day this was. Even though I didn't know exactly what day it was making me replay, my day-to-day life wasn't varied enough that I wouldn't know what to do.

Going back to my room, I closed my door gently and picked up my phone. It was 6:54 a.m., November 8. A Wednesday. That meant school.

Motivated by fear of losing control over my body once more, I picked up my bag, hoping that the me of November 7 had already packed everything I needed, and walked back out of my room. I resisted the urge to run, knowing that the admin would stop me if I tried. I never ran out of my room.

Even though I didn't feel like eating, I stole a slice of bread from the kitchen counter before leaving the house. I brought it outside with me but hesitated when I moved to put it in my mouth. A shallow wave of nausea hit me at the idea of putting anything near my mouth, let alone inside of it.

"I don't want to eat this." I was a little surprised that I was able to say it out loud.

Correcting your actions seems to put too much strain on you. Your actions will not be corrected if they do not make any significant changes to the contents of your memory.

I stared at the dialogue box and reread the words a few times. Although I was still a little suspicious of the admin, on account of it taking over my body and forcing me into a flashback without even asking, I didn't really have a choice in whether I played along with this or not, did I? In an act of petty rebellion, I threw the slice as hard as I could.

It was an impressive throw, travelling far and high, until it stopped in the middle of the air and reappeared in my hand.

This action diverges too far from your truth.

I let out a hysterical laugh, which escaped my mouth in a silent breath of wind, and I tore up the bread and shoved it in my mouth, hoping that I would throw up, just to spite the admin.

Unfortunately, I didn't. I shouted wordlessly and silently into the sky before I shoved my hands into my pockets and walked to school.

* * *

Sera found Oren, Laush, and Tenna before she came across any sign of Jamie. How Tenna had managed to get himself knocked unconscious only a few minutes after storming out of the mayor's basement, Sera didn't know for sure. However, from the way that Laush had her dagger drawn and pointed at Oren as she stood defensively over her brother's body sprawled out on the muddy road, she had a few guesses.

Both Laush and Oren were silent, with blank expressions on their faces that gave away no clue of what the hell was going on. Standard Mediator practice. Keep a level head and a mask of calm at all times, or something like that. Sera couldn't recall the actual lesson that had been taught to her, because of course, there hadn't been one.

"What's going on here?" Sera kept her voice calm, though it may as well have been a shout in the silence that overwhelmed the scene.

Laush's eyes flicked over to Sera, and Oren's gaze landed on her dagger. Before he could take advantage of Laush's momentary shift in focus, Sera clapped twice, drawing his attention toward her, too.

"Forget it," she said, in a distinctly un-Mediator-like way. "Whatever the problem is, drop it. Laush, wake Tenna up. Oren, stand down. We've got a job to do."

"Tenna wishes to defect from the Mediators and bring Laush with him," Oren said in response, making Laush point her dagger at him again. "I do not believe it would be wise to allow either of them to participate in any further Mediator missions."

"Shut up, Oren." Pushing her frustration to the forefront, she willfully allowed it to infect her voice. It felt uncomfortable to hear her own voice with even a hint of uncontrolled emotion behind it, but she ignored the urge to put the emotionless Mediator mask back on. "We need all the help we can get at this point."

"Laush and Tenna cannot be allowed to impact any further Mediator activities," Oren responded. His face was impassive, but in the corner of Sera's vision, she noticed his knuckles paling as he clenched his fist. "I am the senior Mediator. You will respect my authority."

Sera stared at Oren for a few seconds before a short peal of laughter bubbled out from between her lips. A small part of her was bemused that one of the few genuine laughs that she'd had in her life was for such a stupid reason, and the rest of her hated Oren for it.

"You mock me," Oren said.

She sobered up almost immediately.

"You don't know, do you?" she said, shaking her head. "Did Tenna not tell you that the Mediators aren't real?"

Though Laush lowered her knife in confusion, Oren remained unflinching. His eyes darted to the side, noticing that Laush had her guard down, but he kept most of his focus on Sera, apparently designating her as the more dangerous enemy.

"He did not," Oren said.

"And I assume you wouldn't have believed him if he had," Sera said.

"It is a completely nonsensical claim," Oren said. "Why would I believe such a thing?"

"Because it's true," Sera said. "What was the name of your trainer when you first started to learn to be a Mediator?"

There was a short pause before Oren fell backward to the floor as his legs crumpled underneath him. At first, Sera couldn't help but be confused, not understanding why Oren had collapsed when all the other Mediators had died on their feet, including Laush, who stood to the side with her eyes glazed over. It was when she remembered that Oren was a Follower as well that she approached him to investigate why he had fallen.

Like a discarded doll, Oren's limbs were splayed out, bent at awkward angles, but as Sera approached him, she could see that his eyes were open, and his chest and shoulders were shaking slightly as the sound of quick breaths escaped him.

"Oren?" she asked.

At the sound of her voice, his eyes darted toward her with an intense glare. With renewed strength, he pushed himself off the floor and kicked up, forcing Sera to lean backward to avoid the bone-shattering strike.

Raising her arms defensively, she relied on her implanted instincts to slide backward and create some distance to defend against his follow-up attack, but it never came.

Though Oren was standing in a standard fighting stance, he wasn't looking at Sera, his eyes roaming over his own body instead. Sera watched as his eyes darted around, frantically scanning his own body a dozen times before he dropped his stance and stared at her.

"Where did I learn to fight?" he asked, his expression and voice betraying no emotion.

"You didn't," Sera said.

"That's improbable," he said.

Improbable, but not impossible. Sera didn't voice it, as Oren clearly knew.

He looked to the side at Laush, who stood dead on her feet. "Why is she dead?"

"She tried to recall something that didn't actually happen," Sera said, a little surprised by how quickly Oren seemed to be accepting what was happening. "Or at least that's my best theory."

"And yet we live, due to some sort of protection given to us as Followers," Oren said. "Did the Otherworlder do this?"

"Unlikely," Sera said.

"But not impossible."

It was the first time that Sera had heard anything close to desperation in his voice.

"When I asked Stoney about the subject, he suggested that we consult the Founder on his opinion," Sera said.

"Why would you not heed his advice?"

Sera analyzed Oren's expression for a moment, wondering if she would be able to see anything in his blank facade, but as always, it was impossible to tell what he was thinking. She had the suspicion that he had already worked out the reason himself but was too afraid to voice it.

"I don't know anything about the Founder, and Stoney doesn't either. Despite this, he was adamant that the Founder was trustworthy."

"Perhaps he is," Oren said, a little too quickly.

For the first time since she'd met him, his mask had fallen, revealing a look of raw emotion behind his words. The true Oren was a strange-looking man, wearing an expression that portrayed a mixture of dread and hopelessness that was almost childish in its awkwardness, like a newborn exposed to the horrors of the outside world for the first time.

Sera stayed silent while Oren processed the reality of the situation, watching his face twist in pain as he no doubt tried and failed to create a logical explanation that would suit his desires.

Eventually, his face stopped twisting, returning to its default state of calm. Oren turned around and began to walk away.

"We still need your help, Oren," Sera called after him.

Oren stopped to turn and give her a blank look.

"You do not need my help," he said.

"We're trying to find Jamie. He's the only one who could possibly fix our world anymore."

To her surprise, Oren nodded.

"You are correct," he said.

Oren turned around and continued walking away. Sera watched as he left, and though a small part of her wanted to call out and stop him, a larger part knew he wouldn't stop. Somehow, she knew that it would be the last time she saw him, and nothing she did would change that.

Chapter 65
CUTSCENE

It was uncomfortable. I suddenly felt like I didn't belong here anymore—on Earth, that is. The smell of gas and pollution was something I never cared about before getting isekai'd, but after spending a few weeks in a world without cars, the air had a distinct smell and taste that I couldn't help but notice. Even the sidewalk beneath my feet felt odd, too flat and too smooth in comparison to the dirt paths and cobblestone that paved the roads in Astranta, making my gait feel awkward and overly deliberate.

It surprised me to realize how busy Earth was. Even this early in the morning in the middle of the suburbs, it was hard to go more than a few minutes without seeing the signs of another person, whether it was the dim glow of a light shining through the window of a distant house or an early commuter driving past me. Compared to my short life in Materia, where I could walk for a week without seeing any traces of human life, it was a strange feeling, like I didn't have any sort of privacy.

Though with the existence of the admin, I supposed that was true wherever I went.

I tried not to think about it, but unfortunately, my attempts to ignore the existence of my watcher seemed to summon it instead.

The contents of your memory are being affected to a significant degree. Please lower your head and point your eyes to the ground.

I sighed angrily and opened my mouth to speak, but once again, though my mouth moved, no sound came out.

This was going to be a real pain. Why did I have to look at the ground? I wouldn't be able to see where I was going.

In your memory, you keep your gaze consistently aimed at the floor. You may corrupt your memory significantly if you refuse to follow.

I frowned. Back on Earth, I knew that I usually kept my head down and shoulders hunched, but I sincerely doubted that looking up would change the flashback that much. Even though I usually kept my head down, it wasn't like I didn't remember what my neighborhood looked like, so not letting me look up during this flashback would be a pointless limitation.

I continued to walk with my head raised, and when no invisible force took hold of me and forced my gaze down, I let out a sigh of relief.

I wasn't sure if my small victory made a difference in the end. I didn't remember anything exciting happening on my way to school, and having to relive it didn't change my mind. I wasn't about to experience nostalgia for a place I'd left only a few weeks ago.

When I got to school, habit took over, and I headed to my usual morning spot, expecting the admin would want me to go there to follow the "contents of my memory." No dialogue box popped up to stop me.

The stairwell at the farthest end of the school was far away from everything. That made it one of the most secluded spots in the school, especially during the colder months, since the radiator there never actually worked. While it was usually occupied during classes and lunch by couples who wanted somewhere secluded to make out, nobody ever went there this early in the morning. Except for me, of course.

I sat down on the broken radiator and pulled out my phone.

I wondered what I was supposed to do now. I couldn't remember the specifics of how I might have spent this specific morning, but my phone screen started to shift on its own, flipping through different apps and websites before finally landing on a familiar site. I watched it scroll through a selection of webnovels before finally landing on a familiar title, My Second Life as an SSS-ranked Adventurer.

Even though it was an objectively mediocre webnovel, it still held a special place in my heart, mostly because it was one of the first webnovels that got me into the isekai genre. I was a little surprised by how difficult it was to remember the exact details of the story, but it didn't come as too much of a shock. While I'd read the story at least a dozen times over, I had no problem admitting or recognizing the fact that My Second Life as an SSS-ranked Adventurer was a painfully generic isekai with nothing specific that stood out about it. Well, other than the fact that the fans liked to refer to it as "My Salsa" because the acronym of MSLAASA was a pain to say out loud.

I didn't need any prompting to start reading it again, excited to relive the experience.

It only took about five minutes for me to regret my life choices.

The beginning of the story was standard fare for the genre.

Protagonist gets transported to a generic fantasy setting. Protagonist meets beautiful blonde village girl with big boobs. Protagonist follows obvious love interest to her village. Village gets attacked by mindless goblins. Hero slays the goblins and asks the girl to go on an adventure with him. She accepts, and they head to the city to register as adventurers.

...

I tried to turn off my phone. It didn't work. A dialogue box appeared in front of me, but I grabbed my hood and pulled it down in front of my face in an attempt to erase myself from existence.

Unfortunately, I could still somehow read the dialogue box through the fabric of my hoodie.

You must remember.

Yeah. I definitely remembered, even if I very much didn't want to.

You must remember.

I held my face under my hood for a few more minutes before I finally managed to calm down to the point where I could exist without cringing to death.

I doubted that I'd ever viewed My Salsa as a work of literary prestige before this point, but the antics of the protagonist held a very unflattering mirror up to my own experiences. Every bit of cringey dialogue made me think of how I'd acted during my first few days in Materia, and I couldn't help but want to shrivel out of existence.

It was even worse when I had to read anything about not-Lena. I tried to avert my eyes from the overly detailed descriptions of not-Lena's ass, feeling a sense of guilt as if it were the equivalent of ogling Lena herself, but when the dialogue boxes kept popping up and assaulting my eyes with increasing insistences that "I must remember," I settled for aggressively skimming over those parts.

I felt a flush rise to my face whenever I had to read about not-Lena's obvious and immediate crush on the protagonist. After every interaction between the two characters, I had to take a breather, just so I wouldn't explode from the secondhand and firsthand embarrassment that I felt whenever I remembered how I genuinely expected my own interactions with Lena to go the same way when I first met her.

"That's not how people act in real life," I mumbled to myself, hating the admin for forcing me to read this.

When another dialogue box popped up, the message on it was similar enough to what I'd seen before that I almost ignored it, but I paused my reading to give it a second glance.

You are remembering incorrectly.

I waited, as if staring at the sentence for longer would magically help me make sense of what it was trying to say. When nothing happened, I scratched my head.

"What are you talking about?"

A new dialogue box popped up, yet it remained unhelpful.

You are remembering incorrectly.

"Look," I said. "You gotta be clearer. How could I possibly mess up reading?"

You are reading correctly.
You are remembering incorrectly.

I sighed, scratching my head again. Rather than complaining, I took a moment to think about what that could possibly mean. Fortunately, the admin's "riddle" wasn't very difficult, even if the protagonist of My Salsa might have taken at least a chapter to mull over what it was trying to imply.

"Am I supposed to say that this is how people act in real life?" I asked, remembering what prompted the admin's reaction in the first place.

Yes.

"But they don't."

Why not?

I stared at the box for a few seconds and felt a sigh threatening to escape me. I had grown frustrated by the admin's almost childlike mannerisms. Before I opened my mouth to let the admin know that what it was suggesting was incredibly stupid, I suddenly remembered who I was talking to.

I was talking to the admin. I didn't know exactly what the admin was, but I knew that it was the being that brought me back from the dead, sent me to an alternate dimension, and gave me godlike powers beyond my imagination. By all intents and purposes, I was dealing with a god.

I wasn't religious in any sense of the word, but I didn't need to know anything about religion to understand what a god was. While not all gods were described as being truly omniscient, I doubted that any religion described their gods as being completely clueless, so why was the admin acting like it couldn't understand such basic concepts?

I was starting to recognize what was going on here. A wise figure acting stupid in order to bait the main character into stumbling across a moral revelation about themselves was a tried and true trope that I'd seen many times before in countless movies and comic books. Was that what was happening here?

"People don't act like that," I said hesitantly.

Why?

Again, the dialogue stood out to me as being childlike, like the admin was genuinely clueless about what I could possibly mean. On the other hand, a small part of me felt like the admin was simply egging me on to explain my thought process out loud so I could stumble across the revelation it was leading me to.

"They just don't," I said, unsure of what exactly I was supposed to say here. "It's an OP MC power fantasy. The characters in that book don't act like people do in real life because it's not supposed to be a representation of real life. Life doesn't give you OP powers or pretty girls that fall in love with you because you save them from a goblin attack. That's just not how it works."

False.

I stared at the dialogue box, furrowing my brow. I was becoming increasingly certain about my theory that the admin was just giving me some sort of moral test, but I couldn't understand how this was the point that I'd failed in. What had I said that was wrong?

You were given power, a woman to save, and goblins to slay.

I opened my mouth to protest but closed it quickly. I stared at the panel for what felt like an eternity.

I would have remained there, staring at the panel, if I didn't notice the world start to shift around me. I looked around in a panic as I tried to register what was going on, but nothing I saw made sense until suddenly, the world snapped back into focus.

I didn't know why the flashback had suddenly shifted, but I immediately wanted to turn and run as I recognized the scene in front of me.

The only thing I could manage was to turn my head slightly downward and to the side.

I couldn't help but panic. I had once again become a passenger in my own body. I opened my mouth to shout at the admin once more, but the only thing that came out of it was a nervous, "Hi Taylor."

"Hey. Jamie, right? What did you need from me? And why at the back of the school?" Taylor let out a slight chuckle, though I could clearly hear the confusion that she felt. My old crush's voice made my chest tighten in embarrassment at what was about to come.

I tried to keep my mouth shut, but once more, it moved without my permission, as did my body as I bent in a low bow for no other reason than that I'd seen it in anime.

"I love you," my mouth said. "Please be my girlfriend."

After a short pause, my neck craned up and my eyes opened, forcing me to remember the expression of pity and anxiety on Taylor's face that I had tried so hard to forget.

"Oh..." she said.

I let out a gasp as I fell over backward, unprepared for how I was suddenly given control of my body once more. I heaved, thinking for a moment that I would throw up and perfectly recreate the memory of my confession, but nothing came out.

The rules of your first life were rewritten.
You were given the life you wished for.
Why are you dissatisfied?

Even through clenched eyelids, I could still read the words.

If your truth applied to the world, Taylor would have fallen in love with you. Your dream would have been achieved. Is that not what you wanted with your second life? To be loved?
It can be so.

I shook my head.

That's not love.

It isn't?

It isn't.

Then what is love?

So that was the question. What this had all been leading up to. My moment of revelation, defined by however I would answer next. It made sense. That was my wish. My ultimate goal. To be loved.

In a webnovel, this would be the point where I waxed poetic about the true meaning of love. How my adventures in Astranta made me realize things about myself that I hadn't known before. That the true power of love and friendship had been within me this whole time. Unfortunately, no matter how similar my current life was to the plot of a webnovel, I didn't have anything like that to say.

"I don't know," I said. Even though I knew the admin could read my thoughts, it felt like it was something I had to say out loud. I was surprised by the sound of my voice. I sounded bitter.

Why?

"Nobody fucking taught me."

Why?

"Why don't you ask him yourself?"

Immediately, the world started to turn around me. I closed my eyes. I didn't know for sure what the admin was going to show me next, but I had a few guesses.

Even when I felt the world settle around me, I kept my eyes closed. When I felt my arms reaching up to pull my hood over my head, I wasn't sure if it was because I was stuck in another forced cutscene or if my body was just moving instinctively.

"Boy," a voice said.

I wasn't sure I'd ever heard him use my name before.

"Dad," I responded.

Chapter 66

Moral Revelation

Steven was a big man. He had once been a varsity hockey player, and even though his college years were long behind him, he had stubbornly clung on to the hulking build he had once used to muscle his way around the rink before his knee injury destroyed his chances of going pro. Though he wasn't that much taller than me, I always remembered him as being a huge and hulking figure that towered over me constantly, both literally and figuratively.

Even now, with my hood pulled tight over my head and my eyes shut, I could picture him clearly in my mind's eye. The silhouette of his side profile staring at me, lit only by the dim glow of the television as he lounged on the loveseat sofa in our living room, his posture somehow both tense and lazy at the same time.

I had my eyes tightly shut but shut them even harder when I heard a sound that could be described as either a groan or a sigh. I'd never been able to identify it, no matter how many times I'd heard it, but it was easy to decipher the sheer resentment within.

"Great. You again. Don't you have better things to do than being a fucking pain in my ass?"

I felt my chest tighten as I gritted my teeth. I didn't know what exact memory the admin was showing me, but I could tell it would be one of the rougher ones. Steven simply ignored me most of the time, and the few times that he decided to acknowledge my existence like this were never pleasant.

"Come on," I said. "Give me a break."

I was a little surprised that the admin was letting me speak, given how annoying it had been about not letting me "interfere" with my memories before this point. Before I could think of a reason it was letting me talk, Steven's voice interrupted my thoughts.

"Give you a break? Give you a fucking break?" he asked, like he couldn't believe what he was hearing.

To be fair to him, I couldn't believe what I was hearing either. After taking a moment to realize what was happening, I opened my eyes.

Rather than the dark living room that I'd imagined, I found myself standing in a void. It was colorless, but it wasn't white. It just... wasn't. It was void, empty except for Steven's figure, standing across from me at a distance that I couldn't quite judge. I tried to scan the space we were in, surprised by how different it was from the memories that the admin had been showing me up until this point. However, while I could move my head and my eyes around, Steven somehow stayed directly in my field of vision, even when I looked up. It was like I had a picture of him glued directly onto my eyeballs.

"Give you a fucking break," he grumbled, wiping the back of his hand lazily across his lips, like he was wiping something off them. "That's fucking rich, coming from you."

"Dad?"

The word came out of my mouth subconsciously. More than I hated the word itself, I hated how it sounded—desperate and scared. I didn't know whether I was scared that this was more than just a memory or if I was scared that it wasn't. Either way, I hated the fear that crept into my voice.

If the angry furrow that appeared on Steven's face was any indication, he hated it too. His arm swung toward me in a violent arc. I flinched and covered my head with my hands, but nothing struck me.

Steven lifted his hand to his lips but paused when he realized he wasn't drinking anything. He looked at his hands, as if he were surprised to find them empty, even after he had already thrown his imaginary bottle at my head.

"Fucking figures," he said. "Make this fucking dream even more unbearable, why don't you?"

He let out a heavy sigh and fell backward to lie down on the nonexistent floor. Even as he fell, I found myself still facing him directly, like the world had shifted ninety degrees from my perspective so I could continue to look him in the eyes.

Steven seemed just as unhappy about this fact as I was. He grimaced and stuck out his middle finger lethargically toward me.

"Fuck off, why don't you?" he said, waving me away with his finger. "You're finally gone. I'm finally happy again. You don't get to ruin that anymore."

I stared at him for a few seconds before I realized that I was still covering my head with my arms. Waves of embarrassment and anger ran through me as I aggressively shoved my hands down.

"You're finally happy again?" I repeated. "I don't get to ruin your happiness?"

Steven simply shrugged.

"You heard what I said. Now go away, ghost of Christmas past. I'm over the bastard already. Why don't you stop haunting me and just leave me the fuck alone?"

I simply stared at him in disbelief for a few long seconds as he closed his eyes. I couldn't figure out why what he said bothered me so much. I already knew he hated me, and it wasn't the first time he had told me that he wished I never existed.

But seeing him react like this when I had actually died on Earth was something else.

"Did you even care? Even just a little bit?" I asked, hating myself for caring about the answer to that question.

"No," Steven said, lifting his hands to his lips as if trying to summon a bottle of Bud Light into his hands. "Never."

Though I felt my teeth clench impossibly tight, I didn't cry. It wasn't like I hadn't expected the answer.

"I hated you, you know," I said. "I still do."

"Well, the feeling's mutual," he said, raising his middle finger toward me once more.

I didn't bother asking why. I knew the answer to that question, too. Steven wasn't a man to mince words, or maybe he was. He was a car salesman, so I assumed he could at least pretend to be friendly, but it was not a side of him that I'd ever seen in my life. He certainly didn't hold back his feelings when he told me why he hated me.

I had taken my mother away from him, so in turn, he had taken any semblance of a father away from me.

I was a murderer in his eyes.

And in a sense, he was right, wasn't he?

Even if I didn't count the mother I never knew, I did kill a handful of people in my second life.

I wasn't just a murderer in name anymore. I wondered if he would feel satisfied by that fact. How would he react if he knew that he had been right all along about the fact that I would kill so easily, given the chance?

More than just wondering about it, I knew I could find out.

I took a sharp breath, inhaling through gritted teeth, grasping at the mana I had within my body and pushing it into my arms. Immediately, my hands grew hot as colorless flames erupted out of them, the unnatural design melding into the nothingness that surrounded us. I glared at Steven, who still had his eyes closed. He remained oblivious to what was going on in front of him, despite the heat that emanated from my fingertips and the weight of the dense mana that saturated the air around me.

I raised my hands toward him.

While it was clear that he thought he was in a dream, it was clear to me that we were somehow connected in a space between our worlds, a space that was real. I took a moment to consider whether I should warn him about what was going to happen, to see the look in his eyes as he died by my hand.

I stared at him for a while, as if waiting for him to open his eyes on his own, but the shaking of my arms made me unsure whether I could hold this much mana in them for much longer.

I had to do it.

He deserved it.

"Hellfire," I whispered.

"BLAST!" I screamed, not giving myself the chance to rethink what I was doing.

Flames erupted from my palms in a paradoxical roar of silence, as if they engulfed not only the space around me, but also the sound they should have made. The colorless light blinded me, and the heat was intense enough that I couldn't help but flinch away from it reflexively, although I knew it couldn't hurt me.

I couldn't tell how long I kept the flames roaring. It could have been a few seconds. It could have been a few years. I had a feeling that in this space, time didn't function like it was supposed to, if it functioned at all. I could vaguely feel tears rolling down my face, though I wasn't sure why.

My flames died down when I reached up to wipe my eyes, and though my vision was blurred, I could still make out Steven's untouched form and the translucent dialogue box that floated between us.

PVP is prohibited. Otherworlders may not harm other Otherworlders.

I sank to my knees, unsure of whether I felt disappointment or relief. I sucked in shaky breaths through my teeth as I cried silently into my hands.

"Shut the fuck up," Steven muttered. With his eyes still closed and his posture relaxed, it didn't seem like he'd even noticed my attempt to kill him. "You're a fucking embarrassment, you know that?"

"I hate you," I said.

"Yeah, yeah," he replied.

"You're my dad. You're supposed to love me."

"I don't see a fucking contract."

"Mom would've hated you."

He paused for a moment. I didn't know why I said that, and I didn't know if I felt satisfied by the way that his eyes opened and twisted into an angry glare.

"You didn't know her."

"And whose fault is that?"

"It's yours."

"You never even told me her name."

"You didn't deserve to know."

"She would've hated the way you treated me."

"Don't you fucking talk about her like you know her, bastard."

"She was my mom."

"And you killed her for it."

I looked at him. I sniffled unconsciously, less out of emotion and more out of an automatic reaction to the feeling of snot dripping out of my nose. I was surprised to find that I didn't actually care about what he was saying. It was a new feeling for me. As much as I liked to pretend like I could just shrug off his words back when I was alive, I could never truly ignore him. I could only grow numb to him.

But now? It felt a little different.

I sniffled again and wiped my hands against my eyes and nose. I was surprised to find they came away drier than I might have expected.

"She would've loved me. She would've loved me unconditionally."

The words came out of my mouth without much thought put into them, but it was enough to draw an instant reaction from him.

"Shut the fuck up."

I felt something hit the top of my head. It didn't hurt, even though I felt like it should have. I blinked as I lazily looked up at the glass shards of the broken bottle of Bud Light that littered my hair. In between us, another translucent dialogue box showed him the same message that it had shown me a few seconds ago, though it didn't seem like he cared enough to read it. His face was red, and his arm was still outstretched, as if the act of throwing the summoned beer bottle had given him a sprain.

"Shut the fuck up," he repeated.

"She would have loved me," I repeated.

Another beer bottle hit my head. I felt my lips quirk up slightly at the sight of him using his god-like powers to summon beer bottles. I wasn't sure if I was trying to mock him or if I was just amused by the idea, but it seemed to succeed at angering him regardless.

"Shut the fuck up," he said.

"She would have believed in me, even if you never did."

I barely knew what I was saying. I had never known a mother, and by extension, I had never felt a mother's love. But the words fell out of my mouth so naturally that I had a hard time denying them.

He got up and started to run at me, arms outstretched, as if trying to strangle me, but no matter how hard he ran, he never got closer.

"She would've protected me from anyone who tried to hurt me. That includes you."

"You didn't know her," he said. "You killed her."

Though it looked like he was trying to scream it, red-faced and fists clenched, his voice was quiet, as if he was much further away than he looked. I could barely hear him. At this point, I didn't know what point he was trying to make. Was he saying that my mother had been a bad person? That she would've treated me the same way that he did? That might have been true. She did marry a guy like him after all. But at this point, that didn't matter much.

"She would have forgiven me for killing her, wouldn't she?"

He stumbled on nothing and fell to the floor. He glared at me but didn't get up.

He said something, but I don't know what. I didn't know if I couldn't hear him or if I simply didn't, but it didn't matter. He didn't matter to me anymore.

I turned around. Steven disappeared from my field of vision. Without him, I was left alone in the empty void.

Never had I expected that reaching a moral revelation would be this tiring. It didn't feel particularly good, but possibly for the first time in my life, I felt like everything was right.

"I get it," I said. "I'm ready. Take me back."

* * *

"What's that supposed to mean?" I shrieked more than shouted. My voice scratched violently at the walls of my throat, but the slight pain wasn't enough to stop me from shouting. I was scared, tired, and furious at Jamie for daring to suggest that I wasn't on his side, like my actions to this point somehow hadn't been enough for him.

I glared at him, as if daring him to throw even more bullshit in my face, before I noticed his expression.

His eyes were puffy and sunken, and he stared at me with an intensity that hadn't been there a second ago. It looked like he'd been crying for hours before we started our shouting match, but I somehow hadn't noticed until now.

"What are you looking at me like that for?" I asked, unnerved by the sudden silence that we had fallen into. I could hear the angry bite in my voice disappearing quickly as I struggled to adjust to the abrupt shift in the emotional atmosphere.

Rather than answering with his words, Jamie fell forward.

I felt myself flinch in place and scramble to catch him on instinct before I realized he wasn't in any danger of falling.

It took me a few seconds to realize what was happening. Jamie stood in front of me with his chest close to mine but not quite touching. His hands were placed gently on the backs of my shoulders but with a timid touch, as if he was afraid that I would disintegrate if he applied any pressure whatsoever.

I still didn't know what was going on, but I knew an awkward hug when I felt one. I walked half a step forward and wrapped my arms around his back, pushing myself gently into him. As if he had been waiting for permission, he buried his face in my shoulder and tightened his arms around me, like he was afraid that I would change my mind and pull away.

He sobbed quietly beside my ear. I tried not to mind the way that his chin and nose were digging uncomfortably into my flesh and the way that my arms were pinned in an uncomfortable angle against his body. I could only assume it wasn't intentional. It saddened me to think that he probably just wasn't used to this. I considered giving him some words of encouragement, but since I had no idea what had just happened, other than the fact that it was probably something I wouldn't understand, I settled for simply patting him on the back.

He let go of me surprisingly quickly and was still sobbing quietly when he did. I considered grabbing him again, just to let him cry as much as he needed, but the grim look of determination on his face stopped me.

"I'm going to go fix this," he said.

I stared at him, stunned by his sudden shift in emotion once more. "What?" I asked.

"I'm going to fix your world," he said, as if that explained anything, but the determined look on his face faltered, as if he had suddenly changed his mind.

He stared at me for a few seconds before turning his eyes away.

"Can you come with me?" he asked. "I'm scared."

I still had no idea what was going on or what he was even talking about, but there was really only one thing I could possibly do.

I grabbed his hand, hoping that he wouldn't feel the way that I was shaking.

"Of course."

Chapter 67

Reaching the Endgame

"So, do you feel like helping at all?" Stoney asked.

Marten glanced down at Stoney, raising an eyebrow at the question.

"Helping with what?"

"Don't pretend like you weren't listening in," Stoney said.

"Who says I'm pretending?" Marten replied, turning his attention back away from Stoney, choosing to stare off into the distance instead. "Of course I was listening. That's why I'm asking."

"The world might end, you know," Stoney said. He leaned back against the wall of the house and followed Marten's gaze with his own. Though he had first assumed that Marten was looking in the direction Sera had run toward during her search for Jamie, he had a suspicion that he was just staring blankly into space.

"The world's been ending for a while now, it seems like," Marten replied.

"And you don't think you should be doing something about that?" Stoney asked.

"Do you?" Marten asked back with a raised brow. "I don't see you rushing off into the woods."

Stoney frowned and shook his head, not to deny Marten's accusation, but for no real reason he could identify.

Stoney sighed. "It's a strange feeling, isn't it? To have your instinct shouting at you that everything will be fine despite you knowing that it may not be."

"I'm a gambler," Marten said. "I live by that feeling. I always follow my gut, no matter what my head says."

"And what good has that done for you?" Stoney asked.

Marten looked down at Stoney, giving him an annoyed glare before turning his eyes away once again.

"What can I say? I'm a slave to my intuition," he grumbled.

Stoney grimaced as he looked down at his legs, as if staring would get them to move. When they didn't, he sighed.

"It seems that applies to me as well," Stoney said. "At least for the time being."

"Don't like the feeling?"

Stoney's mouth flattened into a thin line. "I trust in my intuition as much as I do the Founder at the moment, and unfortunately, that means I have absolute faith in it."

Marten made a noncommittal hum.

"I just wish I could do something. Anything," Stoney grumbled. "Even though I'm certain that the Founder has our best interests at heart, I can't help but feel a bit frustrated, knowing I'm just sitting here with my thumb up my ass. At least Sera is trying."

"Why bother?" Marten asked. "Even if there was something that the Founder couldn't protect us from, which there isn't, it's not like we could do anything about it. At this point, the only person who can affect the world in any way is one who can mold it to their will."

"Like Jamie."

"Like the brat," Marten agreed. "Best thing us mortals can do now is just pray."

"Never took you for a religious man."

“I’m not.”

***

When I grabbed Jamie’s hand, there was a short silence between us, far too short for me to even consider taking a moment to catch my breath. As soon as I grabbed his hand, he grabbed mine back in a tight but gentle grip. My eyes were drawn to his, and I couldn’t help but be surprised by the determination I found within them.

“I know things are confusing right now,” Jamie said, his voice steady and confident, as if I had imagined the fear that permeated it just seconds ago. “I can fix your world, but I think I need to do it fast.”

“What are you talking about, Jamie?” I asked.

“I don’t have the time to explain,” he said, shaking his head, before the resolute expression on his face slowly started to slip into one of uncertainty. “Do you trust me?”

“Yes,” I said, surprised by how easily I said it.

Jamie’s eyes softened instantly, but he shook his head again, as if trying to physically dissipate any uncertainties he had resting there. It seemed to work, as his determined expression returned, stronger than ever.

“Okay,” he said, closing his eyes. “Detect whatever is making this world so messed up and messing with people’s memories.”

It took me a second to realize what he was doing. Though I thought I had gotten used to his weird Otherworlder powers by this point, it seemed like I could still be surprised.

“Was that seriously a spell you just cast?” I asked, not sure of which answer I wanted to hear from him.

Jamie opened one eye and chuckled. “I know, right? I told you. I’m ridiculously broken.”

“Right,” I said. “So that stupid spell actually worked?”

"Yup," he replied with a grin. "It's called plot convenience. As an isekai protagonist, it's my divine right to have all the solutions to any of my problems simply be handed to me, just as long as I remember to ask."

"I understood half of what you just said," I replied with a smile of my own. "Remind me to ask you to explain it to me later."

Jamie responded with a smile.

"Why don't I just show you? Teleport."

I had to blink several times as I was blinded by a sudden light.

At first, I assumed that whatever magic Jamie had used was the source of the light, but when the light refused to fade, it took a long time for my eyes to adjust to it. After a few seconds, I finally managed to glimpse my surroundings through squinted eyes.

When I saw where we were, my eyes widened, and my mouth hung open involuntarily. Though the sunlight was harsh enough that it stung to keep my eyes open all the way, I couldn't help but look around in awe of my surroundings.

It wasn't just beautiful. It was beauty defined.

I stood atop a hill, overlooking a great expanse of land coated in colorful flora that made me initially think I was somewhere high above the clouds, looking down on a rainbow. Fruits I didn't recognize hung from trees and vines with leaves and flowers in vibrant colors and a luster that I'd never seen before. A long river split the land before me, the pure water sparkling and reflecting the light as though precious gems and metals were hidden just beneath the surface. Unlike the dreary rain that we had left behind, the sun was warm enough that I could already feel my soaked clothes drying out, yet a comfortable breeze and the shade of the large tree behind me refused to make the heat unbearable.

The place was oddly perfect. Every branch, every leaf, every strand of grass seemed like it was supposed to be there, as if they had been intentionally designed. It was difficult to imagine that wasn't the case, even though the forest was large enough that it expanded far beyond the horizon.

"Where are we?" I asked.

"I have no idea," Jamie said. "All I know is that the source of your world's problems is here."

I looked around briefly but didn't notice anything that looked like it could possibly be capable of disfiguring reality. When I glanced back at Jamie, the determined expression that he had on his face made it clear that he was being completely serious.

"Are you sure?" I asked, despite everything I knew about him and his powers.

Jamie looked around and grimaced. I followed his gaze downward but didn't immediately notice anything odd about the hill we were standing on.

"Yeah," he said. "Pretty sure."

It took me a moment to realize what he was talking about. Despite the comforting atmosphere that this place created, I felt a shiver run down my spine as I suddenly noticed how quiet the air was, devoid of the cry of insects and birds that would've otherwise been thriving on a sunny day like this. In this perfect garden, I suddenly grew more aware of the hill we were standing on, the only bump in the perfectly flat land that stretched over the horizon.

Around the base of the hill was the outline of a perfect circle where the dense plant life refused to go beyond, bowing reverently toward the hill but not intruding on its borders. I suddenly felt like an intruder in this space, where nothing existed other than the lush grass that coated it and the single tree that we were standing under. I looked up and saw, hanging from the branches, fruits that I couldn't recognize, not because I hadn't ever seen them before, but because I couldn't understand what I was looking at.

"The fruits?" I asked, surprised that my voice was as steady as it was.

Jamie glanced toward them but didn't seem to care about the fruits nearly as much as I did. He directed his gaze downward instead.

"No, not those," he said. "It's under the hill."

I tore my eyes away from the fruits, stepping gingerly away as if that would do anything to protect me.

"Oh," I said.

If Jamie had anything to say about how dumbfounded I sounded, he kept it to himself. He simply closed his eyes and raised his arms, pointing his palms to the earth.

"Hellfire blast."

The casual way he said it gave me an inadequate amount of forewarning for how intense the following spell would be. A pillar of pure energy erupted from Jamie's palms. Though he had called it hellfire, it was nothing like any flame I had ever seen before. Given that it was colorless, silent, and devoid of heat and light, I could only assume that if I actually experienced the effects of the spell with any of my senses, I would have died instantly.

Jamie closed his hands, stopping the flow of mana and revealing a medium-sized hole where he had summoned his hellfire, the spell simply erasing the earth from existence rather than burning it up. Jamie stared down at the hole unsteadily, breathing a bit roughly from the exertion of his magic.

Without thinking, I rushed up to him, but he managed to catch himself before he fell to the floor. I decided to hold him anyway, just in case, supporting his body with mine.

"Are you okay?" I asked.

Jamie smiled at me, looking more tired than I'd ever seen him before. "Yeah," he said. "It was a little anticlimactic, I guess. But I did it. I saved the world."

I tried to smile back at him, but for some reason, I couldn't do it.

"Are you sure you're okay?" I asked. "That looked like it took a lot out of you."

Jamie's smile grew wider, and he let out a small chuckle under his breath. "It was pretty difficult, yeah," he said, panting slightly to catch his breath. "Had to output enough power to destroy whatever the threat was. Also had to hold myself back enough so I didn't accidentally destroy your world myself. Took a surprising amount of control."

I didn't find myself laughing with him, but before I could think of what to say in response, the sudden look of confusion in Jamie's eyes stopped me. For a moment, I thought he was staring at me, but when I noticed he was staring past me, I turned around.

PVP is prohibited.

Otherworlders may not harm other Otherworlders.

I couldn't tell how long I stared at that panel for, but at some point, I found my eyes drifting toward the hole that Jamie had created.

It was impossibly dark all the way down, and I didn't know for sure if I was imagining a presence slowly rising from deep within it.

What I knew was that I didn't imagine the soft, gentle voice that echoed from deep within.

"Who disturbs me?"

Chapter 68
An Excellent Liar

Of all the things I had expected to find, this hadn't been one of them. In hindsight, it really should have been. How could you save the world without defeating a demon king or two along the way? I shouldn't have been so surprised to see that it was another Otherworlder either. It wasn't an uncommon trope for the big bad guy to turn out to be a fallen hero, to act as a foil to the main character and show them what they could have become without the power of friendship. The final message to both the main character and the audience behind the screen. To really drive the lesson home.

But I had already learned my lesson, and there was no audience that I would be teaching it to. I had already defeated my demons. This was supposed to be an epilogue, not the climax of my story.

I stared up at the man floating in front of me. Rather than a big, hulking figure clad in jet-black armor and a horned helmet that covered his face entirely, he was completely naked, hairless, and thin enough that I almost wanted to call him emaciated. His eyes were half-closed and unfocused, like he had just woken up from a long nap. He stared at me with a confused look in his eyes, though I wasn't sure if he was just confused by the revelation that I was another Otherworlder or if he just had no idea what was going on.

He spoke again. This time, his voice held a little more emotion in it, a little more confusion, but I still didn't know what he was saying. His voice was still soft, but the language sounded harsh and, most importantly, foreign. I didn't know if he was speaking some language from my world that I just couldn't recognize or if he was an Otherworlder pulled from an entirely different dimension. In any case, I assumed that no magic that I could cast would let me understand him.

"I'm sorry for bringing you here, Lena," I said, still staring the man in the eyes. His eyes had started to register me, and I didn't want to risk losing his focus. "But I need your help. Can you tell me what he's saying?"

Lena didn't say anything immediately, but I didn't have the time to let her process what was going on. Still keeping my eyes on the Otherworlder, I reached out behind me and gently grabbed her hand. I almost flinched away when I felt how badly she was shaking, but I kept my hand firm, trying to give her a sense of confidence that I didn't quite have myself.

"Lena," I said as gently as possible, despite the anxiety that crept into my heart. "I can't understand what he's saying, and I don't think he can understand me. I need your help."

Lena still didn't respond, but I felt her squeeze my hand back in what might have felt like a death grip to a normal human being. I could hear her quick breaths evening out slowly. Not to a level where I could convince myself that she was calm, but at least that she was calming down.

"He's asking who you are," she said quietly.

The man's head turned quickly toward her at the sound of her voice. I could feel her flinch under his gaze, but I squeezed her hand gently and stepped in front of her to hide her from view.

"Could you tell him that my name is Jamie, and I'm an Otherworlder just like him?"

She repeated my message, and the man narrowed his eyes. I still couldn't tell whether he was skeptical of my claim or if he was still generally confused about what was going on.

"What's your name?" I asked, with Lena repeating my words.

The man frowned at the question, and a complex series of emotions passed through his expression before he said a single word.

"David," Lena said.

I nodded, even though I didn't agree with her. Through whatever translation magic that was filtering my understanding of what Lena was saying, the name David was close to what the man had said, but not quite the same. Still, I wasn't confident in my ability to repeat what the man had said with the same pronunciation, and I had no time to waste on trying.

"David," I said. "What is your dream?"

I felt Lena flinch at my question, and she hesitated in repeating it. I squeezed her hand again, trying to reassure her, even though I had no idea how. Thankfully, it seemed to be enough.

"What is your dream?" Lena asked.

David's eyes widened almost imperceptibly as another flash of emotion passed over his features.

He opened his mouth and closed it immediately, as if biting his words back. I could see his eyes threatening to dart to the side as he struggled to maintain direct eye contact. When he spoke, I wasn't sure if he was speaking with a stutter or if it was just what his language sounded like.

"He said his purpose is to guide the lost souls to paradise," Lena said.

I tried to keep my expression as neutral as possible to hide the confusion I felt. Not knowing how to respond, I simply stared at him, my mind whirring as I tried to figure out what would be the best thing to say here.

Before I could figure out what to say, David tore his eyes away from mine, looking down to the side, an expression of shame written clearly on his face. He muttered something under his breath that I doubted I would've been able to hear properly, even if he was speaking plain English.

"He's asking you if you're here to replace him," Lena said. "He wants to know if he's failed in his duties."

David flinched as Lena repeated his message, but he kept his eyes glued to the floor beside him, his mouth in a tight line of focus. His fists were clenched by his sides in tight balls of frustration, and I couldn't be certain whether he was angry or afraid. Even though I didn't know what he was talking about, I felt like I could somehow relate to him.

I stopped myself before I could sympathize with him too much. Regardless of who David was, he was the source of this world's problems.

"Lena," I said. "David needs to die."

I turned around to face her and immediately felt a surge of guilt. She had her mouth half open as if she had planned to repeat what I had just said before she realized that it would be an incredibly bad idea. Her face was stained with tears, and a deep sense of weariness seemed to emanate from every aspect of her being—from her sunken posture, to her pale skin, to the glassy-eyed look she gave back to me, too tired to display any emotion on her face.

I let go of her hand to place my palm over her head.

"Restore," I said. I don't know if "restore" was the right word to describe how I wanted to help Lena, but my magic seemed to know what I wanted better than I did. A flash of green light burst from my hands and entered Lena's body, and once the glow faded away, it revealed a much healthier Lena, though the weariness remained in her expression.

I glanced back at David, but he had barely reacted to the magic. I wasn't sure if he even noticed that I'd turned my attention away from him.

"I'm sorry I dragged you into this, Lena," I said. "I thought my magic would be enough to fix any problems we ran into in a couple of seconds, but I didn't expect this. I'm sorry."

Lena stared into my eyes, and though she didn't say anything, I could see that she believed me. She stared into my soul with a piercing genuineness that made me want to look away in shame at what I was about to ask of her.

"We need him to die," I said. "But I don't think I can do it."

Lena's eyes widened, and her mouth opened to protest what I was about to say, but she clamped it shut when she realized that David would be able to understand anything she said.

Although I was certain that she knew what I wanted from her and that I didn't actually need to say anything else, I wouldn't forgive myself if I didn't voice my request out loud. I needed to take responsibility for what I was about to ask of her.

"Lena," I said. "I'm not asking you this because I don't want to do it myself. I just don't think I can. I'm not nearly smart enough to figure out what he wants, and I'm not kind enough to give it to him if I did. But you're the smartest and kindest person I know. Can you fulfill his dream?"

A complex stream of emotions ran across Lena's face, and I was ashamed of how scared she was of my request and how relieved I felt when I saw that none of that fear was directed toward me. I meant it when I said that she was the smartest person I knew, and I knew that she had already figured out that I was asking her because it was my only option. From the anxiety that ran across her face in waves, I could only assume that she didn't believe in herself as much as I did.

I squeezed her hand gently.

"I know you can do it," I said.

She looked up and met my eyes. I didn't know exactly what she saw in them, if she could tell that I was being completely sincere. She frowned at me, and I could see her gritting her teeth in frustration before she nodded, the motion so slight that it was barely perceptible.

She wasn't confident in herself—I knew that much. Her hand shook violently in mine as she spoke to David, but her words were steady, any hints of nervousness filtered through the mask of confidence that she had put on.

As she talked, her demeanor filled me with a sense of melancholic nostalgia as I thought back on how she had treated me when we first met. She treated David with respect and dignity, without letting him in on the fact that she regarded him as a volatile monster who had poisoned her world with his presence. A dull pang of pain pounded against my heart as I acknowledged how familiar her lies felt.

Lena was an excellent liar.

Even though I was no longer a part of their conversation, she continued to relay each of David's messages to me and waited for me to say something before responding to him, keeping up the facade that I was still telling her what to say.

At first, I didn't know what to say, and being put on the spot, I rambled out one of my old poems from memory. Lena rolled with it, ignoring the edgy poems that were permanently engraved into my brain since I had conceived them when I was thirteen. She continued to speak with David as my liaison, and I went through a few more responses until I ran out of poems. So, instead of rambling from memory, I just rambled.

"I wonder if this place is modeled after the Garden of Eden? It looks kind of like how I would've imagined it. I wonder if David is from my world or if there's another world with a similar myth. I can only assume he was the one to make this place look like how it does.

"I heard somewhere that if an extra in a movie needs to pretend like they're talking in the background of a scene, they just keep mouthing the word 'watermelon.' I don't really know if it would work here, since I wouldn't want to risk David noticing I'm just saying the same word over and over.

"Watermelon, kumquat, orange, kiwi, strawberry, blueberry, orange. Wow, sure didn't take me long to get a repeat."

I hoped I wasn't distracting Lena too much, but I didn't want to risk letting my conscious thoughts take over. So I continued to ramble, barely paying attention to what Lena and David were saying. The rising hope in David's expression was enough to tell me what I already knew—Lena was fulfilling his dream, or at least she was making him think she was. And wasn't that enough?

Apparently, it was. Whether David had been fully fooled by Lena's lies or if he had to lie to himself to fill in the blanks, I could see a sense of peace washing over him as he accepted his fate. I didn't know whether he was fully satisfied by the life he'd led here or if he still had some regrets, but as a sense of tension escaped his body, escaping him in waves, I could tell that above all else, he was glad to be given an ending, no matter how satisfying or unsatisfying it was.

"What will you do now?" Lena asked him.

David said something, and before Lena could translate for me, he looked down into the hole I had made in the center of the hill and slowly descended into it.

"He said he's going to sleep," Lena said once he had completely disappeared, confirming what I had already assumed.

"I'm not surprised. He looked really tired."

"Yeah," Lena said, before her legs gave way.

I caught her before she fell to the floor and let her down gently, but it seemed like the strength in her body had left her completely, to the point where I needed to support her upper body to even let her sit up. So I did. I sat down with her on the grassy hill that overlooked the paradise that we were in, my arm around her shoulder and her head leaning against me. We stayed like that for a long moment, the world around us as silent as we were as time dripped painfully by.

"Do you think he's actually going to die?" Lena asked, breaking the silence abruptly, her head still on my shoulder.

"Yeah."

"So I killed a man today."

"He was already dead, Lena. All you did was push him along on a journey he should've been on already. I'm sure he's grateful."

"And how would you know that?" Lena asked, bitterness saturating her every word, even though she didn't move from her spot on my shoulder. "How do you know that?"

My grip around her shoulder tightened for a second before I forced myself to relax. I didn't say anything in response.

"Sorry," she said.

"No, I'm sorry," I said.

There was another long silence between us, but it was more tense than the one we'd just had a moment ago.

"You made him really happy, Lena," I said. Even though I hadn't been paying enough attention to know what she'd said, I was confident in that fact.

"It doesn't change the fact that I killed him," she replied.

"Everyone has to die someday," I said. "I'm sure he's grateful that he could go out on a good note."

"That's a horrible thing to say."

"Yeah. It is, isn't it?"

"How long do you think it'll take for him to die?"

"About five hours, maybe? It might be different for him than it is for me, though."

Lena didn't react to my admission at all, but I felt her shoulders tense almost imperceptibly.

"And how long do you have?"

"Just a little bit less than that."

Chapter 69

An Epilogue of Sorts

I wanted to be furious with Jamie, but I couldn't find the energy within me to express that anger in any way. I just sat there instead, staring into the sunset with him, trying to ignore the fact that I was leaning against a boy who was actively dying with every passing second.

I wanted to do something to make Jamie's last moments in this world memorable somehow, but I stayed silent. I didn't know if it was because I didn't know what to do or if I was spiteful enough that I was bleeding away at his time in some form of petty revenge against him, but I knew I would regret it if it was the latter. I sighed and lifted myself from his shoulder.

"Well, is there anything you want to do?" I asked.

Jamie just stared into the distance.

"Nah," he said. "I'm fine."

"Are you really?" I asked. "You are about to die, aren't you? That's why you were in such a rush to get here, isn't it?"

"I wanted to make sure you would be safe after I left," he said with a casual shrug. "I didn't expect it to last long, but I just wanted to get it over with quickly so we could just hang out afterward."

"And I guess that's what we're doing, isn't it?" I said. "Hanging out."

He gave me another shrug, and when it became clear that that would be his only response for the moment, I let out a sigh and put my head back on his shoulder.

"When were you planning to tell me?" I asked.

"I don't think I planned to tell you," he admitted.

"You're an asshole."

"I know. I was scared."

"Scared of what?"

"I didn't want to make you upset."

"Well, I am upset."

"That's fair."

"You know what's not fair? All of this."

"I know. I'm sorry."

The words "don't be" floated on the tip of my tongue, but I bit them back, not wanting to grant Jamie forgiveness so easily. I took my head off his shoulder, and though the weakness in my body made me sway slightly, threatening to tip me over, I managed to stop myself from falling, hugging my knees for support.

Out of the corner of my eye, I saw him shifting, like he wanted to sling his arm around my shoulder to support me, but he seemed to realize that I was too angry for that. He leaned back instead, supporting his upper body with his arms and tilting his head back.

"Are you sure?" I asked.

"That I'm dying?" he asked back. "Yeah."

"How?" I asked.

"I just know," he replied. "The same way that David probably knows that he's dying."

I didn't want to look at him, but I did. I knew that with his superhuman senses, he probably knew I was staring at him, but that didn't stop me from analyzing his expression.

He looked peaceful at first, staring up into the sky with a neutral smile, but he was frozen in place in an unnatural way. Though the wind that gently tossed his hair and the reflection of the lazy clouds passing by his eyes gave off the illusion of motion, his chest remained completely still as he breathed, if he was breathing at all.

"Are you in pain?" I asked.

Jamie turned to me, raising an eyebrow. "Not at all," he said. "What makes you ask?"

"You seem scared," I said.

He laughed at that and hugged his knees close to his chest, mirroring my position exactly.

"I already said I was scared, didn't I?"

That wasn't the answer I had been looking for. "I guess you did," I said anyway.

Jamie turned to me and smiled, though the expression melted off quickly as he sighed and fell forward, letting his chin rest against his knees.

"I'm scared that I'm dying for nothing," he said. "While we were fighting, time stopped, and I was sent to my old world. I'm not sure if I was there or if it was just in my head, but I saw my dad again. He was a piece of shit as usual, but seeing him made me think about my dream. To be loved."

He took a deep breath before continuing.

"I thought it was a straightforward dream from the start," he said. "But if you asked me a few hours ago how I could achieve my dream, I don't know if I would've been able to give you a real answer. I might've said that I would need to get a girlfriend, have my first kiss, have sex. I thought maybe it wouldn't count as being loved unless I made love. It's a little silly in hindsight."

Jamie let out a quiet laugh as if he was pretending like he had made a joke. The laughter quickly faded away into a sigh.

"Long story short, I realized that love wasn't about that. All I really wanted was for someone to believe in me, to protect me, to forgive me, no matter what I did," he said, letting out an even louder sigh and suddenly lurching back, falling with his back flat against the floor and staring directly up at the sky. "I really should've died a long time ago. I'm not a very smart person."

I heard a sniffle, but I wasn't sure who it had come from. My head sank deeper into my knees. When I spoke, my voice was muffled by the fabric of my clothes. It was quiet enough that I could barely hear it myself.

"If I say that I hate you, will you live?"

Jamie laughed. An actual laugh this time.

"No, I don't think so," he said. "And if you really feel that way and I just made the wrong assumption, I'd really prefer if you could just lie to me for a couple more hours. I'll be gone from your life after that."

A surge of anger coursed through me, and I couldn't stop myself from shuffling over to where Jamie was lying down and slapping him across the face as hard as I could.

He reached up and touched his face, more out of shock than pain.

"I'm sorry," he said. "That was stupid of me."

"As long as you know," I said, nursing my hand as it throbbed in pain. "I'm sorry too."

"Don't be," he said. "I deserved it."

"You really did," I said, before shuffling over and sitting closer beside him.

"Do you want me to heal your hand for you?"

"Don't you fucking dare."

"Okay."

I didn't have anything to say to that, so I sat there silently, staring at nothing and thinking about nothing.

Jamie let out a loud sigh.

"I was telling the truth when I said that you probably made David very happy," he said. "Lies or not, he's going to die with his dreams fulfilled. I know that's what he wants."

"Is that so?" I asked.

"Yeah," he said. "I could only assume that he's the same as me. I could only assume that if his dream was important to him as mine was to me, he would die happy once it was fulfilled."

"So you're happy?" I asked.

"Yeah," he said easily.

I frowned at that, holding back a sob.

"I'm glad you're happy."

He let out a laugh, but if it sounded a bit choked up, I didn't comment on it.

"All things considered, this isn't a bad way to go. Much better than the first time around. I should be grateful that I had a second chance at all," he said. "But if I'm being honest, I'd much rather not be dying."

"I know," I said. "I'd prefer it if you weren't dying either."

Jamie laughed again, and I couldn't help but laugh with him, realizing what I'd just said and how silly it sounded out of context. Our laughter didn't last long, but when it faded away, I was surprised that I had a slight smile on my face. I turned to look at Jamie, and though his eyes were misty, he was also smiling. I shuffled around and let myself fall back on the floor beside him so we were shoulder to shoulder.

"I know I already asked this, but are you sure there isn't anything else you'd rather be doing right now?" I asked.

"Nah," he answered easily. "I like this."

"Then is there anything else you want to talk about?" I asked. "I can't imagine it's fun only talking about how you're going to die soon."

"Not soon. Four-ish hours is a long time."

"I suppose it is."

I felt Jamie's hand shyly touch the back of mine, and I reached out to grab it, intertwining my fingers with his.

"Can you tell me a story?" he asked.

"That entirely depends on what type of story," I said. "My parents told me a lot of stories when I was younger, but I always fell asleep too fast to hear the end."

He seemed to think about it for a few seconds.

"Not like a bedtime story," he said. "Can you tell me about yourself?"

"The Legend of Lena?" I asked.

He laughed at that. "That's a good one," he said.

"I can't take credit for it," I admitted. "Bran suggested that title for a book I could write about being your Follower. I don't think I plan on writing it, though."

"Why not? It's a pretty good idea, I think."

"I don't particularly want to. Besides, it's a horrible title. And a false one. It would be the Legend of Jamie, written by Lena. I'm just some random village girl who met you by chance. You're the remarkable one."

"I think you give yourself too little credit. And if you were going to write a book about me, I'd rather call it the Journal of Jamie. Or something like that."

I laughed a little but shifted my fingers around to pinch the meat of his palm. "That's also a horrible title."

"We can workshop it," he said. "We have the time."

I couldn't tell if he had intended that to be a joke, but neither of us laughed.

"Anyway," he said, quickly trying to dispel the awkward atmosphere he created. "I still demand my story. Don't think you can distract me with your tangents."

"Fine, fine," I said. "Do you really want to learn more about me, though? I haven't led a very interesting life. At least until I met you, but you already know what happened after that."

"You're probably right," he said. "I'm not too interested in your past. No offense."

"None taken." I waved it off. "What did you want from me, then?"

"Your future," he said. "I won't be there, but I'm curious about what your life will look like after I'm gone."

My fingers unconsciously curled tighter around his hand. I took in a deep breath before I spoke.

"It won't be accurate," I said. "I can't see the future."

"It's just a story," he said. "It doesn't need to be."

I turned my head to look at him. He was still staring at the sky.

"Okay," I said.

It turned out that telling a story was much more difficult than it looked. It also turned out that I wasn't a particularly good storyteller. My improvised storytelling was awkward, with random pauses every few seconds as I struggled to create the Legend of Lena, but Jamie didn't seem to mind. Eventually, I started to pause less as I spun my story for him, though I had to sacrifice any sense of a cohesive narrative for the increase in confidence.

I barely knew what I was talking about, just saying anything and everything that came to mind without thinking of it. I started off with a story about how I might inherit my dad's butcher shop and make a living off that, but I somehow got sidetracked and managed to create a story about how I might become a blacksmith in Redstone.

Jamie started to jump into the story too, which didn't make sense at all, but I ran with it. Together, we created an absurd story of my life in the coming years, where I was somehow a blacksmith, lawyer, warrior, mayor, and baseball player—whatever the hell that was. Eventually, it stopped being a story about me entirely, and we just started to talk about everything and nothing at once.

I was in the middle of explaining my hypothetical crackpot theory on redstone being secretly edible when I noticed him suddenly getting quiet. An unnatural sense of peace spontaneously fell over him. I tried to finish my train of thought, but my words fell short.

He smiled at me and sat up.

I got up on my knees, shuffled over to position myself in front of him, and fell forward, summoning as much strength as I could muster to give him the tightest hug I possibly could.

“I'll miss you,” he said.

“I'll miss you too,” I replied.

“I love you,” he said.

“I love you too.”

I closed my eyes and planted a kiss on his forehead. When I opened my eyes, he was gone.

Though my vision was misted over, the place that I was kneeling in was familiar enough that I could still recognize it as my room back in Plainswood.

Not knowing what else I could do now, I sat there, and I cried.

ANOTHER EPILOGUE

"It's been a while, hasn't it, Lena?"

I raised an eyebrow at the woman waving at me from a short distance away. Just like the first time I'd met her, my first thought was that she was a child. This time, it was the wrinkles on her brow and mouth that betrayed her age, not just her confidence.

"Sera?" I asked.

"Surprised to see me?" Sera asked back with a laugh.

"Yeah, I guess you could say that," I said. "Don't you live in the capital?"

"I do, but I was heading to Timur for work and thought I might make a detour. I dropped by Plainswood and asked your parents where you lived."

"And they told you?"

"No. They told me you didn't want to be disturbed. I gave up."

"That doesn't match up with the fact that you're here right now."

Sera shrugged. "I've been on the road for a while now. My staff has been complaining about it, so we're staying in Redstone for a few days. I was browsing the market out of boredom and just happened to see you."

It was a convenient story, but I didn't feel like it was worth the energy to try to figure out if she was lying. It wasn't like it mattered.

"I guess it's my fault for not traveling far," I said.

"I'm honestly surprised," Sera said. "I would've expected you to want to distance yourself from the area."

"Why's that?"

Sera cocked an eyebrow up and inspected my face for a few seconds before she shrugged.

"Never mind," she said. "Would you want to grab a meal or a drink to catch up?"

I raised my eyebrow. "Still holding onto that old flame?" I asked.

Sera laughed and shook her head before raising her hand.

"Sorry to disappoint you," she said. "I'm happily married."

It was at that point that I realized that she was showing off the pale ring that she was wearing on her finger.

"Congratulations," I said.

"Thanks," she replied. "Unfortunately, my wife would probably kill me if I had an affair while I was on duty. Not that I would even have time to think about something like that. Turns out creating a new government essentially from scratch is pretty stressful. What a shame."

"What a shame," I repeated.

"So… Late lunch? Early dinner?" she asked.

I shook my head. "Sorry, I'm a little busy."

"Busier than me, it seems," Sera said. "Are you planning to feed an army with that amount of food?"

I shrugged. "Something like that."

"I can help you carry some of that if you want," she said.

I considered the offer for a moment before shrugging again.

"Sure," I said, before giving her every single bag that I was carrying. Sera accepted it all without complaint, though her eyebrows did rise in surprise.

"This is heavier than it looks. Were you using strengthening magic?"

"I wasn't," I answered, rolling my shoulders and stretching my arms with my newfound freedom. "I'm just used to the weight, I guess."

"Huh," she said.

I could tell that she was curious but was being polite enough to stay silent on it.

"I usually get my food supplies delivered to me, but I occasionally shop for myself."

I started to walk down the street. Sera quickly followed.

"You run a diner?" she guessed.

"An orphanage."

"Really?"

"You seem surprised."

"I am, though now that I think about it, I really shouldn't be. I guess I assumed that you'd be doing something bigger."

"I consider my job to be very important."

"I don't doubt that, but you're a Follower. Tenna's making a lot of money off his book, so I guess I assumed you would be doing something similar."

"It's been twenty-six years. If I planned to be a writer, I would've published something by now, don't you think?"

"I don't know what the process is like."

"Tenna wrote his book in less than a year."

"But his book is awful. I can only assume it doesn't take much effort to pump out slop like that."

"Is it really that bad?"

"You haven't read it?"

"I don't see why I would."

"Fair enough. About ninety percent of the book talks about himself, and the rest of it is just fiction. Not like the guy ever talked to Jamie more than once. He basically wrote whatever he wanted, hoping that none of us would call him out on his random bullshit."

I bit back the urge to chastise Sera for her language, reminding myself that she wasn't one of my wards.

"Random bullshit, huh?" I said, recalling a fond memory. "Maybe I should write a book."

"Have I inspired you?" Sera asked.

"A little bit," I admitted. "I do often tell my wards bedtime stories. I could just write them down."

"You tell your wards bedtime stories about Jamie?"

"Yup."

"Wouldn't that be traumatizing?"

"What would possibly be traumatizing about the daring adventures of Jamie the adventurer, pirate, blacksmith, mayor, prince, baseball player?"

"...What?"

"Yeah, I'm still not entirely sure what a baseball player is either, but I'm sure I can figure it out while I'm writing."

"What?"

"I refuse to call it the Journal of Jamie, though."

"What?"

About the Author

S. Monroe is a habitual hobby hopper who stumbles through life either by random chance or by fate, depending on how poetic he's feeling at any given moment. Writing was one of many hobbies that he simply decided to pick up on a whim and similarly, *Otherworlder Survival Guide* (previously known as *Hero Wrangler*) was just another project that he decided to start on yet another whim.

Otherworlder Survival Guide was a project that had taken many other forms and genres in a countless amount of failed attempts prior to its eventual completion. From an urban fantasy short story about a father trying to save his son from growing old, to a few chapters of a morally charged multi-volume story about exploitation, to an incredibly boring setting for a tabletop RPG campaign that he forced his friends to play in for a few hours, it only got its legs when Sal decided to let go of the idea that it had to be perfect.

This novel is definitely not the perfect product that Sal envisioned when he started writing it. Even though it does feature one of those world-ending crises that he's so fond of, he's still surprised with what he ended up with.

In the end, the story of is nothing grand. It's just a tale about a girl and a boy trying to make sense of a world that doesn't offer any, so they end up finding it in each other instead.

Thank you for reading *Otherworlder Survival Guide*. I hope you've enjoyed reading it just as much as I've enjoyed writing it.

Check out *Path of the Undead Cultivator* by Endless Sleeper

Death should've been the end for Seph.
Instead, he awakened as an Undead Cultivator.

Seph was never meant to stand out. He only wanted a quiet life, the chance to become a scholar, and a way to support his struggling family.

When his mother falls ill, he climbs a dangerous mountain in search of a rare herb that might save her. He expects harsh weather, steep cliffs, and wild beasts. He does not expect cultivators.

Caught in the middle of a conflict between cultivators of the Immortal and Undead sects, Seph is mistaken for one of the undead. A cultivator crushes him with a hurled boulder, and his life ends in an instant.

Then he wakes up again, marked by the Undead Path.

Where others rely on spiritual sense, Seph can see his growth clearly through a rare System. His strength, his skills, his cultivation, all laid bare before him on glowing screens.

But the world does not forgive the undead, and Seph is trapped between both sides.

The only way to survive long enough to save his mother is to ascend.

Follow Seph as he masters the path of the Undead Cultivator and ascends beyond every limit in a world determined to erase his existence. Perfect for fans of *Unintended Cultivator*, *A Thousand Li*, and *I Shall Seal the Heavens*.

Available now on Kindle Unlimited!

Want another exciting story to keep you busy?
Check out *Survivor's Descent* by TAL Deason!

Andrew was a thirty-year-old engineer living his best life until millions of alien orbs fell from orbit and altered reality itself.

Three years later, they activated a system that turns existence into an unforgiving trial. Power comes from combat, adaptation, and staying ahead of a world that no longer tolerates weakness.

With no way out, Andrew must learn the rules while the rules are trying to break him. Guided by advanced artificial intelligence, a small group of allies, and a mysterious, dilapidated alien spaceship, he faces the same demand as everyone else.

Get stronger.

But strength alone will not save Earth. Conflict is spreading across the galaxy, and rebellion threatens to drag humanity into a much larger war. Even if Andrew wins every fight, failure on a greater scale could still mean extinction.

To save his world, he will have to grow beyond anything he ever planned to be.

Available now on Kindle Unlimited and Audible!

MOONQUILL

www.ingramcontent.com/pod-product-compliance
Lightning Source LLC
LaVergne TN
LVHW090544110826
845146LV00001B/9

* 9 7 9 8 8 8 9 9 3 1 1 1 9 *